# Telling Tales

## The Clarion West 30th Anniversary Anthology

Edited by **Ellen Datlow**

Featuring stories by
award-winning &
highly acclaimed
Clarion West alumni

**Clarion West**
Writers Workshop

Hydra **HH** House

Seattle

Telling Tales
Edited by Ellen Datlow
Copyright © 2013 Hydra House.

Hydra House
1122 E Pike St. #1451
Seattle, WA 98122
www.hydrahousebooks.com/

Cover art by Todd Lockwood.
Cover titling by Choo Ling Howle.
Interior and back cover design by Vicki Saunders.
Copyediting by Shannon Page.

978-0-9848301-9-0 (ebook)
978-0-9848301-6-9 (paper)
978-0-9890828-0-8 (hardcover)

Library of Congress Control Number: 2013933034

Library of Congress Cataloging-in-Publication Data
Telling tales : the Clarion West 30th anniversary anthology / edited by Ellen Datlow.
     pages cm
  ISBN 978-0-9848301-6-9 -- ISBN 978-0-9848301-9-0 (ebook)
  1. Science fiction, American. 2. Fantasy fiction, American. 3. American fiction--20th century. 4. American fiction--21st century. I. Datlow, Ellen, editor of compilation.
  PS648.S3T426 2013
  813'.0876608--dc23
                    2013008311

Printed through Lightning Source

First softcover edition

0 9 8 7 6 5 4 3 2 1

v1.1

# Copyright Acknowledgments

"I attended Clarion West as a student and in six weeks I learned more about myself than any other time in my life. Teaching the workshop taught me even more. Those experiences can't be replicated, but this book does a great job of sharing the best that the Clarion West Writers Workshop offers. Invaluable."

Gordon Van Gelder

"The miracle about this book of stories by Clarion West graduates is that is is not a book of Clarion West stories. The miracle is that Clarion West does not produce a particular kind of writer. What we see here is 16 stories by men and women who have learned that the first and most important thing about writing is not what you want to say but knowing how to say what you want to say. Not one of the superb tales given to us here is like any other in this big generous volume. The only thing they have in common is the Knowledge. They know themselves."

John Clute

# Contents

# Endings and Beginnings

## Vonda N. McIntyre

The Clarion Writers Workshop was going to end.

Robin Scott Wilson had attended Damon Knight and Kate Wilhelm's Milford peer workshop for professional writers. Realizing it could be adapted for new writers, he did exactly that and directed it for three years at Clarion State College in Clarion, Pennsylvania.

1970 was its third and final year in Pennsylvania. Robin had a new job in Chicago, and was, I suspect, a bit burned out by running the workshop for three years.

The workshop was a peak experience for me. I'd sold a handful of SF stories already, but this was the first time I ever got any face-to-face positive feedback on my work. I'd taken one creative writing class in college, mostly to justify taking a break from calculus and physics to spend some time writing every week. The creative writing class was not a happy one for me, as the professor's regard for SF was somewhere in the imaginary numbers.

Clarion was a completely different experience. Critiques might be tough, but they were honest, and SF/F was considered an honorable genre. I was in the company of wonderful writers—our instructors Robin Scott Wilson, Joanna Russ, Fritz Leiber, Samuel R. Delany, Damon Knight, and Kate Wilhelm, and fellow students who included George Alec Effinger and Octavia Butler.

I found it awfully difficult to think that Clarion would end after 1970. James Sallis felt the same. Robin gave his blessing to both of us, Jim in New Orleans and me in Seattle, to continue the workshop.

Clarion West ran for three years, in the summers of 1971-1973, in Seattle. The New Orleans Clarion ran for one year, 1971. After 1971, Clarion ran in East Lansing, Michigan, and several years ago moved to San Diego.

I remember Clarion West through a fog of exhaustion, but with fondness. Several of the students and instructors became lifelong friends. I'm glad I didn't know, at the time, about the roof-climbing adventures on our Tudor-style dorm, but in retrospect it would have been fun to climb up there to try to figure out how to steal the gargoyles. (I hasten to add that forty years later the gargoyles are still safely in place.)

After the 1973 workshop, I was fairly burned out. I had fled screaming from graduate school, was more or less allergic to the academic environment, and was living four miles down a logging road in a charming creekside cabin courtesy of friends. Clarion West had ended, but Robin's workshop continued at the Michigan branch.

Ten years later, J.T. Stewart (a Seattle poet who had been a Clarion West student) and Marilyn J. Holt (a fellow Seattle writer) told me that they would like to revive Clarion West.

I told them I knew a good shrink I could refer them to. (This was actually not true, but I get paid for not true.)

They were right and I was wrong: they revived Clarion West (www.clarionwest.org) and it's been running smoothly for thirty years. With the help and support of its amazing volunteers, I expect it to run at least another thirty years.

# Foreword

## Ellen Datlow

I've been privileged to teach at the Clarion West Writers Workshop five times since my first stint in 1991. Clarion West's 30th Anniversary workshop this year will be my sixth. Teaching the workshop is hard work, but not a fraction of how difficult the experience is for the students—not to mention intense and often life changing.

Some students attend Clarion West at great sacrifice—leaving jobs, sometimes permanently, and their families for six long weeks. It's often referred to as boot camp for writers, and that it is. The schedule is strenuous; the students are encouraged to write a story a week for each new author who comes to teach, and on the fifth week, an editor. Students critique all morning; read, write and conference in the afternoon and evening, and then repeat it all over again five days a week for six weeks.

Clarion West cannot make you a writer. What it will do is provide you with essential tools you need as a writer. It might help you realize that you are on the right—or wrong—path. Some graduates will go on to writing careers while others might end up in editing or publishing, or something entirely unrelated. The workshop helps you hone your analytical tools so that you can give and take a good critique and apply what you learn to your own work. For many, it provides lifelong friends and colleagues.

All the authors in this volume graduated from the workshop and went on to write and publish work that has garnered critical acclaim. Each has developed a singular voice, one of the most important components of fine fiction. Many readers of this book will already be aware of the contributors. For those who are not, you're in for a treat.

The sixteen stories, novelettes, and novella are science fiction, fantasy, horror and sometimes a mix of genres. They vary in theme, in treatment, in background, in point of view, and they are a lovely representation of what is possible in fantastic fiction. Enjoy.

# Acknowledgments

Hydra House would like to thank the Clarion West Board for their support of this project. It is our sincere hope that the proceeds from this anthology will continue to benefit Clarion West for years to come.

We would like to acknowledge all of the individuals who gave their time and talent to help bring this collection of stories into the world, including:

Editor Ellen Datlow, for her depth of professional wisdom and unerring eye for good fiction.

Artist Todd Lockwood, for the donation of his amazing artwork.

Vicki Saunders, for her excellent layout and graphic design skills.

Choo Ling Howle, for her work on the cover typeface.

Les Howle, for her support, resource gathering, suggestions, experience, and for helping connect us to the award-winning authors and stories in this anthology.

Neile Graham, for her support, suggestions, and assistance with contacting Clarion West alumni.

Patrick Swenson, for his advice, experience, and knowledge of the publishing industry.

Micaiah "Huw" Evans, who volunteered his assistance whenever assistance was required.

Shannon Page, for her copyediting skill.

... and a special thank you to all of the talented Clarion West graduates who donated their work to this publication as a fund raiser for Clarion West.

Tod McCoy
Hydra House
May 2013

# The Parrot Man

## Kathleen Ann Goonan

## 1988

Janitsu couldn't sleep for the street noise in Lahaina.

Hoots, off-key songs, and the shouted imprecations of tourists freaked on enz or drunk on triple-distilled space-station whisky (Special! Made In Space!) made her feel as if she were right down on the sidewalk instead of on the second floor of the mouldering Pioneer Hotel. The smell of teriyaki cooking somewhere below reminded her that she hadn't eaten since last night. She'd been much too upset. But the unpleasant cacophony made her sorry she'd left the Sphere resort just up the coast, with all its hushed amenities.

Rough sheets, wet with sweat, entangled her legs. She kicked them off. She'd been tossing on the narrow, creaky bed for hours. Lights glared through the open window and the hooked screen door which led onto the balcony. It was too stuffy to pull the shades. Some stupid Polynesian prints hung on the peeling wall opposite the bed.

She didn't have to stay in this cheap place. She still had full benefits—Mijea, her supervisor, had made that clear. But to give her the news at a staff meeting, in front of everyone! She was, effective immediately, pulled off-station ten years early because of bone loss. The worst of it was that now they wouldn't let her go on to Mars, where she had planned to do her next phase of research, where she'd dreamed of eventually retiring. She was Earth-bound forever.

"It's free to hold the parrot," yelled the man who was stationed right under her balcony.

Janitsu rolled out of bed. She had to take another Halcyon or she'd never get to sleep. That damned parrot man was the worst of the noise, unrelenting and tedious. When would he give up and go away?

"Hold the parrot," he said again, as she went into the bathroom, turned on the light, and pawed through her bag for the little vial of pills. She must have heard his standard patter about a hundred times already: "It's free to hold it. What's wrong with your arm? Oh, there's no parrot on it. Only a thousand yen for a holo. This is Ed, this is Gertrude, this is Ichi."

His voice was irritatingly parrotlike, as if the birds had taught him to talk. She found the Halcyons, shook out two of the tiny white pills, thought about it, then put one of them back. His endless patter rose and fell with a flat squawk, ensnaring passers-by, mostly slummers from Sphere out for the night.

She'd started her low-grav hormone work for Sphere on the orbiting Kukanzai station twenty-five years ago, a pioneer, before bone loss was preventable. Was that the real reason she'd been bumped, or just an excuse? Certain people had always been jealous of her, and perhaps her losing the results of the latest experiment had given them a bit of fuel for this purge. Mijea had assured her that Sphere would give her a new Earthside position immediately if she liked, or that she could live at any of the international resorts for as long as she wanted. It was all up to her.

Sure it was. She swallowed the pill and set the glass down on the edge of the sink, turned out the light and stood still in the darkness for a moment. She hoped the anger would subside and let her sleep, but that didn't seem possible. She was sick of Sphere, sick of that well-regulated life. She'd only worked there since she'd been a starry-eyed, gifted kid of sixteen to get to Mars, or even beyond. She had enough questions—important questions—about how the endocrine system would be affected by life on a low-gravity planet to fuel the work of several lifetimes. For years Janitsu and a few other colleagues had led the field. She couldn't do that on Earth, and her competitors knew it.

She found the t-shirt she'd flung on the floor and pulled it on.

"It's free to hold the bird," the parrot man said again, as she stepped out onto the warped floorboards of the hundred-fifty-year-old balcony, remnant of the brief whaler culture. She'd worked with whale hormones, had been in on the entire planetary genome bank project and the resulting endocrine studies from the beginning. After all that work, to be shunted off like this!

She looked down on his pith-helmeted head. His three wing-clipped parrots were bright splashes of color in his spotlight, one green, one red, one blue. Gorgeous creatures. They flapped, but couldn't fly. Like her.

He swooped his hand past their heads, and caught one by its beak. Expertly, he flipped it upright and held it out to some tourists. "Where you from?" They walked past, ignoring him, but he didn't seem daunted. "We have an arrangement here," he said. "A thousand yen to holo all you want." One woman stopped, and stood shyly. Janitsu had to admire his expertise as he talked her into getting a holo. He positioned her inside a square painted on the brick sidewalk. As the parrot man snapped his finger the blue parrot—Ichi?—spread its wings, and Janitsu saw a flash of bright yellow underwing. The parrot man pushed a button on a box which sat next to him on a low wall, and the two laser/mirror spheres, a few inches in diameter each, rose from their positions on opposite sides of the square in a swift spiral around the woman and lodged in the collector above. Janitsu was amused to see that the magnet, from which the working parts of the spheres were shielded, was attached to an overhanging branch.

He motioned the woman aside, reached up and removed one of the spheres, and flicked it open. He took out a small silver disk and slipped it into a plastic box he had in his hand. "That's all," he said. "Works on any standard machine. I hope you enjoy it." The woman handed him some money, smiled, and tucked the box into the pouch slung around her waist.

He stuffed the money in the pocket of his green-and-white checked shirt. He was tall, thin, and brown, and moved with short, jerky motions. When he took his helmet off to wipe sweat from his forehead, a long black ponytail fell halfway to his waist and shimmered in the spotlight. He coiled it up and stuck the helmet on again.

One of the parrots made a sound like the inside gears of her retrieval arm. A long, drawn-out mechanical screech, like the grating of metal on metal just before the damned thing broke and the results of the experiment which would have guaranteed her ticket to Mars spattered against the side of the module. Had that been sabotage? Just the thought of trying to prove it made Janitsu feel quite weary.

She contrasted the noise and confusion of Lahaina with the resort she'd left so abruptly a few hours ago. A high balcony with a pool below, which glittered aqua beneath clear night sky. Roll of surf gleaming white beyond in the full moon, a path to the stars. Or to Mars. Where she'd never go now. Rare wild sushi, not that farm stuff, flanked by green dabs of hot wasabi and long pink curls of daikon, delivered to her room immediately when she brushed the orderscreen in her room. She even had her own hot tub, in which she'd sat nude for two nights, staring at the lush, bright array of stars. So clear here out in the middle of the Pacific. But not as clear as space, as Mars.

This was just riff-raff here, hustlers. The parrot man was an endorphin freak, she decided, smoking too many of the enz which triggered endorphin production. He gave off a weird, brittle energy.

"Here, Ed, take a little nap," he said as he flipped one of the birds onto its back and let it lie placidly on his open hand. He offered it to a man passing by, who looked the other way.

"Where you from, where you from?" he asked over and over. "What do you do there?" Not much of a question, really. Hawaii had been virtually owned by Sphere and its subsidiaries for about twenty-five years.

Then he looked up. She felt like a spy, and shrank back into the shadows. He couldn't see her up here, could he?

The pill was taking effect. She went back inside, let the screen door slam. Between the clicks of the palm fronds, which increased in intensity as the wind picked up, she heard, "Yeah, I holo you, your family, with the parrots, only a thousand yen. Cheap, eh? Use your camera if you like, take a snapshot. Same price."

She closed her eyes. Yellow and red flowers filled her vision, and she poised on the verge of dream.

She was in Mexico, a child. With mother Susan, father Namu. Sunlight spilled onto the screened-in porch where they ate breakfast, miso soup. Her ceramic spoon clanked against the side of the bowl; she hated to pick it up like a cup. The sweet-salty soup burned her tongue. Dad drank coffee, Mom tea. She smelled sweet ginger blossoms and toast.

There were parrots in the trees outside, the jungle close in, so convenient for Mom and Dad to leave her and little sister Keiko with Auntie-san and go out to collect samples. The air was full of harsh bird cries.

One swooped right in under the roof and landed on the back of the empty chair next to Janitsu. A bright blue parrot, with splashes of green and red on its head. It spread its wings, and she was dazzled by the yellow feathers beneath.

She stared into its eyes for a long time without daring to breathe.

"Hold the parrot, hold the parrot," it said. She saw smoke behind it and tried to struggle away from the image, but the pills were too strong, and she entered the nightmare.

She woke just before dawn with a headache. Her t-shirt was soaked with sweat, and she was chilly in the cool, sweet air of morning.

She got out of bed, opened the rickety screen door, let it slam behind her as she stepped onto the balcony with its wood filigrees in the upper corners of the roof support.

The sky was streaked with brief ribbons of pink, then an aqua space appeared over the West Maui mountains, capped by clouds. A thin woman below in a straw hat with fake flowers was hosing down the sidewalk, a cigarette dangling from her mouth.

This is the world, she reminded herself. The world is not little white office cubicles, or a dome full of pleasure-gardens, or jaunts to the moon's nightside where stars glow more pure than earthers could ever imagine. It's not a myriad of wind-and-string pavilions. It's a place where on-leave spacers puke on the sidewalk below your room, and a loud parrot man screeches in your ear all night. You'll be here on Earth forever now.

She stretched and groaned. But it was just ordinary forty-eight-year-old stiffness. Her bones felt all right here. They'd felt all right there, damn it. She'd been tested every year. Why hadn't they detected the unacceptable rate of loss earlier? She should have anticipated it, faked the results. The tests were bullshit anyway. She just should have paid more attention to the backstabbers.

The street was blessedly quiet here. No magtrans—this was the outback. Bicycles only. A slow, lazy electric train made stops for tourists.

The parrot cart was empty, the holo apparatus gone. On the perch, two brown sparrows searched the seedcups with nervous pecks. The banyan tree in the park across the street had dropped so many baby trunks that now uncountable thick branches twined among the others, reaching for support, or holding the others up. It was hard for her eye to follow them down and untangle them, sort them into parent trunk. Some sort of birds—she couldn't see them—reacted to the light with a crescendo of haunting cries which made her think of a remote waterfall deep in some ancient jungle.

Ancient jungle. What was that dream again? She rubbed her eyes and caught its edge—smoke, pain, and birds singing—then felt it recede beyond recall.

What did it matter, anyway? What did anything matter? You'd think that after she'd worked so hard on developing hormonal balance criteria for space travel that she could write her own ticket. They'd wooed her with every perk resort they owned, fifteen years ago. She loved it, loved how Sphere gave her freedom to pursue every interest. Their new star.

But now? She hated golf, chief pursuit of the retired.

She went back inside and rummaged through her bag. She found her tiny black bikini and pulled it on over skin still smooth and unwrinkled. She'd never had children, and her tall, slim body was brown and not bad-looking, she thought. T-shirt, hat, polarizing light-sensitive contacts. Zoris. Set for the day. Tourist in paradise. Flowers. Aqua sea. Slummers, freaks, all kinds, dregs and richies, real life, real world, no more work for you, who cares?

Her vision filmed over and she felt the ache of tears. She sat down on the edge of the bed and tried to calm herself by breathing deeply. But she couldn't keep from crying, crying as if she were were a child.

Her breathing gradually returned to normal. She went into the bathroom, vaguely glad it only took five minutes to get it over with. After the meeting yesterday, she'd run to her room and cried for an hour before checking out.

She stood in front of the mirror, splashed her face, combed her very short, very black hair with a swoop of the comb. Were those reddened eyes shrewd or stupid? She went down to eat breakfast.

The open-air cafe was on the waterfront, and just as old as everything else in town. It was refreshing to be somewhere which hadn't been created within the past twenty years. Nothing made by robots, all human, unpredictable. Real food, too, factored into the ecocycle, eat, shit, pee, be eaten. She looked across to the banyan tree park, with its fringe of hibiscus, yellow in the morning light. Eat $CO_2$, exude $O_2$, little flowers, my sisters.

Little trees, my aunties. Big banyans, my grandmothers. Auntie-san, Mama-san. Protecting, caring for her and Keiko, even after their parents died. "Coffee," she said to the waiter. "Espresso, a double."

She lit one of the enz she'd bought on the street last night before checking in, when she was so mad, felt the hit smooth through her body, watched the world light up. Careful now, don't be a freak. Then she laughed. Why not? Hell, she didn't have to concentrate any more. Nobody needed her.

She glanced up from her newspaper and saw the parrot man come in.

He stood in bright sunlight in the entrance, lime-green shirt with red flowers blooming, room only for about three they were so huge. Darker green leaves twining around. Little vines, my brothers.

Little suns, little stars, my life.

Shit. Don't get upset. Earth is good. Earth is good. You can't stay away from it forever. Little brother vines, little sister trees. Little sister Keiko, running down the jungle path screaming "Hurry Auntie-san, hurry! The heli—the heli—"

And then Janitsu and Auntie-san saw it too, the smoke plume from the pad which must be the ultralight which Auntie-san had hated from the beginning, hated her brother going up in, while he laughed, saying, "O, it's so beautiful from the air, you come too, Kis."

Parrots swooped, screaming, blue, green, red.

"Hello?"

She jumped when he touched her wrist. She still held the smoking enz, which had burned to the stub.

"Are you all right?"

The parrot man removed it from between her fingers very carefully, very gently. She shivered, then tried to laugh.

"I've only done this a few times before," she said. She hadn't thought about the accident in years, had never seen it so clearly. She had only been six when it happened.

"Just take a deep breath, that's it," he said. His voice was different than last night, quiet and reassuring. "Put your head down if you like. Good, you'll feel better in a minute. You've got to be careful with it if you aren't used to it. Endorphins are really powerful to begin with. You get this enhancement stuff on the street here, it can blow you away." She sat up, still a little dizzy, and he pulled out the chair opposite her before she could protest.

He looked into her eyes for a long time. She was surprised that it didn't bother her. It wasn't even as if a human was looking at her. His eyes were hard, birdlike, and they darted across her face with short jerks. Green. Caucasian. Lovely long eyelashes, sharp curve of black eyebrows which echoed the ironic curve of his mouth. There was something familiar—

He blinked, and the feeling went away. "The usual," he said to the waitress when she came. "And you?" he asked.

Rattled, she said, "Rice. Miso soup." Something she was used to.

She wanted to ask him to go away, but that would be rude, after he'd been so nice.

"Where you from?" he asked.

She shrugged.

"You don't have to say," he said. "Ninase. Kukanzai. Or one of the other Sphere space stations. We see station burn-outs here all the time. They get bumped, then go stir crazy up there at Kaanipali."

"Not everyone does," she said, annoyed at being pegged so easily.

"But you have."

The breeze in the open-air pavilion switched some strands of black hair across his green eyes as he watched her, too closely now, she thought. It was true that she'd put up with the regimentation for Mars, but she'd never quite fit, in little ways that bugged everyone else. She supposed it was her American mother. It seemed much easier for those raised entirely in Japan to take. They even liked being programmed from the cradle to the grave. She hadn't—and look what had happened because of it. She'd made too many waves. Couldn't help it. Half of her life wasted, and she didn't know if she could even survive away from Sphere. She looked up to see him still studying her.

"Where are *you* from?" she asked, upset when it sounded belligerent.

His mouth turned downward for a second, then he shrugged. "It doesn't matter. I'm here forever. Stranded." He laughed, and his voice switched to the parrot's laugh, high-pitched and harsh. His nose was straight and long, his cheekbones high. A tan burnished his skin, smooth except for faint lines around his mouth and eyes.

Their food came. She dumped her rice in her soup and he made a face.

"Your food is even worse," she said. "What's that? Just a bunch of seeds."

"Lots of protein," he said. "You ought to try it some time."

She felt more relaxed after eating, and started to read the front page of the *Maui Times*.

"I saw you last night," he said. "You have the room above me. Maybe you should move."

She looked up from her paper. "It's all right. I have pills."

"Pills." He reached over quickly and touched her wrist. "Too many pills aren't good for you. What's wrong? Can I help?" He rubbed his thumb back and forth over the inside of her wrist, tilted his head.

She understood the unspoken part of his question, stared at him, then smiled. "So early in the morning?"

"Early is nice," he said.

They rose and he went with her to her room.

She was surprised at the gentleness with which he drew off her shirt, liked his swift, teasing touches. They changed to long, sweeping caresses which blended in her mind with the sound of the wind in the trees. His silky hair fell forward and brushed her shoulders, and she pulled him close.

She liked the way he moved, so fierce and quick, when they lay side by side on the bed, one of her legs wrapped around him. How long it had been for her! She came quickly, and colors burst inside her closed eyelids.

He got up and went in the bathroom. She heard him open a patch packet and the slap when it hit his neck.

She wondered.

He was back again below her window that evening. She couldn't sleep, couldn't stay awake. Still not on this cycle. Circadians all messed up.

She heard an odd note through the Halcyon fog as she lay in bed, one she hadn't heard the night before. Was it plaintiveness? What did the parrot man yearn for? Besides a quick lay with a tourist? There was something very different about him, but she didn't quite know what. She suspected he was a little crazy, but all the people she'd been around for most of her life were so homogeneous that she wasn't sure she'd know a crazy person if she met one.

He took something, some medicine, to regulate something. She'd sat out on the porch smoking cigarettes earlier, and saw him put on one patch, frown, take it off, look at it, open a little case, and replace it with another. A mistake, one which he could sense immediately. Fast stuff, strong stuff, vital stuff.

"Where you from? Want to hold the bird? It doesn't cost to hold it you know. Hey, it's *mandatory* to hold the bird."

In bed, she closed her eyes, and saw him swoop the parrot around his thin, bony wrist, around and around and around. As it fluttered and grasped with its claws, he turned to a parrot too, and the two of them swirled around each other in a blaze of color, like a yinyang. Then they each spread their wings and flew off in opposite directions, into the velvet night inside her eyes, as if he had been one, and now split into two.

When she passed the cafe and saw him sitting there the next morning, his back was to her. She walked by quickly. She didn't need any crazies in her life. She didn't need anyone. All she needed was Mars, and her work. She could go back, pull strings, get what was her due. Maybe. It would amount to begging. It might be worth it. But not now. Let them stew. Let them realize what they'd lost.

She caught the train and went across the West Maui mountains, through dense jungle dripping with flowers, with sheets of rain blowing against her as she stood in the open section.

The other coast was where the wavesporters skimmed and dared, dropping onto the wave at just the right instant, curling over and over in their forcesuits in a wild, disorienting frolic with death, which would surely occur if they didn't curl at just the right moment, at just the right angle.

She stood on the bright golden beach in front of the deadly, furling waves and watched as the powerful offshore wind kicked up sand which stung her legs, as spellbound as all the other tourists. Death and life combined they called it. A yinyang dance.

Yinyang like the parrot man, not of a whole. Part of him shadowed, hidden by the drugs he took. Jerky, birdlike motions, harsh voice. Birds which did his bidding as if they were linked mind to mind. Mind to mind as no one wholly human could be. Mind to mind as she'd believed could happen, just one result of what had been tried and lost so long ago.

No, she thought. That's silly. He couldn't be. There were only a hundred of them.

She watched the sporters float up, in their brightly colored suits, from out of the foam, and jet back out to the breakline.

When she returned that evening, the parrot man was gone, and she felt an instant's panic. She hadn't even asked his name. Another man was there, far more polite to the tourists. She could see he wasn't as successful.

She was surprised at herself when she called down from her balcony, "Where did the other one go?"

He looked up. "Sentio? He had to take the night off," he said. "Sometimes he don't feel so hot."

She sat on the balcony watching, relieved. He'd be back. The birds misbehaved for his substitute, who kept saying, "No," and squirting them in the face with a plastic jug of water he kept in his hand. Gertrude bit someone's ear; Ed shit on a little boy's arm.

During a lull, the man just walked away. Janitsu wondered where he went.

Ed grabbed the perch with his beak and climbed down to the platform. Then he latched onto that and dropped to the sidewalk. He ambled off.

Janitsu watched nervously as Ichi and Gertrude followed. They beat their wings, scolding with terrible hisses and cries, trying to get off the ground.

"Pick him up," Janitsu yelled to a man who watched Ed step into the street. The train was approaching only a block away.

The man looked up at her.

"Just put your arm in *front* of him. He'll step onto it. He won't hurt you." Ichi and Gertrude followed Ed into the street, stepping down from the curb as carefully as crotchety old folks who needed canes.

"Sure, lady," the man said, and walked away.

"Damn you," Janitsu yelled, and ran out of her room into the hall. She tore down the steps and ran out in the street. She put her arm down and Ed stepped onto it, his claws hard and scratchy. She put out her other arm and got Gertrude. Ichi pecked at her bare foot. It didn't hurt as much as she thought it would. The other man came back with a blue shave ice and saw what was happening.

"Thanks," was all he said, and he took the birds back, stuck them on the perch, and squirted them in the face. They squawked and shook their heads.

Janitsu fumed on the way back upstairs. How could he leave his birds with such an idiot?

She tossed and turned as she listened to his dull, well-mannered voice saying, "Hold the bird?" She couldn't fall asleep without her friend's harsh, aggressive badgering.

She most missed the plaintive note. It was well hidden. But it was there.

She thought she might know why.

She got a message the next morning to check in—Mijea had found her—and ignored it. She knew he just wanted to up her perk ratio as an apology. It made them nervous, her being on the outside for so long, out of their control, not accepting the next step they had offered. Why should she accept a demotion?

She couldn't remember when she had last been on her own, not on some space station or on some every-eyeblink-programmed tour. The hell with them. She could add up all her perks and still not get to Mars. What did she have? No family, nothing, all for the company, all her life. And now no Mars.

She went to the cafe and saw him inside. She hesitated, then walked in. She was almost sure. There were not that many people in a position to know, but she was one of them.

"Parrot man," she said.

He jumped, turned. "I'm not—" he began, a sharp, intense stare in his eyes, then stopped. He smiled, but it wasn't a real smile. "Oh, it's you. Sorry."

"You are, I think. A bird-person. From the biogeneering project. How old are you?"

He took a deep breath, looked down. "I'm not—quite sure."

She nodded as she sat down. "Someone took you. And left you. You've read about it, haven't you?"

He closed his eyes and bent his head for a moment. When he looked up at her again, his eyes were distant. "Why don't you tell me. You seem to know something about it."

Janitsu took a deep breath, put her elbows on the table and linked her fingers. "I don't have anything new to add. The raid was very well-planned. Insider information. All of you were about four years old when you were stolen. Liberated, they called it. They landed on the beach with machine guns. I wasn't there myself, I wasn't on-site all the time, like most of the scientists. My work was more abstract." Think-taking biogeneered humans had been abstract indeed, and extremely heady, she recalled.

She looked down at the stain a coffee cup had left on the table. "They just—they just dropped you into cities, at random. Left you on corners, in subways. Said that way you couldn't be re-collected, and that you weren't human anyway. It was horrible. They claimed that they'd made their point, revealed the operation to the world. Now it's against the law. I was stunned when it happened. All of us were. I went back to the island twice, alone."

"What island?"

"It was a small island in the Gulf of Cortez. Everything was so empty without the kids, so desolate. We'd taken kilometers of film, of course. You wouldn't believe how well-documented everything was. After the second time, I never went back. I made copies of the films and watched them over and over at home. They were all I had left. We were all so hopeful, so excited, and it was my first real project, to monitor hormonal development, stack the data against behavioral information, motor information, cognitive information. But it wasn't really the loss of the experiment that upset me. It was the thought of each of you alone somewhere in the world, wondering what had happened, growing up strange—we didn't know *how* strange—without any of the help we'd meant to give you." Odd, how crazy, how depressed she'd been. She'd cried over those children, memorized those faces, dreamed them for years. Her only children.

Not hers, really, of course not. Hundreds of people had worked on the project, though her research had played a decisive role in making it possible. She'd never let anyone know how she felt, how she watched the films alone, late at night. Such behavior would have been questionable at best. Some had already thought her far too young to be on such a project, and were jealous anyway, looking even then for ways to get rid of the young woman who she now realized must have seemed haughty and distant. She felt now like the children must have felt then: abandoned.

Sphere, to duck the damning publicity, had shifted the lot of them to the space stations, scattered them anonymously among the divisions. She had loved space almost instantly: so straightforward. So constant. So healing.

And now they'd sent her back.

"You're almost thirty," she told Sentio, aware that she was encompassing an entire, fruitful career in those brief words. She took one of her enz from her pocket, lit it, pulled smoke into her lungs. "It was about twenty-five years ago. Never any more of you made. Against God's will, they said. Let this be a lesson." She began to shake, remembering how it had been to be the focus of so much hatred, so many threats.

"Careful now," he said, and she saw real concern in his eyes. He smiled just a bit. "So long ago," he said. "You can see I'm all right."

"Oh, of course you are." She reached over and touched the patch behind his ear. He pulled back and looked away. She said, "Life could be much different for you. Your entire awareness, your way of assimilating information. Hormones are everything."

"I think I know that better than you," he said, and the sarcasm in his voice didn't surprise her. "But my life is just fine, thank you. I'm very happy."

She let that pass. "Where did you get the parrots?"

"All I knew was, I had to have them," he said. "I grew up in L.A. On the street. It was hard. I—saw things differently. Later, when everything was a little more—shall we say, normal—I could tell the difference."

"What was different?" she asked, jealous of all the lost information, lost knowledge. God, the tests they'd prepared, the tests they'd done already, by the time they were abducted.

"Patterns. Energy. Flowers glowing. Oh, so bright. Sounds so sharp and meaningful, even the sound of traffic, the sound of rain, the sound of voices when they don't make words but only music. I couldn't get along with people. Didn't care for them. Felt nothing."

"How do you get the hormones? How do you know what kind, how much?"

His eyes narrowed. "A doc. Friend of mine. Black market. Not very fine-tuned, I'm afraid. It's been a while. He did a profile on me about ten years ago and figured it out, he thought. I never have been really sure." He looked at her bitterly. "Until now. Sometimes," he shrugged, "I don't know. Think maybe I'll stop taking them."

"That's not necessary. Or wise. Things could be much, much better."

"Quite the expert, aren't you?"

Why should she feel defensive? "As a matter of fact, I am."

"Then what are you doing here? Isn't your little vacation over yet? And what good does it do me to screw around with myself with all these patches anyway? Tell me that. What good is it to try and be like everybody else? Too expensive. Too much trouble. The hell with everything." His eyes lit up. "Ever been to the headlands to the north?

Past Kaanapali. Narrow dirt road. A cliff a thousand feet high. Bright blue ocean, tiny white waves so far below. It just looks wrinkled, so far away. The wind—the wind is so strong. It could just take you, you know? Out over the ocean. People die there, good hang gliders. World champions, they come there to die. Oh, God. Oh shit! You damned biogeneers! Tell me, what was the point?"

"One of the offshoots was to be the production of people better adapted to long space journeys. But that was just one—"

"Right," he said. He stared at her for a minute, then went on in a low voice. "Sometimes I wavesport, when I can afford it. Hanglide. Anything." An ironic smile touched his lips, then it crumbled.

She saw that he could cry.

She reached over and took his hands. They were warm, human. His fingers twisted through hers tightly.

It's not my fault, she wanted to say. We had plans for all of you. She pulled him out of his chair, and held him so close that his bony hips hurt her, walked him up the stairs, down the narrow dark hallway to her room. It's not my fault, she tried to say with her hands, her mouth. But it was, and she knew it.

She knew he did too.

That night, he refused to look up at her from beneath his pith helmet. She watched him for several hours, while people danced across the street in an upper-floor, open air nightclub to whale calls rearranged by synthesizers, and amplified, it seemed, a million times.

She'd accessed some perks and sipped hundred-year-old whisky, spiked it with slowly smoked enz. Mexico broke into her mind over and over, a bright window of flowers, clear air laced with bird song. A shining green river and the hot, yellow flames of death. The colors of Earth meant death to her, meant loss. Space, spare black and white, had come to mean life and hope.

She turned from the thoughts each time they intruded. Long ago. Not important. She bent her elbow, took another puff, tasted the whisky again.

She watched the parrots flap their clipped wings. She'd asked again where he'd gotten them—they were endangered—and why no one arrested him, and then was sorry she'd asked. Why should he trust her? He just said in his low, wry voice, "The world is not quite as well-regulated as you think, Janitsu."

Tropical night blossomed around her. The shuffle of feet on the sidewalk below was constant, the smell of grilled fish drifted upward whenever a new couple stopped at the brazier down the block. Business was heavy. It was a good excuse for him to ignore her. Torches flared at a Hawaiian place next door.

"Sentio," she whispered.

He glanced up, surprising her. Sharp ears. "Where you from?" he shouted, and his anger blazed through the air.

She didn't mind. She remembered his thin, sure hands holding her hips, the way he cried out like a bright jungle bird, his green eyes which could weep and see flowers glow.

She couldn't believe that he had survived. How sad to still scrabble for life here on the streets. Who knows what he might have been, might have done, might have *known*, if he hadn't been thrown into the streets like a stray dog. They'd been feeding information to those kids like crazy, using every theory about learning enhancement and then some. And they'd been loved.

She went downstairs, sat next to him on a little brick wall.

"Go away," he said. "You'll ruin my business." He turned away and raised his voice. "Want to hold the parrot? Come on, don't be afraid," he called out. A mother and father turned around to get their daughter, dressed in a tight-fitting station outfit, who gazed at Ed with wide eyes.

"Do you remember anything?" Janitsu asked. "The waterfalls, the beach? The computers? All the toys, the games? Things to climb on, the best designers in all the world created your environment. What fun you had, playing, yelling, running. Oh, we had about five adults for each of you, holding you, watching you, taking care of you, teaching you, learning from you. A real family."

He stared at her for a few seconds, then looked away. "It's free to hold the parrot," he yelled. He stood with his back to her, facing the tourists, and swirled two at once on one arm, laughed angrily, and swooped them onto the perch in an elaborate bow. He didn't say a word, but Ichi reached out, swung on his outstretched finger for an instant, flapped, and landed on the shoulder of a boy who had stopped to watch, one with curly brown hair and a yellow and red striped jumpsuit. He shrieked, then laughed. The parents paid. Sentio handed them their disk.

"Don't be afraid," he shouted, his voice even more grating. A little boy dropped his tofu cone and hid behind his father, who frowned and pulled him down the sidewalk.

Janitsu got up and grabbed Sentio's shoulders, spun him around.

"I'm *not* afraid, don't you understand? I'm not afraid of you."

He shook her off. He knelt and said to a girl with green barrettes in her black hair, "What's wrong with your arm? Oh, it doesn't have a parrot on it. Come closer, young one. That's it. It's very safe, don't worry." He carefully set Ed on her shoulder, swooped around and let Gertrude step onto the other, and put Ichi on her head. The mother and father looked bemused. "Doesn't she look pretty with a parrot? Keep your shoulder up. Want to go for a holo?" They did. Afterwards, they walked on.

"When I was a little girl," Janitsu said to his back, "I lived in the jungle with parrots. I even had one as a pet."

"Oh, really?" he said. "No wonder you like me so much." He turned and smiled, but his eyes were cold. "And I think you agree that my reptile brain works very well, once it is let loose."

She kept looking at him, calm. "I didn't even remember that until that first morning I saw you—remember?"

"Of course," he said in a low voice, then shifted into his high one as another family passed: "Don't be afraid, it's all right. You can hold the parrot."

"My parents died there," she said. "They died in a heli crash. All the parrots flew up out of the jungle, away from the fire, the explosions. I don't think I've seen any parrots since then, not live ones. It seemed like the explosions would never stop. All the fuel was stored right there—" tears filled her eyes, and she was surprised. The third time in three days. The third time in twenty years.

He sat down next to her, and deftly transferred Ichi to her right arm, Gertrude to her left. He kept Ed. He pressed the release button and touched his nose to hers in the holo, looking straight into her eyes. "Go get some sleep," he said.

She left the door to her room unlocked. Later, when the street was still, he woke her, ran his hands up to her breasts, slipped into bed beside her.

"What have you done to me?" he whispered.

She woke later because he was holding her so tightly it hurt. She stirred, and he loosened his arms a bit, but didn't wake. His hair, which lay across them, slipped from her shoulder and brushed her breast. The street was quiet at last, and the room was a jumble of shadow and fragments of surfaces lit by the streetlight.

His face was very close, and she studied the slant of his eyebrow. His long eyelashes fell a millimeter short of his cheekbone, which she lightly kissed. Then she closed her eyes and slept.

The next day she went to make some arrangements with Mijea. Credits accessed and transferred. Computer time bought with some, to get all the information she needed. Suppliers, maps.

She couldn't do everything there, though. But she'd met a friendly woman down on Front Street who knew the ropes.

In the end, she was able to get a new name into the system, one which hadn't been there before. It cost, but she could well afford it.

She wondered about the hormone mix, then decided she could handle it later. She ordered everything in the book. They arrived in ten hours, cold in permchill until she needed them.

She sat across from him in the cafe the next morning. She was sure he'd patched just for her, because he smiled, a genuine smile. Very much this side of human. She smiled back.

"There are a few places in the world where parrots still live," she said.

"Mexico, perhaps?" he asked. Why did he always sound so ironic?

"I've booked passage for us on the next hover. It leaves tonight. Here's a new passport, and a ticket." She reached over and tucked the envelope into his pocket, tried to ignore the look in his eyes she was afraid might be anger. "We can take the birds." She stopped, suddenly aware of the weight of her assumptions, tried to think of how to share with him her certainty that this was right, and why.

He nodded once. "A big gift, from you," he said. "Why did you do it? Why didn't you ask me? I don't want to be on anyone's system. Not even yours. What's in that box?"

"Hormones," she said. "I want to show you what I ordered and you can let me know if there's anything else I ought to bring. This won't be hit or miss. I can—"

He interrupted in a quiet voice. "I see. Yes. You can. You can make me whatever you want. You can mix my heart and mind together and take them apart again. I know. I've done it myself. You can turn me into a bird and back into a man again. What fun."

"No," she said, "that's not—I don't have to—"

"So you intend to go to Mexico. Leave Sphere? Who are you kidding? Have you ever lived on your own?" His eyes were challenging, but Janitsu sensed fear behind his arrogance.

"What about you?" she flung back. "This isn't a real life you have here, Sentio. It's an absurd life."

"It always has been, don't you think? And whose fault is that?" He pushed his chair away from the table and stood up. "Do you suppose I'll have a real life with you? You and your little painting box of hormones? At least, here, I and my parrots are one," he said. "At least I don't manipulate and control them, the way you want to control everything in your path. Isn't that what you've done all your life?" His voice was harsh again, high. He reached behind his neck and pulled a patch off, flung it down, began to talk so quickly she could barely understand what he said. "How do I know you are who you say you are? Maybe you've tracked me down, maybe Sphere wants me for experiments." His eyes were wide and glittery. He blinked, and took a deep breath which he let out slowly.

He turned away, hands on his hips, and stared out at the harbor. After a moment he said so quietly that she had to strain to hear above the clatter of silverware and chatter, "I'm sorry. I do know. You are who you say you are. That's not a problem. I wonder, though, if you could help just—being yourself. If you can even see me as a person." He sighed, put his hand in his pocket, and opened the little container he pulled out. He chose two packets, opened them, and put them on his neck.

He turned back to her, and sat on the edge of his chair. Sweat shone on his forehead as he spoke. "You know, I saw something in your eyes that first morning. Like my parrots, something clipped inside of you, some flight gone. Whirling on my wrist, holding onto me with their fine, hard beaks, holding on so tight. Like you." He looked at her for a few seconds. "I have to feed my friends now," he said. He squeezed her hand and left.

She walked distractedly through Lahaina that day, coming down from too many enz, watching the play of light zigzag through palm frond filters.

Was he right? Did she always have to play with life?

Maybe she should go back to Sphere. Safe, cared for. She could really write her own ticket, except for Mars. Silly to get so wrought up over politics. She could come here often, visit Sentio …

At six, after a long anxious day of buying odd things she thought she might need, she went up to her room. Sentio had vanished. She hadn't seen him once since the morning, though she'd tried to find him.

She opened and slammed drawers. She'd bought some new shorts and shirts, some heavy boots, but it still only took her ten minutes to stuff everything into her duffel. Supplies and equipment would be waiting when she got there.

Only the hormones, in their permchill box, still lay out on the rumpled bed when she was finished. She put the box in a net bag, picked everything up, took one look around the room, and stepped into the hall.

Where was Sentio? If he were going, he would be here by now. She stood beside the open door, wondering what to do.

If he didn't come, what was the point? Why take this long voyage by herself? To unearth long-dead memories, to stir up the pain of the past?

Why not stay? If she did, Sentio would let her do whatever she wanted with his hormones. She knew he would. She would do good things, change him in ways he would be happy about, the ways he wanted to be changed.

Yes, and soon he would *want* to come with her, to those bright jungles where he belonged, full of parrots, that place she had to see again. Wouldn't he? How could she not make sure of that? It was right that they go together. It fit, it made sense. She could make that happen, and he would thank her, once he saw what was possible.

Exactly.

Ah, how could he know her so well, so soon? It was frightening, to be so thoroughly understood, to know that someone could see her quite clearly, see all the flaws she'd always refused to acknowledge. She'd never imagined that it could be so.

Perhaps it was just as frightening for him.

She walked to the railing at the end of the corridor and stood for a moment, watched birds settle into the banyan tree for the night with their customary cries. To the right, she saw the hover, anchored on water that seemed smoothed by the pink and gold of sunset which colored the slow-moving swells. A boy, silhouetted against the swiftly darkening sky, ran down the dock with a fishing pole and bucket. "Hurry, Dad," she heard him yell, and any answer was drowned out by the engine of a brightly-lit dinner boat which pulled out of its slip laden with tourists.

She set the hormones down, watched the net bag collapse onto the worn green carpet, then descended the stairs.

The hover, with room for only eight passengers, was open for boarding. It was the only one, not hard for him to find. She stowed her small bag and stood up top, waiting.

The unsailed masts of yachts bobbed in the harbor lights. The speedway for the hover was lit with phosphorescent biolights which glimmered just below the surface, making pure, cool, green circles of light.

A few passengers trooped on and went to their rooms. An attendant closed a hatch next to her. She said, "You can stay up here for the first ten minutes or so, until we leave the channel. After that you have to go below while we accelerate. I'll let you know."

Then she was alone.

She looked at the wharf. Empty.

She went to the other side of the hover and sat on a bench with a view of Lanai, the island across the channel. The hover rocked gently on the harbor chop.

It would take just twenty-four hours to reach the coast of Mexico. Another three days of increasingly difficult travel to reach the place she had in mind. The place where she knew he would feel at home.

But he wasn't coming.

She was surprised at the tears which burned her eyes. She kept her back to empty wharf and watched the green and red gulches of Lanai lose detail during the swift, still minutes of sunset. One engine revved, then another, as the crew checked them out. She didn't move when the hover hummed with the sound of the gangplank retracting.

They maneuvered out into the bay. Her hair lifted in the breeze. Soon they would leave the sound of the engines behind, and only the hiss of wind would skim the edge of the cabin. Another engine roared to life.

She fingered the bright red abort button, for emergencies, set into the railing next to her. The other passengers would be annoyed at the delay, but it was still a possibility. She could go back.

She clenched her hand, jammed it into her pocket, and jumped at a touch on her shoulder.

She turned, and Sentio was there. His hair, hanging free, blew against her face and he grabbed it and held it back with one hand.

"It took a long time to persuade those parrots that they would be all right in the room. They told me it was number five. I hope it's the right cabin." He looked at her directly, but in the green glare of the biolights she couldn't read the expression in his eyes.

Then he held up the net bag with the permchill pack.

"I tripped over this in the hallway when I went to look for you," he said. He paused a moment, and she felt something alien, hard to identify, something that reminded her of sitting on the porch with her parents and Keiko in a pool of light, brushed by the ginger-scented breeze while her spoon clanked against the side of the bowl.

"I think it's yours," he said.

**Kathleen Ann Goonan** attended Clarion West in 1988, and she credits this experience with her transformation into a professional writer. Since then, she has published over thirty short stories and seven novels. *Queen City Jazz*, her first novel, was a *New York Times* Notable Book, and her other novels have been shortlisted for the Arthur C. Clarke Award, the British Science Fiction Association Award, the Nebula Award, and others. *In War Times*, her sixth novel, was the American Library Association's Best SF Novel of the Year, and it won the John W. Campbell Award for Best Novel of the Year. She is presently Professor of the Practice at Georgia Institute of Technology, where she teaches Creative Writing and the history of science, technology, literature, and culture.

# Greg Bear
# on Kathleen Ann Goonan

A real treat arising out of my involvement with Clarion West over the years has been meeting new and prominent writers at the beginnings of their careers. I've watched with affection and undue pride the progress of my former students.

Yet that word—student—rings oddly. One fact that almost everyone acknowledges, in the writing biz, is that writing cannot be taught: it can only be encouraged and informed. Some clues can be provided, but not all clues work for all writers. Encouragement often comes in the form of realizing that not everything you are told by other writers applies to you or your writing. A writing career is personal, specific, delicate. And that breeds individuality, inner conviction, sometimes inner strength. Or it breeds confusion and anxiety.

I've described Clarion West as a boot camp for writers. If you don't like what you see and hear during this workshop, you either move on and make your own writing reality—or you find another line of work.

The writers I worked with at Clarion became friends, colleagues, people who, inexplicably, sat and listened to my blather in classrooms for almost an entire week. I have to admit that my memory of those day-to-day discussions are hazy at best. I remember mostly faces, voices. Laughter. I remember talking too much.

Astrid and I have sponsored a fourth-week Clarion party at our house since the late 1980s, adding to my confusion! Sometimes, to my embarrassment, I jumble one year with another, one class with another, one party with another ...

But in the years since, I've kept in touch with nearly all the writers that grew out of the Clarion sessions I taught. A dizzying assortment!

Kathy Goonan's Clarion class was awash with novelists. One isn't allowed to pick favorites, and in fact, I admire all of them, and keep their books—again with undue pride—in my library, where I have been known to point them out to visitors and say, "Look! This one listened to me," or, "Look! This one paid no attention at all, and now, all these excellent books!"

But the one thing I do remember saying, in my week of blather, was "Write novels. And try very hard to write science fiction novels, because really good science fiction novels are rare and much in demand."

And so many did listen!

Kathleen Ann Goonan has specialized in writing fine science fiction novels. She laid down a distinctive voice with her debut novel, *Queen City Jazz*, and ever since has demonstrated both a personal and regional touch, drawing richly from her own biography, enthusiasms and experience in books that have won many loyal readers, accolades, and awards. Her most recent novels, *In War Times* and *This Shared Dream*, add a great deal of personal detail to the already-rich Nanotech Quartet. And this in some of the most challenging times in American publishing!

But it's very clear from "The Parrot Man" that she has also mastered an equally difficult length of story—some say more difficult. The accumulation of sensual details, familiar but slightly skewed in both technology and language, the reflection of an eternal quandary in a future looking-glass, dreams and hopes frustrated, then recast ... Classic science fiction, classic short story.

So it's a treat to say, again, with undue pride, that Kathy is still surprising, still growing, still learning. And in that way, every good writer—and Kathy is a very good writer—is indeed a student, and remains a student for life.

A student of life.

**Greg Bear** is the author of more than thirty books of science fiction and fantasy, including *Blood Music*, *The Forge of God*, *Darwin's Radio*, *Hull Zero Three* and *Mariposa*. He has received five Nebula Awards, one in every category, two Hugo Awards, and numerous award nominations.

# Absalom's Mother

## Louise Marley

## 1993

The dome is dark above my head as I trot down the narrow lane toward the storage depot. The air chills my neck. I'm a few minutes late, and I don't want the others to think my courage failed. It took all my strength to leave the peace of my home, my bed, my partner's warmth beside me, to rouse Carly with a whispered warning, to pretend to be calm.

As I round the last corner, I see through the gloom that the others are already gathered in the red-brick plaza beneath the steps of the storage depot. I slow my steps to pass through the line of women, counting. They are all there. Everyone is shivering with cold and with dread, as I am. Some of them speak in low, uneasy voices. Several speak my name in hushed tones. One or two faces are streaked with tears. I stop near the front, hugging my jacket around me.

I have not slept at all. Jem and I wept together last night, long into the darkness. We clung together, grieving, but even when I felt his tears on my shoulder I did not tell him what we planned. When he finally fell asleep, gripping my hand in his, I lay staring at the low ceiling of our residence cabin until it was time.

Keisha, by tacit agreement the leader of this—this—thing that we're doing, that we're attempting, Keisha jumps up to stand on the edge of a foamcast planter. She holds up one hand, pale in the gloom, and calls in a quiet, commanding voice, "This is it, my friends. Remember, we stand together, that's the important thing. The only thing. No one flinches, no one runs."

"Right, Keisha," someone calls. I turn and see Maria at the back, her arm around Jasmine. Jasmine keeps her face turned into Maria's shoulder.

"That's right," someone else drawls. I turn the other way, and see Ebony, tall and black and strong. My own skin is an indeterminate brown, but Ebony's skin is the true satiny black of an earlier age. I asked her once how she came by such pure blood, and she only shrugged, and said, "Lucky." Ebony looks like a soldier.

I don't look like a soldier at all. I'm small. My arms and shoulders are thin, and the shade of my skin comes from ethnicities nobody remembers now. But I'm as determined as Keisha is. As we all are. We have to be.

Unity is our only weapon.

Keisha gestures to me. "Come up here, will you, Vivi?"

"Okay." I move into the fourth position. My legs feel weak, and I'm shaking inside my jacket. I thrust my hands in the pockets so no one will see them tremble.

Keisha is second in line, and Ebony is right behind her. We determined all this, working in the communal kitchens, speaking out of the sides of our mouths as if we were prisoners. In a way, we are prisoners. Every community, even tiny poor ones like ours, is subject to the power of Central Council. Central controls the air, the water, the clothes and food we import, the fabricated materials we export. It all comes from Central, along with Directives, and Rulings, and Resolutions, and Policies. And Recruitment Orders, which bring us here on this cold, dark morning.

First in our shivering line is Avery.

Avery, among us all, does not seem to be afraid. But then, Avery has a cabinet full of powerful drugs, pain relievers, tranquilizers, narcotics. The medics give her anything and everything they can think of, because they can't do anything else for her.

We all treat Avery with reverence. She volunteered to be first. When we all said, No, Avery, you're too ill, she insisted.

She said, when the Orders came from Central and we began to talk about this rebellion, she said, "I want my death to count for something."

Keisha said at the time, "Avery, they shouldn't take Johnny anyway, not with you so sick. We should tell them—tell them about you."

And Avery, in a faint voice, said, "They called them all, Keisha. They won't care. They don't care about us."

I look up again, to the very top of the dome. The light has reached it at last, a silvery, hesitant glimmer. The panels will pick it up, and the streets and squares of 78th Grange will brighten. By the time everyone comes out of their cabins to begin work, the dome will be warm. I wonder where we—all of us gathered here—where will we be by then?

Avery leans against one of the tall planters with her eyes closed. I look past her, up the steps to the doors of the storage depot. Silos and bolt rooms and parts storage facilities fill its two floors. At one side of the small lobby is a desk, with a wallscreen behind it. This is called the Extension Office, and it's usually empty. Central sends someone to sit behind the desk only when they've made a Ruling or issued a Directive. 78th Grange is so small, and produces so little, that we have no Councilor of our own. We have a proxy, but only one-half vote.

The storage depot is built into the curve of the dome right by the two northern access locks. The main lock opens directly into the monorail. The other lock, leading outside, is for the people who repair the dome or the rails or the silo feeders, or inspect the vacuum-growth filaments. From my position, fourth in line behind Avery, I can see the cabinets beside the locks, where the vacuum suits are stored. I can't read the signs from here, but I know what they say. I grew up in 78th Grange, and all of us memorized those warning messages before we learned to read. No one is to step into the outside lock without a suit on, and the suit has to be thoroughly checked by someone qualified, someone who knows how to be certain all the seals are sealed and the slender oxygen cylinders properly adjusted and connected. Thinking of the locks, and the instructions I've known since babyhood, makes my heart pound. I look away.

Keisha has left her place, and is working down the line, arranging us in descending order of courage, as she sees it. The most fearful will be at the end, probably Jasmine. Jasmine is terrified of everything, but she can't help it. A lot of terrible things have happened to her. She says this is the worst.

Avery moans, and I hurry up the steps to stand beside her. "Avery, are you okay?"

Her eyelids flutter, and she rolls her head a little against the foamcast.

"Avery," I say. "You could sit down for now. Until—until they come."

She lifts her eyelids, and I see that her pupils are expanded so much the brown irises are almost swallowed up. She laughs. "Oh, Vivi," breathlessly, "am I still here? I thought—I'm so stoned, I thought I was already gone."

"Are you in pain, Avery?"

She shakes her head, and her dark hair catches on the trailing vine in the planter. "No pain," she murmurs, and gives a high, breathy laugh. "No, no pain at all."

I stay by her until Keisha returns, and then I move down two steps to my place in line. I look out over the cramped square and see that Keisha has put everyone in order. I count, to be certain they are all there.

Everyone is. Thirteen women. Mothers.

Central made a gross error, of course. If they had only called a few of our children, or even half of them, this would probably not have happened. Those whose children were safe would not risk themselves. Those who managed to have their children's names left off the list through influence, or bribery, or threats, or any of the things wealthy and educated and powerful people come up with, would never have come out to stand exposed in the square in the early morning. They would have no need.

But this is 78th Grange, and there is no power or wealth here. Central called all of them, every child of 78th Grange who was recruitment age. My own Carly had just reached it. We celebrated her eleventh birthday two months ago.

When the Order came down, flashed from Central to the Extension Office, Keisha had come around to read it to us. "In this time of crisis," she read, her voice tight with anger, "all citizens share the burden of maintaining the peace."

"What peace?" Ebony growled. We were all at work in the kitchens, stirring the great vats of soup, shredding the salad greens for dinner, stacking bowls and plates to be laid on the long tables. Only Avery was missing. She was too sick to work.

Keisha's eyes flashed at Ebony, and she kept reading. "Quotas will be met by all communities. The lowering of the age of induction, mandated by the Council to reduce frivolous deferments, will make it possible to maintain the current levels in the workforce while supplying the manpower needs of the militia for the foreseeable future ..."

Her voice went on, reading the entire Order, but I could no longer hear her. My heart pounded in my ears, and my knees turned to jelly. In fact, I think I collapsed, but I don't remember exactly. The next thing I remember clearly is Ebony holding me up with her long, hard arms and saying, "No. No. Don't worry, Vivi. They can't do this."

But they can do this. When the age of induction was lowered again, we heard there were demonstrations everywhere, people marching, people shouting their views on street corners, people chaining themselves to things or destroying government offices. Central Council responded by saturating the news with tales of dictators, torture, labor camps, shattered domes, poisoned water. There is always an enemy, there always has been. Enemies are as interchangeable as—well, as Councilors.

Carly was six, then, and I was busy with my work in the kitchen, where everyone has to take a turn, and the school, where I helped teach the little ones to learn fabrication techniques suited to their small hands. I let the news swirl around me, and prayed it would all pass.

Now I know you can't do that. It doesn't pass. It never passes. I don't know if all those horrible stories Central put about were true or not, but I do know that old people in power always send young, powerless people out to fight their battles for them. It has been true for millennia, and it doesn't change.

Until now. Until today, here in 78th Grange.

Because we agreed, we thirteen mothers. Because we have no dissenters.

The biggest problem was where to hide the children.

78th Grange has few hiding places. We live in nested cabins, crowded beneath the dome, with narrow streets too tight for anything but walking or cycling. And we decided not to consult the fathers, because we doubted there would be unity. Some would agree, no doubt, but some would not. Some people think Recruitment is a good idea. They agree that every community has to make sacrifices.

We were simply lucky that the thirteen of us, at this particular time, were of one mind. There were no arguments, that day in the kitchen, or the days following, when we whispered our questions, our ideas, and our plans.

The children are waiting, this morning, in the maternity area. 78th Grange has no doctor, of course. Letha is our midwife, and her Mark is one of the children on Central's list. There are no pregnancies in 78th Grange at the moment. No one goes in the maternity area unless they're delivering a baby. We worry about the children being unsupervised, but we are more worried about them being loaded onto the monorail and taken away from us.

We know how inducted children change. Militia training turns gentle, soft-eyed young people into weapons. It teaches them not to care, not to feel. To follow orders. Not to think.

Lowering the induction age, we are told, helps the children. They get an early start. They get an education. They learn to be independent, to rely on themselves. To be strong. But we know the truth.

First Central lowered the induction age to seventeen, a small change. Then they lowered it to fifteen, and then to thirteen. Finally, they dropped it to eleven. An eleven-year-old can't get a college deferment, or a marriage or pregnancy or essential function deferment. Few eleven-year-olds have suffered injuries that can interfere with their service. They are, according to Central Council, perfect.

And so, as we stirred the soup vats, we decided we would not comply. We don't want our children twisted, molded into something fierce and hard. We didn't suffer through pregnancy and childbirth, the nurturing, exhausting years of babyhood, the worries of early childhood, to supply Central with weapons to fight its countless and unending wars. This is not a 'current' crisis. This is a perpetual crisis.

And now as I look up at Avery, I see she has sunk to the cold concrete of the steps. Her forehead rests on her knees. Daylight begins to brighten the dome. Soon partners will be rising, wondering why the mothers have left their cabins so early. People will go to the kitchens, and there will be a buzz when they don't find us there. The citizens are expecting to come to the Extension Office to say goodbye to the recruits. When they come into the plaza, they will see us standing here, a line of women, waiting for the delegate from Central, but no children.

Jem, Carly's father, will understand immediately what we're doing. I dread seeing his fear, and the look of hurt on his face because I didn't tell him. I couldn't tell him.

There is no doubt in my mind that Jem would stand with me, if I gave him the chance. But we can't take the chance, we thirteen mothers. Our only power is in our unity.

Inside the dome, we don't hear the hum of the monorail's powerpack as it approaches, but we can feel the vibration through our feet. I whirl, and watch it fly toward 78th Grange on its shining rail. It doesn't slow until the last moment, always looking as if it's about to plow right through the fused silica of the dome. The monorail is pulling five cars, and one of them—the middle one—is a passenger car. The lead car slides swiftly and neatly into the lock. We hear the snick and hiss of the seals as they secure themselves, and the lock opens. Keisha lifts Avery to her feet. Avery leans against her, her head falling back, her lips slack and her eyes rolling. Avery, at least, will feel nothing. Briefly, I envy her.

Every citizen of 78th Grange knows what exposure does to an oxygen-breathing being. There are pictures, and we've all seen them, hideous, terrifying pictures.

I am terrified now.

I stand stiffly, my arms folded. Jem will be along soon. I have to stand with the others, tell him nothing, and hope that later he will forgive me. If there is a later.

I am relieved to have the waiting be over, though my legs tremble so I'm afraid I might fall. The sun is up now, gleaming on the red bricks of the plaza, the gray cement of the steps and the foamcast of the planters, the varicolored cabin roofs. The delegate from Central emerges from the lock just as the first curious citizens, our partners, come up the narrow lane from the kitchens. I can hear a few voices, calling our names: "Ebony?" "Jasmine?" "Keisha?" And then, Jem's sweet voice, dry with worry: "Vivi! Oh, Vivi. What are you all doing out here? Where's Carly?"

I turn briefly to Jem, kiss my fingers to him, and then turn forward again, facing the delegate. I drop my arms to my sides, and try to stand like a soldier.

I'll go, if they'll take me. If they'll give me a chance. I don't think they'll take me, or take any of us, but if they will, I'll do it. What I won't do is stand here, in the cramped plaza of 78th Grange, and watch Carly leave without me.

The delegate is a woman. She's not much taller than I am, but her body is square and strong-looking. She wears the militia uniform, green and brown, and a cap with a hard visor. She stares down at the line of thirteen women for a long moment, and we stare back.

"What's going on here?" she asks. Her voice is clear and carrying. She has a rather pleasant face. She's frowning, but she seems more confused than angry. "Where are my recruits?"

Avery, in front, is too far gone to answer.

Keisha speaks for her. Her voice is a little rough, and I know she's afraid, too. "We're right here," she says loudly. I hear a couple of the partners, standing in the lane watching us, draw noisy breaths.

The delegate looks at Keisha, and then at the rest of us, not understanding. "What are you talking about? Who are you?" She puts her fists on her hips, and for the first time, she really looks like a soldier. I think she must be about my own age.

Keisha says, "We're your recruits, Sergeant." I wouldn't have known she was a sergeant. It's the sort of thing Keisha knows. "We're the recruits from 78th Grange."

The sergeant's chin juts at us. "Ridiculous. Where's your proxy?" She pauses, and takes a comm from her pocket to glance at it. "James, right? Joletta James. Where is she?"

We left Joletta in the maternity area, with the children. We slipped her one of Avery's drugs, last night at dinner. Letha thinks she'll be out for another six hours.

Ebony shrugs. "She musta gone out for the day."

"I don't think so." Now the sergeant's spine stiffens. "Who's in charge here?"

"We are." This is Ebony again. She stands at her full height, which is impressive, and looks down her nose at the delegate. "We told you, Sergeant, we're your recruits."

The sergeant takes a step forward. "Look, folks."

Behind me I can hear the fathers calling out to us. "Maria! What's happening?" And Avery's husband, with tears in his voice, "Oh, God, Avery, what are you doing? You need to be in bed."

A toddler, held in one of the fathers' arms, wails for its mother. I hear a muffled sob from somewhere behind me, Carrie or Tamlen or maybe Pat. I don't dare look. If I meet Jem's eyes, fixed on me, I'm afraid I, too, will weep.

"Look," the sergeant says again. "78th Grange has thirteen fine young recruits on the list for induction. Let's bring 'em out here, okay? And load 'em on the monorail. We'll process 'em at Central."

I feel Carrie press close against my back, and I know the line is tightening, pushing forward. This is good, it feels good. I feel stronger because of it.

Keisha says, "We're all you get today, Sergeant. Take us, or leave."

The sergeant's voice drops to a growl. "Look, ma'am, I'm not leaving without my recruits. I have the list right here—" She brandishes her comm. "Central will send support if I need it, but that shouldn't be necessary." She puts the comm in her pocket, and pulls her jacket away from her weapon. "Come on, now, citizens." She glances past our line to the others standing below us in the square, staring, muttering among themselves.

Maria's partner shouts up at her. "Hey! Maria! For chrissakes, where's Matty? I'll go get him now, if you'll just tell me ..."

Jasmine whimpers, and Maria tightens her arm around her. I can see Maria's lips press hard together. I know her partner to be a hard man. And a militia veteran.

"Come on, Maria. I served, why shouldn't he? What the hell are you doing?"

Suddenly Maria turns on her heel, making Jasmine stumble backward. "What am I doing?" Maria shouts, her voice shrill with tension. "I'm stopping my son from turning into you, that's what the hell I'm doing!"

Her partner stares at her, his jaw dropping. The men and women around him step a little away, as if he might explode. Jasmine sobs, and Maria gathers her into her arms again, patting her shoulder.

"Look," the sergeant calls now, loudly enough to reach everyone in the square. "Look, some of you people out there go find my recruits, and we'll just let this go. I understand this is an emotional moment, but you can all be proud, doing your duty, being patriotic."

Some of the workers turn and look at each other. Maria's partner growls something to the man next to him, who steps even further away. Jem's eyes are wide, his head lifted to meet my gaze. I shake my head, just slightly, and he nods in return. I can feel his pain from where I stand. I will him to understand why I couldn't tell him about this, why we had to do this alone.

The sergeant's face has gone red. She pulls out her comm again. "Okay, people," she says in a rough voice. "You leave me no choice."

We know what will happen when she calls Central. They have all sorts of ways to force compliance. They can cut off services, shut down transportation, stop the imports we depend on. But all that takes time. She's more likely to call for the militia, who will come with more weapons than she carries, and who will search the whole dome.

That takes time, too, time that we will use. Time is part of our plan.

Keisha helps Avery to her feet. She speaks in a low tone, but I am so close, I hear her perfectly. "Avery," she says. My heart twists in my chest. "Avery, sweetheart, it's time."

Avery's head droops, and her eyes are almost closed. "Now?" she whispers.

"Now."

The sergeant turns toward Keisha and Avery, taking a stiff step forward.

Keisha says, "This is it."

"Help me," Avery says. I can't breathe. I stare at her, and she seems to glow with purpose.

Keisha says, "I will." She loops Avery's arm around her neck. It's only a few steps to the access lock, but their progress is slow, Avery's legs rubbery, her steps uncertain. We press into a tight line, as disciplined as any militia platoon.

Tears burn in my throat, and I grip my hands together so hard the fingers hurt.

"Hey!" the sergeant calls. "Where do you think you're going?"

Keisha says over her shoulder, flatly, "Central. To be inducted."

Just as Keisha and Ebony said she would, the sergeant moves ahead of us, trotting, although we're moving at Avery's glacial pace. The sergeant blocks the monorail access lock with her body. Just as we expected.

Keisha leads Avery right up to it, as if she might shove the sergeant aside, or dare her weapon. The sergeant plants her feet, and seems, oddly, to grow taller as Keisha approaches.

Avery straightens her neck with a huge effort. Keisha steps behind her, her strong hands supporting Avery's back. We hold our breaths to hear what Avery says.

"Militia," she says, her voice thin and quavering. "Me. Not my child."

"Yeah," the sergeant says scornfully. "You'd make some soldier, ma'am."

Avery takes another step, her face right in the sergeant's.

The sergeant puts up a hand, and shoves Avery backward, so that Keisha has to catch her with both arms. My throat closes tight. I know what will happen next. We all know.

The sergeant has the monorail access blocked. The other lock, the one beside the cabinets full of pressure suits, is to our left, the sergeant's right. It leads outside into near-vacuum, low oxygen, high carbon dioxide. Seven millibars of atmosphere. A person could survive perhaps half a minute. If the person held her breath. If the person didn't freeze before someone dragged her inside.

I tremble with last-minute doubts. We all have them, of course. But we swore to each other, in secret, passionately, sharing our strength in our weakest moments. And Avery—our first martyr—chose this.

She staggers to her left, pulls on the lever to open the hatch of the access lock.

It doesn't open. She hasn't enough strength. I hear, among the women, the intake of anguished breath.

Keisha, with a muttered oath, has to step up beside Avery to help her. The sergeant shouts something at them, something wordless, but she can't leave the lock she's guarding. Someone from the square shouts, too. It may be Avery's partner, I don't know. There's a little commotion, as if someone is trying to push forward, to get to her. I feel Carrie press even closer against my back, as if the crowd is pushing at our line. I brace my feet, try not to shove Ebony.

Avery is in the lock now, and as Keisha shuts the inner hatch, Avery puts all her body weight on the lever for the outer hatch. This one rotates smoothly. The hatch opens.

The sergeant, in a surprisingly feminine gesture, covers her mouth with both hands. Her weapon hangs at an odd angle before her face, dangling from her fingers.

I barely register this. I watch Avery, numb with shock and horror. It doesn't matter, now, how often we talked about how this would be, how we would feel. My stomach turns, and my throat closes.

Avery stumbles out of the hatch, casting one tragic look backward so that we see her face flood with color as the blood vessels blossom and break. She squeezes her eyes shut, and turns her face away.

I hear the anguished cry of Avery's partner just as Avery releases her held breath. As she exhales, the precious air from her lungs freezes almost into a crystalline fog around her head. There will be no indrawn breath. There is nothing to breathe.

Twenty to twenty-five seconds. That's the time we have to suffer with Avery, the time we've been told it takes for a person to lose consciousness after exposure, if the person is not pulled back into the hatch, given oxygen, wrapped in thermal blankets. Avery's partner is sobbing, loudly, desperately, behind me. I can't look at him. I stare, transfixed, at Keisha's tall figure. She turns her back to the access lock, making it clear no one can pass her. Her courage stuns me.

And now everyone, including the sergeant from Central, falls silent, as Avery's body slips slowly to the icy ground beyond the curving wall of the dome. She sits, and then collapses to one side, a huddle of uninhabited flesh. Her partner cries, hopeless and helpless. With deliberation, Keisha turns her face to the sergeant.

"One," she says, biting off the word. She folds her arms across her chest.

"What the hell ... ?" The sergeant stares at her, turns to stare at all of us. "What have you done? Why did she ... I mean, my God!"

There is a long, awful silence, broken only by the weeping of Avery's partner. The sergeant waits for one of us to say something, to do something. We look back at her. My eyes burn, wanting to cry, to mourn Avery's passing. But we are not yet finished here.

The sergeant has her comm in one hand, her weapon in the other. She speaks swiftly, in an undertone, and listens to an answer, then speaks again. We know she is asking for orders, desperately asking for someone to tell her what to do. When she puts the comm away, she levels the weapon at Keisha. "No one else moves," she says. Tension makes her voice high and tight. "Central is sending the militia. You can't get away with this kind of crap."

"Crap?" Ebony cries. "Recruit us! We're ready to go!"

The sergeant doesn't lower her weapon, but her eyes swivel to Ebony. "I have my orders. I'm not leaving 78th Grange without the ch—without the inductees."

"You still have twelve of them, right here," Ebony says. "Take us, or go away."

"Can't do that, and you know it." The sergeant turns her eyes back to Keisha, whose hands are now on the hatch lever. "Don't move," she says. "That's an order."

Keisha, incredibly, manages. "What are you going to do, Sergeant?" she asks. "Kill me?" And she turns on her heel, deliberately, and reaches for the lever to open the lock again.

"Stop!" the sergeant orders. Her hand tightens on the little black weapon. Keisha sneers at her over her shoulder, and pushes the lever.

The sergeant's hand wavers, and her face crumples with indecision.

From the crowd behind our line, another shout rises, this time from Keisha's partners. Only Keisha, of all of us, could manage two partners. "No! Keisha, no!" they shout. She casts them a glance full of sorrow, shaking her head, and then steps into the access lock.

The sergeant discharges her weapon just as the hatch door closes. The narrowly focused beam flashes uselessly, glimmering on the silica surface. Keisha presses on the lever for the outer hatch, and wails arise from the crowd. I sense it pushing forward, men and women running to their partners, seizing their arms. Jem is beside me, his hands on my shoulders. I close my eyes, and shrug him off. What I want to do is throw myself into his arms, run back to our cabin, return to our life. But it will not be our life without Carly. And Avery has made her sacrifice, the ultimate gesture. How can any of us dishonor that by giving in now?

"Vivi," Jem says urgently. "You're not going to ... you wouldn't ..." I can't look at him. I'm watching Keisha.

The sergeant has left the monorail access, and taken the three long steps to the other lock. She puts her hand on the lever for the inner hatch, but she is too late. The outer one is lifting up and out of its housing now, and the inner one won't open.

It takes much longer for Keisha, our friend and our leader, to die. She is so much stronger than Avery, and she's not ill. She turns to face us—no, to glare at the sergeant, who falls back a step, her mouth dropped in horror. We watch Keisha's eyes glaze, her face darken. She grimaces with the involuntary effort to hold her breath. It seems an eternity before, at last, her breath escapes her. Her mouth opens, and works, like a fish out of water. Her knees give way. Still facing us, she collapses, her forehead braced against the outer wall of the dome. I press the heels of my hands to my burning eyes. When I take them down, Keisha has toppled beside Avery, her eyes open, frozen, staring.

Behind me someone is speaking in a high, clear voice. As I watch the cloud of Keisha's last breath dissipate, I listen with disbelief as Jasmine, quiet, anxious Jasmine, orders the citizens of 78th Grange to step back, to leave us alone. Keisha's partners, who have run forward to the dome, slump against it now, just opposite where she has gone down. The sergeant, her hands hanging, her weapon pointed at the ground, stares dumbly at the two bodies outside.

Ebony steps to the top of the stairs, and the rest of us take a step forward too. There is a steady rush of sound around us, some sobs, some curses. Most of our citizens are shocked into silence. Ebony shouts, "Two! How many more, Sergeant?"

When the sergeant turns to face her, I feel a spasm of sympathy. The woman's eyes are huge, her face gray with shock. She must have expected an entirely different job today, a monorail trip with thirteen frightened children. She was unprepared to watch two women commit deliberate suicide. "Look," she says, her voice breaking. She has to clear her throat and try again. "Look, this doesn't do any good. I'm nobody, I'm just following orders, and no one will believe—" She breaks off, and makes a shaky gesture that includes the bodies outside, Keisha's two partners, weeping on each other's shoulders. "Who would believe you'd do this? Please, citizens ... no more! Please!"

At that very moment I become aware that Jem, my Jem, is recording everything. He's standing on the edge of the planter, where Keisha stood to call us to order, and he's running the little recorder we use when there are events to report to Central. It's kept in the proxy's office, usually. I don't know how, or when, Jem got hold of it, but everything it records is automatically received at Central. I wonder if anyone is watching.

The sergeant looks up at Jem. She turns, if possible, even paler than before. "Give me that," she says hoarsely. Once again, she lifts her weapon, though her hand is shaking so badly I doubt she can aim it.

"Jem," I warn, but he gives me one of those dark, close looks I know so well.

He has the recorder balanced against the foamcast of the pillar, snugged between his shoulder and his jaw. "You have to let me do this, Vivi," he says. "Carly is mine, too."

The sergeant is clearly confused. Ebony has already taken a step toward the access lock, and the weapon swings toward her, and then, wavering wildly, back to Jem. "Stop," she croaks. "Please, give me that. You'll ruin me."

I cry, without meaning to, "No!"

Several other men step forward, as if to follow Jem's example, but Ebony throws up her arm, and it is her turn to shout, "No!"

Jem's eyes flicker at the weapon. I can see the amber flash, then the green, as it fastens on him. The sergeant's hand shakes, and the light turns amber again as she loses her target.

Ebony takes another step. The noise from the square intensifies, cries and calls, and our line of mothers is swallowed up by citizens pressing forward, trying to interfere, to stop us, to stop the sergeant. My heart flutters. It is all just as Keisha said it would be, noisy and confused and frightening. She had predicted all of it.

Except for Jem.

The sergeant sees Ebony approaching, and her thoughts are as plain as if they were written across her face. Two women dead already. Another about to commit suicide. And one man, a recorder on his shoulder, sending it all to Central.

"Jem! Stop! Come down!" I cry. He refuses, a short, sharp shake of the head. And I know why.

I am fourth in line. If Ebony succeeds in following Avery and Keisha, if the sergeant doesn't give in, I will be next.

The sergeant demands, "What is it you want? What do you want me to do?" Her voice has gone shrill.

Ebony stops where she is. "Take us as your recruits, or go away," she says.

"I can't!" the sergeant wails. "If I go away, they'll just send someone else, you know that! The Recruitment Order ... "

"You can't have them." I am startled to hear my own voice, usually rather soft, ring out across the square. "We decided, all of us together. You can't have our children."

"But I can't take you!" the sergeant cries. She waves the weapon around, at me, at Jem, at Ebony.

Ebony takes another step, right into the sergeant's face. Ebony is a head taller, her shoulders broader, her arms longer. She stiff-arms the sergeant to one side, and reaches for the hatch lever.

The sergeant points her little weapon at Ebony, but Ebony only laughs, a bitter sound that grates on my bones. I ache with tension. Ebony leans on the lever.

Jem shouts, from his perch, "How many more, Sergeant?"

As the hatch opens, the sergeant falls back a step. She shakes her head, a little wordless sound escaping her as Ebony steps into the lock and the hatch closes behind her. Someone screams, "No! Stop her!" The sergeant shakes her head again, and groans.

Jem shouts again. "How many?"

The sergeant whirls, pointing her weapon at him. The recorder hums, pointing back at her. Her hand on the weapon steadies, and the amber light goes red.

"Jem!"

She fires.

They trained her for this. I suppose she was an inductee, too, though she may have volunteered. There are those who volunteer for the militia, and I have never understood why. Perhaps they simply want to get away from their homes, travel, live more exciting lives than they can in the granges. Or perhaps they like to use weapons, to play war games ... to kill.

Jem freezes, and the recorder falls from his shoulder. His face goes white, and then slack. Slowly, slowly, he crumples, and tumbles from the planter's edge to fall on the cement with a great sigh. The sergeant, his killer, whimpers as she lowers her weapon.

Bedlam erupts around me.

"Jem!" I scream. My voice is lost in the tumult that rises from the plaza. Men rush forward, and some women. Ebony's partner pulls open the inner hatch door before she can push the lever on the outer one, and he drags her over the sill and out of the access lock. Two strong men lift Jem's nerveless body from the cement, and carry him past me down the steps. I almost fall, but someone, one of the other women, holds me with her arms around my waist. We try, all of us, to hold our line, but we are buffeted by the rest of the 78th Grange citizens, everyone shouting, crying. I want to go after Jem, but I hold my place. I know it's useless, in any case. Those weapons—the ones they expect our children to use—deal certain death.

I want to weep for my partner, my best friend, but there is no time.

Ebony leaps up to the planter where Jem had stood before. She has the recorder in her hands. She lifts it to her shoulder. Bit by bit, the square falls silent.

The sergeant spreads her hands. "Listen to me! I'm only following orders! These are my orders!"

"Go home, Sergeant." This is Maria, I know her deep voice. "Go back to Central and tell them we refused."

"You can't refuse!" the sergeant whines. Her face is a mask of shock and revulsion. "No more, please! My god, three people are dead here!"

"How many of our children would be dead?" Maria shouts.

"Go home," Ebony repeats, and the rest of the citizens shout it, too. "Go home! Tell them! Go home!"

The crowd bulges, surges toward the sergeant, past our diminished line of women. She cowers back against the curving wall of the dome, her weapon wavering around, trying to choose a target. I think, this could have been Carly, firing at her own people, and I experience a spasm of sympathy for the sergeant.

Our citizens stop short of her position. She stares at them, white-faced, one hand at her neck. Then, with a hopeless cry, she thrusts her weapon into its holster, and backs into the access lock to the monorail. The hatch closes behind her. For a long moment she stares out at us, and then she throws a switch, and the monorail cars, in reverse, begin to move.

Ebony is still recording. Sooner or later someone at Central will see these images. What will they do? Can we resist the next wave that will come, and the next? We don't know. But our citizens gather around us, stand by us. We stand together, we remaining eleven, with our partners and friends, and we watch the monorail cars disappear over the horizon. Ebony records until it is gone, and then switches off the machine.

And then we hear a new sound, the sound of running feet on the bricks. They're coming, released at last from the maternity center, dashing up the narrow lane with the strength and energy of youth. Our children.

The mothers turn with cries of gladness. Ebony commands, "Don't let them see!" Several men hurry into vacuum suits, to go out to retrieve the bodies.

I see Carly, dark hair flying, eyes wide and dark with fear, and I rush to her.

The militia will return, of course, in force. Central can't let 78th Grange defy the Recruitment Order. More soldiers will come next time, and they'll be ready. No element of surprise.

I look above Carly's head and see Ebony with the recorder cradled in her arms. Jem's last gift to us is the record of what happened here this morning.

Ebony's eyes meet mine, and she nods as if we have already spoken of what to do, how to disseminate the recording, to spread the word of what thirteen mothers did in 78th Grange. Thirteen mothers, and one father, who refused to give up their children.

Central will punish 78th Grange, we know that. They will find a way. But something has changed here today, something that can never change back. A precedent has been set. Obedience will no longer be automatic.

I squeeze Carly tight, and we cry together. I hope she will understand, someday, why we did what we did. And I hope she will forgive me for being the one who's still here.

*When King David learned that his son had been killed in battle, he lamented, "O my son Absalom, my son, my son Absalom! Would God I had died for thee, O Absalom, my son, my son!"*

2 Samuel 18:33

**Louise Marley** is a graduate of Clarion West 1993. In 1995 her first novel, *Sing the Light,* was published by Ace, and since that time she has produced fifteen more novels of fantasy, science fiction, historical fiction, and young adult fiction, published by Ace, Viking, Puffin, and Kensington Books. She is a two-time winner of the Endeavour Award, and was a Campbell Award nominee. A former concert and opera singer, many of her books have musical and historical themes.

# Pat Murphy
# on Louise Marley

I remember meeting Louise Marley more than two decades ago, at the 1993 Clarion West workshop where I was an instructor for a week. At the time, I was struck by her elegance and poise, characteristics I don't generally associate with science fiction writers. (As a group, I'd say we tend more toward eclectic and scrappy.) Louise did not, at that first meeting, seem like the sort of woman who would rip your heart out.

But she is.

Consider this story—fierce, passionate, and deeply felt. Harsh, but only in the sense that a bright light is harsh—shining into shadows and revealing what some might prefer remain hidden. The story has an edge—razor sharp and painful. And yet in that pain and through that pain, her work offers hope. The way forward is not easy, but there is a way.

Yes, Louise is capable of ripping my heart out—and I thank her for that.

**Pat Murphy** is a writer, a scientist, and a toy maker. Her fiction has won the Nebula, the Philip K. Dick Award, the World Fantasy Award, and the 2002 SEUIN Award.

# Mulberry Boys

**Margo Lanagan**

1999

So night comes on. I make my own fire, because why would I want to sit at Phillips's, next to that pinned-down mulberry?

*Pan-flaps, can you make pan-flaps?* Phillips plopped down a bag of fine town flour and gave me a look that said, *Bet you can't. And I'm certainly too important to make them.* So pan-flaps I make in his little pan, and some of them I put hot meat-slice on, and some cheese, and some jam, and that will fill us, for a bit. There's been no time to hunt today, just as Ma said, while she packed and packed all sorts of these treats into a sack for me—to impress Phillips, perhaps, more than to show me favour, although that too. She doesn't mind me being chosen to track and hunt with the fellow, now that I'm past the age where he can choose me for the other thing.

We are stuck out here the night, us and our catch. If I were alone I would go back; I can feel and smell my way, if no stars and moon will show me. But once we spread this mulberry wide on the ground and fixed him, and Phillips lit his fire and started his fiddling and feeding him leaves, I knew we were to camp. I did not ask; I dislike his sneering manner of replying to me. I only waited and saw.

He's boiled the water I brought up from the torrent, and filled it with clanking, shining things—little tools, it looks like, as far as I can see out of the corner of my eye. I would not gratify him with looking directly. I stare into my own fire, the forest blank black beyond it and only fire-lit smoke above, no sky though the clouds were clearing last I looked. I get out my flask and have a pull of fire-bug, to settle my discontentments. It's been a long day and a weird, and I wish I was home, instead of out here with a half-man, and the boss of us all watching my every step.

"Here, boy," he says. He calls me *boy* the way you call a dog. He doesn't even look up at me to say it.

I cross from my fire to his. I don't like to look at those creatures, mulberries, so I fix instead on Phillips, his shining hair-waves and his sharp nose, the floret of silk in his pocket that I know is a green-blue bright as a stout-pigeon's throat, but now is just a different orange in the fire's glow. His white, weak hands, long-fingered, big-knuckled— oh, they give me a shudder, just as bad as a mulberry would.

"Do you know what a loblolly boy is?"

He knows I don't. I hate him and his words. "Some kind of insulting thing, no doubt," I say.

"No, no!" He looks up surprised from examining the brace, which is pulled tight to the mulberry's puffed-up belly, just below the navel, when it should dangle on an end of silk. "It's a perfectly legitimate thing. Boy on a ship, usually. Works for the surgeon."

And what is a surgeon? I am not going to ask him. I stare down at him, wanting another pull from my flask.

"Never mind," he says crossly. "Sit." And he waves where; right by the mulberry, opposite himself.

Must I? I have already chased the creature five ways wild today; I've already treed him and climbed that tree and lowered him on a rope. I'm sick of the sight of him, his round stary face, his froggy body, his feeble conversation, trying to be friendly.

But I sit. I wonder sometimes if I'm weak-minded, that even one person makes such a difference to me, what I see, what I do. When I come to the forest alone, I can see the forest clear, and feel it, and everything in it. If I bring Tray or Connar, it becomes the ongoing game of us as big men in this world—with the real men left behind in the village, so they don't show us up. When I come with Frida Birch it is all about the inside of her mysterious mind, what she can be thinking, what has she noticed that I haven't about some person, some question she has that would never occur to me. It's as if I cannot hold to my own self, to my own forest, if another person is with me.

"Feed him some more," says Phillips, and points to the sack beside me. "As many as he can take. We might avoid a breakage yet if we can stuff enough into him."

I untie the sack, and put aside the first layer, dark leaves that have been keeping the lower, paler ones moist. I roll a leaf-pill—the neater I make it, the less I risk being bitten, or having to touch lip or tongue. I wave it under his nose, touch it to his lips, and he opens and takes it in, good mulberry.

Phillips does this and that. Between us the mulberry's stomach grumbles and tinkles with the foreign food he's kept down. Between leaf-rollings, I have another pull. "God, the smell of that!" says Phillips, and spares a hand from his preparations to wave it away from his face.

"It's good," I say. "It's the best. It's Nat Culloden's."

"How old are you anyway?" He cannot read it off me. Perhaps he deals only with other men—I know people like that, impatient of the young. Does he have children? I'd hate to be his son.

"Coming up fifteen," I say.

He mutters something. I can't hear, but I'm sure it is not flattering to me.

Now there's some bustle about him. He pulls on a pair of very thin-stretching gloves, paler even than his skin; now his hands are even more loathsome. "Right," he says. "You will hold him down when I tell you. That is your job."

"He's down." Look at the spread cross of him; he couldn't be any flatter.

"You will hold him *still*," says Phillips. "For the work. When I say."

He pulls the brace gently; the skein comes forth as it should, but—"Hold him," says Phillips, and I hook one leg over the mulberry's thigh and spread a hand on his chest. He makes a kind of warning moan. Phillips pulls on, slowly and steadily like a mother. "*Hold* him," as the moaning rises, buzzes under my hand. "Christ above, if he makes this much of a fuss *now*."

He pulls and pulls, but in a little while no more silk will come. He winds what he has on a spindle and clamps it, tests the skein once more. "No? Well. Now I will cut. Boy, I have nothing for his pain." He looks at me as if *I* forgot to bring it. "And I need him utterly still, so as not to cut the silk or his innards. Here." He hands me a smooth white stick, of some kind of bone. "Put that crosswise between his teeth, give him something to bite on."

I do so; the teeth are all clagged with leaf-scraps, black in this light. Mulberries' faces are the worst thing about them, little round old-children's faces, neither man nor woman. And everything they are thinking shows clear as water, and this one is afraid; he doesn't know what's happening, what's about to be done to him. Well, I'm no wiser. I turn back to Phillips.

"Now get a good weight on him, both ends."

Gingerly I arrange myself. He may be neither man nor woman, but still the creature is naked, and clammy as a frog in the night air.

"Come on," says Phillips. He's holding his white hands up, as if the mulberry is too hot to touch. "You're plenty big enough. Spread yourself out there, above and below. You will need to press here, too, with your hand." He points, and points again. "And this foot will have some work to do on this far leg. Whatever is loose will fight against what I'm doing, understand?"

So he says, to a boy who's wrestled tree-snakes so long that his father near fainted to see them, who has jumped a shot stag and ridden it and killed it riding. Those are different, though; those are wild, they have some dignity. What's to be gained subduing a mulberry, that is gelded and a fool already? Where's the challenge in that, and the pride upon having done it?

"Shouldn't you be down there?" I nod legs-wards.

"Whatever for, boy?"

"This is to let the food out, no?"

"It is to let the food out, *yes*." He cannot speak without making me lesser.

"Well, down there is where food comes out, yours and mine."

"Pity sake, boy, I am not undoing all *that*. I will take it out through his silk-hole, is the plan."

Now I am curled around the belly, with nowhere else to look but at Phillips's doings. All his tools and preparations are beyond him, next to the fire; from over there he magics up a paper packet. He tears it open, pulls from it a small wet cloth or paper, and paints the belly with that; the smell nips at my nostrils. Then he brings out a bright, light-as-a-feather-looking knife, the blade glinting at the end of a long handle.

"Be ready," he says.

He holds the silk aside, and sinks the blade into the flesh beside it. The mulberry-boy turns to rock underneath me; he spits out the stick, and howls to the very treetops.

Mulberry *boys* we call them. I don't know why, for some begin as girls, and they are neither one nor the other once they come out of Phillips's hut by the creek. They all look the same, as chickens look all the same, or goats. *Nonsense,* says Alia the goat woman, *I know my girls each one, by name and nature and her pretty face.* And I guess the mothers, who tend the mulberries, might know them apart. This one is John Barn, or once was called that; none of them truly have names once they've been taken.

Once a year I notice them, when Phillips comes to choose the new ones and to make them useful, from the boys among us who are not yet sprouted towards men, and the girls just beginning to change shape. The rest of the year, the mulberries live in their box, and the leaves go in, and the silk comes out on its spindles, and that is all there is to it.

They grow restless when he comes. Simple as they are, they recognise him. *They can smell their balls in his pocket,* says James Pombo, and we hush him, but something like that is true; they remember.

Some have struggled or wandered before, and these are tied to chairs in the box, but you have to watch the others. Though they have not much equipment for it, they have a lot of time to think, and because their life is much the same each day and month and year, they see the pattern and the holes in it through which they might wangle their way.

Why the John Barn one should take it into his head after all these years, I don't know. He was always mulberry, ever since I knew to know, always just one of the milling amiables in that warm box.

*Oh, I remember him, says Pa. Little straw-haired runabout like all them Barns. Always up a tree. Climbed the top of Great Grandpa when he couldn't have been—what, more than three years, Ma? Because his sister Gale did it, and he told him he was too little. That'll send a boy up a tree.*

Last year when I was about to sprout, it was the first year Phillips came instead of his father. When he walked in among us we were most uneasy at the size of him, for he is delicately made, hardly taller than a mulberry himself, and similar shaped to them except in lacking a paunch. Apart from the shrinkage, though, you would think him the same man as his father. He wore the same fine clothes, as neat on him as if sewn to his body directly, and the fabrics so fine you can hardly see their weave. He had the same wavy hair, but brown instead of silver, and a beard, though not a proper one, trimmed almost back to his chin.

The mothers were all behind us and some of the fathers too, putting their children forward. He barely looked at me, I remember, but moved straight on to the Thaw children; there are lots of them and they are very much of the mulberry type already, without you sewing a stitch on them. I remember being insulted. The man had not *bothered* with me; how could he know I was not what he wanted, from that quick glance? But also I was ashamed to be so obviously useless, so wrong for his purposes—because whatever those purposes were, he was from the town, and he was powerfuller in his slenderness and his city clothes than was any bulky man among us, and everyone was afraid of him. I wanted a man like that to recognize me as of consequence, and he had not.

But then Ma put her arm over my shoulder and clamped me to

her, my back against her front. We both watched Phillips among the Thaws, turning them about, dividing some of them off for closer inspection. The chosen ones—Hinny and Dull Toomy, it was, that time, those twins—stood well apart, Pa Toomy next to them arms folded and face closed. They looked from one of us to another, not quite sure whether to arrange their faces proudly, or to cry.

Because it is the end of things, if you get chosen. It is the end of your line, of course—all your equipment for making children is taken off you and you are sewn up below. But it is also the end of any food but the leaves—fresh in the spring and summer, sometimes in an oiled mash through autumn if you are still awake then. And it is the end of play, because you become stupid; you forget the rules of all the games, and how to converse in any but a very simple way, observing about the weather and not much more. You just stay in your box, eating your leaves and having your stuff drawn off you, which we sell, through Phillips, in the town.

It is no kind of life, and I was glad, then, that I had not been taken up for it. And Ma was glad too, breathing relieved above me as we watched him sort and discard and at length choose Arvie Thaw. I could feel Ma's gladness in the back of my head, her heart knocking hard in her chest, even though all she had done was stand there and seem to accept whatever came.

While we tracked John Barn today, I was all taken up impressing Phillips. The forest and paths presented me trace after trace, message after message, to relay to the town-man, so's he could see what a good tracker I was. I felt proud of myself for knowing, and scornful of him for not—yet I was afraid, too, that I would put a foot wrong, that he would somehow catch me out, that he would see something I had missed and make me a nobody again, and worthy of his impatience.

So John Barn himself was not much more to me than he'd always been; he was even somewhat less than other animals I hunted, for he had not even the wit to cut off the path at any point, and he left tracks and clues almost as if he wanted us to catch him, things he had chewed, and spat out or brought up from his stomach, little piles of findings—stones, leaves, seed-pods—wet-bright in the light rain. He might as well have lit beacon-fires after himself.

Climbing up to him in the tree, I could see his froggy paunch pouching out either side of the branch, and his skinny white legs around it, and then of course his terrible face watching me.

"Which one are you?" he said in that high, curious way they have. They can never remember a name.

"I am George," I said, "of the Treadlaws."

"Evening's coming on, George," he said, watching as I readied the rope. This was why I had been brought, besides for my tracking. Mulberries won't flee or resist anyone smaller than themselves (unless he is Phillips, of course, all-over foreign), but send a grown man after them and they will throw themselves off a cliff or into a torrent, or climb past pursuing up a tree like this. It is something about the smell of a grown man sets them off, which is why men cannot go into the box for the silk, but only mothers.

I busied myself with the practicalities, binding Barn and lowering him to Phillips, which was no small operation, so I distracted myself from my revulsion that way. And then, when I climbed down, Phillips took up all the air in the clearing and in my mind with his presence and purposefulness, which I occupied myself sulking at. Then when I had to press the creature down, to lie with him, lie *on* him, everything in me was squirming away from the touch but Phillips's will was on me like an iron, pinning me as fast as we'd pinned the mulberry, and I was too angry and unhappy at being made as helpless as John Barn, to think how he himself might be finding it, crushed by the weight of me.

But when he stiffened and howled, it was as if I had been asleep to John Barn and he woke me, as if he had been motionless disguised in the forest's dappled shadows, but then my eye had picked out his frame, distinct and live and sensible in there, never to be unseen again. All that he had said, that we had dismissed as so much noise, came back to me: *I don't like that man, George. Yes, tie me tight, for I will struggle when you put me near him. It's getting dark. It hurts me to stretch flat like this. My stomach hurts. An apple and a radish, I have kept both down. I stole them through a window; there was meat there too; meat was what I mostly wanted. But I could not reach it. Oh, it hurts, George.* I had done as Phillips did, and not met the mulberry's eye and not answered, doing about him what I needed to do, but now all his mutterings sprang out at me as having been said by a person, a person like me and like Phillips; there were three of us here, not two and a creature, not two and a snared rabbit, or a shot and struggling deer.

And the howl was not animal noise but voice, with person and feeling behind it. It went through me the way the pain had gone through John Barn, freezing me as Phillips's blade in his belly froze him, so that I was locked down there under the realising, with all my skin a-crawl.

I stare at Phillips's hands, working within their false skins. The fire beyond him lights his work and throws the shadows across the gleaming-painted hill-round of Barn's belly. Phillips cuts him like a cloth or like a cake, with just such swiftness and intent; he does not even do as you do when hunting, and speak to the creature you have snared or caught and are killing, and explain why it must die. The wound runs, and he catches the runnings with his wad of flock and cloth, absentmindedly and out of a long-practiced skill. He bends close and examines what his cutting has revealed to him, in the cleft, in the deeps, of the belly of John Barn.

"Good," he says—to himself, not to me or Barn. "Perfect."

He puts his knife in there, and what he does in there is done in me as well, I feel so strongly the tremor it makes, the fear it plays up out of Barn's frame, plucking him, rubbing him, like a fiddle-string. His breath, behind me, halts and hops with the fear.

Phillips pierces something with a pop. Barn yelps, surprised. Phillips sits straighter, and waves his hand over the wound as he waved away the smell of my grog before. I catch a waft of shit-smell and then it's gone, floated up warm away.

He goes to his instruments. "That's probably the worst of it, for the moment," he says to them. "You can sit up if you like. Stay by, though; you never know when he'll panic."

I sit up slowly, a different boy from the one who lay down. I half-expect my own insides to come pouring out of me. John Barn's belly gapes open, the wound dark and glistening, filling with blood. Beyond it, his flesh slopes away smooth as a wooden doll between his weakling thighs, which tremble and tremble.

Phillips returns to the wound, another little tool in his hand—I don't know what it is, only that it's not made for cutting. I put my hand on Barn's chest, trying to move as smoothly and bloodlessly as Phillips.

"George, what has he done to me?" John Barn makes to look down himself.

Quick as light, I put my hand to his sweated brow, and press his head to the ground. "He's getting that food out," I say. "If it stays in there, it'll fester and kill you. He's helping you."

"Feed him some more," says Phillips, and bends to his work. "Keep on that."

So I lie, propped up on one elbow, rolling mulberry pills and feeding them to Barn. He chews, dutifully; he weeps, tears running back over his ears into his thin hair. He swallows the mulberry mush down his child-neck. *Hush*, I nearly say to him, but Phillips is there, so I only think it, and attend to the feeding, rolling the leaves, putting them one by one into Barn's obedient mouth.

I can't help but be aware, though, of what the man is doing there, down at the wound. For one thing, besides the two fires it is the only visible activity, the only movement besides my own. For another, for all that the sight of those blood-tipped white hands going about their work repels me, their skill and care, and the life they seem to have of their own, are something to see. It's like watching Pa make damselfly flies in the firelight in the winter, each finger independently knowing where to be and go, and the face above all eyes and no expression, the mind taken up with this small complication.

The apple and the radish, all chewed and reduced and cooked

smelly by John Barn's body's heat, are caught in the snarled silk. Phillips must draw them, with the skein, slowly lump by lump from Barn's innards, up into the firelight where they dangle and shine like some unpleasant necklace. Sprawled beside John Barn, in his breathing and his bracing himself I feel the size of every bead of that necklace large and small, before I see it drawn up into the firelight on the shining strands. Phillips frowns above, fire-fuzz at his eyebrow, a long streak of orange light down his nose, his closed lips holding all his thoughts, all his knowledge, in his head—and any feelings he might have about this task. Is he pleased? Is he revolted? Angry? There is no way to tell.

"Do you have something for their pain, then," I say, "when you make them into mulberries?"

"Oh yes," he says to the skein, "they are fully anaesthetized then." He hears my ignorance in my silence, or sees it in my stillness. "I put them to sleep."

"Like a chicken," I say, to show him that I know something.

"Not at all like that. With a chemical."

All is quiet but for fire-crackle, and John Barn's breath in his nose, and his teeth crushing the leaves.

"How do you learn that, about the chemicals, and mulberry-making? And mulberry-fixing, like this?"

"Long study," says Phillips, peering into the depths to see how the skein is emerging. "Long observation at my father's elbow. Careful practice under his tutelage. Years," he finishes and looks at me, with something like a challenge, or perhaps already triumph.

"So *could* you unmake one?" I say, just to change that look on him.

"Could I? Why *would* I?"

I make myself ignore the contempt in that. "Supposing you had a reason."

He draws out a slow length of silk, with only two small lumps in it. "Could I, now?" he says less scornfully. "I've never considered it. Let me think." He examines the silk, both sides, several times. "I could perhaps restore their digestive functioning. The females' reproductive system *might* re-establish its cycle, with a normal diet, though I cannot be sure. The males' of course ... " He shrugs. He has a little furnace in that hut of his by the creek. There he must burn whatever he cuts from the mulberries, and all his blood-soaked cloths and such. Once a year he goes in there with the chosen children, and all we know of what he does is the air wavering over the chimney. The men speak with strenuous cheer to each other; the mothers go about thin-lipped; the mothers of the chosen girls and boys close themselves up in their houses with their grief.

"But what about their ... Can you undo their thinking, their talking, what you have done to that?"

"Ah, it is coming smoother now, look at that," he says to himself. "What do you mean, boy, 'undo'?" he says louder and more scornfully, as if I made up the word myself out of nothing, though I only repeated it from him.

I find I do not want to call John Barn a fool, not in his hearing as he struggles with his fear and his swallowing leaf after leaf, and with lying there belly open to the sky and Phillips's attentions. "They ... haven't much to say for themselves," I finally say. "Would they talk among us like ourselves, if you fed them right, and took them out of that box?"

"I don't know what they would do." He shrugs again. He goes on slowly drawing out silk, and I go on hating him.

"Probably not," he says carelessly after a while. "All those years, you know, without social stimulus or education, would probably have impaired their development too greatly. But possibly they would regain something, from moving in society again." He snorts. "Such society as you *have* here. And the diet, as you say. It might perk them up a bit."

Silence again, the skein pulling out slowly, silently, smooth and clean white. Barn chews beside me, his breathing almost normal. Perhaps the talking soothes him.

"But then," says Phillips to the skein, with a smile that I don't like at all, "if you 'undid' them all, you would have no silk, would you? And without silk you would have no tea, or sugar, or tobacco, or wheat flour, or all the goods in tins and jars that I bring you. No cloth for the women, none of their threads and beads and such."

Yes, plenty of people would be distressed at that. I am the wrong boy to threaten with such losses, for I hunt and forage; I like the old ways. I kept myself fed and healthy for a full four months, exploring up the glacier last spring—healthier than were most folk when I arrived home, with their toothaches and their coughs. But others, yes, they rely wholly on those stores that Phillips brings through the year. When he is due, and they have run short of tobacco, they go all grog and temper waiting, or hide at home until he should come. They will not hunt or snare with me and Tray and Pa and the others; take them a haunch of stewed rabbit, and if they will eat it at all they will sauce it well with complaints and wear a sulking face over every bite.

"And no food coming up, for all those extra mouths you'd have to feed," says Phillips softly and still smiling, "that once were kept on mulberry leaves alone. Think of that."

What was I imagining, all my talk of undoing? The man cannot make mulberries back into men, and if he could he would never teach someone like me, that he thought so stupid, and whose folk he despised. And even if he taught us, and worked alongside us in the unmaking, we would never get back the man John Barn was going to be when he was born John Barn, or any of the men and women that the others might have become.

"You were starving and in rags when my father found you," says Phillips, sounding pleased. "Your people. You lived like animals."

"We had some bad years, I heard." *And we are animals, I nearly add, and so are you. A bear meets you, you are just as much a meal to him as is a berry-bush or a fine fat salmon. What are you, if not animal?*

But I have already lost this argument; he has already dismissed me. He draws on, as if I never spoke, as if he were alone. Good silk is coming out now; all the leaves we've been feeding into John Barn are coming out clean, white, strong-stranded; he is restored, apart from the great hole in him. Still I feed him, still he chews on, both of us playing our parts to fill Phillips' hands with silk.

"Very well," says Phillips, "I think we are done here. Time to close him up again."

I'm relieved that he intends to. "Should I lie on him again?"

"In a little," he says. "The inner parts are nerveless, and will not give him much pain. When I sew the dermal layers, perhaps."

It is very much like watching someone wind a fly, the man-hands working such a small area and mysteriously, stitching inside the hole. The thread, which is black, and waxed, wags out in the light and then is drawn in to the task, then wags again, the man concentrating above. His fingers work exactly like a spider's legs on its web, stepping delicately as he brings the curved needle out and takes it back in. I can feel from John Barn's chest that there is not pain exactly, but there is sensation where there should not be, and the fear that comes from not understanding makes Phillips's every movement alarming to him.

I didn't quite believe that Phillips would restore John Barn and repair him. I lie across Barn again and watch the stitching-up of the outer skin. With each pull and drag of thread through flesh Barn exclaims in the dark behind me. "Oh. Oh, that is bad. Oh, that feels dreadful." He jerks and cries out at every piercing by the needle.

"He's nearly finished, John," I say. "Maybe six stitches more."

And Phillips works above, ignoring us, as unmoved as if he were sewing up a boot. A wave of his hair droops forward on his brow, and around his eyes is stained with tiredness. It feels as if he has kept us in this small cloud of firelight, helping him do his mad work, all the night. There is no danger of me sleeping; I am beyond exhaustion; Barn's twitches wake me up brighter and brighter, and so does the fact that Phillips can ignore them so thoroughly, piercing and piercing the man. And though a few hours ago I would happily have left Barn to him, now I want to be awake and endure each stitch as well, even if there is no chance of the mulberry ever knowing or caring.

Then it is done. Phillips snips the thread with a pair of bright-gold scissors, inspects his work, draws a little silk out past all the layers of stitching. "Good, that's good," he says.

I lever myself up off Barn, lift my leg from his. "He's done with you," I tell him, and his eyes roll up into his head with relief, straight into sleep.

"We will leave him tied. We may as well," says Phillips, casting his used tools into the pot on the fire. "We don't want him running off again. Or getting infection in that wound." He strips off his horrid gloves and throws them in the fire. They wince and shrivel and give off a few moments' stink.

I feel as if I'm floating a little way off the ground; Phillips looks very small over there, his shining tools faraway. "There are others, then?" I say.

"Others?" He is coaxing his fire up to boil the tools again.

"'Careful practice,' you said, by your father's side. Yet we never saw you here. So there are other folk like ours, with their mulberries, that you practiced on? In other places in the mountains, or in the town itself? I have never been there to know."

"Oh," he says, and right at me, his eyes bright at mine. "Yes," he says. "Though there is a lot to be learned from ... books, you know, and general anatomy and surgical practice." He surveys the body before us, up and down. "But yes," he says earnestly to me. "Many communities. Quite a widespread practice, and trade. Quite solidly established."

I want to keep him talking like this, that he cares what he says to me. For the first time today he seems not to scorn me for what I am. I'm not as clear to him as John Barn has become to me, but I am more than I was this morning when he told Pa, *I'll take your boy, if you can spare him.*

"Do you have a son, then," I say, "that you are teaching in turn?"

"Ah," he says, "not as yet. I've not been so blessed thus far as to achieve the state of matrimony." He shows me his teeth, then sees that I don't understand. Some of his old crossness comes back. "I have no wife. Therefore I have no children. That is the way it is done in the town, at least."

"When you have a son, will you bring him here, to train him?" Even half-asleep I am enjoying this, having his attention, unsettling him. He looks as if he thought *me* a mulberry, and now is surprised to find that I can talk back and forth like any person.

"I dare say, I dare say." He shakes his head. "Although I'm sure you understand, it is a great distance to come, much farther than other

... communities. And a boy—their mothers are terribly attached to them, you know. My wife—my wife *to be*—might not consent to his travelling so far, from her. Until he is quite an age."

He waits on my next word, and so do I, but after a time a yawn takes me instead, and when it is over he is up and crouched by his fire. "Yes, time we got some rest. Excellent work, boy. You've been most useful." He seems quite a different man. Perhaps he is too tired to keep up his contempt of me? Certainly *I* am too tired to care very much. I climb to my feet and walk into the darkness, to relieve myself before sleep.

I wake, not with a start, but suddenly and completely, to the fire almost dead again and the forest all around me, aslant on the ridge. Dawn light is starting to creep up behind the trees, and stars are still snagged in the high branches, but here, close to me, masses of darkness go about their growing, roots fast in the ground around my head, thick trunks seeming to jostle each other, though nothing moves in the windless silence.

I am enormous myself, and wordless like the forest, yet full of burrows and niches and shadows where beasts lie curled—some newly gone to rest, others about to move out into the day—and birds roost with their breast-feathers fluffed over their claws. I am no fool, though that slip of a man with his tiny tools and his sneering took me for one. I see the story he spun me, and his earnest expectation that I would believe it. I see his whole plan and his father's, laid out like paths through the woods, him and his town house and his tailor at one end there, us and our poor mulberries at the other, winding silk and waiting for him. A widespread trade? No, just this little pattern trodden through from below. Many communities? No, just us. Just me and my folk, and our children.

I sit up silently. I wait until the white cross of John Barn glimmers over there on the ground, until the smoke from my fire comes clear, a fine grey vine climbing the darkness without haste. I think through the different ways I can take; there are few enough of them, and all of them end in uncertainty, except for the first and simplest way that came to me as I slept—which is now, which is here, which is me. I spend a long time listening to folk in my head, but whenever I look to Barn, and think of holding him down, and his trembling, and his dutiful chewing of the leaves, they fall silent; they have nothing to say.

A red-throat tests its call against the morning silence. I get up and go to Barn, and take up the coil of leftover cord from beside him.

Phillips is on his side, curled around what is left of his fire. His hands are nicely placed for me. I slip the cord under them and pin his forearms down with my boot. As he wakes, grunts—"What are you at, boy?"—and begins to struggle, I loop and loop, and swiftly tie the cord. "How *dare* you! What do you think—"

"Up." I stand back from him, all the forest behind me, and in me. We have no regard for this man's thin voice, his tiny rage.

Staring, he pushes himself up with his bound hands, is on his knees, then staggers to his feet. He is equal the height of me, but slender, built for spider-work, while I am constructed to chop wood and haul water and bring down a running stag. I can do what I like with him.

"You are just a boy!" he says. "Have you no respect for your elders?"

"You are not my elders," I say. I take his arm, and he tries to flinch away. "This way," I say, and I make him go.

"Boy?" says John Barn from the ground. He has forgotten my name again.

"I'll be back soon, John. Don't you worry."

And that is all the need I have of words. I force Phillips down towards the torrent path; he pours *his* words out, high-pitched, out-raged, neat-cut as if he made them with that little knife of his. But I am forest vastness, and the birds in my branches have begun their morning's shouting; I have no ears for him.

I push him down the narrow path; I don't bully him or take any glee when he falls and complains, or scratches his face in the under-brush, but I drag him up and keep him going. The noise of the torrent grows towards us, becomes bigger than all but the closest, loudest birds. His words flow back at me, but they are only a kind of odd music now, carrying no meaning, only fear.

He rounds a bend and quickly turns, and is in my arms, banging my chest with his bound purple hands. "You will not! You will not!" I turn him around, and move him on with all my body and legs. The torrent shows between the trees—that's what set him off, the water fighting white among the boulders.

Now he resists me with all that he has. His boots slip on the stones and he throws himself about. But there is simply not enough of him, and I am patient and determined; I pull him out of the brush again and again, and press him on. If he won't walk, I'm happy for him to crawl. If he won't crawl I'm prepared to push him along with my boot.

The path comes to a high lip over the water before cutting along and down to the flatter place where you can fill your pots, or splash your face. I bring him to the lip and push him straight off, glad to be rid of his flailing, embarrassed by his trying to fight me.

He disappears in the white. He comes up streaming, caught already by the flow, shouting at the cold. It tosses him about, gaping and kicking, for a few rocks, and then he turns to limp cloth, to rubbish, a dab of bright wet silk draggling across his chest. He slides up over a rock and drops the other side. He moves along, is carried away and down, over the little falls there, and across the pool, on his face and with blood running from his head, over again and on down.

I climb back up through the woods. It is very peaceful and straight-forward to walk without him, out of the water-noise into the birdsong. The clearing when I reach it is quiet without him, pleased to be rid of his fussing and displeasure and only to stand about, head among the leaves while the two fires send up their smoke-tendrils and John Barn sleeps on.

I bend down and touch his shoulder. "Come, John," I say, "time to make for home. Do I need to bind you?"

He wakes. "You?" His eyes reflect my head, surrounded by branches on the sky.

"George. George Treadlaw, remember?"

He looks about as I untie his feet. "That man is gone," he says. "Good. I don't like that man."

I reach across him to loosen his far hand. "Oh, George," he says "You smell bad this morning. Perhaps you'd better bind me, and walk at a little distance. That's a fearsome smell. It makes me want to run from you."

I sniff at a pinch of my shirt. "I'm no worse than I was last night."

"Yes, last night it started," he says. "But I was tied down then and no trouble to you."

I tether him to a tree-root and cook myself some pan-flaps.

"They smell nice," he says, and eats another mulberry leaf, watching the pan.

"You must eat nothing but leaves today, John," I tell him. "Anything foreign, you will die of it, for I can't go into you like Phillips and fetch it out again."

"You will have to watch me," he says. "Everything is very pretty, and smells so adventurous."

We set off home straight after. All day I lead him on a length of rope, letting him take his time. I am not impatient to get back. No one will be happy with me, that I lost Phillips. Oh, they will be angry, however much I say it was an accident, a slip of the man's boot as he squatted by the torrent washing himself. No one will want to take the spindles down to the town, and find whoever he traded them to, and buy the goods he bought. I will have to do all that, because it was I who lost the man, and I will, though the idea scares me as much as it will scare them. No one will want to hunt again, in years to come as the mulberries die off and no new ones are made; no one will want to gather roots and berries, and make nut flour, just to keep us fed, for people are all spoilt with town goods, the ease of them and the strong tastes and their softness to the tooth. But what can they do, after all, but complain? *Go down to the town yourselves*, I'll tell them. *Take a mulberry with you and some spindles; tell what was done to us. Do you think they will start it again? No, they will come up here and examine everything and talk to us as fools; they might take away all our mulberries; they might take all of us away, and make us live down the town. And they will think we did worse than lose Phillips in the torrent; they will take me off to jail, maybe. I don't know what will happen. I don't know.*

"It is a fine day, George of the Treadlaws," John Barn says behind me. "I like to breathe, out here. I like to see the trees, and the sun, and the birds."

He is following behind obedient, pale and careful, the stitches black in his paunch, the brace hanging off the silk-end. Step, step, step, he goes with his unaccustomed feet, on root and stone and ledge of earth, and he looks about when he can, at everything.

"You're right, John." I move on again so that he won't catch up and be upset by the smell of me. "It's a fine day for walking in the forest."

**Margo Lanagan** has written five collections of short stories: *White Time, Black Juice, Red Spikes, Cracklescape* and *Yellowcake*, and two dark fantasy novels, *Tender Morsels* and *The Brides of Rollrock Island*. She is a four-time World Fantasy Award winner, for Short Story, Collection, Novella, and Novel. Lanagan lives in Sydney, and works as a contract technical writer. She was an instructor at Clarion South in 2005, 2007 and 2009, and at Clarion West in 2011.

# Howard Waldrop
# on Margo Lanagan

## Margo Lanagan: Bass*ackwards

Years when I taught Clarion West, I didn't want to know anything about the classes til the day I walked in and saw what they put on paper and how they critiqued in the workshop sessions.

Years I didn't teach I (and others, whose names would frighten you) did some of the preliminary reading that led to acceptance in Clarion West.

I was teaching in '99, so I had no idea who or what anyone was, or where their writing was, or if they even knew what a story was.

What I didn't know was that Margo Lanagan had already had 14 novels published in her native Australia, and that she was coming to Clarion West to learn how to write short stories.

The stories she turned in first at Clarion West had the usual problems of someone shifting gears (writing short stories is not like writing novels—most people just manage their careers the other way round—first, short stories then a novel or two.)

In other words, because the stories weren't exactly working right, I didn't know she'd had all that work published, and it was a case of new forms, not uncertainty and lack of fundamentals (like some of the rest of her class).

She got with it, I believe, about week 3 and things showed great improvement from then on.

(I'm such a tough cop: I'm telling you this when 6 of her Clarion West stories were in her first collection. (From Allen & Unwin, no less.))

Once she got her traction, there was no holding her back. She won the World Fantasy Award for both short story AND best collection in 2005. (Something I've never done.)

It was a pleasure to have her as part of the '99 class (like, she needed our help!) and watching a writer change the modal setting in mid-career and becoming just as good a short-story writer as novelist. You don't get to see that often, and it makes me sleep better at nights.

**Howard Waldrop** has been called "a national treasure" by those who love his multi-award winning alternate and secret history short stories and novellas such as "The Ugly Chickens," "Flying Saucer Rock and Roll," and "A Dozen Tough Jobs". His work has received twenty Hugo, Nebula, and World Fantasy nominations alone and he has won both the Nebula and World Fantasy Awards, among others.

# The Fate of Mice

## Susan Palwick

## 1985

I remember galloping, the wind in my mane and the road hard against my hooves. Dr. Krantor says this is a false memory, that there is no possible genetic linkage between mice and horses, and I tell him that if scientists are going to equip IQ-enhanced mice with electronic vocal cords and teach them to talk, they should at least pay attention to what the mice tell them. "Mice," Dr. Krantor tells me acidly, "did not evolve from horses," and I ask him if he believes in reincarnation, and he glares at me and tells me that he's a behavioral psychologist, not a theologian, and I point out that it's pretty much the same thing. "You've got too much free time," he snaps at me. "Keep this up and I'll make you run the maze again today." I tell him that I don't mind the maze. The maze is fine. At least I know what I'm doing there: finding cheese as quickly as possible, which is what I'd do anyhow, anytime anyone gave me the chance. But what am I doing galloping?

"You aren't doing anything galloping," he tells me. "You've never galloped in your life. You're a mouse." I ask him how a mouse can remember being a horse, and he says, "It's not a memory. Maybe it's a dream, Maybe you got the idea from something you heard or saw somewhere. On TV." There's a small TV in the lab, so Dr. Krantor can watch the news, but it's not even positioned so that I can see it easily. And I ask him how watching something on TV would make me know what it *felt* like to be a horse, and he says I *don't* know what it feels like to be a horse, I have no idea what a horse feels like, I'm just making it up.

But I remember that road, winding ahead in moonlight, the harness pulling against my chest, the sound of wheels behind me. I remember the three other horses in harness with me, our warm breath steaming in the frosty air. And then I remember standing in a courtyard somewhere, and someone bringing water and hay. We stood there for a long time, the four of us, in our harness. I remember that, but that's all I remember. What happened next?

Dr. Krantor came grumbling into the lab this morning, Pippa in tow. "You have to behave yourself," he says sternly, and deposits her in a corner.

"Mommy was going to take me to the *zoo*," she says. When I stand on my hind legs to peer through the side of the cage, I can see her pigtails flouncing. "It's *Saturday*."

"Yea, I know that, but your mother decided she had other plans, and I have to work today."

"She did *not* have other plans. She and Michael were going to take me to the *zoo*. You just hate Michael, Daddy!"

"Here," he says, handing her a piece of graph paper and some colored pens. "You can draw a picture. You can draw a picture of the zoo."

"You could have gotten a *babysitter*," Pippa yells at him, her chubby little fists clenched against her polka-dot dress. "You're *cheap*. A babysitter'd take me to the *zoo*!"

"I'll take you myself, Pippa." Dr. Krantor is whining now. "In a few hours. I just have a few hours of work to do, okay?"

"*Huh*," she says. "And I bet you won't let me watch TV, either! Well, *I'm* gonna talk to Rodney!"

Pippa calls me Rodney because she says it's prettier than rodent, which is what Dr. Krantor calls me: The Rodent, as if in my one small body I contain the entire order of small, gnawing mammals having a single pair of upper incisors with a chisel-shaped edge. Perhaps he intends this as an honor, although to me it feels more like a burden.

I am only a small white mouse, unworthy to represent all the other rodents in the world, all the rats and rabbits and squirrels, and now I have this added weight, the mystery Dr. Krantor will not acknowledge, the burden of hooves and mane.

"Rodney," Pippa says, "Daddy's scared I'll like Michael better than him. If you had a baby girl mouse and you got a divorce and your daughter's Mummy had a boyfriend, would *you* be jealous?"

"Mice neither marry nor are given in marriage," I tell her. In point of fact, mice are non-monogamous, and in stressful situations have been known to eat their young, but this may be more than Pippa needs to know.

Pippa scowls. "If your daughter's Mommy had a boyfriend, would you keep her from seeing your daughter *at all*?"

"Sweetheart," Dr. Krantor says, striding over to our corner of the lab and bending down, "Michael's not a nice person."

"Yes he *is*."

"No he's not."

"Yes he is! You're just saying that because he has a picture of a naked lady on his arm! But I see naked ladies in the shower after I go swimming with Mommy! Michael doesn't always ride his motorcycle, Daddy! He promised to take me to the zoo in his *truck*!"

"Oh, Pippa," he says, and bends down and hugs her. "I'm just trying to protect you. I know you don't understand now. You will someday, I promise."

"I don't *want* to be protected," Pippa says, stabbing the paper with Dr. Krantor's red pen. "I want to go to the zoo with Mommy and Michael!"

"I know you do, sweetheart. I know. Draw a picture and talk to the rodent, okay? I'll take you to the zoo just as soon as I finish here."

Pippa, pouting, mumbles her assent and begins to draw. Dr. Krantor, who frequently vents his frustrations when he is alone in the lab, has told me about Pippa's mother, who used to be addicted to cocaine. Supposedly she is drug-free now. Supposedly she is now fit to have joint custody of her daughter. But Michael, with his motorcycle and his naked lady, looks too much like a drug dealer to Dr. Krantor. "If anything happened to Pippa while she was with them," he has told me, "I'd never forgive myself."

Pippa shows me her picture: a stick-figure, wearing pigtails and a polka-dot dress, sitting in a cage. "Here's my picture of the zoo," she says. "Rodney, do you ever wish you could go wherever you wanted?"

"Yes," I say. Dr. Krantor has warned me that the world is full of owls and snakes and cats and mousetraps, innumerable kinds of death. Dr. Krantor says that I should be happy to live in a cage, with food and water always available; Dr. Krantor says I should be proud of my contribution to science. I've told him that I'd be delighted to trade places with him—far be it from me to deny Dr. Krantor his share of luxury and prestige—but he always declines. He has responsibilities in his own world, he tells me. He has to take care of his daughter. Pippa seems to think that he takes care of her in much the same way he takes care of me.

"I'm *bored*," she says now, pouting. "Rodney, tell me a story."

"Sweetheart," says Dr. Krantor, "the rodent doesn't know any stories. He's just a mouse. Only people tell stories."

"But Rodney can *talk*. Rodney, do you know any stories? Tell me a story, Rodney."

"Once upon a time," I tell her—now where did that odd phrase come from?—"there was a mouse who remembered being a horse."

"Oh, *goody!*" Pippa claps her hands. "Cinderella! I love that one!"

My whiskers quiver in triumph. "You do? There's a story about a mouse who was a horse? Really?"

"Of course! Everybody knows Cinderella."

I don't. "How does it end, Pippa?"

"Oh, it's a happy ending. The poor girl marries the prince."

I remember nothing about poor girls, or about princes, either, and I can't say I care. "But what about the horse who was a mouse, Pippa?"

She frowns, wrinkling her nose. She looks a lot like her father when she frowns. "I don't know. It turns back into a mouse, I think. It's not important."

"It's important to me, Pippa."

"Okay," she says, and dutifully trudges across the lab to Dr. Krantor. "Daddy, in Cinderella, what happens to the mouse that turned into a horse when it turns back into a mouse?"

I hear breaking glassware, followed by Dr. Krantor's footsteps, and then he is standing above my cage and looking down at me. His face is oddly pale. "I don't know, Pippa. I don't think anyone knows. It probably got eaten by an owl or a cat or a snake. Or caught in a trap."

"Or equipped with IQ boosters and a vocal synthesizer and stuck in a lab," I tell him.

"It's just a story," Dr. Krantor says, but he's frowning. "It's an impossible story. It's a story about magic, not about science. Pippa, sweetheart, are you ready to go to the zoo now?"

"Now look," he tells me the next day, "it didn't happen. It *never* happened. Stories are about things that haven't happened. Somebody must have told you the story of Cinderella—"

"Who?" I demand. "Who would have told me? The only people I've ever talked to are you and Pippa—"

"You saw it on TV or something, I don't know. It's a common story. You could have heard it anywhere. Now look, rodent, you're a very suggestible little animal and you're suffering from false memory syndrome. That's very common too, believe me."

I feel my fur bristling. Very suggestible little animal, indeed!

But I don't know how I can remember a story I've never heard, a story that people knew before I remembered it. And soon I start to have other memories. I remember gnawing the ropes holding a lion to a stone table; I remember frightening an elephant; I remember being blind, and running with two blind companions. I remember wearing human clothing and being in love with a bird named Margalo. Each memory is as vivid and particular as the one about being a horse. Each memory feels utterly real.

I quickly learn that Dr. Krantor doesn't want to hear about any of this. The only thing he's interested in is how quickly I can master successively more complicated mazes. So I talk to Pippa instead, when she comes to visit the lab. Pippa knows some of the stories: the poem about the three blind mice, the belief that elephants are afraid of mice. She doesn't know the others, but she finds out. She asks her mother and her friends, her teachers, the school librarian, and then she reports back to me while Dr. Krantor is on the other side of the lab, tinkering with his computers and mazes.

All of my memories are from human stories. There are also a witch and a wardrobe in the story about the lion; the mouse who is in love with the bird is named Stuart. Pippa asks her mother to read her these stories, and reports that she likes them very much, although the story with the bird in it is the only one where the mouse is really important. And while that story, according to Pippa, ends with Stuart looking for his friend Margalo, the story never says whether or not he ever finds her. The fate of mice seems to be of little importance in human stories, even when the mouse is the hero.

I begin to develop a theory. Dr. Krantor believes that language makes me very good at running mazes, that with language comes the ability to remember the past and anticipate the future, to plan and strategize. To humor him, I talk to myself while I run the mazes; I pause at intersections and ask myself theatrical questions, soliloquizing about the delicious cheese to be found at the end of the ordeal, recounting fond anecdotes of cheeses past. Dr. Krantor loves this. He is writing a paper about how much better I am at the mazes than previous mice, who had IQ boasting but no vocal synthesizers, who were not able to turn their quests for cheese into narrative. Dr. Krantor's theory is that language brings a quantum leap in the ability to solve problems.

But my theory, which I do not share with Dr. Krantor, is that human language has dragged me into the human world, into human tales about mice. I am trapped in a maze of story, and I do not know how to reach the end of it, nor what is waiting for me there. I do not know if there is cheese at the end of the maze, or an elephant, or a lion on a stone table. And I do not know how to find out.

And then I have another memory. It comes to me one day as I am running the maze.

In this memory I am a mouse named Algernon. I am an extremely smart mouse, a genius mouse; I am even smarter than I am now. I love this memory, and I run even faster than usual, my whiskers quivering. Someone has told a story about a mouse like me! There is a story about a very smart mouse, a story where a very smart mouse is important!

Pippa comes to the lab after school that day, scowling and dragging a backpack of homework with her, and when Dr. Krantor is working on his computer across the room, I tell her about Algernon. She has never heard of Algernon, but she promises to question her sources and report back to me.

The next day, when she comes to the lab, she tells me that the school librarian has heard of the Algernon story, but says that Pippa isn't old enough to read it yet. "She wouldn't tell me why," Pippa says. "Maybe the mouse in the story is naked?"

"Mice are always naked," I tell her. "Or else we're never naked, because we always have our fur, or maybe we're only naked when we're born, because we're furless then. Anyway, we don't wear clothing, so that can't be the reason."

"Stuart wears clothing."

"But the three blind mice don't." My personal opinion is that Stuart's a sell-out who capitulated to human demands to wear clothing only so that he could be the hero in the story. It didn't work, of course; the humans couldn't be bothered to give him a happy ending, or any ending at all, whether he wore clothing or not. His bowing and scraping did him no good.

I suspect that Algernon is non-monogamous, or perhaps that he eats his young, and that this is why the librarian considers the story unsuitable for Pippa. But of course I don't tell her this, because then her father might forbid her to speak to me altogether. I must maintain my appearance of harmlessness.

Am I a sell-out too? I don't allow myself to examine that question too closely.

Instead I tell Pippa, "Why don't you ask your mother to find the story and read it to you?" Since Pippa's mother doesn't mind letting her see naked women in the shower, she may not share the librarian's qualms about whatever misconduct Algernon commits in the story. It makes perfect sense to me that a very smart mouse would do things of which humans would not entirely approve.

"Okay," Pippa says. "The story's called 'Flowers for Algernon,' so it must have a happy ending. Mommy gets flowers from Michael on her birthday."

"Oh, that's lovely!" I tell Pippa. I've never seen humans eating flowers—Pippa favors chocolate and once gave me a piece, which I considered an entirely inadequate substitute for seeds and stems—but my opinion of people rises slightly when I learn this. I'm very optimistic about this story.

The next day, Pippa tells me cheerfully that her mother found a copy of the story, but is reading it herself before she reads it to Pippa, just in case the librarian had a good reason for saying that Pippa shouldn't read it. This frustrates me, but I have no choice but to accept it. "I told her that you'd had a good dream about it," Pippa says happily. "She was glad."

The next day, Pippa does not come, and Dr. Krantor makes me run the maze until my whiskers are limp with exhaustion. The day after that, Pippa returns. She tells me, frowning, that her mother has finished reading the story, but agrees with the school librarian that Pippa shouldn't read it. "But I told her she had to: I told her it wasn't fair not to let me know what happens to Algernon." Her voice drops to a whisper now. "I told her she was being like Daddy, trying to keep me from knowing stuff. And that made her face go all funny, and she said, okay, she'll start reading it to me tonight."

"Thank you," I tell Pippa. I'm truly touched by her persistence on my behalf, but also a little alarmed: What in the world could have shocked both a staid school librarian and Pippa's unconventional mother?

It takes me a while to find out. Pippa doesn't come back to the lab for a week. Dr. Krantor is frantic, and as usual when he's worried, he talks to me. He paces back and forth in front of my cage. He rants. "She says it's because she has too much homework, but she can do her homework here! She says it's because her mother's taking her to the zoo after school, but how can that be true if she has all that homework? She says it's because she and her mother and Michael have to plan a trip. A trip! Her mother's brainwashing her, I know it! Michael's brainwashing both of them! I'm going to lose Pippa! They'll flee the country and take her with them! He's probably a Colombian druglord!"

"Just calm down," I tell Dr. Krantor, although I'm worried too. The string of excuses is clearly fake. I wonder if Pippa's absence has anything to do with Algernon, but of course I can't talk about that, because Dr. Krantor doesn't approve of my interest in human stories.

"Don't tell me to calm down, rodent! What would you know about it? You don't have children!"

And whose fault is that? I think sourly. Often have I asked for a companion, a female mouse, but Dr. Krantor believes that a mate would distract me from his mazes, from the quest for cheese.

He storms back to his computer, muttering, and I pace inside my cage the same way Dr. Krantor paced in front of it. What in the world is wrong with Pippa? What in the world happened to Algernon? Was he eaten by a cat, or caught in a trap? Right now I would welcome even the mazes, since they would be a distraction, but Dr. Krantor is working on something else. At last, sick of pacing, I run on my exercise wheel until I am too exhausted to think.

Finally Pippa returns. She is quieter than she was. She avoids me. She sits at the table next to Dr. Krantor's computer, all the way across the lab, and does her homework. When I stand up on my hind legs, I can see her, clutching her pencil, the tip of her tongue sticking out in concentration. And I see Dr. Krantor frowning at her. He knows she is acting oddly, too. He stands up and looks down at her workbook. "Pippa sweetheart, why are you working so hard on that? That's easy. You already know it. Why don't you go say hello to the rodent? He missed you. We both missed you, you know."

"I have to finish my homework," she says sullenly.

"Pippa," Dr. Krantor says, frowning even more now, "your homework is done. That page is all filled out. Pippa, darling, what's the matter?"

"Nothing! Leave me alone! I don't want to be here! I want to go home!"

I'm afraid that she's going to start crying, but instead, Dr. Krantor does. He stands behind her, bawling, his fists clenched. "It's Michael, isn't it! You love Michael more than you love me! Your mother's brainwashed you! Where are they taking you, Pippa? Where are you going on this trip? Whatever your mother's said about me is a lie!"

I stare. Dr. Krantor has never had an outburst like this. Pippa, twisted around in her chair, stares too. "Daddy," she says, "it has nothing to do with you. It's not about *you*!"

He snuffles furiously and swipes at his face with a paper towel. "Well then," he says, "why don't you tell me what it's about?"

"It's about Algernon!" she says, and now she's crying, too.

I'm very afraid. Something even worse than a trap or a cat must have happened to Algernon.

It's Dr. Krantor's turn to stare. "Algernon? Who's Algernon? Your mother has a new boyfriend named Algernon? What happened to Michael? Or she has *two* boyfriends now, Michael *and* Algernon? Pippa, this is terrible! I have to get you out of there!"

"Algernon the *mouse*, Daddy!"

Dr. Krantor squints at her. "What?"

And the whole story comes out. Pippa breaks down and tells him everything, hiccupping, as I cower in my cage. Pippa's upset, and it's my fault. Dr. Krantor's going to be furious at me. He won't let me have any more cheese. He'll take away my exercise wheel. "That's why

I've been staying away," Pippa says. "Because of Algernon. Because of what happens to Algernon. Daddy—"

"It's just a story," Dr. Krantor says. It's what I expect him to say. But then he says something I don't expect. "Pippa, you have to tell the rodent—"

"His name's Rodney, Daddy!"

"You have to tell Rodney what happened, all right? Because he's been waiting to find out, and he can hear us talking, and not knowing will make him worry more. It's just a story, Pippa. Nothing like that has happened to my mice, the ones here in the lab. I promise. Come on, I'll help you."

Astonished, I watch Dr. Krantor carry Pippa across the lab to my cage. "Pippa," he says when he gets here. "Rodney's missed you. Say hello to Rodney. Do you want to hold him?"

She snuffles and nods, shyly, and Dr. Krantor says, "Rodney, if Pippa holds you, you won't run away, right?"

"No," I say, even more astonished than I was before. Pippa's never been allowed to hold me before, because Dr. Krantor's afraid that she might drop me, and I represent a huge investment of research dollars. But now Dr. Krantor opens the top of the cage and lifts me out by my tail, the way he does when going to put me in the maze; but instead he puts me in Pippa's cupped palms, which are very warm. She peers down at me. Her breath is warm too, against my fur, and I see tears still shining in the corners of her eyes. Dr. Krantor tells her, "Rodney's a very healthy mouse. He's fine, Pippa. There's nothing wrong with him, even though he's smart."

I don't understand this, and nobody's answering the main question. "What happens to Algernon?" I ask.

"He dies," Pippa says in a tiny voice.

"Oh," I say. Well, I'd deduced as much. "A cat gets him, or a mouse-trap?" And Pippa's face starts to crumple as she strokes my back, and I hear Dr. Krantor sigh.

"Rodney," he says, "in the story 'Flowers for Algernon,' the mouse Algernon has been IQ boosted, the way you are. Only the story was written before that was really possible. Anyway, in the story, the mouse dies as a result of the experiment."

"He dies because he's smart," Pippa says mournfully. "Except he gets stupid first. The experiment wears off, and he gets stupid again, and then he dies! The flowers are for his grave!"

"Right," Dr. Krantor says. "Now listen to me, you two. It's *just a story*. None of my mice have died prematurely as a result of the IQ boosting, and the IQ boosting hasn't worn off on any of them. All my mice stay smart, and they don't die any sooner than they would anyway. If anything, they live longer than non-enhanced mice. Okay? Does everybody feel better now?"

"But how did they die?" I ask, alarmed. "How could they die if they were here in their cages, where there aren't any owls or cats or snakes or mousetraps?"

Dr. Krantor shakes his head. "They just died, Rodney. They died of old age. All mice die, sometime. But they had good lives. I take care of my animals."

"What?" I say stupidly. All mice die? "I'm going to die? Even if there aren't any cats?"

"Not anytime soon," Dr. Krantor says. "Everything dies. Didn't you know that?" A drop of water splashes on me, and Dr. Krantor says, "Pippa, sweetheart, you don't have to cry. Rodney's fine. He's a healthy little mouse. Pippa, dear, if you're going to drown him, you'd better put him back in his cage."

And he helps her put me back in my cage, and he says he's going to take her out for ice cream, and he'll bring back some special cheese for me, and I won't even have to run a maze to get it, and they'll be back in a little while. All of these words buzz over me in a blur, as I huddle in my cage trying to make sense of what I've just learned.

I'm going to die.

I'm going to die. All mice die. That's why the stories about mice never say what happened to them, because everyone knows. The mice died. The mouse who became a horse died, and the mice who freed the lion died, and Stuart Little died. I curl into a ball in a corner of my cage and think about this, and then I uncurl and run very hard on my exercise wheel, so I won't have to think about it.

You have taught me language, and my profit on it is, I know how to fear.

Where did that line come from? I don't know, and it's not even really true. I feared things before I knew that I must die; I feared cats and snakes and mousetraps. But fear was always a reason to avoid things, and now I fear something I cannot avoid. I run on the exercise wheel, trying to flee the thing I have learned I cannot escape.

Dr. Krantor and Pippa come back. He has brought me a lovely piece of cheese, an aged cheddar far richer than what I usually find at the end of the maze. He and Pippa sit and watch me nibble at it, and then he says, "Are you all right, Rodney? Do you feel better now?"

"No," I tell him. "You aren't really protecting me by keeping me in this cage, are you? You can't protect me. I'm going to die anyway. You aren't keeping me safe from death; you're denying me life." I think of my memories, the joy of galloping down the road, of chewing through rope, of loving a bird. "You're depriving me of experience. Dr. Krantor, please let me go."

"Let you go?" he says. "Rodney, don't be ridiculous! There are still cats and snakes and mousetraps out there. You'll live much longer this way. And you represent a huge investment of research dollars. I can't let you go."

"I'm not an investment," I snap at him, "I'm a creature! Let me go!"

Dr. Krantor shakes his head. "Rodney, I can't do that. I really can't. I'm sorry. I'll buy you a new exercise wheel, okay? And a bigger cage? There are all kinds of fancy cages with tunnels and things. We can make your cage ten times bigger than this one. Pippa, you can help design Rodney's new cage. We'll go to the pet store and buy all the parts. It will be fun."

"I don't want a new exercise wheel," I tell him. "I don't want a new cage. I want to be free! Pippa, he says he can't let me go, but remember when he said you couldn't go to the zoo? It's the same thing."

"It's not the same thing at all," Dr. Krantor says. His voice isn't friendly anymore. "Rodney, I'm getting very annoyed with you. Pippa, don't you have more homework to do?"

"No," she says. "I already did my homework. The page is all filled out."

"Well then," Dr. Krantor says. "We'll go to the pet store—"

"I don't want you to go to the pet store! I want you to let me go! Pippa—"

"Stop trying to brainwash her!" Dr. Krantor bellows at me.

I can feel my tail flicking in fury. "You're the one brainwashing her!"

"Stop it," Pippa says. She's put her thumb in her mouth, muffling her words, and she looks like she's going to cry again. "Stop it! I hate it when you fight!"

We stop. I feel miserable. I wonder how Dr. Krantor feels. Pippa goes back to the table where her homework is, and Dr. Krantor goes back to his computer, and I nibble disconsolately on the excellent cheddar. No one says anything. After a while, Dr. Krantor comes back over to my cage and asks wearily, "All right, Rodney. Ready for the maze?"

"Are you out of your mind? I'm not going to run any more mazes! Why should I? What's in it for me?"

"Cheese!"

"I've had enough cheese today." I'm being ungracious, I know. I should thank him for the excellent cheddar. But I'm too angry to mind my manners.

"It's for my research, Rodney!"

"I don't care about your research, you imbecile!"

Dr. Krantor curses; Pippa, at her table, has covered her ears. Dr. Krantor reaches into my cage. He lifts me by the tail, none too gently, and plunks me down at the beginning of the maze. "Go," he says.

"Go groom yourself!"

He stomps away. I sit in the maze and clean my whiskers, fastidiously, and then I curl into a ball and take a nap.

I wake to feel myself being lifted into the air again. Dr. Krantor puts me back in my cage, even more roughly than he took me out, and says, "All right, Rodney. Look, this has all been a terrible mess, and I'm very sorry, but if you aren't willing to work tomorrow, we're going to have a problem."

"Going to?" I say.

Dr. Krantor rubs his eyes. "Rodney. Don't do this. You're expendable."

"I am? Even though I represent a tremendous investment of research dollars? Well then, you should have no problem letting me go."

He glares down at me. "Don't do this. Please don't do this. There are things I can do to make you compliant. Drugs. Electric shocks. I don't want to do any of that, and I know you don't want me to either. I want to keep a good working relationship here, all right, Rodney? Please?"

"You're threatening to torture me?" Outrage makes my voice even squeakier than usual. "Great working relationship! Hey, Pippa, did you hear that? Did you hear what your father just said?"

"Pippa isn't here, Rodney. Her mother came to pick her up while you were asleep. They were going to a birthday party. Rodney: Will you run the maze tomorrow, or will I have to resort to other methods?"

I'm frightened now. Dr. Krantor's voice is calm, reasonable. He's very matter-of-fact about the prospect of torturing me, and Pippa isn't here as a witness. He's probably bluffing. Coercion would probably compromise his data. But I don't know that for sure.

"Rodney?" he says.

"I'll think about it," I tell him. I have to buy myself time. Now I know why Stuart bowed and scraped. People are so much bigger than we are.

"Good enough," he says, his voice gentler, and reaches into the cage to give me another piece of the excellent cheddar. "Have a good night, Rodney." And then he leaves.

I stay awake all night, fretting. I try to find some way to escape from my cage, but I can't. I wonder if I could escape from the maze; I've never tried, but surely Dr. Krantor has made the mazes secure, also. I don't know what to do.

I dread the morning.

But in the morning, when Dr. Krantor usually arrives, I hear three sets of footsteps in the hallway outside, and two voices: Dr. Krantor's and a woman's.

"Why do you have to take her on this trip in the middle of the school year?" Dr. Krantor says. "And why do you have to talk to me about it now?"

"I already told you, Jack! Michael's family reunion in Ireland is in a month, so if we go we have to go then, and I need you to sign this letter saying that you know I'm not kidnapping her. I don't want any trouble."

Dr. Krantor grumbles something, and the lab door opens. Dr. Krantor and the woman—Pippa's mother!—come inside, still arguing. Pippa comes inside too. Pippa's mother walks to the computer; Pippa races to my cage.

"How *do* I know you aren't kidnapping her?" Dr. Krantor says. "Pippa, there's more of the new cheese over here, if you want to give Rodney a nice breakfast."

"Pippa," I whisper, "he threatened to torture me! Pippa—"

"Shhhhh," she whispers back, and opens my cage, and reaches into one of her pockets. "Don't make any noise, Rodney."

She's holding a mouse. A white mouse, just like me. Pippa puts the new mouse in the cage and we stare at each other in surprise, nose to nose, whiskers twitching, but then I feel Pippa grasp the base of my tail. She lifts me, and I watch the new mouse receding, and then she puts me in her pocket. I hear the cage close, and then we're walking across the room.

"All right, Jack, here's the itinerary, see? Here on this map? Jack, look at the map, would you? I'll tell you every single place were going; it's not like we're spiriting her away without telling you."

"But how do I know you'll really go there? You could take her to, to, Spain or the South Pole or—"

"Michael doesn't have a family reunion in Spain or the South Pole. Jack, be reasonable."

"I'm bored," Pippa says loudly. "I'm going outside."

"Stay right by the front door, sweetheart!" That's Dr. Krantor, of course.

"I will," she says, and then I hear the lab door open and we're out, we're in the hallway, and then we go through another door and I smell fresh air and Pippa lifts me out of her pocket. She sits down on a step and holds me up to her face. "Mommy and I went to the pet store last night, Rodney, and we got another mouse who looks just like you. He was in the cage of mice that people buy to feed to their snakes. Being here is better for him. Daddy won't feed him to a snake."

"But your father will torture the other mouse," I say, "or worse. When he realizes it's just an ordinary mouse he'll be very angry. Pippa, he'll punish you."

"No, he won't," she says cheerfully, "or Mommy and Michael will say he isn't taking good care of me." She puts me down on the warm cement step. I feel wind and smell flowers and grass. "You're free, Rodney. You can have your very own adventures. You don't have to go back to that stupid maze."

"How will I find you?" As much as I yearned for freedom before, I'm terrified. There really are cats and snakes and mousetraps out here, and I've never had to face them. How will I know what to do? "Pippa, you have to meet me so I can tell you my stories, or no one will know what happens to me. I'll be just like all those other mice, the ones whose stories just stop when they stop being useful to the main characters. Pippa—"

But there are footsteps now from inside, forceful footsteps coming closer, and Dr. Krantor's voice. His voice sounds dangerous. "Pippa? Pippa, what did you do to the rodent? It won't talk to me! I don't even think it's the same mouse! Pippa, did you put another mouse in that cage?"

I find myself trembling as badly as I would if a cat were coming. Pippa stands up. The sole of her sneaker is the only thing I can see now. From very far above me I hear her saying, "Run, Rodney."

And I do.

**Susan Palwick** is an Associate Professor of English at the University of Nevada, Reno. She has published four novels: *Flying in Place, The Necessary Beggar*, *Shelter*, and *Mending the Moon*. "The Fate of Mice" is included in her collection of the same name, published by Tachyon Publications. She remembers her time at Clarion West very fondly and is grateful to all of her instructors and fellow students.

# Samuel R. Delany
# on Susan Palwick

Over the years, most Clarion West students tend to blend in with one another. They're all generally smart. They're all generally talented. They're all generally committed. But now and again, one does stand out. Susan Palwick was such a student. Shortly after her graduation from Clarion West, she was working on the staff of a poetry journal— David Hartwell's *The Little Magazine*—that met weekly in my living-room for several years, so that from then on, remembering was ... what do I say? A lot easier. That persisted through the early parts of her writing career, right through her first novel, *Flying in Place*. Susan is a wonderful writer and a wonderful person. I'm proud and happy to have had even a small bit of input in the process. For the last years I know she's been teaching and writing—and now and again arguing passionately and intelligently on various blogs' comment threads, over a whole variety of socially important topics. Though we haven't seen each other for a while, I still think of her as a good friend.

And it's a pleasure to say a few words of introduction about her and her work. What she had to say was always worth listening to, and her writing was (and is) always lucid and precise.

**Samuel R. Delany** is an author, professor, and literary critic. His work includes novels, as well as memoir, criticism, and essays on sexuality and society. His science fiction novels include *Babel-17*, *The Einstein Intersection*, *Nova*, *Dhalgren*, and the Return to Nevèrÿon series. After winning four Nebula awards and two Hugo awards over the course of his career, Delany was inducted into the Science Fiction Hall of Fame in 2002. Since January 2001 he has been a professor of English and Creative Writing at Temple University in Philadelphia, where he is Director of the Graduate Creative Writing Program.

# My She

## Mary Rosenblum

## 1988

I wait outside the speaking chamber, where the young Speakers learn to Hear and Speak. The walls and carpeted floor are purest white, the color of this God place and the Speakers who live here walk by, all dressed in white like the walls and the floor, their palms on the shoulders of their guides. They all look the same with their pale hair and pale eyes. Only their smell tells me who they are. I am a guide for my Speaker. Until she puts on the robe and is sent to another place to Speak between the worlds for the citizens. Then I will have a new pup to raise. I will miss this puppy. Her scent comes to me from beneath the door of the learning room, smelling of trying hard and not sure.

She is never sure, my she, not since I first came to her, when she was just small. I sometimes smell her silent tears at night and slip into her room from my cubicle to lie beside her. She strokes the fur on my head and shoulders and it comforts her. It is our secret—kept secret, I think, because she does not know if it is permitted for me to sleep on her bed at night. I, myself, do not know, even after all these years here. Never before have I slept beside a pup in my charge. Perhaps there is nothing wrong. Perhaps there is. But it is our secret and it binds us. When I sleep in her bed, I hear my litter-brother in my dreams and I like that. I miss him always.

I will miss her, when she leaves. Unless they finally send me with her, the way they sent my litter-brother with his Speaker. But they say

I am good at raising puppies and they have not sent me with a newly-robed Speaker yet.

While I wait for her, I pull out my brother's last mail to me. The tiny disk feels cool and hard in my palm. Disk-mail is not expensive, but it is slow. This disk traveled in four ships before it found its way here from the colony world where my brother now lives. But we guides are servants and servants are not entitled to use the Speakers; they are for citizens only. Perhaps they think that because we mostly smell to each other that we do not need to speak with words. But we cannot smell between the stars. I would like to speak to my litter-brother and hear his answer. I will never see him again, except on my she's bed. There, he speaks to me, tells me how he misses me. We used to wrestle in the meadow around the school where we were raised, chasing each other into the creek, splashing and laughing. Sometimes it snowed and I still dream of snow, cold and white, stinging my palms and the soles of my feet, tingly as it melted in my fur.

There is no snow in the convent. Only spring, forever.

The door opens and I have been dreaming of snow and my brother. I am not ready. I leap to my feet, ears going flat.

"Siri? Where are you?"

Her hand goes out and I step beneath it so that my shoulder fur comes up against her palm. I feel the tickle of her mind finding my eyes and the white-walled corridor blurs just a bit as our minds share my eyes.

I wonder if that is how I speak to my brother when I sleep in her bed? "I had a mail from my litter-brother," I tell her.

She understands litters. The Speaker puppies are born in litters of ten. We walk down the hall and I see that she is heading for the garden in the center of the convent. Sadness darkens her scent and I reach up to touch her hand lightly, wanting to make the smell go away.

"You don't understand." She shrugs me off but she does not smell angry. "What if I fail?"

Fail? The word chills me. My puppies to do not fail. Have never failed. We step out into sunlight, soft and gentle through the dome. Water trickles and the rich tapestry of dirt smells, the small beings that inhabit this space, the breath of the water itself make me dizzy. Most of the convent is clean of such smells. She sits on a bench covered with bright chips of color and I squat beside her, leaning lightly against her thigh because that comforts her. Her fingers slide into the long fur on the back of my neck and that makes me shiver. "Who said you would fail?"

"My Speaker-Mistress." Her words are low and she smells sharp, unhappy. "The one who ... trains me. I ... Hear more than the voice I'm tuning to. I can't shut the others out. But I don't listen to them." She smells distress and a tinge of anger. "I am good. I would not listen to any other voice. I would not Speak the God Words to another. Not ever."

I wince—I cannot stop myself—because her fingers digging in hurt me. She lets go and covers her face with her hands.

"I am not trying to Hear them. I listen only for the voice that speaks to me. Too sensitive she said, the Speaker-Mistress." Her voice is hard to hear, but she smells frightened. "She said it could not be, that my genes will not permit it."

I shiver as if I am a puppy again and have played too long in the snow.

"Will they make me leave?"

She does not understand. Maybe none of them do. Speaking only the God Words, Hearing the God Words is all there is for them. Only Speakers live here in the convent. And we servants.

No one leaves, except on a ship, to Hear and Speak in another place, so that the citizens can talk between the stars. The way my brother left with the new Speaker assigned to him.

I try to distract her. I can smell the vanilla orchids opening and she loves them. Even she can smell them with her poor dead nose and she loves the touch of their thick petals. So I take her to them. And she puts on a face that means she is happy. But she smells sad.

And I smell afraid.

She is my puppy. She was given to me to raise. And none of my puppies have ever failed.

If she fails, I will no longer speak to my litter-brother in my dreams.

☙

I wake in darkness and smell her tears. I leave my cushion and pad across the carpet in the soft, warm darkness, slipping onto the soft mattress beside her. She puts her arm around me and buries her face in the fur that covers my shoulders. I can feel the wetness of her tears as they soak my fur, like the melting snow, so long ago. But warm. She reeks of sorrow but not fear.

How can she truly know fear?

I envy her that.

"Tell me about snow," she says.

"It is frozen water. It falls from the skies."

"Tell me more. Tell me about when you were a child."

She is using her command voice and it's hard, very hard, to say no to her, even though we do not speak of things outside. Not in here. The God of Speakers will be angry. The God of Speakers is only angry at you one time.

But if she has failed? So I shrug. What can it hurt now? "I was never a child." The tail stub that doesn't show under my coveralls wriggles in amusement. "But my litter was born in a place where winter—the cold time when snow falls—lasts a very long time. So we were old enough to play in it before we were old enough to be sent to our homes."

"You were young. So you were a child."

"We are not called children when we are young." I flatten my ears, uneasy. Never has one of my young Speakers talked to me like this. I suddenly want to tell her. "Our people have forever served yours. Even as I serve you now."

"I do not understand." But she has stopped thinking about it and she smells wistful. "I keep wondering what type of world they will send me to. I dreamed of snow, you know. Snow. White, fluffy flakes falling from a gray sky. And two furry creatures chasing each other through humps of white. Was that you?" She smells happy. "Did I dream of you?"

I flatten my ears and nod.

"I hoped they would send me to a world with snow." She buries her face in my fur again. "But will they send me anywhere now?"

My ears are tight to my head and my nose quivers. I want to point to the moon that I remember but cannot see here and want to howl.

I have not howled since I was a puppy far younger than my she. Instead I kiss her cheek and let her soak my fur with her warm-snowmelt tears and my howl fills my belly. When she is gone, my litter-brother will be gone, too.

I dream of my brother. We are playing chase in the snow and it glitters like stardust from a thousand frozen galaxies as he catches me and we tumble over and over in the cold, dry whiteness. Then we are curled together in our sleeping place, warm, dreaming. That was a long, long time ago, before we learned to be servants, before we left to guard the Speaker pups. I will never forget the smell of him. *How can I forget you?* He blinks green eyes in the darkness and his tongue curls over his white, white teeth. *We dream together every night.*

Once, in his mail, he sent me a map of the place where he is, a sweep of glittering stars with their silent planets. He had flagged the world he was on, a mote of darkness in that sea of light. *You are younger than I now, could be my puppy,* I tell him and nuzzle his ears. *That is what happens when you sleep on the slow ships that carry living things.*

*You look like you always look,* he says, and then we romp off to play in the snow.

My she stirs and wakes and stares up into the darkness. My dream is gone, my litter-brother's voice is gone, and even when she finally falls asleep again, it does not return.

She is quiet this morning. I take her to the dining room, her hand on my shoulder. She is not using my eyes, is looking inward, walking in darkness, trusting me to guide her feet. I bring her breakfast and take my own plate to squat along the wall with the others like me. Their ears flick and flatten as I pass and they smell sympathy for me. Ah, well, we know before anyone else, always. I have no appetite for my roll this morning but I eat it. I am a good servant.

Each litter of young Speakers sits at its own table, ten together, the oldest and tallest near the front, the young ones with their servants close in the rear, near the big doors. The room is light and warm. I have made many trips across it over the years, moving from the door to the front of the room, then back to the door as my puppy assumes the Speaker's gown and departs and I am assigned to a new puppy.

Now, my she sits at the front table with her litter, all identical, with the same, white-gold hair braided down their backs, the same white coveralls that mark them as Speakers-in-Training. The same faces and pale, lavender, unseeing eyes. Only the smell identifies them.

My she smells sad.

And this morning ... afraid.

Perhaps, even among the Speakers, the news is spreading. Perhaps even they, with their nearly-dead noses, can smell failure.

The litters rise together at their tables, the youngest first, to return to their meditation where they can learn to Hear the words of God across the space between the stars. One after another, we rise as we smell our puppy and we follow. And it occurs to me as they pass— identical hair, identical pale, sightless eyes, identically curved spines and graceful fingers—that they are as created as we are.

That is a blasphemous thought because we are taught that citizens are not created. Servants are. I rise to join my she and I feel her arm brush against my shoulder. Secretly. I smell sympathy from the other servants, and think that she is like us.

I should not think it, but I do.

After breakfast we go to the room where she learns to Hear the God words. But when she gets there, an old one like she waits for her, wearing the full robe of a Speaker. Her servant flicks his ears at me then flattens them slightly and my own flatten in return. I want to squeeze against my she and comfort her. She lowers herself before the Speaker, like any pup. Respectfully. But her fear stings my nose and my ears flick back and forth.

"Your presence is requested at Council." The Speaker offers a hand.

"The DNA analysis came back?" My she doesn't move.

I take her hand, place it in the Speaker's hand. It feels dead, heavy without life.

"Yes." The Speaker closes her hand around my she's and then releases it, walking away with her hand on her servant's shoulder.

The Council room is white but the table and the chairs are brown, made of dead trees from the Home World. I was not born on the Home World, I know. That world is at the far end of the stars, too far to visit, farther even than my litter-brother. But the Speakers can Speak there. They can Hear a whisper on the far, far away world.

I am proud to be a servant to Speaker pups.

But the scent of the room keeps my ears flat and the others along the wall smell sympathy for me as we come in. Three Speakers wait at the table, their robes all around their feet, their faces creased and wrinkled like a pile of clothes that has been slept on. They smell very old. And of power.

The fur on my neck stirs and rises even though that is not permitted here. I flatten my ears but I cannot make my fur lie down. I sit along the wall with the others.

"The power to Speak is all," they murmur, all together. "The power to Hear is all." They bow their heads. Except my she. She has seated herself but her eyes are on the far wall.

"The Speaker is a pure being." The Speaker who smells oldest, the one who made my fur stand up, speaks. "In a thousand years, the purity has been maintained. Only those of that purity can Speak between the worlds with the words of God. What is the holy trinity?"

She speaks command and my throat wants to answer her.

"A pure life, a pure mind, and a pure body." My she's voice is so soft even I can barely hear it.

"You have never compromised the purity of your life, nor of your mind." The powerful Speaker whispers on. "But even in the sanctity of the convents, purity must be defended. Always."

"How can I be impure?" My she rises, smelling of anger now. "I came into being here. I have nine siblings. They are pure. You cannot have found anything wrong."

"It is a tiny mutation." Another of the powerful old ones speaks. "A small thing. It occurred late in gestation, after our final test pre-decantation. We will expand our testing after this and we have alerted the other convents."

"I can block out the other voices. I can concentrate on the one I'm supposed to Hear."

"Communication is the neurosystem that holds our civilization together. Flesh and blood, impure as we are, we must emulate the purity of electronics. Interpretation, alteration, destroys purity."

"But I don't ... "

"The quantum effect is doubled by the mutation. That is why you Hear more than the voice you tune to."

"But I can—"

"Communication must be pure, perfect. *Private*. There is no room for impurity." The old-smelling, power-smelling one stands.

Even her standing is a command. The others stand with her and their servants leap into position. My she does not react as I reach her side, refusing my sight, keeping her face turned to the wall as the others file out. The last one out the door, the one who came to summon her, smells sad. Only she.

We stand there for a long time after the others have left. My fur no longer stands up, but my ears are still flat to my head and the howl that has troubled me has returned to knot in my gut. Finally, she stirs and the room shimmers as she takes my sight. She strides out of the room and I have to almost trot to stay with her. It is dinner time and my stomach growls as we pass the corridor that leads to the dining room and the scent of fish stew wafts out. But my she marches on past servants like myself moving floaters piled with laundry or stacked with goods that came in as tithe from the citizen communities around the convent. We pass into the old hallways in the center of the convent, the ones that were built long ago, perhaps before my gene-line even existed, when my ancestors still ran on four feet and ate from the floor. I know where she is going. We come here, sometimes. And she always smells thoughtful. It is after these visits that she often wants me to creep onto the bed with her.

At last we reach it, the center of the old convent, the room with eight sides and the old, dark screens that once, my she told me, offered information the way a holographic window does now. And in the very center of that center room stands the statue. She stops in front of it.

It is of two women standing palm to palm. I don't know what it is made from—none of the materials in the convent smell like it and I never smelled anything like it when I was a pup. Even the taste, when I once licked it, is strange. But it is smooth and milky and the eyes of the two women seemed to gleam with faint light, the same pale lavender as the Speakers' eyes, as my she's eyes.

"Once upon a time, more than a millennium ago, a pair of identical twins were born. They were born disabled because at that time, people couldn't read DNA well enough ... to fix it." Her words stumble here and her smell of sadness makes me want to kiss her cheek, but when I lean gently against her, she steps away.

"No one else could do what they did so they ... preserved the gene-line. And thus was the origin of the convents. Purity of thought, word, and deed. You must not know the words you Hear, you must only repeat them perfectly, and only to the one you are tuned to."

Her face is dry but she smells like crying. I want to press against her, but I stay still.

"I am impure." Her voice grows softer, deeper. "Perhaps my DNA has betrayed me, but my mind betrayed me first. Making me wonder why. Why can we not know history? Why can we not know the world outside the dome? Why can we not simply Speak when we choose? To whom we choose? Why only here, only the words that are given us, without understanding what those words mean?"

She smells angry again now. And I flick my ears forward and back, fighting an urge to crouch low.

"The convents exist on every inhabited planet." Her face looks strange and tight. "And there are no Speakers other than at the convents. Communication is ... valuable."

I don't understand, but her angry smell makes my neck fur rise, wanting to protect her.

"How can I think such thoughts?" She clenches both her pale hands now. "No wonder my DNA betrayed me. My impure thoughts must have warped it. Where will I go now? What can I do if I cannot Speak to the stars? Who will I Speak to?"

The howl knotted in my gut nearly escapes, but I flatten my ears and crouch in spite of myself, forcing it down. Even when she uses my eyes she cannot see me without a mirror, and for that I am now grateful. There are no mirrors here and if she looked in my eyes she would see the truth.

"Perhaps I'll end up a servant like you." Her shoulders droop. "Cleaning the gardens or cooking in the kitchen. I've never seen one of our type as a servant before. Not many fail, I suppose."

Not many fail.

I shiver, glad that she is not touching me to feel my crouch, my shiver, glad that she cannot smell.

I am old, but the Speakers that smell old tell me that I am a good puppy raiser. Will they give me a new small one tomorrow? Next week? Then I will sit at the table nearest the door with my small puppy while she learns how to eat, and walk, and Speak. Will I ever need to slip onto her bed at night? Will she ever wet my neck fur with warm snow-melt tears?

Will I ever speak with my litter-brother again, nested in our dreams?

Perhaps she is right and she is impure.

We are all impure, us servants here. We cannot Speak and we know far too much for purity. Perhaps my dreams have made her impure.

"We've missed dinner." She gropes for me finally and I place myself beneath her palm. "Take me to the garden and then you can go to the kitchen and get food. I'm not hungry but I want you to eat."

They are waiting for her, in her room or in the garden. I smell the traces of tension in the air circulating through the room, the smell of distress like bitter smoke in my nose. We always know. She starts forward, knowing the way to the garden without my eyes. I step in front of her and she bumps into me, smelling surprised, stumbling back a step.

"Siri, what happened? What's wrong?"

"Not to the garden," I tell her.

"Why not?"

They will be gentle. They will be kind. The way they are when we grow too old for our duties. That gentleness will come to me sooner rather than later. I am gray now; I have traveled the room many times from back to front. "No Speaker leaves the convent, except to a new world," I say and the howl in my gut thickens the words.

"What do you mean? That I'll be servant here?"

I do not answer and I do not need to. She knows that none of her kind serve here. I smell her sharpening fear.

"There's no way out." Her eyes are round now, reflecting the dim light in the room.

"Where would I go if I could escape? What would I do?"

I take her hand, firmly. The corridor on the far side of the statue smells like old air and long-dead small things. We know everything, we who serve. She shuffles after me, clinging to my hand and I hurry, because if I go slowly, the fear will fill her and she will stop. At the end of the corridor is a narrow space, one that brought air, perhaps, or heat, or some kind of small cargo. We have to crawl and she can only touch me briefly so she loses her sight. But she hurries, perhaps afraid that I might leave her. If she could smell, she would know that I would never leave her. But she cannot smell, so I harden my heart against her fear and hurry. Fear of being left behind will keep her moving.

At the far end of the small corridor, an old, corroded screen gives way reluctantly, tangled in green vines that fill the air with the sweet-sharp scent of their injuries, a shout that fills the night air. But the Speakers have no nose and none of us will tell. I emerge and stand, helping her up. The two moons of this world—small and strange, one blue, one reddish—float against a blazing ceiling of stars.

"Where are we?" she gasps.

I take her hand, pull her. The door is small, not one for cargo, but for the people who must come and go. No one can get in. But the Speakers see no need to lock it from this side. You only go through a door if you have permission.

I do not have permission.

Terror rises up out of my bowels like a black snake, filling me as I place my palm against the door, and I reek into the night air. I wet myself and almost, *almost* turn and flee, releasing that knotted howl into the safe darkness of the convent.

But she has shared my dreams and brought me to my brother. I place both palms against the door, although pain sears me as if it is red hot. It swings open, silent, and I stumble through, falling to my knees. I feel her hands on me and I smell her worry. She is afraid for me. Not for herself.

"I am all right," I tell her, standing up. My whole body shivers with reaction. But her arms around me, her worry *for me* fills me with strength. None of my pups have ever worried about me.

The convent sits in the middle of the city. It has many needs and many of us fill those needs every day. And we all share. So I know the city even though I have never walked it. And it frightens me, how easily we left it. But then, none of them try to leave. Only this one, the puppy who shares my dreams. It is warm this night but her clothes—the white coverall of a Speaker-in-Training—seem to shine like the midday sun. The narrow alley that leads to this door opens into a wide street. I see lights and shops and eating places and smell people, happy and angry and hungry and full. I smell my own kind, too. We servants are everywhere. People have always had servants.

Garden grows along the wall surrounding the convent, like the garden within, but smelling of people and city and no vanilla orchids. I take her to a bench in the deeper darkness against the wall. Her clothes still shine like the moon I remember or the snow my litter-brother and I rolled in. But she will be hard to see from the street. She smells fear, but more than that she smells curious.

"I hear things. I smell food. What is it like—let me see?"

But I am afraid. "I have to find you clothes. So that people don't see you and know what you are."

"What are we going to do, Siri?" The fear smell gets briefly stronger.

I don't know. But I don't want to say that. "I will be back. Stay here and be quiet and you will be safe."

I hurry down the narrow alley to the main street, but there I stroll, sorting the thick woven fabric of scent for what I need. People don't see me, they don't really see any of our kind. Their eyes skate over us and past, as if we live on the other side of an invisible wall, as if we all live within a convent.

I smell my kind, a strong home smell, and I follow it, unraveling it from the tapestry of food and people-lust, of happy smells, and sad smells. It leads me to an alley that opens to another like it, a courtyard of clean paving surrounded by the back side of tall house-buildings and shops. Small apartments line the walls of this small courtyard along with shops lit dimly or not at all, unlike the shops on the main street.

One smells open. I sniff the doorway, smelling food, herbs, dust, invitation. The shopkeeper pricks his ears at me and smells a question. "I need clothes," I tell him in the common tongue, although it is forbidden for me to speak it. I am not supposed to know the common tongue because the Speakers cannot know the words they repeat.

But of course, we servants know everything.

His ears flick another question at me, and he smells surprised. Because, of course, the simple coverall I wear in the convent is quite good. Not worn at all. "Not for me." I flatten my ears in quick apology. "For a friend. A people friend."

Now he smells wary.

"A friend of us."

And he smells truth, so he shrugs and rummages in bins behind his small counter, smelling doubtful, because he does not sell to people, just to us. But he drags a long cloak out into the light and shakes it. I smell old dust, insect wings, and summer and sneeze. I have seen a few cloaks on the street on my way here, enough like this that she will pass and it will hide her convent-whiteness.

He wants money, of course.

I have no money. As the servant for a Speaker-in-training, I have no time of my own to trade with others in the convent, so have not amassed the coins that we use among ourselves. I flatten my ears in apology and smell need for that cloak. Now his ears flatten and he smells thoughtful and crafty.

"Bring your people here," he finally says. And he reeks now of curiosity.

I cannot hide the smell of my relief and that makes his ears prick again. We servants love a good story and clearly I am going to have one to show him, never mind tell. I take the cloak, roll it tightly, and run down the narrow alley-of-us to the main street where I once again stroll—invisible to those people-eyes—to the garden. My ears are flat with worry by the time I reach the convent alley, even though I have been gone a short time. They may be looking for her. Someone may have wandered into the night shadows to see her whiteness.

But she is there, her sightless eyes turned upward, her hands palm up on her thighs. She no longer smells afraid.

I touch her, inviting her to use my eyes and see the cloak and the garden shadows.

"There is no place for me out here." She smells peace as she says these words, but a whiff of darkness lurks behind that peace and it makes the hair on my shoulders bristle.

"We will find you a place," I tell her. And I drape the cloak around her shoulders.

She raises a fold to her nose. "It smells like you. Where are we going to go?"

"To a place." To pay for the cloak that smells of us. "I do not think the convent will look for you there."

I am sure of it. The hair on my face is gray and I have lived all my life among the people in the convent. They will not think that the servant led her. We are eyes only, a tool to use. They will look for her among the people of the city.

I take her hand. People do not walk with their hands on our shoulders, the way they do in the convent. Out here, they have their own eyes. But all she needs is a touch to use my eyes. I feel the effort she makes to walk easily on this strange street and she smells fear even though she does not show it. I am full of pride for this puppy. She is much stronger than any other pup I have raised. She is ... different.

Perhaps it is not my fault. Perhaps I have not contaminated her after all.

I lead her past the shops and through the crowds of people who see only a slight woman wearing a cloak, walking hand-in-hand with her servant. The food-smells make my stomach hurt because it has been a long time since I ate my breakfast roll. But I have no coins and I fear to take her into a shop where someone might speak to her.

Her head tilts and her steps begin to drag. She smells ... shocked.

"They are speaking Words," she whispers to me, almost too low to hear. "The God Words."

"They are speaking the tongue that everyone speaks," I tell her softly. I want to kiss her cheek, to comfort her. "They are only God Words to you."

Now her feet stumble and I pause, smelling fear so strong that for a minute I think that even the people with their dead noses might notice.

"What are we?" she breathes.

My blasphemous thought comes to me, that she is as created as I. Only now, I think that she is *more* created than I. I have been created to be a servant, but she has been created to be a machine.

I relax a bit when we reach the darkness of the alley. By now, the convent must guess that she has left. They probably record our traffic in and out of the small door and now they will know that she left with me.

They will not look for her here. They will not even know that *here* exists.

The shopkeeper's eyes widen as we enter his shop and her hair catches the light from beneath her hood. He reeks curiosity now. "Welcome," he says and flattens himself almost like a puppy in front of her.

"She doesn't understand, any more than she can smell." I shrug. "She has run away."

His eyes narrow and his ears flick nervously, but he smells thoughtful rather than afraid. "Why did you bring her here?"

"She speaks to my litter-brother." My ears flatten in spite of myself and I cannot keep my lips from drawing back from my teeth. "He is on a star a long ship-travel from here. When I sleep next to her, I speak with him." I know my teeth are showing now and his eyes burn bright in the dim light of the shop. My she was wrong when she thought that speaking-across-the-stars brought the convents money.

It brought them power.

"They can speak for us, too." The words sound deep in my throat. Like a growl.

His eyes gleam in the darkness and I think for a moment that I can see the moon of my puppy-hood reflected in them. Only citizens can speak across the stars.

"*She* can speak for *us*."

**Mary Rosenblum** has been publishing her fiction since 1988, when she graduated from the Clarion West Writers Workshop, and has been a finalist for both Hugo and Nebula awards, as well as a winner of the Sideways in Time Award. She writes speculative fiction as Mary Rosenblum and mystery as Mary Freeman, with eight novels out from New York publishers. She has returned to Clarion West twice as an instructor, and divides her time between writing and working as a "literary midwife," http://www.newwritersinterface. com/, for new authors. When she's not working with words, she's flying a small plane as an instrument rated pilot.

# Gardner Dozois
# on Mary Rosenblum

In every Clarion class I've ever taught, there have been several students who clearly had more natural talent than the others, something usually evident from reading the submission stories, and there have also been several students from nearly every class I've ever taught who went on to achieve one level or another of professional success. These are not always the same students by any means, though, and if you'd taken a bet on the first day of class which of the students would establish a successful professional career, you'd often turn out to be wrong. In establishing a writing career, persistence and hard work (and a thick skin, to keep going after the inevitable rejections and bad reviews) often trump natural talent, and sometimes the most talented students from any given class are never heard from again.

Sometimes, though, you get a student with both natural talent and a willingness to work hard and persistently to establish themselves.

Mary Rosenblum was one such student.

In the Clarion West class of 1988, which Mary was part of, there were several students with great natural talent, and several of them did in fact go on to establish a professional presence for themselves, appearing regularly in print to this day. It soon became clear, though, that Mary was one of the ones to bet on, as far as her chances of becoming a selling writer were concerned. Her determination and drive were formidable—she had actually sold her business in order to raise the money to attend Clarion West—she was clear-eyed, hard-headed, and practical, and she was willing to work very, very hard.

As important, though, she wrote about people. Her characters were at the heart of every story, and it was clear that she cared deeply about them, and wanted us to care about what happened to them next. That ability, to establish a character and make us care about finding out what happens to that character next, has been at the heart of the narrator's art since Ice Age storytellers sat around a campfire on a long winter's evening and spun tales. The desire to know what happens next to a character you've invested yourself into caring about, to know their story, is hardwired into the human brain. A natural storyteller, Mary knew that from the start, and worked hard to refine her ability to tell an engrossing story about people you were interested in and cared about.

After the workshop, she submitted a rewrite of one of the stories we'd workshopped to me at *Asimov's*, and it became her first sale: "For a Price," in the June 1990 issue. Subsequently, she went on to sell more than thirty stories to me when I was the editor of *Asimov's*, and has gone right on selling them there under the new editor, Sheila Williams, as well as selling stories to *The Magazine of Fantasy & Science Fiction*, *SCIFICTION*, *Analog*, and *Pulphouse*, to many anthologies such as *Federations*, *The New Space Opera*, *The Dragon Book*, and *Old Mars*, and has won a Sidewise Award for best Alternate History story, won the Compton Crook Award, and been a finalist for the James Tiptree Memorial Award. On the whole, she's sold eight novels (five of them mystery novels, under the name Mary Freeman) and over sixty short stories, and she hasn't stopped selling yet.

I'm not surprised—you only had to be around her for a couple of days to realize that she was going to let nothing stand in the way of getting those stories that bubbled inside of her out where other people could appreciate them too.

**Gardner Dozois** is both an award-winning writer and editor. He edited *Asimov's Science Fiction Magazine* for twenty years, and *The Year's Best Science Fiction Annual Anthology Series* since 1984. He received the Nebula Award for Best Short Story twice and has won 15 Hugo Awards for Best Editor.

# Bitter Dreams

## Ian McHugh

### 2006

The blackfellas brought the body down to the town gate in the grey of morning, when the mist was lifting but hadn't yet burned off. There were four of them and they carried the remains up on their shoulders, on a stretcher made of branches and plates of paperbark.

They didn't wear much, despite the cold, just loincloths and possum-skin shawls and one of them in a pair of cut-off moleskins. They were tall men, as blackfellas are, all ropy muscle, with the long, skinny calves and broad, long feet of runners. In the weak light, when their shadows were faint on the ground, their heavy brows and wide noses still gathered darkness around their eyes. Their hair was matted with clay and their faces, torsos, and limbs were scarred all over with the white lines and dots the blackfellas use in place of pictures and letters.

They left the body outside the gate, wouldn't pass between the posts carved with English runes—couldn't, with the dreams of the land mapped all over their bodies. They turned around without a word and jogged back into the bush, not hurrying, just because that's the way they preferred to move.

Constable Robert Bowley sat on the porch outside the post office with Maise Wallace, drinking tea while Maise worked at her embroidery.

Georgie, Maise's old half-dingo bitch, lay curled up at her mistress's feet.

Bowley toyed with his teacup, gazing at the buildings across the way. Hunched things, all, imposed on but never accepted by the clay and rock they squatted over. Mockeries of Englishness, with their crooked frames and sagging spines, tarred timbers and dark shingles unalleviated by the runes carved into their surfaces. They huddled beneath their roofs, shaded by alien trees and encroached by grass that was never green even in the wettest months.

Only the church was made of stone, not counting the coolroom out the back of the pub, and only it rose higher than the houses, and not by much. And it was even sadder than they, with no priest there since before Bowley had first come to Useless Loop. Its stones had all been shipped from England because local rock refused to take the shape.

He examined his hands around Maise's porcelain cup and saucer: the dirt that would never come out, at the base of his fingernails, in the creases of his knuckles and the fine lines that etched his skin. The cuffs of his uniform jacket, permanently impregnated with clay dust. He ran his thumb across the largest chip in the edge of the saucer, fitted the leathered pad into the shallow cavity.

"Bowls." Alby Tucker stood at the front of the porch, one booted foot propped against the edge of the boards, toe upwards so that Bowley could see the runes scorched into the leather sole. "Mate, you'd better come see what the blackfellas have left outside the gate."

"Bloody hell."

Bowley stood over what was left of Stink McClure, forcing himself to look. He couldn't bring himself to squat down beside Alby and examine the corpse more closely. He rested one hand on his service holster and had the thumb of the other hooked in his belt, both fists closed so no one would see the shake in his fingers. He breathed through his mouth.

Maise stood beside him, her face pale, arms folded across her chest.

Bowley doubted it was because her hands were shaking. Beyond her, German Braun and young Dermott O'Shane watched Alby prod at the corpse, their lips pursed in mirrored expressions of distaste. Their shadows all bunched up close under their boots, reluctant to cast themselves across the corpse.

"Been dead a day or so," said Alby. He poked about under the ribcage with a stick. "His liver's gone as well."

Bowley could see there wasn't as much left inside the open belly as there should've been. There wasn't much left, in fact, to show that the carcass *had* been old Stink, just his grey nest of hair, his crappy old home-made snakeskin boots and that prickly-pear of a nose of his. As well as opening his guts, whatever had eaten him up had chewed off his penis, and dug out his eyes, and ripped apart his cheeks to get at his tongue. His blood-matted beard hung from shreds of skin around his ears. His lower jaw flopped loosely on his chest.

German asked, "Vas it a villyvilly?" Ingrained soot made the furrows of his always-sweaty brow appear even deeper.

Maise said, "Willywilly wouldn't chew him up like that."

She knew. A willywilly had taken her husband, Nev, not a year after Bowley arrived in town, left his carcass with all the hair sucked off it and scattered around. But, with the sun now peeking through the clouds, they could all see that Stink's corpse cast no darkness beneath it, on its bed of bark and sticks. Whatever killed him had drunk up his shadow as well. The body seemed to float, a hair's-width off the ground, cut adrift, as the corpses of the dream-eaten are.

But what the hell kind of dreaming would tear a man up like that? A willywilly wouldn't make a mark on a man, just leave him bald, not needing to devour the parts that anchored him in his flesh in order to pull out his soul. A bunyip or potkoorok might chew a body up, some, but the dreamings that lay in billabongs and creeks didn't have teeth, as such, and tended to crush up the guts and bones and leave the bag of skin that contained them intact.

"Maybe it was dingos, or a goanna, after," said Alby, pressing hands down on thighs to come upright. The ligaments in his knees creaked as he straightened.

Bowley shook his head, doubtfully. He extracted his thumb from his belt and scratched at the edges of his moustache, his skin still raw from the morning's cold-water shave. He wished he'd remembered to put on his uniform cap—still on Maise's outdoor table beside the cold dregs of his tea. He felt vulnerable without it, his lawman's persona incomplete. He realised his hand was still shaking and put it back to his belt.

"Dingo's too smart," he said, "and a goanna's been around long enough to know better."

"What about the blackfellas?" said Dermott O'Shane.

"Why would they bring him in if they'd done it?" said Alby.

The young Irishman shrugged. "Maybe he did something to them. They wanted us to know they'd had their justice."

"Old Stink?" said Bowley. Stink McClure had been a mad old bastard, but he'd known better than most how to stay on the good side of the natives. Although, if it was the blackfellas that'd done it, no one in their right mind, not even a magister, was going to dispute it. That meant case closed, no further problems. Bowley didn't think so.

"We should go out to check on the others," said Maise.

The Del Mar clan, she meant, her blood kin, in their fortified farmstead up the top of the Loop, where the track crossed the ridge and turned to come back down. She had a sister up there, Lucy, and a niece, as well as all her cousins and uncles and aunts. Less important, for her, King James Campbell and White Mitchell with his retarded brother and all the other antisocials prospecting the gullies and creek beds between Del Mar's and the town.

Everyone looked at Bowley, the Queen's Man, the town's sole protector, although he was as mundane as any of them. Useless Loop was too small to maintain its own magister or even a runesmith. Only German, the blacksmith, with the dozen signs he knew that worked on hooves and boot soles. The town had Bowley and the rune posts at the gate and the rune stones laid beneath their houses and in a ring around the town. And they had the runes on their boots and bullets of English silver in their guns. None of which would stop a really strong and bitter dreaming, should the land ever throw one up, just make it angrier.

Alby snuffled back a chunk of phlegm and dug in his vest pocket for a handkerchief. He saved Bowley from having to answer. "Bugger that, Maise."

Bowley nodded, hoping his relief wasn't too obvious. He badly wanted a whiskey, couldn't while he was on duty. He thought he might get away with a gulp or two from the bottle under his desk, later.

"Come crank up the telegraph for us, eh, Maise? We'll get onto Ballarat and see what they say." For a moment he thought she'd argue. Her shoulders were tucked up like they got when she was that way inclined. But she nodded. Bowley waved a hand to encompass Alby, German and O'Shane. "You blokes take the body to the pub and put it in the coolroom."

Alby snorted. "Ulf's going to be bloody happy about that."

"Tell him I've deputised you," Bowley called back over his shoulder, walking after Maise, his shadow stretching ahead and eager to be gone.

*Investigate. Report.* Was the terse reply that came back from Ballarat in the middle of the afternoon.

Bowley had stayed at Maise's for lunch after they sent their telegram, returned, without thinking, to his accustomed seat on the post office's porch. She'd made his food in the same manner, neither his fear nor her anger enough to derail them from their familiar patterns. Neither of them had spoken while they ate. They rarely did say much. Usually, it was because there wasn't all that much to say, just closeness to be had and that was something both of them felt was best taken in silence. Today the crow's feet at the corners of Maise's eyes had been tight with worry. A lot going on inside of her, he could tell, although it was unlikely that much, if any, of it would find its way into words.

Leaning against the frame of the stationhouse door, Bowley

unfolded the paper for the dozenth time and re-read Maise's scrawled transcription. As if, somehow, the message might've changed from the previous eleven times he'd read it. *Investigate. Report.* "Green Christ."

Maise had wanted to ride out right away. Bowley had started to shake his head, to point out that there wasn't time to get out to Del Mar's and back before dark. She'd smelled the whiskey on his breath as soon as he opened his mouth. He'd watched her rigid back as she stalked away.

He watched her now, back on her porch with Georgie sprawled at her feet, both of them sharing the last rays of sun and Maise pretending not to see him watching. He'd always thought, vaguely, that one day he'd make an honest woman of her, although both of them were past childrearing age. He'd never quite gotten around to asking. In truth, he was happy enough to just share the stillness of her front porch and, sometimes, the warmth between her bed sheets, whenever the urgency was enough in both of them to keep him there overnight.

Cold nights alone stretched ahead of him.

His thoughts circled back to worrying at what the hell might've done that to old Stink, like nothing he'd ever seen before—heard about, maybe, but only up north, nowhere nearby—and where it might've come from and how could it, since dreamings didn't move from the patch of land that dreamed them? And how strong was this dreaming? Strong enough to get past the rune stones and the gate? Because if it was, there was no one and nothing here that could stop it from doing to the whole town what it'd done to Stink McClure.

There were dreamings that came that strong, he'd heard, out in the desert, where the land was still wakeful and warlike, that could take over a person, or more than one, and use them as its teeth and claws ... He shuddered, thinking of human teeth tearing up Stink.

Georgie's shadow slunk off under the porch, leaving the dog still asleep in her patch of sun.

Other animal shadows flitted across the dusty clay of the street, looking for dark places to hide. Their frantic owners pursued them. Cats, chooks, a couple of early-rising possums and Ted Wright's brown nanny goat, united in flight. Georgie awoke with a start, twisted wildly about and, with a swallowed yip, followed her shadow under the porch.

The pair of horses hitched at the watering trough in front of the smithy started in alarm as their shadows bucked, shadow-legs stretching with their feet anchored to the runes beneath the horses' shoes. German tumbled out and lunged for the animals' reins. The horses quieted before he even reached them, opting to freeze with flight denied. Bowley could see their ears flicking, trying to pinpoint the threat. German's head swivelled to look down the street, towards the gate. Maise was up out of her chair and looking that way too.

The horse was a dappled grey of the long-necked, spindle-legged variety bred to tolerate sorcery. Its rider wore a battered oilskin coat, with worn and faded edges on its collar, cuffs and hem, and slashes of lighter colour where it had dried out and stiffened in the dust and sun. A rough Hessian shawl draped the man's head and shoulders beneath the sagging brim of his hat.

He reined his horse to a halt in the middle of the street, facing the setting sun. Neither the man nor his horse cast a shadow. They stood, superimposed on the world, but not really fitted to it.

Two days at least for a magister to come up from Ballarat with a company of redcoats in tow, and Bowley's superiors had made it plain that they weren't coming to his aid at all until he could tell them more precisely what they'd be walking into. So who in hell was this, right here and now?

Bowley reached inside the door and took his uniform cap from its peg. Maise looked his way as he stepped outside. He tried a tentative smile. She didn't respond. He pretended not to notice, smoothed his jacket and hitched his gun belt. He straightened his policeman's badge on its silver chain and stepped down from the porch.

He was acutely conscious of the eyes that followed his progress across the rutted clay. Maise and German. Alby, leaning outside the pub with Ulf Erikssen. He could feel his shadow's reluctance to follow, a heaviness in his calves and feet, like his legs had fallen half asleep. He willed it to stay with him.

He was conscious, too, of the awkward weight of his gun, bumping

on his hip with every step. He hooked his thumbs in his belt to keep
it still.

Bony hands folded over the saddle's pommel—pale skinned, with
a greyish tinge, and blotched with darker grey liver-spots, the man
evidently as dappled as his horse. Both the rider's gear and his horse's
tack were curiously blank, unmarked by runes. Bowley could see
nothing on either man or horse to indicate that the rider was, in any
regard, a Queen's Man.

*Bloody hell, a wild spook.*

The cowled head turned towards him as he neared. Bowley could
make out the lines of a gaunt face in the shadows gathered beneath
the man's hat. The shadows seemed to writhe across his cheeks and
down his neck. A long nose protruded into the light, blotched like the
man's hands.

Bowley stopped a distance from the stranger that he hoped might
appear both authoritative and deferential. Queen's Man or not, a
spook was a spook, after all, and Bowley had no wish to have his soul
sucked out of him for the sake of a moment of perceived impertinence.

"I'm Bowley, local constable." It sounded as inadequate as he felt.

The cowl dipped in acknowledgement. Bowley waited, but the man
didn't speak. The silence began to stretch.

Bowley cleared his throat and said, "You got a name, mate?"

The stranger's reply was as oblique as any magister's would be:
"None that's any use." His voice was a surprise, rich and soft.

Bowley tried again, "What brings you to Useless Loop?"

"Land's thrown up a bad dreaming, hereabouts."

Bowley's guts clenched. He tried to keep his reaction off his face
as he said, "How do you know about it?"

The man gave a huff that might've been a laugh. "Land stinks of
it. How do *you* know about it?"

Bowley considered him, disinclined to answer and wracking
his brains for who the hell this wild spook might be and coming
up with nothing. But, damn it all, he was far out of his depth and,
wild spook or not, he was in dire need of magical aid. "Dreaming
killed a man, outside town. Chewed him up something horrible.

Got the body in the coolroom at the pub."

He felt an abrupt increase in the intensity of the other's stare. "Can I see it?"

Bowley hesitated, but knew he'd committed himself now. He tipped his head in the direction of the pub.

He started walking, not waiting for the stranger to dismount. He heard the man land, heard his steps close behind—puffs of dust and the small clinks of shifting pebbles, no thump of boot soles striking earth.

The hair stood up along the length of Bowley's spine. *Bloody spook.*

Ulf and Alby levered themselves off the rail and disappeared inside the pub. Bowley led the stranger down the side and round the back. By the time they arrived, Ulf had unlocked the coolroom door and retreated to the rear porch with Alby.

Bowley let the stranger precede him through the low door. The temperature dropped sharply within the thick stone walls. The man crouched beside the body, his oilskin collapsing towards the floor, as though it were all but empty. He pulled back the tarp that covered Stink and was still for a while, a crumpled pile of shadows in the light from the door. Outside, Ulf muttered something to Alby that Bowley couldn't quite catch.

The stranger flipped the tarp back over the body and rose, turning, the brim of his hat only inches from Bowley's eyes. His coat sleeve brushed Bowley's chest as he exited. Bowley stood in the darkness alone for a moment. His eyes fell on the flattened lump under the tarp. He shuddered.

Ulf and Alby watched silently as he re-emerged. Ulf's expression offered him nothing. Alby widened his eyes a moment. Bowley hurried after the stranger, already striding back up the street. The man walked past his horse and headed for the gate. Intrigued and disturbed, Bowley followed. Maise's porch was empty. Sweat trickled past his belt to lodge in the back of his pants.

The man stopped outside the gate. His shrouded head half turned towards Bowley. "This is where they left the body."

"Yep."

The stranger faced outward. Bowley scanned the surrounding bush, wondering what he saw. For a minute the man was still. Then darkness began to pour from under the fringe of his shawl, out of his cuffs and under his coat tails. Bowley squeaked.

His shadow tore itself free of the runes on his boot soles and fled back into town. The darkness pooled on the ground around the man's feet, its edges reaching and questing. It lapped at Bowley's toes and flowed around his heels, then released him. The man raised his arms and the darkness shattered into a thousand running shadows that raced away into the bush.

The stranger lowered his arms.

Bowley swallowed. *Green bloody Christ.*

The stranger stood like a statue for most of half an hour while his shadows hunted. Bowley waited with him, not daring to walk away, feeling queasy and light-headed without his shadow. At last the hunters returned. They flowed up the man's legs, moving fast, so that Bowley had trouble making out their shapes. He thought he saw men among the dogs and roos and emus and other, smaller forms. The last shadow disappeared beneath the man's coat.

"The town should be safe for tonight."

Bowley nodded, only realising after he'd done so that the man couldn't see the gesture. He gathered up enough composure to say, "There's a lot of prospectors out there, up the Loop."

"Dead."

*Christ.* He'd had a notion there'd be more than just Stink McClure, but the stranger's flat appraisal rocked him, even so. "There's a farmstead, too, up the top. Fortified. Lot of people."

The spook didn't respond.

"My orders are to investigate," Bowley added.

"You're riding out?"

"Tomorrow."

Silence, for a while, then: "I'll come with you. I can defend four men."

A small part of Bowley bristled at the man's presumption. Most of him sagged with relief.

"Have you got any rune-carved bullets?" the stranger asked.

Bowley knew the number precisely: six. He answered cautiously, "Some."

The spook turned, his shrouded face a vague impression amid the shadows. "We'll need more than some. Is there a runesmith in town?"

"Just the blacksmith."

"He'll do."

The man brushed past and strode back into town. Bowley hurried after. The skin on his back crawled. His shadow lunged at him from the shelter of Ted Wright's house, nearest the gate, and re-attached itself to his feet.

The mist was heavier the following dawn. The stranger, on his horse just outside the gate, was discernable only because Bowley knew he was there.

Bowley fumbled another carved silver bullet from his palm and pressed it into the magazine of his service carbine, then shrugged the gun from the crook of his arm into his hand and slotted the magazine home. Alby, German, and young Dermott O'Shane formed a circle with him. German's eyes were so bloodshot he had no whites left to speak of. Bowley knew his own eyes weren't much better, having seen the state of himself in his washstand mirror. He'd spent the whole night out on his porch, his service revolver in his lap, loaded with the six rune-carved bullets he'd been issued a decade before, when he joined the Queen's Constabulary. He doubted any of them had slept much.

Young O'Shane grabbed at a bullet that slipped between his fingers. It bounced off his thumb and tumbled in an arc to strike the ground. The older men flinched and sucked air through their teeth. All three shared a sheepish grin, their reflexes outdated, accustomed to rimfire cartridges. O'Shane scooped up the escapee and stood again, red from forehead to chin.

"No worries, mate," said Bowley, relieved that he'd managed to load his own weapon without dropping anything and made magnanimous because of it. There was still a tremor in his hands, but much less than the day before, now that the moment was upon them.

Alby flipped the magazine cylinder shut on the second of his six-shooter rifles. He sniffled loudly. His cold seemed to be getting worse. "You know anything about this spook, Bowls?"

"Much as you do," said Bowley. "German?"

"Don't ask me, mate," the blacksmith said. "Ve just carved fucking bullets all night."

Young O'Shane piped up, "I heard about a dappled man, once, when I was out Ararat way. Said he came in from the desert, on foot, dressed like a blackfella and spotted all over, like his sire was one of them Dalmatian hounds. That's all I know. Never saw him myself."

Alby spat. "Reckon that's our bloke. We right?"

"Yep."

"Ya."

The O'Shane boy nodded his head.

"No time like the present," said Bowley.

His old brown mare, Clay, looked back at him with wide nostrils and white-rimmed eyes as he shuffled along her side. Her shadow was skittish beneath her, faint as it was, both horse and shade aware of the Dappled Man's presence and keyed-up because of it. Bowley shoved his carbine into the sleeve in front of the saddle and patted her neck.

"Alright, old girl." He unhitched the reins and brought them up to her neck. Alby was already aboard his chestnut mare, Nudge. German heaved himself up onto fat black Bismarck the gelding and O'Shane rose easily into the saddle of his new piebald filly. Bowley put his foot in the stirrup, grabbed a handful of mane and hauled himself up.

"Ah, shit."

Maise, wearing an oilskin and a pair of Nev's old pants, led Ulf's mean-tempered roan up from the direction of the pub. Bowley held his ground while the others retreated. Maise stopped in front of him, Ulf's idiot horse almost pulling her off balance as it danced about.

She didn't wait to hear Bowley's objections. "It's my family, Robert. And I'm a better shot than anyone except you."

He glanced at the others, waiting halfway to the gate. Alby smirked.

Bowley said, "But you can't ride for shit, love. What if we have to move in a hurry? That animal'll break your bloody neck."

"Don't you 'love' me," she snapped. "German can't ride for shit, either."

Of that, Bowley was acutely aware. "No one else volunteered."

"*I'm* volunteering."

"The spook says he can only defend four."

"*You're* the bloody constable—since when are you taking orders from him?"

"It's *because* it's your family out there that I don't want you to come."

"I don't need you to protect me, Robert."

*It's not you I'm protecting, love. It's me.* His desperation crept into his voice, "Maise, please."

Her jaw clenched. She bowed her head, hiding her face from him. She was crying, he knew, and knew too that she wouldn't accept any comfort from him. He dithered for a moment, then pulled Clay's head around and prodded the horse into motion. He didn't need to look back to know she wouldn't follow.

The Dappled Man's hunting shadows already roiled around his horse's hooves, indistinct in the silvery dimness. He waited until the townsmen were a few yards behind him, then clucked his horse forward. His shadows ranged ahead of him, vanishing almost immediately from sight.

The Man's connection to the ground, through his horse's hooves, seemed even more attenuated, today, than it had in strong sunlight. It seemed he might, if he relaxed the will that anchored him, simply drift off into the mist.

None of them looked back as they rode from town. They didn't need to, could feel the moment when it dissolved into the shroud of mist and trees. Their mounted shadows tucked tight beneath the horses hooves. The charms on the horses' tack clinked loudly in the surrounding stillness.

Beside the track grew spiked grass that was only ever the colour of forgotten bones. Trees surrounded them, some twisted, some straight, all of them alien, with their bleached skins—some that leaked thick sap like blood, others with bark hanging in strips and strings as though they'd been flayed. All growing out of ground that was either rock or clay and in both cases unyielding, that gave itself only with bitter resentment to any man who wanted to farm it.

Even under mist or rain, with the air above it saturated, the land remained parched. Bowley could feel it plucking at the edges of his shadow, and knew that the land would drink him up, too, in an instant, should he ever surrender to it.

A couple of miles out of town, they passed a stand of twisted eucalypts, their trunks wound up and bent like wrung towels, that marked a willywilly's hunting ground. Bowley put his left hand to his badge, tracing runes—not that a willywilly was likely to give them trouble when they had a spook in their company. O'Shane pointed. Stink McClure's shack—the old willywilly ground a signpost on the trail. Bowley had been trying not to look. The Dappled Man kept riding, facing straight ahead.

"Bowls," said Alby, softly. "Strikes me that a Queen's magister'll tow a whole company of redcoats around with him. This bloke reckons he can only protect four of us. Makes me wonder, if we come across this thing that did for Stink, whether he'll be able to handle it."

"Alby," Bowley said. "I reckon you think too much, mate."

He slipped a hand inside his jacket, wound the cap off his hip flask with thumb and forefinger, and took a swig. He glanced at Alby, staring pointedly at the flask. Bowley took another mouthful and handed it over. Alby upended it, then passed it around. It came back to Bowley from German, empty.

"Damn," said Bowley, but without much rancour. "Greedy bloody Kraut."

"Vasn't me," said German, "Vas this greedy Irish bastard, here."

Alby sneezed loudly, startling a flock of cockatoos into screeching, deafening flight. Men and horses alike all but jumped off their shadows. Young O'Shane's filly put her head down and pigrooted, nearly planting the Irishman into the dirt. Clay danced sideways, objecting to the younger horse's theatrics. Bowley pulled her head around and made her walk a full circle. He patted her neck as she calmed, his own heartbeat pounding in his ears. The cockies settled in the branches above, white enough to be the spirits of the dead, like the blackfellas believed, but complaining far too loudly to be ghosts.

Neither the Dappled Man nor his horse had reacted to the commotion behind them. The Man reached a fork in the track and unerringly picked the way that led up the Loop.

"Bloodless bastard," O'Shane muttered.

"Reckon this fog might lift?" said Alby.

Bowley looked skywards. "Not for a while, anyway."

The track started to climb. They passed the Mitchell brothers' place shortly after. The Dappled Man ignored that, too. Bowley noted the absence of smoke coming from the chimney pipe. He knew with a sick knotting in his guts what they'd find inside if they looked.

The trees opened out on a shelf of lichen-fringed rock. The clopping of their horses' iron shoes became abruptly louder, but flattened, the echoes smothered by the mist. The flanks of the ranges rose ahead, a blue-green wall vanishing into greyness.

Bowley squeezed Clay's ribs between his knees. When she didn't respond, he gave her a thump with his heels. She broke into a reluctant trot to come level with the Dappled Man, her hooves striking a dissonant staccato on the rock.

The Man sat hunched in his saddle, as if guarding his darkness against leaching away into the grey surrounds. He seemed diminished—not so fearsome, now, when fearsome was what they wanted most.

"You know what we're hunting," Bowley said, flat.

The Hessian fringe turned towards him. The Man whispered a reply, "Broken Hill."

It took Bowley a moment to make the connection. His mouth turned dry. *Broken Hill.* "Christ."

It had been a mining town up in New South Wales, out near the edge of the desert, where the spirit of the land hadn't yet lain down to sleep. Some bitter dream had slithered out of a seam in the rock and into the mines. Possessed by it, the miners had devoured the town and besieged the survivors in the church for four days until the magisters arrived from Sydney Town with a train full of redcoats and organ guns packed with silver grapeshot.

So the story went.

"How?" Bowley asked. "Dreamings don't travel. There's never been any dreamings like that around here."

The Man didn't answer immediately. The trees closed in again around them. There was wood smoke in the mist, blackfellas in the scrub. A camp. Cooking fires smouldered in a second, smaller clearing, enclosed by a half circle of lean-to shelters. The tribe watched them silently between the tree trunks. The women and children stood behind the men, swaddled in possum-skin cloaks and emu feathers. The cloaks were scorched with the same dot-and-line maps that scarred the black-fellas' skins, that connected them to the land's power and protected them from its dreamings. The men leaned on long spears and the hip-high war boomerangs that whitefellas knew as Number Sevens, for the curve and unequal proportions of their arms.

The blackfellas made no gesture or sound, just watched.

"That was a new dreaming, full of anger and strength," said the Dappled Man, when they'd passed. "When the land becomes quiet, as it is here, such dreamings sink down into the rock, and wither away over time. This dreaming, here and now, will be old, from deep in the ground, with little of it left, otherwise it would've attacked the town already."

"But how did it come up? There's no mines."

"Caves?" the Man suggested, and suddenly Bowley saw it all: Del Mar kids with lanterns, daring each other to go further and further into the grottos up the back of the property. Or young Del Mar men, maybe, down there looking for veins in the rock, one of them putting a hand on some old stone, under which a nightmare slept, that would have slumbered away to nothing if one poor fool hadn't happened upon it.

The spook was watching him intently.

"Del Mar's," Bowley said. "Up the top of the Loop."

"How many people there?"

"Maybe forty, plus kids."

"It probably won't have been strong enough to use all of them," the Man said. "But expect there to be children among those it's taken."

Bowley didn't need to ask what would've happened to the rest. He felt a sharp little hurt behind his breastbone. He saw Maise's sister Lucy, putting a hand on his shoulder the last time he'd visited, interrupting his conversation with the Del Mar men to ask him if he wanted tea. A plumper, warmer, motherly version of Maise, almost invariably with a smile on her face. Her daughter Jemima had served the tea, a willowy child with her father's height, barely into womanhood, her cheeks flushing at the gentle teasing of her great-uncle Javier.

Maise's face came to his mind's eye, jaw quaking and eyes brimming before she dipped her head and he turned his back on her and rode away. Bowley's hands were shaking again. He fumbled for his flask, was surprised for a moment to find it empty.

He flung it into the bush. "Fucking hell."

The Del Mar house was an overgrown cousin to the cottages in town—the way a mastiff is to a terrier—a great, brooding thing of raw timbers and tar. Timber roofed, too, with a cavernous loft space where the children slept. They had some talented runesmiths among them, the Del Mars—Oscar had learned the craft in his native Andalusia—so they had no need for English slates to press the building on its runestone foundations. The whole house was covered in a mesh of flowing Arabic script and the angular English runes that Oscar and his sons had learned since they left their homeland. New wings had been added, over the years, as sons and daughters married and brought their wives and husbands back to live. Only a handful, like Maise, had made their lives elsewhere. All of the extensions connected back to the main house, with just the stables and feed barns standing separate, and they were connected to the house with paths of rune-carved corduroy.

It was a fortress town in all but name, Del Mar's, and stronger in its defences than most towns. But perhaps, Bowley thought to himself, its greatest strength was also its weakness. Because dreamings understood matters of blood and hearth—of place—intimately. No dreaming was intelligent, but some were clever. The rare one was strong enough to roam over an area, not tied to a single spot like a willywilly or a bunyip. If a dreaming of that kind got into a man's shadow, then it might ride him to his home and maybe no density of warding signs, English or Arab—or blackfella, for that matter—would keep the contagion out and stop it spreading to his kin.

The Dappled Man reined in at the edge of the cleared ground that surrounded the farm buildings. There was no sign of the cattle that ranged freely over the hills, but which often hung around near the house. The farm was shuttered and silent. Bowley halted Clay beside the Dappled Man. Young O'Shane pulled up beside him and Alby and German on the Man's far side. Alby snuffled into his handkerchief.

Bowley drew his carbine from its sleeve and laid it across his lap. Alby and German followed his example. O'Shane drew two of his four pistols.

The townsmen's horses whickered and danced as the Dappled Man's hunting shadows returned and wriggled up his mount's legs. The Man straightened in his seat, but still he seemed less than he had the day before. A breath of wind rolled curling fingers of mist from the trees beyond the house. Bowley searched the grey above for some sign of a tear in the veil. There was nothing.

The Dappled Man walked his horse a few paces into the open. Another breath of air chilled Bowley's face and ruffled the horses' manes. It tugged the man's coat, collapsing the side of it inwards. Bowley saw him clearly, then: as a scarecrow, a mockery of a man, a creature with limbs and head but only shadow at his centre.

The Man's horse stopped dead in its tracks. Its ears twitched furiously. Clay whickered and tossed her head. Then all the horses were at it, fidgeting and complaining and dancing on their hooves. The air seemed suddenly thin in Bowley's lungs, as though there was a big storm approaching.

The Man's head whipped to the left. Bowley looked that way in alarm, but could make out nothing untoward among the trees. He ran his fingers over the killing runes etched into his carbine's stock. The Man turned the other way, stared.

Bowley thought he heard a whisper of sound, a distant yelping and howling.

"No." The Dappled Man spun his horse on the spot. "Run!" he barked. "We can't face it here."

His horse launched itself towards them.

"*Run!*" the Man cried.

Then he was past them and all of them were cursing, their horses skittering about and bumping into each other while they tried to get them turned around. Bowley glimpsed figures in English clothes racing through the trees. The howling had grown rapidly more distinct. It was in his head, Bowley realised with a stab of horror, but not in his ears.

The riders got themselves moving. Alby and young O'Shane galloped ahead of Bowley, down the slope, Alby riding one-handed, as Bowley was, his rifle pressed across his lap. Bowley glanced back and saw that German was already falling behind, fat Bismarck struggling under his rider's weight, German with one fist in his horse's mane and the other flailing his rifle about for balance. Their conjoined shadows stretched out ahead of them, straining to drag horse and rider along. "Move it, you fat bloody Kraut!" Bowley yelled back, which wouldn't help German at all, but there was nothing practical Bowley could do for him.

Clay jerked her head as something flew past her nose. A second object struck painfully against Bowley's arm. He tucked his head down. In his peripheral vision he saw running figures closing on either side, arms pulled back and whipping forward—throwing rocks as they ran. He caught jumbled impressions of bloody chins and blood-stained shirts, of mouths open wide in silent anguish.

Then he was past them. He looked back. German made it through a heartbeat before the first pursuers spilled onto the track. The black-smith had lost his hat. Bowley saw a splash of red across his forehead. But German was still in his saddle, gritted teeth and wide eyes stark in his dark face.

Clay gained quickly on the three riders ahead. They'd already slowed their horses to a canter. Bowley did the same as he came up to them. The Dappled Man twisted in his saddle. Bowley wished he could see the expression on the spook's face. Alby looked back, too, and gave a shake of his head. Whether the gesture was one of exasperation with Bowley, or the spook, or the situation in general, Bowley wasn't certain.

German hadn't caught up. And wasn't going to, Bowley saw. Bismarck was labouring even harder, now, the horse's gait uneven, favouring a hind leg. Bowley swore under his breath and reined Clay back into a trot. He felt the tug on his flesh as her shadow and his both resisted. The gap between them and the three riders ahead widened again. The mist closed between them.

He scanned the bush around as German caught up. Bismarck didn't need any instruction from his rider to slow to a trot.

"Look's like he's lame."

German dabbed at the cut on his temple with his handkerchief, examined the resulting mess on the white cloth with distaste. "Stone hit him in the leg," he replied. Bowley could see where—a patch of torn hair just above the gelding's hock. German drew a shaky breath and added, "Vell, that vas a vasted trip."

Bowley heard the note of hysteria in the other man's voice, and in his own chuckle in response. "We'll hold a trot for a bit, see if he works the lameness out. We should stay ahead of them at this pace."

German nodded. "Ya, but they vill go straight down the hill vhile ve follow the track."

"Better keep an eye out then, hadn't we?"

German gave a rictus grin. "I notice those other bastards didn't hang around."

"Spook's getting back to town quick," Bowley said. He hoped—to get them ready. By rights, *he* should be riding ahead, too, and leaving German to take his chances. There had been a *lot* of people in the scrub at Del Mar's, enough for it to be the whole damn clan taken by this dreaming. And, Christ, he couldn't get those half-seen faces, or the silent howls of the thing that possessed them, out of his head.

They were—*it* was—coming after them, he was certain, like a tiger snake that'd chase you for a mile even after it'd struck at you once, just because it was pissed at the world and you happened to be a part of it. He hoped like hell this Dappled Man wasn't lighting out on them, that Alby'd shoot the son of a bitch in the back if he was.

They passed the spot where the blackfella tribe had been camped. No sign of them now.

A tortured whispering brushed his mind. He felt a sucking at the soles of his feet. His and Clay's shadows snapped free of the horse's hooves and lit out across the bare rock ahead. German's shadow on Bismarck's was close on their heels.

"*Gruene ...*"

"*... Christ!*"

Running figures emerged from the mist, off to their left. Bowley kicked frantically at his horse's ribs. "Move!"

Clay leapt into a gallop. Bismarck whinnied, in pain, and terrified of the thing that pursued them.

A man lunged out of the trees on their right. Clay's hooves struck the edge of the rock shelf, clattering like gunshots. Behind them, Bismarck screamed.

Bowley looked back. The gelding staggered out onto the open rock. A pick handle hung obscenely from his belly. The horse's eyes bulged as he cried bewilderment and pain.

Bowley hauled back on Clay. Her hooves skidded on the bare stone. Her back end dropped before she found purchase again. Bowley loosed the reins and spun her with his knees.

Bismarck collapsed. German leapt clumsily but got his legs clear of the horse's weight. Bismarck's cries drowned out the dreaming's dingo howls.

The attacker charged out of the trees, empty hands raised like claws. Francisco Del Mar, an iron-haired Andalusian bull. He was barely recognisable, with sticks in his hair and the animal snarl on his face. His feet were bare and he cast no shadow. German was still on his back, no runes between him and the thing that ran beneath Francisco and his kin. Bowley was acutely aware of how vulnerable they were, with their shadows far from their feet.

He brought his carbine to his shoulder. *Christ, Maise's cousin Frank*. He sighted and fired. Missed.

Clay danced on the spot, ears flat.

Bowley swore and sought the cold, marksman's place within himself that used to be so easy to find. He pushed down the carbine's lever to eject the empty shell and chamber the next. It stuck halfway.

"*Shit*!" Bowley pounded the jammed lever with the heel of his hand.

German had his boots under him. Francisco was almost on him. More Del Mars emerged from the trees. German ignored them. He raised his rifle and shot his dying horse through the top of the head. Bismarck's cheek slapped loudly against the rock.

Dingo howling curled through the abrupt quiet.

"German—behind you!"

The blacksmith met Bowley's stare with dazed eyes. He turned, fired at Francisco from the hip. The bullet caught the Del Mar in the shoulder, spun him all the way around and down to the ground.

German swung his rifle towards the approaching horde and kept shooting, not bothering to aim. There were a good forty or fifty people: men, women and children, and more than just Del Mars. Bowley spied White Mitchell's narrow frame among the front ranks. All of them were barefoot, like Francisco, all filthy and bloody and with the same rictus snarl on their faces. Many of them carried farm tools—picks, hatchets and shovels—as weapons. None of them made a sound, only the silent howling of the thing that possessed them.

"Run!" Bowley cried, "You stupid bloody Kraut! *Run!*" He hoped Alby had shot that damn spook, for lighting out and leaving them. He shoved his jammed carbine into its sleeve and fumbled for his service revolver.

German's rifle clicked, empty. The dream-taken were almost on top of him. German started to swing his rifle by the stock, spitting curses in his native tongue. Francisco Del Mar staggered to his feet behind him, his right arm dangling. Bowley shouted a warning.

Too late. Francisco hooked his left arm around German's neck, pulling him off balance just as the rest reached him. They bore him to the ground. Hooked fingers tore at his clothes. Heads dipped, teeth bared, and German's curses turned to screams.

Bile rose in Bowley's throat, spurting out of his mouth before he could swallow it back down. Most of the Del Mars kept coming. Bowley raised his pistol and fired off all six shots without seeing where any of them struck.

He heard the deep 'whooosh-whooosh' before he saw the war boomerangs come spinning out of the scrub. They tore into the dream-taken, snapping human bodies like stalks of wheat.

A rider burst past Bowley. The Dappled Man. Shadows writhed all over both the spook and his horse. The Del Mars fell back, closing ranks before him.

Bowley put his heels to Clay's ribs, and fled. Among the trees, blackfellas whirled like hammer throwers. A second flight of war boomerangs launched into the air.

The Dappled Man caught up with him near Stink McClure's shack. Clay had slowed to a trot of her own accord, and then a walk. The Man had lost his hat and his Hessian shawl was scrunched in one fist. Lank, shoulder-length grey hair framed bony features that receded at forehead and chin from his long nose. The complexion of his face was, indeed, the same unhealthy mottled grey as his hands.

The Man slowed his horse beside Clay. Moving with what seemed to be pained slowness, he shook out his shawl.

"Where the hell were you?" Bowley demanded.

The spook glanced his way, a flash of washed-out grey eyes. He lifted his shawl and put it back over his head. Shadows crawled around his face beneath its fringes. He slumped, evidently exhausted. "I'm sorry. I didn't know you were in danger until your shadows caught up with us."

"Did you kill it?" Bowley asked.

The Man shook his head. "A dreaming can't be killed, only put back in its place. The tribe and I together weren't enough to subdue this dreaming or deter it. When it's done licking its wounds, it'll follow us to town."

"Why did they try and help us?"

Another shake of the head. "Our presence was coincidence. The tribe's witchmen thought a surprise attack might defeat this dreaming. They underestimated its strength."

"So did you," Bowley said. "And now German's dead."

"It wasn't my decision to go hunting for it," the Man replied, softly.

The riposte struck home. *My fault*, Bowley thought. *I shouldn't have let him come.*

The Dappled Man extended a hand. "I have something for you."

Bowley's heart gave a lurch. He stared at the spook's outstretched palm. There was a barely visible tremor in the Man's fingers. Bowley's own hand shook noticeably as he raised it. The Dappled Man's skin was dry as old paper.

Darkness flooded out of the Man's sleeve and up Bowley's arm. Bowley yelped and would've snatched back his hand if the spook hadn't gripped his fingers tightly. The darkness flowed over Bowley's shoulder and down his side, along his leg and then down his horse's to pool on the ground beneath them. It resolved itself into his shadow astride Clay's, before fading in the dull light. The Dappled Man released his hand.

Bowley clutched at his chest. "Green *Christ*."

The Man leaned on his saddle horn, his head bowed. Bowley's

rattling heartbeat slowed to a more normal rate. The Dappled Man spoke again, his voice a bare rasp, "The tribe's intervention has increased our risk when we face this dreaming again. Whenever one of those it has taken is killed, it is freed to steal another shadow."

Bowley watched him, swaying like he could hardly hold his seat, and said, "It took some of yours, didn't it?"

The Man nodded.

*And did you keep German's?* Bowley wondered. *Or did the dreaming take it from you?* His scalp goosepimpled. The spook could as easily have kept his and Clay's, had he wanted. Giving them up had plainly cost him.

"How do we stop it?" he asked.

The cowled head remained lowered, the tattered fringes of the shawl falling forward to hide the Man's face completely. "Kill all of them," he said. "All but the first infected. Each death will be a shock to the dreaming that possesses them. While it's still reeling, I can—perhaps—subdue it and return it to the land."

*Kill all of them.* Bowley's vision blurred. *Oh, Maise.*

The mist had settled at the bottom of the valley, where the town stood, denser than when they'd left. There was a crowd gathered between the posts of the town gate. All men, except for Maise, and all of them armed. Alby and young O'Shane were among them. Bowley watched their faces fall when they realised German wasn't with them.

Bowley gathered his jammed gun and dismounted. He slapped Clay on the rump. The crowd parted to let her by and she skittered off down the street, vanishing quickly into the grey—smart enough, he hoped, to stay inside the rune circle.

"Where's German?" Maise asked.

"Dead," Bowley replied. "Same as old Stink."

She looked away from him, covering her lips with her fingertips and drawing deep breaths.

"We're ready," said Alby. "Everyone else is in the church."

"Uncarved bullets won't hurt the dream-taken," said the Dappled Man, down from his horse now, too. Only an arm's length from Bowley, he seemed to fade into the mist. He stood straight though, and apparently without difficulty.

Bowley looked around at the frightened, determined faces, then back at the spook. "We've got more than four guns loaded with carved bullets," he said.

He pulled his revolver from its holster and reached past Maise to offer it butt-first to Ulf Erikssen, dug in his left pocket for fresh cartridges.

"I can only defend four of you," said the Dappled Man.

"Reckon we'll defend ourselves, mate," said Alby. He handed one of his rifles to Ted Wright. Young O'Shane followed his example.

The spook was still for a minute. His pale eyes glittered beneath the ragged fringe of his shawl, boring into Bowley. Bowley hoped his fear wasn't plain to see on his face. He returned the Man's stare as levelly as he could. At last, the Man said, "Anyone else wants to fight, you'll need weapons with killing runes carved on them."

"The rest get your arses into the bloody church," said Bowley, his knees momentarily weak with relief. Most of the crowd scattered.

Maise glared at him through tears of frustration.

"That includes you, Maise," he said. He was amazed that his voice was steady. "It's your whole bloody family coming down on us, love. What'll you do if you get Lucy in your sights? Or Jemima?"

Her nostrils flared. She pressed her lips white as she, too, tried to stare him down. He put a hand on her arm, pushed her gently. Maise turned away, swayed a little and stumbled on her first step, then walked in the direction of the church.

Bowley took a long breath, felt it chill his lungs. He let it out with a puff. To no one in particular, he said, "I'll be back in a minute."

He strode through the crowd and down the street towards the police station. Inside, he went straight to his desk drawer and retrieved his half-empty bottle of whiskey. He pulled the plug with his teeth and took a long swig. He closed his eyes for a minute while the burn of it spread through his chest.

He rummaged around in the drawer for the screwdriver he thought might be there, found the letter opener and decided that would do. He perched on the desk with the carbine across his lap to try and un-jam it. To his relief, he was able to do so without disassembling the gun. Bootsteps sounded on the boards outside as the lever snapped back into place, chambering the offending cartridge properly, this time.

Alby leaned on the doorpost.

"Didn't know you'd fallen behind, Bowls," he said. "Spook said to keep riding, when we realised."

Bowley passed him the whiskey. "I know," he said. "No worries, mate."

They made their way past empty houses to the church, where the spook had gathered everyone willing to fight below the steps: young O'Shane, Ulf, Ted Wright, half a dozen others busily loading their weapons with the spare bullets Alby and O'Shane had carried. Bowley handed out his spare rifle bullets. A handful of women and kids and shamefaced men huddled in the church's doorway to watch. Dougie MacGill, mad old buzzard that he was, was the only one to turn out without a gun, armed with the rune-carved pike head he'd souvenired when he retired from the redcoats, stuck on its rough cut pole.

The town's rune-stone ring ran across the back of the unwalled churchyard. The world beyond it was invisible in the mist.

Bowley looked down at his hands. They were rock steady. His emotions felt dull and distant—locked out. He cocked his carbine. He heard the creak-and-click repeated around him as the others did the same.

The Dappled Man raised his voice. "Hold your shadows close. Keep the your boot soles on the ground. For every one of its taken that the tribe killed, the dreaming can take one of you. There are worse things than dying, if you fall."

He let that sink in, before adding, "This dreaming has no understanding of guns. That's our advantage. Choose your shots well, because you'll not have enough bullets to finish this task."

"Alright, lads," Bowley said. "Spread out a bit, but stay close to the church. We don't know which way they're going to come."

Somebody shut the church door with a thump, and then only the movements of the men disturbed the silence—the crunch and crackle of their boots on dirt and brittle grass, the creak of oilskin coats—as they positioned themselves in a rough semi-circle, anchored at the corners of the church. Bowley's badge clinked against the top button of his uniform jacket as he took a few paces to position himself behind a headstone.

They waited.

German's death played again in Bowley's mind. He'd frozen, he knew, in the moments before the dream-taken had brought German down. Would it have made a difference, he wondered, if he hadn't? Might he have saved him?

The Dappled Man's spoke: "They're here." The howling began in Bowley's head an instant later.

A stick snapped, out in the mist, from the direction of the town gate. Gravel scraped. All weapons swung in that direction. Another sound cut across the howling.

"Number Sevens!" Bowley cried.

He dropped to his haunches a heartbeat ahead of the men around him. A war boomerang throbbed low overhead, through the space he'd occupied an instant before. A cry, abruptly silenced, told him someone hadn't been fast enough. Dougie MacGill hit the dirt with five feet of bent wood buried in his ribs. War boomerangs clattered against the stone of the church walls.

Somebody loosed a shot.

"Not until you can bloody see them!" Bowley yelled. He peered over the top of the headstone.

Ragged figures materialised out of the mist. Bowley came to his feet, bringing his carbine to his shoulder. For an instant, the sharpness of his perceptions overwhelmed him. He'd seen, in feral dogs, the hurt and desperation that drove them to hurl themselves at the muzzle of a gun. He saw it now in this charging rabble, with grime and gore unwashed from their faces and caked into their cuffs and shirtfronts, axes and shovels clasped in their fists.

Gunshots cracked to his left and right.

His vision narrowed. He was in his marksman's place, where he could act and not feel. Francisco Del Mar came under his sights once again. Bowley's first shot punched through the charging man's face and out the back of his head. The second hit him side-on as he stumbled. The impact took the shattered back of his skull clean off.

Bowley searched for a new target, wondering if he could pick out the first taken, the one who mattered, and avert the worst of the carnage.

He paused, overwhelmed by a sudden feeling of *wrongness*. "Where's the rest of them?"

There were less than twenty attackers in front of him. Half of them were down already and all of them, he saw, carried some kind of injury. He spun on his heel, shouted his question at the Dappled Man, positioned at the foot of the steps.

The Man was already turning, pointing, out where the rune-stone perimeter came closest to the church. Bowley saw movement in the mist.

"Alby! Over there!"

He ran to that side of their line, his gun at his shoulder, as Alby and the others nearest pivoted to meet the new threat.

His sights found a blackfella, running among the Del Mar mob. There were others. The tribe's intervention had cost them. Bowley tracked the blackfella's approach. He fired just as the man passed behind a tall tombstone. The bullet kicked chips off the edge of the stone. Someone else's bullet knocked the blackfella flat.

The new wave of attackers came fast. Bowley put his next two shots into the torso of one of the older Del Mar nephews from less than ten yards away. The twin impacts knocked the Del Mar off his feet, like a giant hand had slapped him flat. The axe handle he'd brandished pin-wheeled between the headstones. Bowley shot little Letitia Del Mar, coming behind, wearing a pinafore brown with blood. Her hair flicked up as the bullet came out the back of her head.

He was dimly aware of Alby beside him, flipping his rifle, already empty, to use as a club. Of Ulf, beyond Alby, with Bowley's service revolver gripped in both hands. Young O'Shane, pumping bullets from his pair of pistols with methodical precision.

A still figure caught Bowley's eye, out beyond the mayhem—a girl, standing straight and tall, her arms raised before her. Jemima Del Mar. Maise's niece. *The first taken*, Bowley realised. In front of the church, the Dappled Man mirrored Jemima's pose.

A woman charged straight at him. It was Maise's sister, Lucy—Jemima's mother. Bowley's finger froze on the carbine's trigger. His pulse pounded in his ears. There was nothing of the woman he'd known in the rictus of Lucy's face. He squeezed the trigger with a jerk, pulling the carbine's muzzle sideways. The bullet hit her high in the chest. She staggered into the arc of Alby's rifle butt. Bone and wood crunched together.

Les Barrett, a senior son-in-law, was hard on Lucy's heels. Bowley flipped his empty carbine in his hands, felt the hot metal sear his fingers and palms, and swung. He met the downward arc of the man's mattock and used the momentum of the blow to push the weapon aside and put his elbow into Barrett's face. Bowley pulled his carbine back over his shoulder and swung. The trigger guard caught Barrett squarely in the side of the head. The blow jarred Bowley's wrists and elbows. Blood crazed beneath the skin of the dream-taken's temple, patterning like shattered porcelain. Bowley adjusted his grip and hit him again. Barrett collapsed.

Ulf went down under the weight of two assailants. Young O'Shane and Ted Wright arrived an instant too late. Ulf started to convulse on the ground. Ted impaled one attacker on the point of Dougie MacGill's pike, belted the other with a long-handled mallet he must've taken from one of her kin. The woman's head rocked on her shoulders. She lunged at Ted, making him stumble. O'Shane shot her, point blank, in the face. Ulf started to rise from the ground at his feet. The Irishman put his second pistol to the publican's forehead and pulled the trigger.

Closer to Bowley, Alby kicked little Tomas Del Mar, all of four years old, under the chin. He raised his boot again and stamped on the child's thin chest as he bounced against the earth.

Hands grappled Bowley from behind. Sharp teeth sank into the side of his neck. He wrenched free and spun. The carbine's stock missed his attacker by a whisker. Javier Del Mar, patriarch of the family, peeled back his bloody lips in a soundless snarl.

A hand snaked over the old man's shoulder and caught him around the face. Alby thrust his hunting knife up under Javier's chin. The Del Mar jerked backwards as the blade penetrated. Alby stumbled and they both started to fall.

"No!" Bowley lunged after them. For an instant, he clutched Alby's coat sleeve. Then the oiled leather slipped through his fingers and Alby's back hit the dirt.

His eyes bulged. His heels drummed the dirt. His shadow flitted away from his stricken body, then it too began to thrash, but only for a moment. Still struggling, it was sucked into the earth.

Alby started to rise. Bowley rammed the carbine's butt into his face. Alby fell back. Bowley hammered down again. Bone gave beneath the blow. Alby's limbs twisted spastically. Bowley swung in a frenzy, as though he could obliterate Alby's identity and, with it, the horror of what he was doing. The carbine's stock snapped. Bowley staggered. Alby's bottom jaw jutted up, above his collar, obscenely intact.

The field was still.

For a while, Bowley leaned on the splintered butt of his gun. His breath rattled in his ears. His neck and his burnt hands throbbed. He slowly pushed himself upright.

Aside from Bowley, only three of the townsmen who'd begun the fight were still on their feet. Young O'Shane was one of them, still with both his pistols in his hands. His face was slack, his eyes closed. Ted Wright crouched with his forehead resting against the pole of Dougie MacGill's pike, one forearm pressed against his belly. Blood dripped between his legs. Bowley began to shake.

One Del Mar still stood amid the carnage. Jemima. Neither she nor the Dappled Man had moved, still confronting each other in their invisible battle of energy and wills. Even in the pale light, Jemima's shadow was dense and dark, many armed and many headed, as though cast by many suns. The Dappled Man's captive shadows writhed across his body.

He took a step forward. Then another. Jemima remained rooted.

The Man walked towards her, each step an obvious effort, like a man wading through mud. He reached out and caught Jemima's chin. Still, she didn't move. Her shadow's many limbs writhed in agitation and it began to shrink towards her feet. Darkness poured out of her mouth and out of her nose and ears and eyes. It ran up the Dappled Man's wrist and into his sleeve. Jemima's body shook violently. The Man bowed his head, his shoulders hunched.

The last bit of shadow drained over Jemima's lip. The Man released his grip on her jaw and they staggered apart. The Man swayed but kept his feet. Jemima crumpled.

A keening sound penetrated Bowley's gun-deaf ears. At first he thought it was the dreaming, howling still, and he wondered how that could be. Then he realised the noise was coming from Jemima—each cry an uninflected blast of anguish, followed by a terrible, wrenching gasp for air, then another long, monotonous cry.

Maise raced across the field, arms outstretched, fingers splayed. She was too slow to catch Jemima before she fell. She skidded to her knees beside the girl and scooped her up. Jemima's face and neck were crimson, veins and ligaments pushed out with the force of the sound coming up her throat.

The Dappled Man stood over them, his shrouded head bowed, leaning a little, like someone who'd taken a bad hurt to the ribs.

His horse picked its way through the slaughter and stopped beside its master. The Man took a moment to react, as though he didn't see it at first. He reached up an arm, then got his foot into the stirrup and lifted himself with painful slowness to slump in the saddle.

The horse moved off again, past the rows of tombstones and out to the rune circle. Blackfellas waited in the fringes of the mist. They fell into step beside the rider as he vanished from sight. They'd see the dreaming put back into the ground, back where Jemima and her kin had found it, to go back to sleep and lie undisturbed until it withered away to nothing. Bowley wondered if he ought to go after them, to be certain it was done with and they'd seen the last of it.

He looked over at Maise, with her eyes screwed shut and her teeth clenched in a grimace, her own body wracked by sobs as she held her niece. What comfort could he offer her? What was there left for him and Maise, with the blood of her family on his hands?

He let the shattered carbine fall from his fingers. He walked towards Maise. Her head was turned away, to where the Man and his escort had gone into the mist. She didn't respond when he knelt beside her, put his hand on her back. He took a grip on her shoulders, pulled her in to him. She didn't resist. Jemima had exhausted her voice, for now, and sprawled in her aunt's arms, panting like a hurt animal. Her eyes were bulged and bloodshot in her still-red face.

Maise pulled away suddenly, and turned to look at him, her face fierce. "You go after them, Robert," she said. "You make sure it's done right."

He didn't want to, started to shake his head, because his place was right here, with all the death and ruin about them to clear away, bodies to bury or burn, and the people needing someone to show the way, and that being down to him, the Queen's Man in Useless Loop. And what would he know, anyway, if he did go, about whether this dreaming was put to rest for good, or not?

But, "Go!" she said, and he staggered up and away from her, propelled by the force in that word.

People stumbled out of the church. Some fell to their knees, some turned away and covered their children's eyes, some vomited. Others hugged each other and wept. A sudden shaft of bright sunshine lit the battlefield in unwelcome light. Bowley hurried past.

He put his fingers to his mouth, barely noticing the salt-metal tang of blood as his whistle shattered the quiet. He whistled again, and saw Clay prick her ears, standing in the street outside the police station. He went to her at a stumbling run, and got her moving at a trot as soon as he was aboard.

He felt the pressure of their eyes, like a physical weight, as he skirted the church yard. He kept his own fixed straight ahead. No one called out to him. Maise didn't look up from rocking her niece. The Dappled Man and his escort had already vanished into the mist. It didn't matter—Bowley knew where they were headed.

He caught up with them quickly enough. The blackfellas ignored him, so he followed a few yards behind, all the way up into the hills behind Del Mars'. The Dappled Man swayed like a man half dead in his saddle. His horse directed itself, or sometimes the blackfellas did, when it seemed unsure. They walked tirelessly, high-stepping over undergrowth and litter from the trees so they rarely needed to check their gait. Bowley watched the patterns of scars on their backs and legs, rippling as they moved, and wondered at the price they paid for living with the land, for not holding themselves apart as whitefellas did.

At the mouth of the caves, they pulled the Man down from his horse and carried him inside, stooping under the low lip of rock. One paused when Bowley got down from Clay and made to follow. He raised a hand, his long, broad-tipped fingers splayed, the palm pink and free of scars. He held Bowley's gaze with brown-black eyes. Shadows gathered beneath his heavy brow. The ridged scars that covered his skin formed a mask that obscured his expression. Once he was certain Bowley wasn't going to follow, the man turned and went after his fellows.

Bowley waited, with only the horses for company. He saw to Clay, but left her saddled, and made himself a small fire. The Man's horse seemed content and Bowley was disinclined to approach it. He hunched beside his fire as night closed in and knew he'd made a mistake, coming here. Knew he should've stayed in town, and been the Queen's Man, no matter what Maise had wanted. But he knew there was no way he could've refused her.

He stared into the flames, trying not to see Alby's head come apart, over and over again. He tried not to hear German's screams as human teeth tore into him. Not to see the grief on Maise's face as she held her niece, nor hear Jemima's wailing, that said saving her was the worst they could've done. Exhaustion eventually let him fall into a light doze.

The blackfellas brought the Dappled Man back out in the grey of morning. He said nothing to Bowley, nor even appeared to recognise his presence, even though Bowley rose to his feet barely an arm's length from where the Man passed.

The blackfellas led him to his horse and put him up in the saddle. One of them took its reins, and another two held the Man's legs to keep him in his seat as they walked away with him into the bush.

Bowley was left alone once again, and wondering what victory had cost the spook, whether he hadn't been able to separate all of himself from the dreaming when they'd put it back into the ground.

He looked back into the cave, felt gooseflesh rise all over his body. He could only hope that the task was done.

He got his skinning knife from his saddle roll, scratched the rune for danger into the rock above the cave mouth. The sign had no power, since he had none to give it, and the shallow marks would fade quickly, but it would serve, for now.

Smoke rose from the churchyard, when he returned to town. A funeral pyre. They'd burned all the bodies together. A few folk watched him walk past on Clay, their faces closed in, looking at him like a stranger. Crows picked among the headstones, hunting for any titbits that might've been overlooked.

There was a cart outside the post office, half loaded with small furnishings and baskets and crates of bric-a-brac. Maise's rocking chair, from the porch, that Nev had made her for a wedding gift, was lashed in pride of place on top of the pile. As Bowley approached, she came out with a basket of clothes. Her eyes flickered over to him. Her expression closed in and she looked away.

Bowley stopped Clay beside the cart and watched for a moment while she worked the basket into a too-small space at the back.

"Maise? You're leaving?"

She didn't look up. "I am."

His eyes were suddenly hot and overfull. "Where are you going, love?" he asked.

"Don't you ..." She caught herself. "I don't know. Away."

Bowley's mouth worked silently for a moment before he could shape more words. "Would you have left before I got back?"

Maise stopped, bowed her head. "I can't do it, Robert," she said, from between her raised arms. "I can't even look at you."

She gave the basket a final shove and turned her back on him. He watched her disappear back inside. She returned a moment later, followed by Dermott O'Shane, carrying Jemima. The younger man glanced at Bowley, and away again, without speaking. Maise climbed up onto the cart's bench, then turned to help O'Shane lift Jemima up beside her. The girl was wrapped in a blanket, so Bowley could discern little more than the fact that she was conscious. She huddled against Maise, tucking her head low. Maise sat straight and rigid, looking neither left nor right, nor back, as she picked up the reins and clucked their horse into motion.

Clay danced a little when the cart started moving. She twisted her neck to watch it, then snorted, and returned her gaze forward, to wait patiently, again, for her master to tell her what to do. O'Shane looked as though he might speak, then shook his head, dissatisfied with the words he might've offered, and walked away.

Bowley sat there for a long time, the words "Can I come with you?" lying bitter on his tongue.

**Ian McHugh** lives in Canberra, Australia. He is a member of the Canberra Speculative Fiction Guild and occasionally teaches fiction writing at writers' centers in and around Canberra. His stories have appeared in professional and other publications around the world, they have won Australia's Aurealis Award and been reprinted in a number of "Year's Best" and "Best Of" anthologies. Most of his past publications can be found free online at his website. "Bitter Dreams" was the first story he wrote at Clarion West in 2006 and it won grand prize in the Writers of the Future contest two years later.

# Maureen F. McHugh
# on Ian McHugh

The year that Ian was at Clarion West was the year of McHughs. There were three of us; Ian from Australia, Maura from Ireland, and me from the United States. I was teaching. I admit to a certain bias towards the other McHughs. I wanted them to do well. To hold up the family name.

Ian suggested he should not be counted on. He had done a stint at art school where he had been diverted by extra-curricular activities. My heart sank a little. Art school. I wondered if I would get conceptual art fiction—long on theory and short on enjoyment.

What he turned in my week was this piece. It generated lots of conversation, including questions from Ian about whether he should use pejoratives like 'blackfellas' but there wasn't any question about how very strong the piece was. I don't ask my students to use their background to write their fiction. It's not like I use Ohio a lot in mine. But Ian's use of the Dreaming, of the Outback and colonialism made something new for us.

It was a fine story then. It's a better story now.

**Maureen F. McHugh** is the author of the critically acclaimed novels *Mission Child*, *China Mountain Zhang*, and *Half the Day is Night*. *China Mountain Zhang* won three awards and was a *New York Times* "Notable Book." Her most recent book is *After the Apocalypse*, a collection of short fiction from Small Beer Press. McHugh received the Hugo for her short story "The Lincoln Train," and other stories have appeared in various magazines and anthologies.

# Leviathan Wept

## Daniel Abraham

## 1998

Good crowd," Pauel said, from Paris.

"Things are weird," Renz said, passing his gaze over that auditorium so that Pauel could see it better. "People are scared."

When Renz had first trained with the link—when he began what Anna called his split-screen life—he had wanted the display windows to show the other people in his cell instead of what they were seeing; to make him feel they were speaking face to face. It had taken months for him to become comfortable with the voices of people he couldn't see and the small screens in his own visual field that showed what they were seeing. Now it lent their conversations a kind of intimacy; it was as if they were a part of him. Pauel and Marquez, Paasikivi and Thorn.

The auditorium was full, agents of CATC—Coordinated Antiterrorist Command—in almost every seat and so many others linked in that the feed was choppy from bandwidth saturation. The air was thick with the heat and scent of living bodies.

Of the other members of his cell, only Marquez was physically present, sitting beside him and tapping the armrest impatiently. Pauel, Paasikivi, and Thorn were linked in from elsewhere. Pauel was in his apartment, lying back on his old couch so that the rest of them were looking up at his dirty skylight and the white-blue Parisian sky. Paasikivi and Thorn were sharing a booth at a Denver coffee shop so that Renz could see each of them from the other's perspective—Thorn small and dark as an Arab, Paasikivi with her barely-graying hair cut short. Renz wondered how long they would all be able to pretend those two weren't lovers, then placed all the window in his peripheral vision so he wouldn't be distracted from the man on the stage.

"Renz. I heard Anna was back in the hospital," Paasikivi said. Her tone of voice made it a question.

"It's just follow-up," Renz said. "She's fine."

The man at the front tilted his head, said something into a private link, and stepped up to the edge of the stage. In Denver, Thorn stirred his coffee too hard, rattling the spoon against the cup the way he did when he was uncomfortable. Renz lowered the volume from the link.

"Good afternoon," the man said. "I'd like to welcome you all here. And I have to say I wish we had this kind of turnout for the budget meetings."

A wave of nervous laughter swept over the crowd. Without meaning to, Renz found himself chuckling along with the rest. He stopped.

"For those of you who don't know me, my name's Alan Andrews. I'm a tactical liaison for the Global Security Council's theoretical branch. Think of me as the translator for the folks in the ivory tower."

"Condescending little pigfuck, isn't he?" Pauel said.

"By now I'm sure you've all heard about the anomalies," the speaker said. "OG 47's experience with the girls in New York, OG 80 and the old woman in Bali, the disruptions at the CATC root databases. I'm here to give you an idea what the theoretical branch has made of them."

"Yes, Pauli," Marquez muttered. "But are you sure about the pig? He looks more a chimp man to me."

"Would you two shut up," Renz said. "I want to hear this."

"The first thing I want to make clear," the man said, holding his hands out to the crowd, palms out, placating, "is that there are no direct ties between these incidents and any known terrorist network. Something's going on, and we all know that, but it's not a conspiracy. It's something else."

The man dropped his hands.

"That's the good news. The bad news is it's probably something worse."

Looking back, the first anomaly had been so small, Renz had hardly noticed it. It had presented as a series of small sounds at a moment when his attention had been a thousand other places. He had heard it and forgotten until later.

The town they had been in at the time was nothing remarkable; the Persian Interest Zone was peppered with places like it. Concrete apartment buildings and ruined mosques mixed with sad, pre-fab western strip malls. The asphalt roads had been chewed by tank treads sometime a decade before and never repaired. But intelligence said that an office building in the run-down central district was still running network servers for the al-Nakba.

Organizational Group 47—Renz, Marquez, Pauel, Thorn, Paasikivi—were in an old van parked on a side street, waiting. Thorn and Pauel—the only two who could pass for local—sat in the front playing the radio and smoking cigarettes. Paasikivi and Marquez squatted in the belly of the machine, using the three-foot-tall degaussed steel case of the EMP coil as a table for Marquez's chess set. Renz kept watch out the tiny tinted windows in the back. Waiting was the hardest part.

The operation was organized in a small-world network, the cells like theirs connected loosely with fifty or a hundred like it around the world and designed to behave organically, adjusting to contingency without need for a central authority.

It gave them, Renz supposed, the kind of flexibility that a war between networks required. But it cost them a solid timetable. They might be called up in the next thirty seconds; they might be waiting for an hour. It might be that allowing the target to survive would be a viable strategy, and they'd all pull quietly out without anyone knowing they'd been there.

Paasikivi sighed, tipped her king with a wooden click, and moved forward in the van, leaving Marquez to chuckle and put the pieces away.

"You're thinking about Anna," Marquez said.

Renz glanced back, shook his head, and turned to the windows again.

"No, I'm winding myself up about the mission."

"Should be thinking about Anna, then. Nothing we can do about the mission right now."

"Nothing I can do about Anna either."

"You going to spend some time with her when this is over?"

"Yeah," Renz said.

"Really, this time?"

It wasn't the sort of question Renz would have taken from anyone but Marquez. He shifted forward, staring out at the sun-drenched street.

"Really, this time," he said.

An out-cell window flashed open. The blond man appearing in it looked harried as an air-traffic controller. Renz supposed the jobs weren't so different.

"OG 47, this is CG 60. Please begin approach to subject. Your target is fifteen minutes."

"Acknowledged," Paasikivi said for them all. Pauel flicked his still-burning cigarette onto the sidewalk and started the van. Renz didn't shift his position at the rear, but as he watched the street flow away behind them, the old electric feeling of adrenaline and anticipation grew in his belly.

There were four stages to the operation: penetration, reconnaissance, delivery, and withdrawal. Or, more plainly, get in, look around, do the thing, and leave. They had all rehearsed it together, and everyone knew what to do.

The van turned the corner two minutes later, angled into a ramp down to underground parking. A security guard at the entrance frowned at Pauel and barked something that wasn't Arabic but might have been Armenian. Pauel replied in Farsi, managing to sound bored and put upon. The guard waved them through. Renz watched the guard turn his back to them.

"Twelve minutes to target," Paasikivi said.

Pauel drove past the stairway leading up to the building proper, around a cinderblock corner, and parked across three parking spaces. The first stage was over; they were in. Without a word, Pauel and Marquez got out and started walking. Renz increased the size of their windows. Marquez, whistling, moved around a corner and deeper into the parking structure. Pauel went up the way they had come, toward the guard and the stairs.

"Pauel, you have something at your ten o'clock."

The window with Pauel's viewpoint shifted. Beside an old white Toyota, a woman in a birka was chiding a wiry man. The man, ignoring her, began walking toward the stairway.

"Civilians," Pauel murmured, hardly loud enough for the link to pick it up.

"Are you sure?" Paasikivi asked.

"Of course not," he said.

"Nine minutes," Thorn said. Hearing the words through the link and in the van simultaneously made them seem to reverberate, carrying a sense of doom and threat they didn't deserve. He felt Thorn tap his shoulder, and, still watching Pauel and Marquez, Renz shifted back, his hands resting on the cool metal carrying handles of the EMP coil, but not gripping them yet.

Marquez's window showed Arabic graffiti, oil-stained concrete, a few cars. More than half the lights were out.

"Looks good here," Marquez said.

In Pauel's window, the guard glanced back, frowning. Renz watched Pauel's hand rise in greeting.

"I'm going to go chat this bastard up, keep him busy," Pauel said. "Apart from him, I think we're clear."

The second stage was complete. Paasikivi slid to the front, into the driver's seat. Renz looked across the steel case to Thorn. Thorn nodded, and Renz leaned forward and pushed the rear door open.

"All right," Thorn said. "Renz and I are coming out. If you see anyone about to kill us, speak up." Renz thought his voice sounded bored. It was only a few steps to the wall, but the coil was heavy. His wrists strained as they snugged the metal against the cinderblock wall.

Renz stepped back as Thorn slid adhesive packs around the base of the coil, and then between the side of the metal case and the wall. He checked the time. Six minutes to target.

There were five small, very similar sounds, quickly but evenly spaced. The guard with Pauel scraped open a pack of cigarettes, the radio in the van beside Paasikivi popped as she put the key in the ignition, Thorn's adhesive packs went off with a hiss, a bit of gravel scraped under Renz's heel, and something like a cough came from deeper in the garage behind Marquez. Each sound seemed to pick up the next. A little musical coincidence that sounded like nothing so much as a man clearing his throat. Renz noticed it, and then was immediately distracted.

"Someone's back here," Marquez said. Renz caught a movement in Marquez's window. Someone ducking behind a car. "I think we may have a problem."

Everything happened at once, improvised and contingent but with the perfect harmony of a team acting together, so practiced it was like a single mind. Renz drew his sidearm and moved forward, prepared to lay down suppressing fire. Pauel, at the front, shot the security guard twice in the chest, once in the head. Paasikivi started the van. Marquez, seeing that Renz was coming, moved quickly backward, still scanning the darkness for movement.

Within seconds, Renz was around the corner, Marquez fifteen or twenty feet ahead of him, a pistol in his hand. Behind them and around the corner, where they couldn't have seen without the link, Thorn had the rear doors of the van opened and waiting, and Paasikivi was turning it around to face the exit. Pauel, at the base of the ramp, was dragging the guard out of the roadway.

Something moved to Marquez's left. Renz shifted and fired while Marquez pulled back past him to the corner. When Renz saw his own back in Marquez's window and Marquez braced to fire in Thorn's, he broke off, turned, and ran as Marquez opened up on the darkness. From listening, it would have been impossible to say when one had stopped shooting and the other started.

On the out-cell link, the blond man from OC 60 was saying that OG 47 had been compromised and Paasikivi was shouting at him that they had not. The coil was in place. They were withdrawing.

Marquez broke off as Renz reached the van, turned, and sprinted toward them, white tombstone teeth bared in what might have been effort or glee. Renz and Thorn both knelt inside the van, guns trained on the corner, ready to kill anyone who came around it.

"Okay," Pauel said from the ramp as Marquez reached the relative safety of the group. "Can you come get me now?"

The van surged forward, tires squealing as they rounded the corner—the van coming into view in Pauel's window; Pauel silhouetted against the blaring light of the street in Paasikivi's.

"Pauel! The stairs!" Renz said almost before he realized he'd seen something. There in Paasikivi's window, coming down from the building. He watched as Pauel shot the girl—five years old? six?

Time slowed. If they had been compromised, Renz thought, the girl could be wired—a walking bomb. There wasn't enough room in the parking structure to avoid her. If she went off, they were all going to die. Fear flushed his mouth with the taste of metal.

He heard Thorn exhale sharply, and the van sped past the stairway. The dead girl failed to explode. A dud.

"Jesus," Marquez said, relief in the sound of the word. "Oh, sweet Jesus."

Paasikivi stopped for less than a second, and Pauel was in the passenger's seat. Renz pulled the rear doors closed and latched them as they went up the ramp and out to the brightness of the street.

They were half a mile from the building when the trigger signal attenuated and the coil sparked out. With a shock like a headache, Renz's link dropped for a half second, leaving the disorienting sensation of only being inside his own head again. It felt like waking from a dream. And then the display windows were back, each showing slightly different views out the front while he alone looked back at a plume of white smoke rising from the town behind them.

By the time they reached the base in Hamburg, the news was on all the major sites. CATC under the orders of the Global Security Council had launched simultaneous attacks on the al-Nakba network, including three opium processing plants, two armories, and a training camp. Also the al-Nakba communications grid and network had suffered heavy damage.

The opposition sites added that a preschool near one of the armories had also been firebombed and that the training camp was a humanitarian medical endeavor. Eighteen innocent bystanders had died, including ten children from the preschool and two teachers.

There was also a girl shot in a minor raid in the Persian Interest Zone. Her name was Samara Hamze. Renz looked at the picture of her on the newsnets—shoulder-length black hair that rounded in at her neck, dark, unseeing eyes, skin fair enough she could have passed in the most racist quarters of Europe if she'd been given the chance. If she'd wanted to.

By the time they'd dropped Pauel off in Paris and found seats in a transatlantic carrier, the news cycle had moved on, and the girl—the dud—was forgotten.

Renz had never expected to see her again.

"That's the good news. The bad news is it's probably something worse," said the man on the stage. "Now, this is going to seem a little off-topic, but we may be in some strange territory before we're done here, so I hope you'll all indulge me. Ask yourselves this: Why aren't we all brilliant neurochemists? I don't mean why didn't we choose to go to med school—there are lots of reasons for that. I mean doesn't it seem like if you're able to *do* something, you must know about it? Aaron Ka can play great football because he knows a lot about football.

"But here we are, all juggling incredibly complex neurochemical exchanges all the time, and we're all absolutely unaware of it. I mean, no one says 'Oops, better watch those calcium channels or I might start getting my amygdala all fired up.' We just take ten deep breaths and try to calm down. The cellular layer just isn't something we're conscious of.

"And you can turn that around. Our neurons aren't any more aware of us than we are of them. If you ask a neuron why it fired or muscle tissue why it flexed, it wouldn't say 'Because it was my turn to run' or 'The bitch had it coming.' Those are the sorts of answers *we'd* give. If our cells could say anything, they'd say something about ion channels and charges across lipid membranes. And on that level—on the cellular level—that would be a fine explanation.

"The levels don't talk to each other. Your neurons don't know you, and you aren't aware of them. And, to torture a phrase, as above, so presumably below."

Renz felt Marquez shift in his seat. It wasn't impatience. Marquez was frowning, his gaze intent on the stage. Renz touched his arm and nodded a question.

"I don't like where this is going," Marquez said.

When Renz got back from the mission, Anna was sitting at the kitchen table—cheap laminate on peeling-chrome legs—scrolling through another web page on her disease. Outside the dirty windows, the streetlights of Franklin Base glowed bright enough to block out the stars. Renz closed the door behind him, went over and kissed his wife on the crown of her head. She smelled of the same cheap shampoo that she'd used since he met her. The sudden memory of her body when it was young and powerful and not quite his yet sent a rush of lust through him. It was embarrassing. He turned away, to the refrigerator, for some soda.

Anna turned off her screen and shifted. Her movements were awkward, disjointed. Her face was pinched and oddly expressionless. He smiled and lifted a bottle of soda. She shook her head—the movement took a second to get going, and it took a second to stop.

"Douglas Harper had Hulme's Palsy too," she said.

"The serial killer?"

"Yup," she said. "Apparently it's old news. Everyone in the support group knew about it. I'm still green compared to all of them. He wasn't symptomatic. They didn't diagnose it until after he'd been executed."

Renz pulled out a chair and sat, his heels on the kitchen table. The air conditioner kicked on with a decrepit hum.

"Do they think what ... I mean, was killing people related?"

Anna laughed. Her eyes wide, she made an overhand stabbing motion like something out of a murder flick. Renz laughed, surprised to find his amusement was genuine.

"They just think if it had progressed faster, some of those girls might have lived," she said.

Renz took a sip of his soda. It was too sweet, and the fizz was already gone, but it was cold. There wasn't more he could ask than cold. Anna dropped her hands to the table.

"I was going to make dinner for you," she said. "But ... well, I didn't."

"No trouble. I can make something," he said. Then, "Bad week?"

She sighed. She was too thin. He could see her collarbone, the pale skin stretched tight over it.

"The new immunosuppressants gave me the shits," she said, "and I think I'm getting another fucking cold. Other than that, just another thrilling week of broadcast entertainment and small town gossip."

"Any good gossip, then?"

"Someone's screwing someone else even though they're both married. I didn't really pay attention to the details. You? The news feeds made things look pretty good."

Anna's eyes were blue and so light that they made him think of icicles when they caught the light from the side. He'd fallen in love with her eyes as much as her tits and the taste of her mouth. He pushed the sorrow away before she could see it.

"We killed a kid. But things went pretty well otherwise."

"Only one kid? That thing with the preschool ... "

"Yeah, them too. I mean *we* killed a kid. My guys."

Anna nodded, then reached awkwardly across the table. Her fingertips touched his wrist. He didn't look up, but he let the tears come. He could pretend they were for the dud.

"So, not such a good week for you either, huh?"

"Had its rough parts," he said.

"You're too good for this," she said. "You've got to stop it."

"I can't," he said.

"Why not?"

He spoke before he thought. Truth came that way; sudden, unexpected. Like illness. "We'd lose the medical coverage."

Her fingertips pulled back. Renz watched them retreat across the table, watched them fold into her flat, crippled fist. The air conditioner hummed, white noise as good as silence. Renz swung his legs down.

"I wouldn't change anything," he said.

"*I* fucking would." There was pain in her voice, and it pressed down on him like a hand.

"You know, boss, I'm not really hungry," he said. "Let's go to bed. We can eat a big breakfast in the morning."

Once she was asleep—her breath slow and deep and even—he got gently out of bed, pulled on his robe, and took himself out the front door to sit on the rotting concrete steps. The lawn was bare grass, the street empty. Renz ran his hands over his close-cropped hair and stared up at the moon, blue-white and pale in the sky. After a while, he turned up his link, seeing if there was anyone online.

Paasikivi and Thorn were both disconnected. Pauel's link was open with the video feed turned off, but it had been idle for three and a half hours—he was probably asleep. Only Marquez was awake and connected. Renz excluded the other three feeds, considering the world from Marquez's point of view. It looked like he was in a bar. Renz turned up the volume and thin country-pop filled his ears.

"Hey, Marquez," he said.

The video feed jumped and then settled.

"Ah! Renz. I thought you were actually here. Is that your street?"

He looked up and down the empty asphalt strip—block houses and thin, water-starved trees. Buffalo grass lawns that never needed mowing. His street.

"I guess so," he said, then more slowly, "I guess so."

"Looks like the same shit as last time."

"It's hotter. There's more bugs."

Marquez chuckled, and Renz wasn't really on the step outside his shitty base housing, Anna dying by inches behind him. Marquez wasn't entirely in the cheap bar. They were on the link together, in the unreal, private space it made, and it removed the distance between them.

"How's Anna?" Marquez asked.

"She's all right. I mean her immune system's still eating her nerves, but apart from that."

"You sound bitter. You're not cutting out on her, are you?"

"No. I said I'd stay, and this time I will. It just sucks. It all just sucks."

"Yeah. I'm sorry. It's hard when your woman's down."

"Not just that. It *all* sucks. That girl we killed. We call her a dud like she wasn't a kid. What's that about?"

"It's about how a lot of those kids have mommies who strap them up with cheap dynamite. You know that."

"Are we soldiers, Marquez? Are we cops? What the fuck are we doing out there?"

"We're doing whatever needs to get done. That's not what's chewing you, and you know it."

It was true, so he ignored it.

"I've been doing this for too many years," Renz said. "I'm getting burned out. When I started, every operation was like an adventure from start to stop. Half the time I didn't even know how what I was doing fit in, you know? I just knew it did. Now I wonder why we do it."

"We do it because they do it."

"So why do they do it?"

"Because of us," Marquez said, and Renz could hear the smile. "This is the way it is. It's the way it's always been. You put people out in the world, and they kill each other. It's the nature of the game. Your problem, man, you never read Hobbes."

"The pissing cartoon kid?"

"Five hundred years ago, this guy named Hobbes wrote a book about how the only way to get peace was to give up all your rights to the state—do what the king said, whether it was crazy or not. Fuck justice. Fuck whether it made sense. Just do what you're told."

"And you read this thing."

"Shit no. There was this lecture I saw on a philosophy site. The guy said you build a government so motherfucking huge, it can *make* peace. Grind peace into people with a fucking hammer. Crush everyone, all the time. He called it Leviathan. He thought it was the only way to stop war."

"Sounds like hell."

"Maybe. But you got a better idea?"

"So we're making them be part of our government. And when we get them all in on it, this'll stop."

Marquez's window panned slowly back and forth—the man shaking his head.

"This shit isn't going to stop until Jesus comes back."

"And if he doesn't?"

"Come on, man. You know all this. I said it before; it's not what's really on your mind."

"And what do *you* know about *my* mind?"

"I spend a lot of time there is all."

Renz sighed and scratched at the welt on his arm growing where a mosquito had drunk from him. The moon sailed slowly above him, the same as it always had, seen or unseen. He swallowed until his throat wasn't so tight.

"She still turns me on," he said at last. "It makes me feel like I'm ... she's crippled. She's dying and I can't fix it, and all I want to do when I see her is fuck."

"So why don't you?"

"Don't be gross."

"She might want to, you know. It's not like she stopped being a woman. Knowing you still want her like that ... might be the kind of thing she needs."

"You're out of your mind."

"There is no sorrow so great it cannot be conquered by physical pleasure," Marquez said.

"That Hobbes?"

"Nah. French girl named Colette. Just the one name. Wrote some stuff was supposed to be pretty racy at the time. It was a long time ago, though. Doesn't do much compared to net porn."

"You read the weirdest shit."

"I don't have anyone to come home to. Makes for a lot of spare time," Marquez said, his voice serious. Then, "Go inside, Renz. Sleep next to your wife. In the morning, make her a good breakfast and screw her eyes blue."

"Her eyes are blue," he said.

"Then keep up the good work."

"Fuck off," Renz said, but he was smiling.

"Good night, man."

"Yeah," Renz said. "Hey, Marquez. Thanks."

"De nada."

Renz dropped the link but sat still in the night for a while, trailing his fingers over flakes of concrete and listening to the crickets. Before he went to bed again, he ate a bowl of cereal standing up in the kitchen and then used her toothbrush to scrape the milk taste off his tongue. Anna had shifted in her sleep, taking up the whole bed. He kissed her shoulder as he rolled her back to her side. To his surprise, he slept.

At 6:30 in the morning, central time, a school bus packed with diesel-soaked fertilizer exploded in California, killing eighteen people and taking out civilian network access for half of the state. At 6:32, a fifteen-year-old girl detonated herself twenty feet away from the CEO of the EU's biggest bank while he was finishing his breakfast at a restaurant in midtown Manhattan. At 6:35, simultaneous brush-fires started outside ten major power transmission stations along the eastern seaboard. At 7:30, Renz was on a plane to New York. At ten minutes before ten, a ground car met him at the airport, and by noon, he was at the site of the attack.

The street should have been beautiful. The buildings soared up around them; nothing in Manhattan was built on less than a cathedral scale—it was the personality of the city. From the corner, he could just catch sight of the Chrysler Building. The café had been elegant once, not very long ago. Two blackened, melted cars squatted at the curbside. The bodies had been taken away long before Renz and the others arrived, but the outlines were there, not in chalk but bright pink duct tape.

"Hey, Renz," Paasikivi said as they took in the carnage. "Sorry about this. I know you wanted to see Anna."

"Don't let it eat you," he said. "This is what they pay me for, right?"

Inside, the window of the café had blown in. Chunks of bulletproof glass three fingers thick lay on the starched linen, the wooden floors polished to a glow. The air still smelled like match heads.

The briefing had been short. OG 47 had done this kind of duty before. Renz pulled up an off-cell window on the right margin of his visual field so the forensics experts could demonstrate what they wanted. The feeds from his cell were stacked on the left. OGs 34 and 102 were security, keeping the area clear while they worked, but he didn't open links to them; things were cluttered enough as it was.

Renz and his cell were the eyes and hands of the deep forensics team—men and women too valuable to risk in the field. A second attack designed to take out agents at the scene was a common tactic. Pauel, still in Paris, joined in not because he was useful, but because he was a part of the cell and so part of the operation. He was good to talk with during the quiet times.

The next few hours were painfully dull. Paasikivi and Thorn, Marquez and himself—the expendables—all took simple instructions from the experts, measuring what they were told to, collecting samples of scorched metal and stained linen, glass and shrapnel in self-sealing bags, and waiting for the chatter of off-cell voices to agree on the next task to be done.

Renz and his cell were the eyes and hands, not the brain. He found he could follow the directions he was given without paying much attention. They drove his body; he waited.

They finished just after 8 p.m. local. There were flights out that night, but Paasikivi argued for a night in the city. Renz could feel Marquez's attention on him like the sensation of being watched as Paasikivi and Thorn changed reservations for the whole cell. Renz almost stopped them, almost said he needed to go home and be with his wife. When he didn't, Marquez didn't mention it. With the forensics team gone, Renz arranged the other in-cell windows at the four corners of his visual field. An hour later, they were scattered over the island.

Marquez was on the edge of Central Park, his window showing Renz vistas of thick trees, their leaves black in the gloom of night. Paasikivi was sitting in a coffee shop at the top of a five-story bookstore, watching the lights of the city as much as the people in the café. Thorn sat in a sidewalk restaurant. Renz himself was walking through a subway station, heading south to SoHo because Pauel told him he'd like it. And Pauel, in the small hours of Paris morning, had taken himself out to an all-night café just to be in the spirit of things.

"I've always wanted to walk through Central Park," Marquez said. "It's probably safe enough, don't you think?"

"Wait until morning," Pauel said. "It's too dangerous at night."

Renz could hear the longing in Marquez's sigh, imagined the way he would stuff his hands into his pockets to hide the disappointment, and found to his amusement that he'd done the same. Marquez's gesture seemed to fit nicely on his own evening. The first breeze of the incoming train started to wash the subway platform, fluttering the fabric of his pants.

"I hate days like this," Thorn said, cutting into a steak. In that window, Renz watched the blood well up around the knife and wondered what it smelled like. "The nights, however, go a long way toward making up for it."

Marquez had turned and was walking now, people on the streets around him that would have been a crowd anywhere else. Paasikivi pushed her coffee cup away, stood and glanced back into the bookstore. In Paris, Pauel's waitress—a young woman with unlikely red hair—brought him his eggs benedict and poured him a cup of coffee. Thorn lifted a fork of bleeding steak to his mouth. The train slid up to the platform, the doors opening with a hiss and a smell of fumes and ozone.

"All I really want ... " Renz began, and then let the sentence die.

The girl came out of the bathroom in Pauel's Parisian diner at the same moment Renz saw her sitting in the back of his half-full subway car. Paasikivi caught sight of her near the music department, looking over the shoulder of a man who was carrying her—he might have been her father. Thorn, looking out the restaurant window saw her on the street. Marquez saw her staring at him from the back seat of a taxi.

In all four windows and before him in the flesh, the same girl or near enough, was staring at him. Pale skin, dark eyes, shoulder-length hair that rounded in at the neck. Samara Hamze. The dead girl. The dud.

As one, the five girls raised a hand and waved. Renz's throat closed with fear.

Thorn's voice, deceptively calm, said, "Well that's odd."

"Pull back," Paasikivi snapped, "all of you get out of there."

"I'm on a moving train," Renz said.

"Then get to a different car."

The others were already in motion. Walking quietly, quickly, efficiently away from the visitations toward what they each hoped might be safety. He heard Paasikivi talking to an off-cell link, calling in the alert. Renz moved to the shaking doors at the front of the car, but paused and turned, his eyes on the girl at the back. There were differences. This girl had a longer face, eyes that made him think of Asia. The woman beside her—the girl's mother, he guessed—saw him staring and glared back, pulling the girl close to her.

"Renz!" Paasikivi said, and he realized it hadn't been the first time she'd said it.

"Sorry. I'm here. What?"

"The transit police will be waiting for you at the next station. We're evacuating the train, but before we start that, I want you out of there."

"This isn't an attack," Renz said, unsure how he knew it. The mother's glare, the protective curve of her body around her child. "I don't know what it is, but it's not an attack."

"Renz," Marquez said. "Don't get heroic."

"No, guys, really," he said. "It's all right."

He stood and walked down the trembling car. Mother and child watched him approach. The mother's expression changed from fierce to frightened and then back to a different, more sincere fierceness. Renz smiled, trying to seem friendly, and squatted in front of them. He took out his CATC agent's ID and handed it to the mother. The darkness outside the windows gave way to the sudden blurred pillars of a station.

"Ma'am," he said. "I'm afraid you and your girl are going to have to come with me."

The doors hissed open. The police rushed in.

"I don't like where this is going," Marquez said.

"Some of you may have heard of the singularity," the man on the stage said. "It's one of those things that people keep saying is just about to happen, but then seems like it never does. The singularity was supposed to be when technology became so complex and so networked, that it woke up. Became conscious. It was supposed to happen in the 1990s and then about once every five years since then. There's a bunch of really bad movies about it.

"But remember what I said before. *Levels can't communicate.* So, what if something did wake up—some network with humans as part of it and computers as part of it. Planes, trains, and automobiles as part of it. This girl is like an individual human cell—a neuron, a heart cell. That man over there is another one. This community is like an organ or a tissue; even before we were linked, there've been constant communications and interactions between people. What if conscious structures rose out of that. Maybe they got a boost when we started massive networking, or maybe they were always there. Call them hive minds. We might never know, just like our cells aren't aware that they're part of us.

"And these hive minds may have been going along at their own level, completely unaware of us for ... well, who knows? How long did we go along before we understood neurochemistry?

"I know we're all used to thinking of ourselves as the top. Molecules make up cells, cells make up tissues, tissues make up organs, organs make up people, but people don't make up anything bigger. Complexity stops with us. Well, ladies and gentlemen, it appears that ain't the case."

"Do any of you understand what the hell this guy's talking about?" Pauel asked. From the murmur of voices in the room, the question was being asked across more links than theirs. The speaker, as if expecting this, stepped back and put his hands in his pockets, waiting with an expression like sympathy, or else like pity.

"He's saying there's a war in heaven," Marquez said.

"No, he isn't," Renz said. "This isn't about angels. It's minds. He's talking about minds."

The man stepped forward again, holding up his hands, palm out. The voice of the crowd quieted, calmed. The man nodded, smiling as if he was pleased with them all.

"Here's the thing," he said. "Some of you have already seen the hole in the model. I said levels of complexity can't talk to each other. That's not quite true. You do it every time you drink a glass of wine or go on antidepressants. We understand neurons. Not perfectly, maybe, but well enough to affect them.

"Well, the only theory that fits the kind of coordinated coincidences we've been seeing is this: something up there—one level of complexity up from us—is starting to figure out how to affect *us*."

When Paasikivi interrupted the debriefing and told him, Renz didn't immediately understand. He kept having visions of bombs going off in the doctor's office, of men with guns. It was the only sense he could make of the words Anna's in the hospital. *She's had an attack.*

Her room stank of disinfectant. The hum and rattle of the air purifier was almost loud enough to keep the noise of the place at bay. White noise, like the ocean. She managed a smile when she saw him.

"Hey," she said. "Did you see? Salmon are extinct again."

"You spend too much time on the net," he said, keeping his voice gentle and teasing.

"Yeah, well. It's not like you take me dancing anymore."

He tried to smile at it. He wanted to. He saw the tears in her eyes, her stick-thin arms rising unsteadily to him. Bending down, he held her, smelled her hair, and wept. She hushed him and stroked the back of his neck, her shaking fingers against his skin.

"I'm sorry," he said, when he could say anything. "I'm supposed to be here fluffing your pillows and stuff, not ... "

"Not having any feelings of your own? Sweetie, don't be stupid."

He was able to laugh again, a little. He set her down and wiped his eyes with his shirtsleeve.

"What do the doctors say?" he asked.

"They think it's under control again for now. We won't know how much of the damage is permanent for another week or two. It was a mild one, sweet. It's no big deal."

He knew from the way she said it, from the look in her eyes, that *It's no big deal* meant *There's worse than this coming.* He took a deep breath and nodded.

"And what about you?" she asked. "I saw there was some kind of attack that got stopped in New York. Did they try a follow-up to the restaurant?"

"No, it wasn't an attack," he said. "It was something else. It's really weird. They've got all the girls who were involved, but as far as anyone can tell there's no connection between them at all. It was some kind of coincidence."

"Girls?"

"Little ones. Maybe five, six years old."

"Were they wired?"

"No, they were all duds. And they weren't linked to any networks. They were just ... people," Renz said, looking at his hands. "I hate this, Anna. I really hate this. All of it."

"Even the parts you like?"

The memory of exhilaration passed through him, of setting the coil, of fear and excitement and success. The feeling of being part of something bigger and more important than himself. The warmth of Anna's body against him as they danced, or as they fucked.

"Especially the parts I like," he said. "Those are godawful."

"Poor sweetie," she said. "I'm sorry, you know. I wouldn't have it like this if I could help it. I keep telling my body to just calm down about it, but ... "

She managed a shrug. It was painful to watch. Renz nodded.

"Well, I wouldn't want to be in depths of hell with anyone else," he said.

"Now *that* was sweet," she said. Then, tentatively, "Have you thought about going to the support group? A lot of the people in my group have husbands and wives in it. It seems like it helps them."

"I'm not around enough. It wouldn't do any good."

"They've got counselors. You should at least talk to them."

"Okay. I'll talk to them. I've got leave coming up soon. I can soldier though until then."

She laughed, looked away. The light caught her eyes just right—icicles.

"What?" he asked.

"Soldiering through. It's just funny. You've got your war, honey, and I've got mine."

"Except you're the enemy too."

"Yeah, it does have that war-between-the-states feel to it," she said, and grinned. "There's a guy in my group named Eric. You'd like him. He says it's like having two people in the same body, one of them trying to live, the other one trying to kill the first one even if it means dying right along with."

"The good him and the bad him," he said.

"That's a matter of perspective. I mean, his immune system thinks it's being pretty heroic. Little white cells swimming around high-fiving each other. Hard to convince those guys to stop doing their jobs."

Renz shook his head. Anna's fingers found his, knitting with them. The air purifier let out a pop and then fell back to its normal grinding.

"Is everyone in your group that grim?"

"They haven't gotten to a place where they divide children into wireds and duds, but yes, there's a grimmish streak to them."

"Sounds like Marquez's kind of people."

"And how is the group mind?" Anna asked.

"Pretty freaked about the New York thing."

"So what exactly happened?"

He wasn't supposed to tell her. He did.

"Something up there—one level of complexity up from us—is starting to figure out how affect *us*," the man said. "The question is what we're going to do about it. And the answer is nothing. What we have to do is *nothing*. Go on with our work, the same as we always have. Let me explain why that's critically important.

"So far, the anomalies all have the same structure. They're essentially propaganda. We see the enemy approaching us in a friendly, maybe conciliatory manner. We start thinking of them as cute little girls and nice old women. Or else we're flooded with death reports that remind us that people we care about may die. That we might.

"And maybe we take that into the field with us. In a struggle between two hive minds, that kind of weakening of the opposition would be a very good move. Imagine how easy it would be to win a fistfight if you could convince the other guy's muscles that they really liked you. The whole thing would be over like that," the man said, snapping.

"We all need to be aware. We all need to keep in mind what's going on, but if we change our behavior, it wins. Let the other side get soft, that's fine, but we can't afford to. If this thing up there fails, it may give up the strategy. If we let it get a toehold—if what it's doing works—there's no reason to think it'll ever stop.

"Now, there is some good news. Some of you already know this. There are chatter reports that these incidents are happening to terrorist brigades too, so maybe one of these things is on our side. If that's the case, we just need to make sure the bad guys get soft before we do."

Renz shook his head. His mind felt heavy, stuffed with cotton. Marquez touched his arm.

"You okay?"

"Why does he think there's two?"

"What?"

The man was going on, saying something else. Renz leaned in to Marquez, whispering urgently.

"Two. Why does he think there are two of these things? If there's only one, then it's not a war. If this is ... why would it be a fight and not a disease? Why couldn't it be telling us that this isn't supposed to be the way things are? Maybe the world's like Anna."

"What's the difference?" Marquez asked.

"With a disease you try to get better," Renz said. "With a war, you just want to win."

"Now before we go on," the man on the stage said, "there are a couple of things I want to make clear."

He raised his hand, index finger raised to make his point, but the words—whatever they were—died before he spoke them. Renz's link dropped, Pauel and Paasikivi and Thorn vanishing, Marquez only a body beside him and not someone in his mind. There was a half-second of dead silence as each agent in the room individually realized what was happening. In the breathless pause, Renz wondered if Anna was on the net and how quickly she would hear what had happened. He heard Marquez mutter *shit* before the first explosions.

Concussion pressed the breath out of him. The dull feeling that comes just after a car wreck filled him, and the world turned into a chaos of running people, shouted orders, the bright, acidic smell of explosives. Renz stumbled toward the exits at the side of the hall, but stopped before he reached them. It was where they'd expect people to go—where many of the agents were going. Marquez had vanished into the throng, and Renz reflexively tried to open the link to him. Smoke roiled at the high ceiling like storm cloud. Another more distant explosion came.

The auditorium was nearly empty now. A series of bombs had detonated on the right side of the hall—rows of seats were gone. The speaker lay quietly dead where he'd stood, body ripped by shrapnel. Fire spread as Renz watched. He wondered if the others were all right—Paasikivi and Thorn and Pauel. Maybe they'd been attacked too.

There were bodies in the wreckage. He went through quickly, the air was thickening. Dead. Dead. Dead. The first living person was a man a little older than he was, lying on the stairs. Salt-and-pepper hair, dark skin, wide hands covered in blood.

"We have to get out," Renz said. "Can you walk?"

The man looked at him, gaze unfocussed.

"There's a fire," Renz said. "It's an attack. We have to get out."

Something seemed to penetrate. The man nodded, and Renz took his arm, lifted him up. Together they staggered out. Someone behind them was yelling, calling for help.

"I'll be back," Renz called over his shoulder. "I'll get this guy out and I'll be right back."

He didn't know if it was true. Outside, the street looked like an anthill that a giant child had kicked over. Emergency vehicles, police, agents. Renz got his ward to an ambulance. The medic stopped him when he turned to go back.

"You stay here," the medic said.

"There's still people in there," Renz said. "I have to go back. I'm fine, but I have to go back."

"You're not fine," the medic said, and pulled him gently down. Renz shook his head, confused, until the medic pointed at his arm. A length of metal round as a dime and long as a pencil stuck out of his flesh. Blood had soaked his shirt.

"Oh," Renz said. "I ... I hadn't noticed."

The medic bent down, peering into his eyes.

"You're in shock," he said. "Stay here."

Renz did as he was told. The shapes moving in the street seemed to lose their individuality—a great seething mass of flesh and metal, bricks and fire, moving first one way and then another. He saw it as a single organism, and then as people, working together. Both interpretations made sense.

Firemen appeared, their hoses blasting, and the air smelled suddenly of water. He tried to link to Marquez, but nothing came up. Someone bound his arm, and he let them. It was starting to hurt now, a dull, distant throbbing.

He caught sight of a girl as she slipped into a doorway. So far, no one else seemed to have noticed her. Renz pushed himself up with his good arm and walked to her.

But she wasn't the same—not another ghost of Samara. This child was older, though only by a year or two. Her skin was deep olive, her hair and eyes black. Flames glittered in her eyes. Her coat was thick and bulky even though it was nearly summer. She looked at him and smiled. Her expression was beatific.

"We have to stop this," he said. "It's not war, it's a sickness. It's a fever. We're all part of the same thing, and it's dying. How are we going to make this *stop*?"

He was embarrassed to be crying in front of a stranger, much less a child. He couldn't stop it. And it was stupid. Even in his shock, he knew that if there was something up there, some hive mind sick and dying in its bed, he could no more reach it by speaking to this girl than by shouting at the sky. Could no more talk it out of what was happening than he could save Anna by speaking to her blood.

Renz saw the girl before him shift inside her coat, and understood. An Arab girl in New York in a bulky coat. A second attack to take out the emergency services answering the first one.

"Please. We have to *stop* this," Renz said. "You and me, we have to stop." The girl shook her head in response. *No, we don't.*

"God is great," she said, happily. Like she was sharing a secret.

Since attending Clarion West, **Daniel Abraham** has published sixteen novels and over two dozen short stories. He also writes as MLN Hanover and (with Ty Franck) as James S A Corey. He has been nominated for the Hugo, Nebula, and World Fantasy awards, and won the International Horror Guild award.

# Lucy Sussex
# on Daniel Abraham

At Clarion West, 1998, I was the odd instructor out. I had come from the underside of the world, via Japan, thus blowing the Clarion travel budget, and I talked strangely. At the time, *The Lord of the Rings* film franchise was yet to flood the Academy Awards' stage with New Zealand and Australian accents, and I would find Americans listening to me intently, trying to work out what I said. 'You have the weirdest vowel sounds,' an American science fiction writer told me. Yes—a mixture of Kiwi, Aussie, and British.

At Clarion West, I was the friendly alien. Conversely, Seattle and its surrounds looked very familiar, the topography of fjords, glaciers, and volcanoes seeming like New Zealand, transplanted up and across the Pacific. I had taught workshops before, but never so out of my comfort zone. Knowing full well what they were doing, the Clarion powers had allotted me the week where traditionally the students went feral. And now for something completely different: a writer from the far south! It worked, for the students were hospitable and amiable, the craziness contained during the week—for which I was very thankful.

Workshop groups are artificial constructs mixing competitiveness and creativity. Each one is different. Sometimes there are obvious stars, who can either burn brightly, or burn out. In 1998 there were two, Ellen Levy Finch and Daniel. He was the youngest in the group, something of a pet—I saw another student affectionately ruffle his hair. But he was also very focused. His submission letter was little more than two paragraphs, listing experience, his early publications, and the comment that he "would really enjoy spending a few weeks working with and talking to people who are serious about writing quality science fiction and fantasy."

Very few workshop stories are brilliant. At best they demonstrate competence—and once that has been achieved the really imaginative ideas can emerge, now that the writer has the skills to show them at their best. Daniel's tales began well, and improved during the Clarion weeks. Ellen Datlow took a story from him, he kept getting published, even to the extent of collaborating on a novel with two of his Clarion instructors, George R. R. Martin and Gardner Dozois.

When I accepted this gig, I half expected fantasy from Daniel, but what we have here is science fiction, with a very contemporary edge. Unusual reading is shown: few sf writers would name check both Hobbes' *Leviathan* and Colette. It looks at the big picture, global terrorism, and also the microcosm of peoples' lives, a tough job endured for the medical insurance, a good marriage actually strengthened by illness. The ideas are big enough for a novel, but can also function well at snapshot length.

Above all, as Daniel continues his astral career, this piece shows how he has matured and changed as a writer. It also shows how America has changed, for the Seattle summer of 1998 seems like the calm before the storm that followed 9/11. The science fiction Daniel wrote then is quite different from this 2004 work. It represents what all good writers do, both adapt to and reflect their challenging times. More power to him, then, and to his future shining!

Award-winning New Zealand/Australian writer **Lucy Sussex** has edited or written twenty books, including five collections of short stories, most recently *Thief of Lives* (Twelfth Planet, 2011).

# Start the Clock

## Benjamin Rosenbaum

### 2001

The real estate agent for Pirateland was old. Nasty old. It's harder
to tell with Geezers, but she looked to be somewhere in her Thirties.
They don't have our suppleness of skin, but with the right oils and
powders they can avoid most of the wrinkles. This one hadn't taken
much care. There were furrows around her eyes and eyebrows.

She had that Mommystyle thing going on: blue housedress, frilly
apron, Betty Crocker white gloves. If you're going to be running
around this part of Montana sporting those gigantic, wobbly breasts
and hips, I guess it's a necessary form of obeisance.

She said something to someone in the back of her van, then hurried
up the walk toward us. "It's a lovely place," she called. "And a very
nice area."

"Look, Suze, it's your mom," Tommy whispered in my ear. His
breath tickled. I pushed him.

It was deluxe, I'll give her that. We were standing under the fifty-
foot prow of the galleon we'd come to see. All around us a flotilla of
men-of-war, sloops, frigates, and cutters rode the manicured lawns and
steel-gray streets. Most of the properties were closed up, the lawns
pristine. Only a few looked inhabited—lawns bestrewn with gadgets,
excavations begun with small bulldozers and abandoned, Pack or
Swarm or Family flags flying from the mainmasts. Water cannons
menacing passerby.

I put my hands in my pants pockets and picked at the lint. "So
this is pretty much all Nines?"

The Thirtysomething Lady frowned. "Ma'am, I'm afraid the Anti-Redlining Act of 2035—"

"Uh-huh, race, gender, aetial age, chronological age, stimulative preference or national origin—I know the law. But who else wants to live in Pirateland, right?"

Thirtysomething Lady opened her mouth and didn't say anything.

"Or can afford it," Shiri called. She had gone straight for the rope-ladder and was halfway up. Her cherry-red sneakers felt over the side for the gunnel running around the house. Thirtysomething Lady's hands twitched in a kind of helpless half-grasping motion. Geezers always do that when we climb.

"Are *you* poor?" Tommy asked. "Is that why you dress like that?"

"Quit taunting the Lady," Max growled. Max is our token Eight, and he takes aetial discrimination more seriously than the rest of us. Plus, he's just nicer than we are. I don't think that's aetial; I think that's just Max. He's also Pumped Up: he's only four feet tall, but he has bioengineered muscles like grapefruit. He has to eat a pound or two of medicated soysteak a day just to keep his bulk on.

Thirtysomething Lady put her hand up to her eyes and blinked ferociously, as if she were going to cry. Now that would be something! They almost never cry. We'd hardly been mean to her at all. I felt sorry for her, so I walked over and put my hand in hers. She flinched and pulled her hand away. So much for cross-aetial understanding and forgiveness.

"Let's just look at the house," I said, putting my hands in my pockets.

"Galleon," she said tightly.

"Galleon then."

Her fingers twitched out a passkey mudra and the galleon lowered a boarding plank. Nice touch.

Frankly, we were excited. This move was what our Pack needed—the four of us, at least, were sure of it. We were all tired of living in the ghetto—we were in three twentieth-century townhouses in Billings, in an "age-mixed" area full of marauding Thirteens and Fourteens and

Fifteens. Talk about a people damned by CDAS—when the virus hit them, it had stuck their pituitaries and thyroids like throttles jammed open. It wasn't just the giantism and health problems caused by a thirty-year overdose on growth hormones, testosterone, estrogen, and androgen. They suffered more from their social problems—criminality, violence, orgies, jealousy—and their endless self-pity.

Okay, Max liked them. And most of the rest of us had been at least entertained by living in the ghetto. At birthday parties, we could always shock the other Packs with our address. But that was when all eight of us were there, before Katrina and Ogbu went south. With eight of us, we'd felt like a full Pack—invincible, strong enough to laugh at anyone.

I followed the others into the galleon's foyer. Video game consoles on the walls, swimming pool under a retractable transparent super-ceramic floor. The ceiling—or upper deck, I guess—was thirty feet up, accessible by ropeladders and swingropes. A parrot fluttered onto a roost—it looked real, but probably wasn't. I walked through a couple of bulkheads. Lots of sleeping nooks; lockers, shelves; workstations, both flatscreen and retinal-projection. I logged onto one as guest. Plenty of bandwidth. That's good for me. I may dress like a male twentieth-century stockbroker, double-breasted suit and suspenders, but I'm actually a found footage editor. (Not a lot of Nines are artists—our obsessive problemsolving and intense competitiveness makes us good market speculators, gamblers, programmers, and bio-techs; that's where we've made our money and our reputation. Not many of us have the patience or interest for art.)

I logged out. Max had stripped and dived into the pool—or maybe it was meant as a giant bathtub. Tommy and Shiri were bouncing on the trampoline, making smart-aleck remarks. The real estate agent had given up on getting anyone to listen to her pitch. She was sitting in a floppy gel chair, massaging the sole of one foot with her hands. I walked into the kitchen. Huge table, lots of chairs and sitballs, enormous programmable foodcenter.

I walked out, back to the Lady. "No stove."

"Stove?" she said, blinking.

I ran one hand down a suspender. "I cook," I said.

"You cook?"

I felt my jaw and shoulders tense—I'm sick of being told Nines don't cook—but then I saw her eyes. They were sparkling with delight. Indulgent delight. It reminded me of my own mother, oohing and aahing over brick-hard cookies I'd baked her one winter morning in the slums of Maryland, back when my aetial age was still tied to Nature's clock. My mother holding up the wedding dress she'd planned to give me away in, its lacy waist brushing my chin. One evening in college, when I'd looked up at the dinner table, halfway through a sentence—I'd been telling her about *The Hat On The Cat*, my distributed documentary (a firebrand polemic for Under-Five Emancipation; how cybernetics would liberate the Toddlers from lives of dependence)—and saw in her eyes how long ago she'd stopped listening. Saw that I wasn't Nine to her, but nine. Saw that she wasn't looking at me, but through me, a long way off—towards another now, another me: a Woman. Big globes of fatty breasts dangling from that other-me's chest; tall as a doorway, man-crazy, marriageable; a great sexualized monster like herself, a walking womb, a proto-Mommy. She was waiting for that Susan, Woman-Susan, who would never show up.

"I cook," I said, looking away from the Lady's eyes. Putting my hands in my pants pockets. I could have used a hug, but Max was underwater and Tommy and Shiri were trying to knock each other off the trampoline. I went outside.

"We could bring in a stove module," the Lady called.

Outside, a pigeon was poking through the lawn. It was mangy and nervous enough to be real. I stood for a while watching it, then my earring buzzed. I made the Accept mudra.

"Suze?" Travis said.

"Why are you asking, Travis? Who do you think is wearing my earring?"

"Suze, Abby's gone."

"What do you mean, gone?"

"She's not picking up. Her locator's off. I can't find her anywhere."

When Travis was nervous, his voice squeaked. Now he sounded like a mouse caught in a trap.

I looked at the active tatoo readout on my left palm. Travis was home. I made the mudra for Abby. No location listed. "Stay there, Travis. We're on our way."

I ran up the plank. Max was dressed again, rubbing his dreadlocks with a towel from the poolside toweltree. Tommy and Shiri were sitting at a table with the Real Estate Lady, looking over paperwork in the tabletop display.

"We've got to go. A personal emergency has come up," I said. Max was at my side instantly.

"Listen, we want this place," Shiri said.

"Shiri, we all have to talk about it," I said.

"What's to talk about?" Tommy said. "It's *awesome*."

"This is the first place we've looked at," I said.

"So?"

The Real Estate Lady was watching us with a guarded expression. I didn't want to say that Abby was missing. Not in front of her. Not in front of that can-you-really-be-trusted-to-look-after-yourselves-all-on-your-own-without-any-grownups attitude that came off her like a stink. I took my hands out of my pockets and balled them into fists. "You're being totally stupid!" I said.

"What's the emergency?" Max said quietly.

"I know what Travis and Abby would say," Tommy said. "They totally want a place like this. Let's just get it and we'll have the rest of the day free."

"We can go windgliding," Shiri said.

"Travis and Abby didn't even agree to getting a *house* yet, never mind *this* house," I said. I felt Max's hand on my shoulder.

"That's because they haven't seen it," Tommy said.

"What's the emergency?" Max said.

"There's probably been a train wreck and Suze has to make sure she's the first ghoul at her flatscreen," Shiri said.

"Screw you," I said and walked out of the house. I was shaking a little with adrenaline. I got in our clowncar and clicked on the engine.

Max hurried out the door behind me. I slid over to the passenger seat and he got in to drive.

"We can pick them up later," he said. "Or they can take a cab. What's up?"

I made the Abby mudra and showed him my palm. "Abby's missing. Travis hasn't seen her, and she's not picking up."

Max pulled out into the street. "She left the house this morning early, with that old black-and-white camera you got her. She was going to shoot some pictures."

I flipped open the flatscreen in the passenger-side dash and logged in. "That's no reason for her to turn off her locator. I hope she didn't stay near the house—a Nine walking around alone in the ghetto, taking photographs—imagine how that looks."

We hummed and whooshed out of Pirateland, up a ramp onto I-90. "Abby wouldn't be that dumb," Max said. But he didn't sound too sure. Abby's impetuous, and she'd been melancholy lately. "Police?" he asked, after a moment.

I shot him a sharp look. The police are Geezers—height requirements keep Under Twelves out of their ranks, and the Teens are mostly too uneducated and unruly. I didn't have any strings to pull with them, and neither did Max. "We wait until we have more data," I said. "Now shut up and let me work. Head home."

Most people have the notion that the public footage is this permanent, universal, easily searchable archive of everything that ever happens, clearly shot, from any angle. It's the job of people in my profession to help perpetuate that illusion. Actually, the networks are surprisingly spotty. There are millions of swarmcams wandering around in any major urban area, but they have a high failure and bug rate, and their pictures are grainy and indistinct—only a lot of imaginative algorithmic reconstruction makes them viewable. There are plenty of larger cameras linked to the net, but often hidden in a byzantine maze of permissions and protocols. And there are billions of motion sensors, audio pickups, locator tags, and data traffic monitors added to the mix, but they're not well correlated with each other. In a few hours on a Sunday morning, one square mile of downtown Billings generates enough data to fill all the computers of the twentieth century, plus all the paper libraries of the centuries before. It's hell to search.

But I'm good. I had enough footage of Abby on file to construct a good bloodhound, and then I spawned a dozen of them and seeded them well. Pretty soon the hits started coming back. Abby had crossed the street in front of our house at 09:06, and turned her locator tag off—on purpose, I imagined, since there was no error log. She'd stopped for bagels and udon in a deli on Avenue C at 09:22; shot pictures in the park until 09:56. She'd talked to a couple of Fifteens there and taken something from them. I couldn't see what, in the grainy gray swarmcam pictures, but it made the hair on the back of my neck rise.

From 10:03 I lost her; she'd gone up an elevator in a bank and disappeared. There's a network of private walkways and an aerial tram in that part of Billings that are poorly monitored. I had a cold feeling in my gut; that was a great way to lose me, if you were trying to.

I searched all the exits to those walkways and the tramway for Abby, buying a bunch of extra processing power on the exchange to run it faster. Nothing.

Max had entered among the spires and alleys of Billings. Dappled shadows of metal and translucent plastics and ceramics rippled over the clowncar. I looked out at the people walking through the corridors around us, all ages and sizes and colors. An old woman was walking slowly on a slidewalk just above us—she must have been an aetial Ninety, which made her a hundred and twenty or so. Walking, slowly, under her own steam. You don't see that every day.

I went back to some old footage I had of a birthday party and grabbed a sequence of Abby walking. I built an ergodynamic profile of her and fed that to my bloodhounds.

Bingo. At 10:42, Abby had left the aerial tramway in disguise. Platform shoes, trenchcoat, false breasts and hips and shoulders—she was impersonating a Fourteen or so. It looked ridiculous, like Halloween. She'd consulted a piece of paper from her pocket.

By 10:54 she was in a bad area. "Head for 30th and Locust," I told Max.

"Shit," he said. "No police?"

"I don't have anything yet that would warrant their attention. Nothing that proves she was coerced."

"So we need other backup," Max said grimly.

"Yeah." I looked up. "Can you get it?"

"I think so," he said. He made some Call mudras with one hand and started talking. "Hey, Dave, how you doing? Listen, man—" I tuned him out as he made his calls.

My last shot of Abby was at 11:06. She was being hustled into a doorway by a gargantuan Fifteen. His hand was on her elbow. Biodynamic readouts from a few stray hospital swarmcams confirmed that her pulse was elevated. Should I send this to the police? Would it prove Abby was coerced? But what was she doing with the weird disguise and the sneaking around? Just slumming? Or would I get her in trouble?

Was Abby buying drugs?

"Parkhill and 32nd," I said to Max. My fingers were still and I was just looking at that last picture, Abby and the giant, him pulling her into darkness.

"Can you meet us at Parkhill and 32nd?" Max was saying. "Damn, I know, man—that's why we need you ... "

When we got there, five of Max's friends were waiting. Four were clearly from his gym. Two of them were probably Nines or Tens (one swarthy, one red-haired and freckled) and they were even musclier than Max, their heads perched like small walnuts on their blockbuster bodies. The other two were Pumped Up Teens—maybe Fifteen or Sixteen. Their blond, slavic-boned faces sat on bodies like overstuffed family room sofas or industrial refrigerators: fingers the size of my forearm, thighs the size of my entire body. I wasn't sure how we were going to get them in the building.

And then there was the fifth—an Augmented Three. She stood a little apart from the others, her tiny arms at her sides. They were clearly afraid of her. One soft brown eye scanned the clouds, and she had a beatific smile on her face. Her other eye was the glistening jewel of a laserlight connector, and there were other plugs and ports glistening in her brown scalp among her cornrows.

Max stopped the car.

"Who's the Three?" I asked.

Max turned to me. He looked nervous, like he thought I was going to make fun of him. "That's my sister, Carla."

"Cool," I said quickly. He got out before I could say anything yet stupider, like "how nice that you've stayed close."

I opened my door and froze—Carla was running toward us. "Max!" she warbled, and flung her arms around his waist, burying her face in his stomach.

"Hi, honey-girl," he said, hugging her back.

I glanced at my palm readout. It had gone blank. So had the flatscreen in the car. It was a safe bet nothing near Carla would be recorded. You could sometimes tell where Augmented Threes and Twos were in the public footage by tracking the blank areas, the little blobs of inexplicable malfunction that followed them around. I once did an experimental documentary on Under-Five Augmentation using that blanked-out footage. It was called *Be Careful What You Wish For*—kind of a rueful, years-later followup to *The Hat On The Cat*.

"Carry me!" Carla said, and Max dutifully swung her tiny body onto his shoulders.

"Carla, this is Suze," Max said.

"I don't like her," Carla announced. Max's face went slack with fear, and my heart lurched. I grabbed the car door so hard my fingernails sank into the frame.

Carla exploded in giggles, then started to hiccup. "Just—*kidding*!" she choked out between hiccups. "You guys are so *silly*!"

I tried to smile. Max turned, slowly, towards the door. It was a formidable steel monstrosity, the kind with a biodynamic access plate governing its security system. Those things are supposed to be off-net, more or less invulnerable to cybernetic hacking. Carla waved at it and it popped open. The four muscleboys crowded their way inside—eager to get to Abby, and away from Carla—and the three of us brought up the rear, Carla still perched on Max's shoulders.

The stairway was dark and rank—it smelled like Teenagers, all their glands and excretions, smeared and sour. Most of the wallglow was dead, and one malfunctioning patch at the top of the stairs was flashing green and red, so that the bodies of the muscleboys ascended the stairs in strobed staccato.

The freckled gymrat was first to the doorway at the top. As he reached for the doorknob, we heard a long moan, and then a series of grunts. Almost snarls. And then, softer, a whimper—a high, female whimper—like the sound of someone tortured, someone in despair.

Carla started to cry. "I don't like it!"

"What is it, honeybaby?" Max said, his voice afraid. "*What's behind that door?*"

"Don't ask her that!" I barked. "Distract her, you idiot!"

"Max, should I make it go away?" Carla wailed. "Should I make them stop, Max?"

"No!" Max and I shouted at the same time.

"Max," I said as pleasantly as I could manage, "why don't you and Carla go play a nice game in the car?"

"But maybe I should—" Max said, looking at me from between Carla's tiny, shaking knees.

"Now!" I barked, and pushed past them.

Panting came from under the door, panting and groans. The muscleboys looked at me nervously. I heard Max's shoes clumping down the stairs behind me, and he started singing "The Itsy-Bitsy Spider."

"In!" I hissed, pointing at the door. The two overmuscled Nines threw their shoulders against it. It strained and buckled, but held. From inside the door came a strangled scream. The two Pumped-Up Teens braced themselves against the wall and each other, bent their knees, and crouched down with their shoulders under the Nine's butts. "Ready—now!" called the biggest, and all four of them pushed. The door shot open, and the muscleboys tumbled and collapsed through it. I sprinted over their bodies, springing from a buttock to a shoulder to a back to another shoulder, and I was through.

On a tiger-skin throwrug in the midst of a pile of trash, two huge naked Fifteens looked up. The male's skin was a mass of pimples and grease; shaggy hair fell over his shoulders and muscles. The female was pinned under him, her gigantic breasts flopping to either side of her thin ribcage, her knees pinioned around his hips. Between the wiry forests of their pubic hair, a portion of the male's penis ran like a swollen purple bridge.

"Ewww!" I shouted, as they flopped down, pulling the tigerskin over themselves. "WHERE'S ABBY??"

"Hi Suze," said Abby drily from an overstuffed chair to my left. She wearing a white jumpsuit, and holding a pen and a paper notebook.

"What the hell are you doing?" I shouted.

"I might ask you the same." She motioned to the pile of muscle-boys, who were struggling to their feet with dazed expressions.

"Abby! You disappeared!" I was waving my arms around like a Macromuppet. "Locator—bad area—disguise—scary—aargh!"

"Are you going to follow me around with a small army every time I turn off my locator?"

"Yes!!"

She sighed and put down her pencil and paper. "I'm really sorry," she called to the Fifteens. "My time was almost up anyway. Um, do you mind if we talk in here for a few minutes?"

"Yes!" gurgled the female.

"Abby, come on," I said. "They can't just stop in the middle. They have to, you know, finish what they were—doing. Until it's finished their brains won't work properly."

"Okay," Abby said. "All right, ah—thanks."

In the stairway, I said, "You couldn't just watch a porn channel?"

"It's not the same," she said. "That's all packaged and commercial. I wanted to interview them before and after. I have to know—what it's like."

"Why?"

She paused on the stairs, and I stopped too. The muscleboys, muttering, went out onto the street, and we were alone in the flashing green and red light.

"Suze, I'm going to start the clock."

Like she'd poured a bucket of ice water down my spine. "You're
what?"

"I'm going to take the treatments." She spoke quickly, as if afraid
I'd interrupt her. "They've gotten much better in the past couple of
years, there are basically no side effects. They're even making headway
with infants. In five years, it looks like most babies won't have any
arrestation effects at all, and—"

Tears had sprung to my eyes. "What are you talking about?" I
cried. "Why are you talking like *them*? Why are you talking like being
like us is something to be *cured*?" I punched the wall, which hurt my
hand. I sat down on the step and cried.

"Suze," Abby said. She sat down next to me and put her hand on
my shoulder. "I love being like us—but I want—"

"That?" I shouted, pointing up to the top of the stairs, where they
were grunting again. "That's what you want? You'd rather have that
than us?"

"I want everything, Suze. I want every stage of life—"

"Oh, every stupid *stage*, as designed by stupid God, who also gave
us death and cancer, and—"

She grabbed my shoulders. "Suze, listen. I want to know what *that*
up there is like. Maybe I won't like it, and then I won't do it. But Suze,
I want to have babies."

"Babies? Abby, your eggs are forty years old—"

"Exactly! Exactly, my eggs are only forty years old, and most of
them are still good. Who do you want to have the babies, Suze? The
Geezers? The world is starting again, Suze, and I—"

"The world was fine!" I pulled away from her. "The world was
just fine!" Snot and tears were running down my nose into my mouth,
salty and gooey. I wiped my face on the sleeve of my stockbroker's
suit, leaving a slick trail like a slug. "We were fine—"

"This isn't about us—"

"Oh baloney!!" I lurched to my feet, grabbing the railing for
balance. "As if you're going to live with us in a galleon and fire water
cannons and go to birthday parties! You're just not, Abby, don't kid
yourself! You're going to be *that*!" I pointed up the stairs. "Sexual

jealousy and sexual exchange economy and cheating and mutual-exploitation-and-ownership and serial monogomy and divorce and the whole stupid crazy boring ... ”

“Suze—” she said in a small voice.

“Just don’t!” I said. “Don’t drag it out! If you want to do it, do it, but then leave us alone! Okay? You’re not welcome.” I turned and headed down the stairs. “Get the hell out.”

Max was standing at the bottom of the stairs. I didn’t like the way he was looking at me. I brushed past.

The boys from the gym were in the car, eating yard-long submarine sandwiches with great gusto. Carla sat on the front steps, talking to a rag doll. She looked up, and her red jewel of an eye flashed—for a moment it was as bright as looking into the sun at noon. Then she looked past me, into the sky.

“What are you afraid of?” she asked.

I leaned against the doorframe and said nothing. A wind came down the street and crumpled sheets of paper danced along it.

“I’m afraid of cows,” she volunteered. “And Millie”—she held up the rag doll—“is afraid of, um, um, you know the thing where if you take all the money people spend and the way they looked at each other that day and you put it inside what the weather’s going to do and then you can sing to cats and stuff? She’s afraid of that.”

I wiped my eyes on my sleeve. “Can you see the future, Carla?”

She giggled, and then she looked serious. “You guys are all wrong about that. It’s just a game you made up. There isn’t any future.”

“Do you like being Augmented?” I asked.

“I like it but Millie doesn’t like it. Millie thinks it’s scary but she’s just silly. Millie wishes we were like people and trees and we didn’t have to make things okay all the time. But then we couldn’t play with bolshoiye-gemeinschaft-episteme-mekhashvei-ibura.”

“Okay,” I said.

“Max is coming out with Abby four thousand five hundred and sixty-two milliseconds after I finish talking right now and projected group cohesion rises by thirty-six percent if you don’t have a fight now so you should take the clowncar and I’ll give them a ride and I’d love to live with you but I know I'm too scary but it's okay but can I visit on Max's birthday?"

"Yes," I said. "You can visit on my birthday too."

"I can? I can?" She jumped up and hugged me, flinging her arms around my waist, pressing her cheek into my chest. "Wow, I didn't even know you'd say that!" She pulled away, beaming at me, then pointed to the car. "Okay, quick, go! Bye!"

I got in the car and clicked on the engine. Carla waved and she held Millie's arm and waved it too. The door behind her opened, I saw Max's shoe, and I drove off.

A quarter mile away from Carla, the flatscreen blinked on again, and my earring started buzzing like crazy. I told it to let Travis through.

"Abby's fine," I said. "She's with Max. They'll be coming home."

"Cool," Travis said. "Whew! That's a relief!"

"Yeah."

"So Tommy and Shiri sent me video of the house. It looks *awesome*. Do you love it too?"

"Yeah, I love it." I was on I-90 now. Beyond the spires and aerial trams of Billings, I could see the funhouse suburbs spreading out before me—windmills, castles, ships, domes, faerie forests.

"Cool, because I think they signed some papers or something."

"What? Travis, we all have to agree!" As I said it, it occurred to me that the only one who hadn't seen the place was Abby. I gripped the wheel and burst out crying.

"What? What?" Travis said.

"Travis!" I wailed. "Abby wants to start the clock!"

"I know," Travis muttered.

"What? You *know*??"

"She told me this morning."

"Why didn't you say anything?"

"She made me promise not to."

"Travis!"

"I was hoping you'd talk her out of it."

I took the exit for Pirateland, swooshing through an orange plastic tunnel festooned with animated skeletons climbing out of Davy Jones' lockers. "You can't talk Abby out of anything."

"But we've got to, Suze, we've got to. C'mon, we can't just fall apart like this. Katrina and Ogbu—" he was doing his panic-stricken ratsqueak again, and suddenly I was very sick of it.

"Just shut up and stop whining, Travis!" I shouted. "Either she'll change her mind or she won't, but she won't, so you'll just have to deal with it."

Travis didn't say anything. I told my earring to drop the connection and block all calls.

I pulled up outside the galleon and got out. I found a handkerchief in the glove compartment and cleaned my face thoroughly. My suit, like the quality piece of work it was, had already eaten and digested all the snot I'd smeared on it—the protein would probably do it good. I checked myself in the mirror—I didn't want the Real Estate Lady to see me weepy. Then I got out and stood looking at the house. If I knew Tommy and Shiri, they were still inside, having discovered a rollerskating rink or rodeo room.

Parked at the side of the house was the Real Estate Lady's old-fashioned van—a real classic, probably gasoline-burning. I walked over to it. The side door was slid open. I looked in.

Inside, reading a book, was a Nine. She was tricked out in total Kidgear—pony tails, barettes, t-shirt with a horse on it, socks with flashy dangly things. Together with the Lady's Mommystyle getup, it made perfect, if twisted, sense. Personally I find that particular game of Let's-Pretend sort of depressing and pitiful, but to each her own kink.

"Hey," I said. She looked up.

"Um, hi," she said.

"You live around here?"

She wrinkled her nose. "My mom, um, kinda doesn't really want me to tell that to strangers."

I rolled my eyes. "Give the roleplaying a rest, would you? I just asked a simple question."

She glanced at me. "You shouldn't make so many assumptions

about people," she said, and pointedly lifted her book up in front of her face.

The clop-clop of the Lady's shoes came down the drive. My scalp was prickling. Something was not altogether kosher in this sausage.

"Oh, hello," the Lady said brightly, if awkwardly. "I see you've met my daughter."

"Is that your actual daughter, or can the two of you just not get out of character?"

The Lady crossed her arms and fixed me with her green-eyed stare. "Corintha contracted Communicative Developmental Arrestation Syndrome when she was two years old. She started the treatments seven years ago."

I realized my mouth was hanging open. "She's a clock-started Two? She spent twenty-five years as an unaugmented two-year-old?"

The Lady leaned past me into the van. "You okay in here, honey?"

"Great," said Corintha from behind her book. "Other than the occasional ignoramus making assumptions."

"Corintha, please don't be rude," the Lady said.

"Sorry," she said.

The Lady turned to me. I think my eyes must have been bugging out of my head. She laughed. "I've seen your documentaries, you know."

"You *have*?"

"Yes." She leaned up against the van. "They're technically very well done, and I think some of what you have to say is very compelling. That one with all the blanked out footage—that gave me a real feeling for what it's like for those children who are wired up into the Internet."

An odd and wrongheaded way of putting it, but I limited myself to saying, "Uh—thanks."

"But I think you're very unfair to those of us who didn't Augment our children. To watch your work, you'd think every parent who didn't Augment succumbed to Parenting Fatigue and sent their toddlers off to the government daycare farms, visiting only at Christmas. Or that they lived some kind of barbaric, abusive, incestuous existence." She looked over at her daughter. "Corintha has been a joy to me every day of her life—"

"Oh, mom!" Corintha said from behind her book.

"—but I never wanted to stand in the way of her growing up. I just didn't think Augmentation was the answer. Not for her."

"And you thought you had the right to decide," I said.

"Yes." She nodded vigorously. "I thought I had the obligation to decide."

The Suze everyone who knows me knows would have made some sharp rejoinder. None came. I watched Corintha peek out from behind her book.

There was silence for a while. Corintha went back to reading.

"My friends still inside?" I asked.

"Yes," the Lady said. "They want the place. I think it fits six very comfortably, and—"

"Five," I said huskily. "I think it's going to be five."

"Oh," the Lady looked nonplussed. "I'm—sorry to hear that."

Corintha put her book down. "How come?"

The Lady and I looked at her.

"Oh, is that a rude question?" Corintha said.

"It's a bit prying, dear," the Lady said.

"Ah—" I said. I looked at Corintha. "One of us wants to—start the clock. Start the conventional biological aging process."

"So?" Corintha said.

"Honey," said the Lady. "Sometimes if people—change—they don't want to live together any more."

"That's really dumb," said Corintha. "If you didn't even have a fight or anything. If it's just that somebody wants to grow up. I would never get rid of my friends over that."

"Corintha!"

"Would you let her talk? I'm trying to respect your archaic ideas of parent-child relationships here, Lady, but you're not making it easy."

The Lady cleared her throat. "Sorry," she said after a moment.

I looked out at the mainmast and the cannons of our galleon. The rolling lawn. This place had everything. The trampolines and the pools, the swingropes and the games. I could just imagine the birthday parties we'd have here, singing and cake and presents and dares, everyone getting wet, foamguns and crazy mixed-up artificial animals. We could hire clowns and acrobats, storytellers and magicians. At night we'd sleep in hammocks on deck or on blankets on the lawn, under the stars, or all together in a pile, in the big pillowspace in the bow.

And I couldn't see Abby here. Not a growing-upwards Abby, getting taller, sprouting breasts, wanting sex with some huge apes of men or women or both. Wanting privacy, wanting to bring her clock-started friends over to whisper and laugh about menstruation and courtship rituals. Abby with a mate. Abby with children.

"There's a place over by Rimrock Road," the Lady said slowly. "It's an old historic mansion. It's not quite as deluxe or as—thematic as this. But the main building has been fitted out for recreation-centered group living. And there are two outbuildings that allow some privacy and—different styles of life."

I stood up. I brushed off my pants. I put my hands in my pockets. "I want us to go see that one," I said.

**Benjamin Rosenbaum's** fiction has appeared in *Asimov's Science Fiction, The Magazine of Fantasy and Science Fiction, Harper's Magazine, McSweeney's, Strange Horizons, Nature,* and been nominated for the Hugo, Nebula, Sturgeon, BSFA and Locus Awards.

He has been a party clown, day care worker on a kibbutz, synagogue president, rugby flanker, stay-at-home dad, and programmer for Silicon Valley startups, the U.S. government, online fantasy games, and the Gnomes of Zurich. He lives in Basel Switzerland with his wife and his two children. More at http://benjaminrosenbaum.com.

# Connie Willis
# on Ben Rosenbaum

One of the chief delights of teaching Clarion West—or actually, maybe the only one since everything else about Clarion West is reading endless manuscripts, writing volumes of critique notes, and trying to survive on too much caffeine and too little sleep—is listening to your students talk. It's like conversation heard nowhere else, and sort of like what I've imagined it must have been like to sit at the Algonquin Round Table and listen to Dorothy Parker and Robert Benchley and Alexander Woolcott and Harpo Marx (and yes, of course he could talk—and play the harp.) Just like the members of the Round Table, Clarion West students are full of ideas, opinions, snark, unusual insights, and rapier-sharp wit. And all kinds of plans for changing the face of science fiction.

My student Ben Rosenbaum was (and is) one of my favorite people to listen to. Hearing him talk was like watching a fireworks display—ideas and intelligence and enthusiasm flew off from him in all directions, fizzing and sparking and exploding into glittering sentences, and you always had the feeling you shouldn't stand too close or you might be hit by a fireball whizzing by. "Oh, my gosh!" I remember thinking during one particular conversation, "if he can somehow get all this Roman-candle dazzle and pop into his stories, he'll really light up the skies!"

And, as "Start the Clock," his red-and gold-and green-flashing starburst of a story about viruses and pirate ships and childhood, about growing up and growing, period, shows, he clearly has.

Careful, don't stand too close!

**Connie Willis** has been awarded 11 Hugo Awards, 11 Locus Poll Awards, and six Nebula Awards. In 2011 she won a Hugo Award for *Blackout/All Clear*. Willis was inducted to the Science Fiction Museum and Science Fiction Hall of Fame in 2009 and received the Damon Knight Memorial Grand Master Award in 2011.

# I Hold My Father's Paws

## David D. Levine

**2000**

The receptionist had feathers where her eyebrows should have been. They were blue, green, and black, iridescent as a peacock's, and they trembled gently in the silent breath of the air conditioner. "Did you have a question, sir?"

"No," Jason replied, and raised his magazine, but after reading the same paragraph three times without remembering a word he set it down again. "Actually, yes. Um, I wanted to ask you ... ah ... are you ... transitioning?" The word landed on the soft tailored-grass carpet of the waiting room, and Jason wished he could pick it up again, stuff it into his pocket, and leave. Just leave, and never come back.

"Oh, you mean the eyebrows? No, sir, that's just fashion. I enjoy being human." She smiled gently at him. "You haven't been in San Francisco very long, have you?"

"No, I just got in this morning."

"Feathers are very popular here. In fact, we're having a special this month. Would you like a brochure?"

"No! Uh, I mean, no thank you." He looked down and saw that the magazine had crumpled in his hands. Awkwardly he tried to smooth it out, then gave up and slipped it back in the pile on the coffee table. They were all recent issues, and the coffee table looked like real wood. He tested it with a dirty thumbnail; real wood, all right. Then, appalled at his own action, he shifted the pile of magazines to cover the tiny scratch.

"Sir?"

Jason started at the receptionist's voice, sending magazines skidding across the table. "What?"

"Would you mind if I gave you a little friendly advice?"

"Uh, I ... no. Please." She was probably going to tell him that his fly was open, or that ties were required in this office. Her own tie matched the wall covering, a luxurious print of maroon and gold. Jason doubted the collar of his faded work shirt would even button around his thick neck.

"You might not want to ask any of our patients if they are transitioning."

"Is it impolite?" He wanted to crawl under the table and die.

"No, sir." She smiled again, with genuine humor this time. "It's just that some of them will talk your ear off, given the slightest show of interest."

"I, uh ... Thank you."

A chime sounded—a rich little sound that blended unobtrusively with the waiting room's classical music—and the receptionist stared into space for a moment. "I'll let him know," she said to the air, then turned her attention to Jason. "Mr. Carmelke is out of surgery."

"Thank you." It was so strange to hear that uncommon name applied to someone else. He hadn't met another Carmelke in over twenty years.

Half an hour later the waiting room door opened onto a corridor with a smooth, shiny floor and meticulous off-white walls. Despite the art—original, no doubt—and the continuing classical music, a slight smell of disinfectant reminded Jason where he was. A young man in a nurse's uniform led Jason to a door marked with the name Dr. Lawrence Steig.

"Hello, Mr. Carmelke," said the man behind the desk. "I'm Dr. Steig." The doctor was lean, shorter than Jason, with brown eyes and a trim salt-and-pepper beard. His hand, like his voice, was firm and a little rough; his tie was knotted with surgical precision. "Please do sit down."

Jason perched on the edge of the chair, not wanting to surrender to its lushness. Not wanting to be comfortable. "How is my father?"

"The operation went well, and he'll be conscious soon. But I'd like to talk with you first. I believe there are some ... family issues."

"What makes you say that?"

The doctor stared at his personal organizer as he repeatedly snapped it open and shut. It was gold. "I've been working with your father for almost two years, Mr. Carmelke. The doctor-patient relationship in this type of work is, necessarily, quite intimate. I feel I've gotten to know him quite well." He raised his eyes to Jason's. "He's never mentioned you."

"I'm not surprised." Jason heard the edge of bitterness in his own voice.

"It's not unusual for patients of mine to be disowned by their families."

Jason's hard, brief laugh startled both of them. "This has nothing to do with his ... transition, Dr. Steig. My father left my mother and me when I was nine. I haven't spoken to him since. Not once."

"I'm sorry, Mr. Carmelke." He seemed sincere; Jason wondered if it were just professional bedside manner. The doctor opened his mouth to speak, then closed it and stared off into a corner for a moment. "This might not be the best time for a family reunion," he said finally. "His condition may be a little ... startling."

"I didn't come all the way from Cleveland just to turn around and go home. I want to talk with my father. While I still can. And this is my last chance, right?"

"The final operation is scheduled for five weeks from now. It can be postponed, of course. But all the papers have been signed." The doctor placed his hands flat on the desk. "You're not going to be able to talk him out of it."

"Just let me see him."

"I will ... if he wants to see you."

Jason didn't have anything to say to that.

Jason's father was lying on his side, facing away from the door, as Jason entered. The smell of disinfectant was stronger here, and a battery of instruments bleeped quietly.

He was bald, with just a fringe of gray hair around the back of his head. The scalp was smooth and pink and shiny, and very round—matching Jason's own round head, too big for the standard hard hats at his work site. "Big Jase" was what it said on his own personal helmet, black marker on safety yellow plastic.

But though his father's head was large and round, the shoulders that moved with his breathing were too narrow, and his chest dropped rapidly away to hips that were narrower still. The legs were invisible, drawn up in front of his body. Jason swallowed as he moved around to the other side of the bed.

His father's round face was tan, looking more "rugged" than "wrinkled." Deep lines ran from his nose to the corners of his mouth, and the eyebrows above his closed eyes were gray and very bushy. It was both an older and a younger face than what Jason had imagined, trying to add twenty years to a memory twenty years old.

Jason's gaze traveled down, past his father's freshly-shaved chin, to the thick ruff of gray-white fur on his neck. Then further, to the gray-furred legs that lay on the bed in front of him and the paws that crossed, relaxed, at the ankles, with neatly trimmed nails and clean, unscuffed pads.

His father's body resembled a wolf's, or a mastiff's, broad and strong and laced with muscle and sinew. But it was wrong, somehow. His chest, narrow though it was, was still wider than any normal dog's, and the fur looked fake—too clean, too fine, too regular. Jason knew from his reading on the plane that it was engineered from his father's own body hair, and was only an approximation of a dog's natural coat with its layers of different types of hair.

He was a magnificent animal. He was a pathetic freak. He was a marvel of biotechnology. He was an arrogant icon of self-indulgence.

He was a dog.

He was Jason's father.

"Dad? It's Jason." Some part of him wanted to pet the furry shoulder, but he kept his hands to himself.

His father's eyes flickered open, then drifted closed again. "Yeah. Doctor told me." His voice was a little slurred. "What the hell're you doing here?"

"I ran into Aunt Brittany at O'Hare. I didn't recognize her, but she knew me right away. She told me all about ... you. I came straight here." *It's my father,* he'd told his boss on the phone. *He's in the hospital. I have to see him before it's too late.* Letting him draw the wrong conclusion, but not too far from the truth.

His father's nose wrinkled in distaste. "Never could trust her."

"Dad ... *why?*"

He opened his eyes again. They were the same hard blue as Jason's, and they were beginning to focus properly. "Because I can. Because the Consti ... *tu*tion gives me the right to do whatever the hell I want with my body and my money. Because I want to be pampered for the rest of my life." He closed his eyes and crossed his paws on the bridge of his nose. "Because I don't want to make any more damn decisions. Now get out."

Jason's mouth flapped open and closed like a fish. "But Dad ... "

"Mr. Carmelke?" Jason looked up, and his father rolled his head around, to see where Dr. Steig stood by the door. Jason had no idea how long he had been there. "Excuse me, I meant Jason." Jason's father put his paws over his face again. "Mr. Carmelke, I think you should leave your father alone for a while. He's still feeling the effects of the anesthetic. He may be more ... open to discussion in the morning."

"Doubt it," came the voice from under the crossed paws.

Jason's hand reached out—to stroke the forehead, to ruffle the fur, he wasn't sure which—but then it pulled back. "See you tomorrow, Dad."

There was no response.

As soon as the door closed behind him, Jason leaned heavily

against the wall, then slid down to a sitting position. His eyes stung and he rubbed at them.

"I'm sorry." Jason opened his eyes at the voice. Dr. Steig was squatting in front of him, holding a clipboard in his hands. "He's not usually like this."

"I've never understood him," Jason said, shaking his head. "Not since he left. We had a good life. He wasn't drinking or anything. There weren't any money problems—not then, anyway. Mom loved him. I loved him. But he said, 'There's nothing here for me,' and he walked out of our lives."

"You mentioned money. Is that what this is about? You know he's given most of it to charity already. What remains is just enough to pay for the craniofacial procedure, and a trust fund that will cover his few needs after that."

"It's not the money. It was never the money. He even offered to pay alimony and child support, but Mom turned it down. It wasn't the most practical decision, but she really didn't want anything to do with him. I think it was one of those things where a broken love turns into a terrible hate."

"Does your mother know you're here?"

"She died eight years ago. Leukemia. He didn't even come to the funeral."

"I'm sorry," the doctor said again. He sat down, let his clipboard clatter to the shiny floor next to him. They sat together in silence for a time. "Let me talk with him tonight, Mr. Carmelke, and we'll see how things go in the morning. All right?"

Jason thought for a moment, then bobbed his head. "All right."

They helped each other up.

Jason's father jogged into the doctor's office the next morning, his lithe new body bobbing with a smooth four-legged gait, and hopped easily up onto a carpeted platform that brought his head to the same level as Jason and the doctor. But he refused to meet Jason's eyes.

Jason himself sat in the doctor's leather guest chair, fully seated this time, but still not fully comfortable.

"Noah," Dr. Steig said to Jason's father, "I know this is hard for you. But I want you to understand that it is even harder for your son."

"He shouldn't have come here," he said, still not looking at Jason.

"Dad ... how could I not? You're the only family I have left in the world, I didn't even know if you were dead or alive, and now ... this! I had to come. Even if I can't change your mind, I ... I just want to talk."

"Talk, then!" His face turned to Jason at last, but his blue eyes were hard, his mouth set. "I might even listen." He lowered his head to his paws, which rested on the carpeted surface in front of him.

Jason felt the little muscles in his legs tensing to rise. He could stand up, walk out ... be free of this awkwardness and pain. Go back to his lonely little house and try to forget all about his father.

But he knew how well that had worked the last time.

"I told them you were dead," he said. "My friends at school. The new school, after we moved to Cleveland. I don't know why. Lots of their parents were divorced. They would have understood. But somehow pretending you were dead made it easier."

His dad closed his eyes hard; deep furrows appeared in the corners of his eyes and between his brows. "Can't say I blame you," he said at last.

"No matter how many people I lied to, I still knew you were out there somewhere. I wondered what you were doing. Whether you missed me. Where did you go?"

"Buffalo."

Jason waited until he was sure no more details were forthcoming. "Is that where you've been all this time?"

"No, I was only there for a few months. Then Syracuse. Miami for a while. I didn't settle down for a long time. But I've been in the Bay Area for the last eleven years." He raised his head. "Selling configuration management software for Romatek. It's really exciting stuff."

Jason didn't care about his father's job, but he sensed an opening. "Tell me about it."

They talked for half an hour about configuration management and source control and stock options—things that Jason didn't understand and didn't want to understand. But they were talking. His dad even managed to make the topic seem interesting. A wry smirk came to Jason's lips when he realized he was getting a sales presentation from a dog. A dog with his father's head.

Jason and his father sat in the courtyard behind the clinic, under a red Japanese maple that sighed in the wind. The skyscrapers of San Francisco were visible above the fence, which was painted with a colorful abstract mural. A few birds chirped, and the slight mineral sting of sea salt flavored the air, reminding Jason how far he was from home.

A phone with two large buttons was strapped to his father's left foreleg. He could push the buttons with his chin to summon urgent or less-urgent assistance. He sat on the bench next to Jason with his legs drawn up beneath him, his head held high so as to look Jason as much in the eye as possible.

"I would have had to have something done with the knees one way or the other," he said. "They were just about shot, before. Arthritis. Now they're like new. I was taking laps this morning, before you showed up. Haven't been able to run like that in years. And being so close to the ground, it feels like a hundred miles an hour."

Jason translated that into kilometers and realized his dad wasn't speaking literally. "But what about ... I dunno, restaurants? Museums? Movies?"

"After they do the head work I'll have different tastes, and I'll get nothing but the best. Museums—hell, I never went to museums before. And as far as movies, I'll just wait for them to come out on chip. Then I'll curl up with my handler and go to sleep in front of them."

"Of course, the movie will be in black and white to you."

"Heh."

Jason didn't mention—didn't want to think about—the other changes that the "head work" would make in his father's senses, and his brain. After the craniofacial procedure, his mind would be as much like a dog's as modern medicine could make it. He'd be happy, no question of that, but he wouldn't be Noah Carmelke any more.

Jason's dad seemed to recognize that his thoughts were drifting in an uncomfortable direction. "Tell me about your job," he said.

"I work for Bionergy," Jason replied. "I'm a civil engineer. We're refitting Cleveland's old natural gas system for biogas ... that means a lot of tearing up streets and putting them back."

"Funny. I was a civil engineer for a while, before I hired on at Romatek."

"No shit?"

"No shit."

"I was following in your footsteps, and I didn't even know it."

"We thought you were going to be an artist. Your mom was so proud of those drawings of the barn, and the goats."

"Wow. I haven't done any sketching in years."

They stared at the mural, both remembering a refrigerator covered with drawings.

"You want me to draw you?"

Jason's father nodded slowly. "Yeah. Yeah, I'd like that."

Someone from the clinic managed to scare up a pad and some charcoal, and they settled down under the maple tree. Jason leaned against the fence and began to sketch, starting with the hindquarters. His father sat with his hind legs drawn up beneath him and his forelegs stretched straight out in front. "You look like the Sphinx," Jason said.

"Hmm."

"You can talk if you like, I'm not working on your mouth."

"I don't have anything to say."

Jason's charcoal paused on the page, then resumed its scratching. "Last night I read a paper I found in the restaurant. The *Howl*. You know it?" The full title was *HOWL: The Journal of the Bay Area Transpecies Community*. It was full of angry articles about local politicians he'd never heard of, and ads for services he couldn't understand or didn't want to think about.

"I've read it, yeah. Buncha flakes."

"I found out there are a lot of different reasons for people to change their species. Some of them feel they were born into the wrong body. Some are making a statement about humanity's impact on the planet. Some see it as a kind of performance art. I don't see any of those in you."

"I told you, I just want to be taken care of. It's a form of retirement."

The marks on the page were getting heavy and black. "I don't think that's it. Not really. I look at you and I see a man with ambition and drive. You wouldn't have gotten all those stock options if you were the type to retire at 58." The charcoal stick snapped between Jason's fingers, and he threw the pieces aside. "Damnit, Dad, how can you give up your *humanity?*"

Jason's dad jumped to his four feet. His stance was wide, defensive. "The O'Hartigan decision said I have the right to reshape my body and my mind in any way I wish. I think that includes the right to not answer questions about it." He stared for a moment, as though he were about to say something else, then pursed his lips and trotted off.

Jason was left with a half-finished sketch of a sphinx with his father's face.

He sat in the clinic's waiting room for three hours the next day. Finally Dr. Steig came out and told him that he was sorry, but his father simply could not be convinced to see him.

Jason wandered the lunchtime crowds of San Francisco. The spring air was clear and crisp, and the people walked briskly. Here and there he saw feathers, fur, scales. The waiter who brought his sandwich was half snake, with slitted eyes and a forked tongue that flickered. Jason was so distracted he forgot to tip.

After lunch he came to the clinic's door and stopped. He stood in the hall for a long time, dithering, but when the elevator's ping announced the arrival of two women with identical Siamese cat faces he bolted—shoving between them, ignoring their insulted yowls, hammering the Door Close button. As the elevator descended he gripped the handrails, pushed himself into the corner, tried to calm his breathing.

He landed in Cleveland at 12:30 that night.

The other hard-hats at his work site gave him a nice card they had all signed. He accepted their sympathies but did not offer any details. One woman took him aside and asked how long his father had. "The doctor says five weeks."

Days passed. Sometimes he found himself sitting in the cab of a backhoe, staring at his hands, wondering how long he had been there.

He confided in nobody. He imagined the jokes: "Good thing it isn't your mother ... then you'd be a son-of-a-bitch!" Antacids became his favorite snack.

The little house he'd bought with Maria, back when they thought they might be able to make it work, became oppressive. He ate all his meals in restaurants, in parts of town where he didn't know anyone. Once he found a copy of the local transpecies paper. It was a skinny little thing, bimonthly, with angry articles about local politicians and ads for services he wished he didn't know anything about.

Four weeks later, on a Monday evening, he got a call from San Francisco.

"Jason, it's me. Your dad. Don't hang up."

The handset was already halfway to the cradle as the last three words came out, but Jason paused and returned it to his ear. "Why not?"

"I want to talk."

"You could have done that while I was there."

"OK, I admit I was a little short with you. I'm sorry."

The plastic of the handset creaked in Jason's hand. He tried to consciously relax his grip. "I'm sorry too."

There was a long silence, the two of them breathing at each other across three thousand kilometers. It was Jason's father who broke it.

"The operation is scheduled for Thursday at 8 a.m. I ... I'd like to see you one more time before then."

Jason covered his eyes with one hand, the fingers pressing hard against the bones of his brow. Finally he sighed and said, "I don't think so. There's no point to it. We just make each other too crazy."

"Please. I know I haven't been the best father to you ... "

"You haven't been any kind of father at all!"

Another silence. "You've got me there. But I'd really like to ... "

"To what? To say goodbye? Again? No thanks!" And he slammed down the phone.

He sat there for a long while, feeling the knots crawl across his stomach, waiting for the phone to ring again.

It didn't.

That night he went out and got good and drunk. "My dad's turning into a dog," he slurred to the bartender, but all that got him was a cab home.

Tuesday morning he called in sick. He spent the day in bed, sometimes sleeping. He watched a soap opera; the characters' ludicrous problems seemed so small and manageable.

Tuesday night he did not sleep. He brought out a box of letters from his mother, read through them looking for clues. At the bottom of the box he found a picture of himself at age eight, standing between his parents. It had been torn in half, the jagged line cutting between him and his father like a lightning bolt, and crudely taped together. He remembered rescuing the torn photo from his mother's wastebasket, taping it together, hiding it in a box of old CD-ROMs. Staring at it late at night. Wondering why.

Wednesday morning he drove to the airport.

There was a strike at O'Hare and he was rerouted to Atlanta, where he ate a bad hamburger and floated on a tide of angry, frustrated people, thrashing to stay on top. Finally one gate agent found him a seat to LAX. From there he caught a red-eye to San Francisco.

He arrived at the clinic at 5 a.m. The door was locked, but there was a telephone number for after-hours service. It was answered by a machine. He stomped through menus until he reached a bored human being, who knew nothing, but promised to get a message to Dr. Steig.

He paced the hall outside the clinic. He had nowhere else to go.

Fifteen minutes later an astonished Dr. Steig called back. "Your father is already in prep for surgery, but I'll tell the hospital to let you see him." He gave Jason the address. "I'm glad you came," he said before hanging up.

The taxi took Jason through dark, empty streets, puddles gleaming with reflected streetlight. Raindrops ran down the windows like sweat, like tears. Jason blinked as he stepped into the hard blue-white light of the hospital's foyer. "I'm here to see Noah Carmelke," he said. "I'm expected."

The nurse gave him a paper mask to tie over his nose and mouth, and goggles for his eyes. "The prep area is sterile," she said as she helped him step into a paper coverall. Jason felt like he was going to a costume party.

And then the double doors slid open and he met the guest of honor.

His father lay on his side, shallow breaths raising and lowering his furry flanks. An oxygen mask was fastened to his face, like a muzzle. His eyes were at half-mast, unfocused. "Jason," he breathed. "They said you were coming, but I didn't believe it." The sound of his voice echoed hollowly behind the clear plastic.

"Hello, Dad." His own voice was muffled by the paper mask.

"I'm glad you're here."

"Dad ... I had to come. I need to understand you. If I don't understand you, I'll never understand myself." He hugged himself. His face felt swollen; his whole head was ready to implode from sadness and fatigue. "*Why*, Dad? Why did you leave us? Why didn't you come to

Mom's funeral? And why are you throwing away your life now?"

The bald head on the furry neck moved gently, side to side, on the pillow. "Did you ever have a dog, Jason?"

"You know the answer, Dad. Mom was allergic."

"What about after you grew up?"

"I've been alone most of the time since then. I didn't think I could take proper care of a dog if I had to go to work every day."

"But a dog would have loved you."

Jason's eyes burned behind the goggles.

"I had a dog when I was a kid," his father continued. "Juno. A German Shepherd. She was a good dog ... smart, and strong, and obedient. And every day when I came home from school she came bounding into the yard ... so happy to see me. She would jump up and lick my face." He twisted his head around, forced his eyes open to look into Jason's. "I left your mother because I couldn't love her like that. I knew she loved me, but I thought she deserved better than me. And I didn't come to the funeral because I knew she wouldn't want me there. Not after I'd hurt her so much."

"What about *me*, Dad?"

"You're a man. A man like me. I figured you'd understand."

"I *don't* understand. I never did."

His father sighed heavily, a long doggy sigh. "I'm sorry."

"You're turning yourself into a dog so someone will love you?"

"No. I'm turning myself into a dog so I can love someone. I want to be free of my human mind, free of decisions."

"How can you love anyone if you aren't *you* any more?"

"I'll still be me. But I'll be able to *be* me, instead of thinking all the time about being me."

"Dad ..."

The nurse came back. "I'm sorry, Mr. Carmelke, but I have to ask you to leave now."

"Dad, you can't just leave me like that!"

"Jason," his father said. "There's a clause in the contract that lets me specify a family member as my primary handler."

"I don't think I could ..."

"Please, Jason. Son. It would mean so much to me. Let me come home with you."

Jason turned away. "And see you every day, and know what you used to be?"

"I'd sleep by your feet while you watch movies. I'd be so happy to see you when you came home. All you have to do is give the word, and I'll put my voiceprint on the contract right now."

Jason's throat was so tight that he couldn't speak. But he nodded.

The operation took eighteen hours. The recovery period lasted weeks. When the bandages came off, Jason's father's face was long and furry and had a wet nose. But his head was still very round, and his eyes were still blue.

Two deep wells of sincere, doggy love.

**David D. Levine** is a lifelong science fiction reader whose midlife crisis was to take a sabbatical from his high-tech job to attend Clarion West in 2000. It seems to have worked. He made his first professional sale in 2001, won the Writers of the Future Contest in 2002, was nominated for the John W. Campbell award in 2003, was nominated for the Hugo Award and the Campbell again in 2004, and won a Hugo in 2006 (Best Short Story, for "Tk'Tk'Tk"). A collection of his short stories, *Space Magic*, from Wheatland Press, won the Endeavour Award in 2009. In January of 2010 he spent two weeks at a simulated Mars base in the Utah desert. He lives in Portland, Oregon, with his wife, Kate Yule, with whom he edits the fanzine *Bento*, and his website is at http://www.daviddlevine.com.

# Geoff Ryman
# on David Levine

David Levine came to Clarion West in 2000 and made his first fiction sale in 2001. In 2006 he won a Hugo for the story 'Tk'tk'tk'. Observe and learn how it's done.

> The receptionist had feathers where her eyebrows should have been. They were blue, green, and black, iridescent as a peacock's, and they trembled gently in the silent breath of the air conditioner.

You won't find description as precise or detailed as that in a lot of literary fiction (LF). In an age of Raymond Carver and paring back, some LF doesn't bother helping us see its world, at least not in the space of a short story. In science fiction, readers want to be able to experience your wonders. Detailed description also helps you to show differences between your world and ours without having to explain them. You play to the reader's desire to build a world up from clues you give them. Genre is about what your readers want and do. (Which makes LF a genre as well).

So a fantasy and science fiction writer needs to be able to imagine wonders clearly and then describe them. It's a core job skill.

David Levine had that skill readymade when he walked into Clarion. Unassuming, pleasant—a nice guy as SF writers so often are. Proof in pudding—it was clear from that week's story that he didn't just speculate about things. He saw them. And he knew what specific details would make us see them and believe them.

I'd like to think we helped develop the craft skills to get those visions down on paper. But he was pretty much there anyway without us.

> The word landed on the soft tailored-grass carpet of the waiting room, and Jason wished he could pick it up again, stuff it into his pocket, and leave. Just leave, and never come back.

More fun with description: the carpet is grass. But here is another difference between LF and SF protocols. When normal English students try to write SF, they do what LF does with emotion: hide it. It's tucked away hidden in the dialogue, or revealed in a twitch of body language. LF readers like to decode behavior the way you have to in real life: despite all the efforts of people to mask what they feel. Young LF writers can have a horror of unsubtlety and melodrama, so they bury feeling and conflict. If you hide the emotions when writing an SF story, the reader has way too much to decode—both the world and the people.

Fantasy and science fiction needs to foreground emotions. Feelings and motives need to be understandable and easy to identify with, otherwise made up worlds will be irrelevant and dull. The feelings of the characters pull us with them into their world and through the story. No embarrassment. And that means a fantasy or science fiction writer must have an extra ability to nail feelings without explaining them. The writing must be what we call 'deeply felt'.

I get Jason's embarrassment though I have no idea why in his culture asking about transitioning makes people tense. Levine takes us right into the character's heads, we hear Jason think. He's the one who says 'just leave and never come back'. Levine delves deeply and unambiguously into the core of painful conflict. An estranged father is about to become a dog; this is Jason's last chance to talk to him. A medical curiosity is made into heartfelt drama. This is what SF does best and uniquely: turn science into pain, conflict, resolution.

"You're turning yourself into a dog so someone will love you?"
"No. I'm turning myself into a dog so I can love someone. I want to be free of my human mind, free of decisions."

Again, David came into Clarion West with the ability to imagine what other people feel. He could be direct about it in prose but in such a way that the feeling is communicated. He was not embarrassed by conflict. He knew the difference between melodrama and drama.

And he knew to how to allude. Transitioning, San Francisco ... there are whiffs there of other things: gender change, sexual politics, social revolution. Different generations are not just LIKE different species: here they are. Metaphor is built in.

SF emphasizes change on both the individual and social level. For SF, literature is prose fiction in which something changes deeply and for good.

I could analyze other things: the way Levine generates suspense and the way he releases information so that, for example, we know a new dog must have a long term master. How both the reader and the characters are surprised at the same time by turns of events; or the wonderful way the story resolves into a comedy with both characters getting what they most need.

Go back and re-read. Observe and learn how it's done.

**Geoff Ryman** is a Canadian-born writer who has resided in Britain most of his adult life. He has published 10 books, numerous stories, and won 14 awards, including the World Fantasy Award, the Arthur C. Clarke Award, the British Science Fiction Award, the James Tiptree, Jr. Award, and the Philip K. Dick Award. He teaches creative writing at the University of Manchester.

# Beluthahatchie

## Andy Duncan

### 1994

Everybody else got off the train at Hell, but I figured, it's a free country. So I commenced to make myself a mite more comfortable. I put my feet up and leaned back against the window, laid my guitar across my chest and settled in with my hat tipped down over my eyes, almost. I didn't know what the next stop was but I knew I'd like it better than Hell.

Whoo! I never saw such a mess. All that crowd of people jammed together on the Hell platform so tight you could faint standing up. One old battle-hammed woman hollering for Jesus, most everybody else just mumbling and crying and hugging their bags and leaning into each other and waiting to be told where to go. And hot? Man, I ain't just beating my gums there. Not as hot as the Delta, but hot enough to keep old John on the train. No, sir, I told myself, no room out there for me.

Fat old conductor man pushed on down the aisle kinda slow, waiting on me to move. I decided I'd wait on that, too.

"Hey, nigger boy." He slapped my foot with a rolled-up newspaper. Felt like the Atlanta paper. "This ain't no sleeping car."

"Git up off me, man. I ain't done nothing."

"Listen at you. Who you think you are, boy? Think you run the railroad? You don't look nothing like Mr. George Pullman." The conductor tried to put his foot up on the seat and lean on his knee, but he gave up with a grunt.

I ran one finger along my guitar strings, not hard enough to make a sound but just hard enough to feel them. "I ain't got a ticket, neither," I bit off, "but it was your railroad's pleasure to bring me this far, and it's my pleasure to ride on a little further, and I don't see what cause you got to be so astorperious about it, Mr. Fat Ass."

He started puffing and blowing. "What? What?" He was teakettle hot. You'd think I'd done something. "What did you call me, boy?" He whipped out a strap, and I saw how it was, and I was ready.

"Let him alone."

Another conductor was standing outside the window across the aisle, stooping over to look in. He must have been right tall and right big too, filling up the window like that. Cut off most of the light. I couldn't make out his face, but I got the notion that pieces of it was sliding around, like there wan't quite a face ready to look at yet. "The Boss will pick him up at the next stop. Let him be."

"The Boss?" Fat Ass was getting whiter all the time.

"The Boss said it would please him to greet this nigger personally."

Fat Ass wan't studying about me anymore. He slunk off, looking back big-eyed at the man outside the window. I let go my razor and let my hand creep up out of my sock, slow and easy, making like I was just shifting cause my leg was asleep.

The man outside hollered: "Board! All aboard! Next stop, Beluthahatchie!"

That old mama still a-going. "Jesus! Save us, Jesus!"

"All aboard for Beluthahatchie!"

"Jesus!"

We started rolling out.

"All aboard!"

"Sweet Je—" And her voice cut off just like that, like the squawk of a hen Meemaw would snatch for Sunday dinner. Wan't my business. I looked out the window as the scenery picked up speed. Wan't nothing to see, just fields and ditches and swaybacked mules and people stooping and picking, stooping and picking, and by and by a porch with old folks sitting on shuck-bottomed chairs looking out at all the years that ever was, and I thought I'd seen enough of all that to last me a while. Wan't any of my business at all.

When I woke up I was lying on a porch bench at another station, and hanging on one chain was a blown-down sign that said Beluthahatchie. The sign wan't swinging cause there wan't no breath of air. Not a soul else in sight neither. The tracks ran off into the fields on both ends as far as I could see, but they was all weeded up like no train been through since the Surrender. The windows over my head was boarded up like the bank back home. The planks along the porch han't been swept in years by nothing but the wind, and the dust was in whirly patterns all around.

Still lying down, I reached slowly beneath the bench, groping the air, till I heard, more than felt, my fingers pluck a note or two from the strings of my guitar. I grabbed it by the neck and sat up, pulling the guitar into my lap and hugging it, and I felt some better.

Pigeons in the eaves was a-fluttering and a-hooting all mournful-like, but I couldn't see 'em. I reckon they was pigeons. Meemaw used to say that pigeons sometimes was the souls of dead folks let out of Hell. I didn't think those folks back in Hell was flying noplace, but I did feel something was wrong, bad wrong, powerful wrong. I had the same crawly feeling as before I took that fatal swig—when Jar Head Sam, that harp-playing bastard, passed me a poisoned bottle at a Mississippi jook joint and I woke up on that one-way train.

Then a big old hound dog ambled around the corner of the station on my left, and another big old hound dog ambled around the corner of the station on my right. Each one was nearbouts as big as a calf and so fat it could hardly go, swanking along with its belly on the planks and its nose down. When the dogs snuffled up to the bench where I was sitting, their legs give out and they flopped down, yawned, grunted, and went fast to sleep like they'd been poleaxed. I could see the fleas hopping across their big butts. I started laughing.

"Lord, the hellhounds done caught up to me now! I surely must have led them a chase, I surely must. Look how wore out they are!" I hollered and cried, I was laughing so hard. One of them broke wind real long, and that set me off again. "Here come the brimstone! Here come the sulfur! Whoo! Done took my breath. Oh, Lordy." I wiped my eyes.

Then I heard two way-off sounds, one maybe a youngun dragging a stick along a fence, and the other maybe a car motor.

"Well, shit," I said.

Away off down the tracks, I saw a little spot of glare vibrating along in the sun. The flappity racket got louder and louder. Some fool was driving his car along on the tracks, a bumpety-bump, a bumpety-bump. It was a Hudson Terraplane, right sporty, exactly like what Peola June used to percolate around town in, and the chrome on the fender and hood was shining like a conk buster's hair.

The hound dogs was sitting up now, watching the car. They was stiff and still on each side of my bench, like deacons sitting up with the dead.

When the car got nigh the platform it lurched up out of the cut, gravel spitting, gears grinding, and shut off in the yard at the end of the porch where I was sitting. Sheets of dust sailed away. The hot engine ticked. Then the driver's door opened, and out slid the devil. I knew him well. Time I saw him slip down off the seat and hitch up his pants, I knew.

He was a sunburnt, bandy-legged, pussel-gutted li'l peckerwood. He wore braces and khaki pants and a dirty white undershirt and a big derby hat that had white hair flying out all around it like it was attached to the brim, like if he'd tip his hat to the ladies his hair would come off too.

He had a bright-red possum face, with beady, dumb black eyes and a long sharp nose, and no chin at all hardly and a big goozlum in his neck that jumped up and down like he couldn't swallow his spit fast enough. He slammed the car door and scratched himself a little, up one arm and then the other, then up one leg till he got to where he liked it. He hunkered down and spit in the dust and looked all unconcerned like maybe he was waiting on a tornado to come along and blow some victuals his way, and he didn't take any more notice of me than the hound dogs had.

I wan't used to being treated such. "You keep driving on the tracks thataway, hoss," I called, "and that Terraplane gone be butt-sprung for sure."

He didn't even look my way. After a long while, he stood up and leaned on a fender and lifted one leg and looked at the bottom of his muddy clodhopper, then put it down and lifted the other and looked at it too. Then he hitched his pants again and headed across the yard toward me. He favored his right leg a little and hardly picked up his feet at all when he walked. He left ruts in the yard like a plow. When he reached the steps, he didn't so much climb 'em as stand his banty-weight self on each one and look proud, like each step was all his'n now, and then go on to claim the next one too. Once on the porch, he sat down with his shoulders against a post, took off his hat and fanned himself. His hair had a better hold on his head than I thought, what there was of it. Then he pulled out a stick and a pocketknife and commenced to whittle. But he did all these things so deliberate and thoughtful that it was almost the same as him talking, so I kept quiet and waited for the words to catch up.

"It will be a strange and disgraceful day unto this world," he finally said, "when I ask a gut-bucket nigger guitar player for advice on autoMO-bile mechanics, or for anything else except a tune now and again." He had eyes like he'd been shot twice in the face. "And furthermore, I am the Lord of Darkness and the Father of Lies, and if I want to drive my 1936 Hudson Terraplane, with its six-cylinder seventy-horsepower engine, out into the middle of some loblolly and shoot out its tires and rip up its seats and piss down its radiator hole, why, I will do it and do it again seven more times afore breakfast, and the voice that will stop me will not be yourn. You hearing me, John?"

"Ain't my business," I said. Like always, I was waiting to see how it was.

"That's right, John, it ain't your business," the devil said. "Nothing I do is any of your business, John, but everything you do is mine. I was there the night you took that fatal drink, John. I saw you fold when your gut bent double on you, and I saw the shine of your blood coming up. I saw that whore you and Jar Head was squabbling over doing business at your funeral. It was a sorry-ass death of a sorry-ass man, John, and I had a big old time with it."

The hound dogs had laid back down, so I stretched out and rested my feet on one of them. It rolled its eyes up at me like its feelings was hurt.

"I'd like to see old Jar Head one more time," I said. "If he'll be along directly, I'll wait here and meet his train."

"Jar Head's plumb out of your reach now, John," the devil said, still whittling. "I'd like to show you around your new home this afternoon. Come take a tour with me."

"I had to drive fifteen miles to get to that jook joint in the first place," I said, "and then come I don't know how far on the train to Hell and past it. I've done enough traveling for one day."

"Come with me, John."

"I thank you, but I'll just stay here."

"It would please me no end if you made my rounds with me, John." The stick he was whittling started moving in his hand. He had to grip it a little to hang on, but he just kept smiling. The stick started to bleed along the cuts, welling up black red as the blade skinned it. "I want to show off your new home place. You'd like that, wouldn't you, John?" The blood curled down his arm like a snake.

I stood up and shook my head real slow and disgusted, like I was bored by his conjuring, but I made sure to hold my guitar between us as I walked past him. I walked to the porch steps with my back to the devil, and I was headed down them two at a time when he hollered out behind, "John! Where do you think you're going?"

I said real loud, not looking back: "I done enough nothing for one day. I'm taking me a tour. If your ass has slipped between the planks and got stuck, I'll fetch a couple of mules to pull you free."

I heard him cuss and come scrambling after me with that leg a-dragging, sounding just like a scarecrow out on a stroll. I was holding my guitar closer to me all the time.

I wan't real surprised that he let those two hound dogs ride up on the front seat of the Terraplane like they was Mrs. Roosevelt, while I had to walk in the road alongside, practically in the ditch. The devil drove real slow, talking to me out the window the whole time.

"Whyn't you make me get off the train at Hell, with the rest of those sorry people?"

"Hell's about full," he said. "When I first opened for business out here, John, Hell wan't no more'n a wide spot in the road. It took a long time to get any size on it. When you stole that dime from your poor old Meemaw to buy a French post card and she caught you and flailed you across the yard, even way back then, Hell wan't no bigger'n Baltimore. But it's about near more'n I can handle now, I tell you. Now I'm filling up towns all over these parts. Ginny Gall. Diddy-Wah-Diddy. West Hell—I'd run out of ideas when I named West Hell, John."

A horsefly had got into my face and just hung there. The sun was fierce, and my clothes was sticking to me. My razor slid hot along my ankle. I kept favoring my guitar, trying to keep it out of the dust as best I could.

"Beluthahatchie, well, I'll be frank with you, John, Beluthahatchie ain't much of a place. I won't say it don't have possibilities, but right now it's mostly just that railroad station, and a crossroads, and fields. One long, hot, dirty field after another." He waved out the window at the scenery and grinned. He had yellow needly teeth. "You know your way around a field, I reckon, don't you, John?"

"I know enough to stay out of 'em."

His laugh was like a man cutting tin. "I swear you are a caution, John. It's a wonder you died so young."

We passed a right lot of folks, all of them working in the sun. Pulling tobacco. Picking cotton. Hoeing beans. Old folks scratching in gardens. Even younguns carrying buckets of water with two hands, slopping nearly all of it on the ground afore they'd gone three steps. All the people looked like they had just enough to eat to fill out the sad expression on their faces, and they all watched the devil as he drove slowly past. All those folks stared at me hard, too, and at the guitar like it was a third arm waving at 'em. I turned once to swat that blessed horsefly and saw a group of field hands standing in a knot, looking my way and pointing.

"Where all the white folks at?" I asked.

"They all up in heaven," the devil said. "You think they let niggers into heaven?" We looked at each other a long time. Then the devil laughed again. "You ain't buying that one for a minute, are you, John?"

I was thinking about Meemaw. I knew she was in heaven, if anyone was. When I was a youngun I figured she musta practically built the place, and had been paying off on it all along. But I didn't say nothing.

"No, John, it ain't that simple," the devil said. "Beluthahatchie's different for everybody, just like Hell. But you'll be seeing plenty of white folks. Overseers. Train conductors. Sheriff's deputies. If you get uppity, why, you'll see whole crowds of white folks. Just like home, John. Everything's the same. Why should it be any different?"

"'Cause you're the devil," I said. "You could make things a heap worse."

"Now, could I really, John? Could I really?"

In the next field, a big man with hands like gallon jugs and a pink splash across his face was struggling all alone with a spindly mule and a plow made out of slats. "Get on, sir," he was telling the mule. "Get on with you." He didn't even look around when the devil come chugging up alongside.

The devil gummed two fingers and whistled. "Ezekiel. Ezekiel! Come on over here, boy."

Ezekiel let go the plow and stumbled over the furrows, stepping high and clumsy in the thick dusty earth, trying to catch up to the Terraplane and not mess up the rows too bad. The devil han't slowed down any—in fact, I believe he had speeded up some. Left to his own doin's, the mule headed across the rows, the plow jerking along sideways behind him.

"Yessir?" Ezekiel looked at me sorta curious like, and nodded his head so slight I wondered if he'd done it at all. "What you need with me, boss?"

"I wanted you to meet your new neighbor. This here's John, and you ain't gone believe this, but he used to be a big man in the jook joints in the Delta. Writing songs and playing that dimestore git fiddle."

Ezekiel looked at me and said, "Yessir, I know John's songs." And I could tell he meant more than hearing them.

"Yes, John mighta been famous and saved enough whore money to buy him a decent instrument if he hadn't up and got hisself killed. Yes, John used to be one high-rolling nigger, but you ain't so high now, are you John?"

I stared at the li'l peckerwood and spit out: "High enough to see where I'm going, Ole Massa."

I heard Ezekiel suck in his breath. The devil looked away from me real casual and back to Ezekiel, like we was chatting on a veranda someplace.

"Well, Ezekiel, this has been a nice long break for you, but I reckon you ought to get on back to work now. Looks like your mule's done got loose." He cackled and speeded up the car. Ezekiel and I both walked a few more steps and stopped. We watched the back of the Terraplane getting smaller, and then I turned to watch his face from the side. I han't seen that look on any of my people since Mississippi.

I said, "Man, why do you all take this shit?"

He wiped his forehead with his wrist and adjusted his hat. "Why do you?" he asked. "Why do you, John?" He was looking at me strange, and when he said my name it was like a one-word sentence all its own.

I shrugged. "I'm just seeing how things are. It's my first day."

"Your first day will be the same as all the others, then. That sure is the story with me. How come you called him Ole Massa just now?"

"Don't know. Just to get a rise out of him, I reckon."

Away off down the road, the Terraplane had stopped, engine still running, and the little cracker was yelling. "John! You best catch up, John. You wouldn't want me to leave you wandering in the dark, now would you?"

I started walking, not in any gracious hurry though, and Ezekiel paced me. "I asked 'cause it put me in mind of the old stories. You remember those stories, don't you? About Ole Massa and his slave by name of John? And how they played tricks on each other all the time?"

"Meemaw used to tell such when I was a youngun. What about it?"

He was trotting to keep up with me now, but I wan't even looking his way. "And there's older stories than that, even. Stories about High John the Conqueror. The one who could—"

"Get on back to your mule," I said. "I think the sun has done touched you."

"—the one who could set his people free," Ezekiel said, grabbing my shoulder and swinging me around. He stared into my face like a man looking for something he's dropped and has got to find.

"John!" the devil cried.

We stood there in the sun, me and Ezekiel, and then something went out of his eyes, and he let go and walked back across the ditch and trudged after the mule without a word.

I caught up to the Terraplane just in time for it to roll off again. I saw how it was, all right.

A ways up the road, a couple of younguns was fishing off the right side of a plank bridge, and the devil announced he would stop to see had they caught anything, and if they had, to take it for his supper. He slid out of the Terraplane, with it still running, and the dogs fell out after him, a-hoping for a snack, I reckon. When the devil got hunkered down good over there with the younguns, facing the swift-running branch, I sidled up the driver's side of the car, eased my guitar into the back seat, eased myself into the front seat, yanked the thing into gear and drove off. As I went past I saw three round O's—a youngun and the devil and a youngun again.

It was a pure pleasure to sit down, and the breeze coming through the windows felt good too. I commenced to get even more of a breeze going, on that long, straightaway road. I just could hear the devil holler back behind:

"John! Get your handkerchief-headed, free-school Negro ass back here with my auto-MO-bile! Johhhhnnn!"

"Here I come, old hoss," I said, and I jerked the wheel and slewed that car around and barreled off back toward the bridge. The younguns and the dogs was ahead of the devil in figuring things out. The younguns scrambled up a tree as quick as squirrels, and the dogs went loping into a ditch, but the devil was all preoccupied, doing a salty jump and cussing me for a dadblasted blagstagging liver-lipped stormbuzzard, jigging around right there in the middle of the bridge, and he was still cussing when I drove full tilt onto that bridge and he did not cuss any less when he jumped clean out from under his hat and he may even have stepped it up some when he went over the side. I heard a ker-plunk like a big rock chunked into a pond just as I swerved to bust the hat with a front tire and then I was off the bridge and racing back the way we'd come, and that hat mashed in the road behind me like a possum.

I knew something simply awful was going to happen, but man! I slapped the dashboard and kissed my hand and slicked it back across my hair and said aloud, "Lightly, slightly, and politely." And I meant that thing. But my next move was to whip that razor out of my sock, flip it open and lay it on the seat beside me, just in case.

I came up the road fast, and from way off I saw Ezekiel and the mule planted in the middle of his field like rocks. As they got bigger I saw both their heads had been turned my way the whole time, like they'd started looking before I even came over the hill. When I got level with them I stopped, engine running, and leaned on the horn until Ezekiel roused himself and walked over. The mule followed behind, like a yard dog, without being cussed or hauled or whipped. I must have been a sight. Ezekiel shook his head the whole way. "Oh, John," he said. "Oh, my goodness. Oh, John."

"Jump in, brother," I said. "Let Ole Massa plow this field his own damn self."

Ezekiel rubbed his hands along the chrome on the side of the car, swiping up and down and up and down. I was scared he'd burn himself. "Oh, John." He kept shaking his head. "John tricks Ole Massa again. High John the Conqueror rides the Terraplane to glory."

"Quit that, now. You worry me."

"John, those songs you wrote been keeping us going down here. Did you know that?"

"I 'preciate it."

"But lemme ask you, John. Lemme ask you something before you ride off. How come you wrote all those songs about hellhounds and the devil and such? How come you was so sure you'd be coming down here when you died?"

I fidgeted and looked in the mirror at the road behind. "Man, I don't know. Couldn't imagine nothing else. Not for me, anyway."

Ezekiel laughed once, loud, boom, like a shotgun going off.

"Don't be doing that, man. I about jumped out of my britches. Come on and let's go."

He shook his head again. "Maybe you knew you was needed down here, John. Maybe you knew we was singing, and telling stories, and waiting." He stepped back into the dirt. "This is your ride, John. But I'll make sure everybody knows what you done. I'll tell 'em that things has changed in Beluthahatchie."

He looked off down the road. "You'd best get on. Shoot—maybe you can find some jook joint and have some fun afore he catches up to you."

"Maybe so, brother, maybe so."

I han't gone two miles afore I got that bad old crawly feeling. I looked over to the passengers' side of the car and saw it was all spattered with blood, the leather and the carpet and the chrome on the door, and both those mangy hound dogs was sprawled across the front seat wallowing in it, both licking my razor like it was something good, and that's where the blood was coming from, welling up from the blade with each pass of their tongues. Time I caught sight of the dogs, they both lifted their heads and went to howling. It wan't no howl like any dog should howl. It was more like a couple of panthers in the night.

"Hush up, you dogs!" I yelled. "Hush up, I say!"

One of the dogs kept on howling, but the other looked me in the eyes and gulped air, his jowls flapping, like he was fixing to bark, but instead of barking said:

"Hush yourself, nigger."

When I looked back at the road, there wan't no road, just a big thicket of bushes and trees a-coming at me. Then came a whole lot of screeching and scraping and banging, with me holding onto the wheel just to keep from flying out of the seat, and then the car went sideways and I heard an awful bang and a crack and then I didn't know anything else. I just opened my eyes later, I don't know how much later, and found me and my guitar lying on the shore of the Lake of the Dead.

I had heard tell of that dreadful place, but I never had expected to see it for myself. Preacher Dodds whispered to us younguns once or twice about it, and said you have to work awful hard and be awful mean to get there, and once you get there, there ain't no coming back. "Don't seek it, my children, don't seek it," he'd say.

As far as I could see, all along the edges of the water, was bones and carcasses and lumps that used to be animals—mules and horses and cows and coons and even little dried-up birds scattered like hickory chips, and some things lying away off that might have been animals and might not have been, oh Lord, I didn't go to look. A couple of buzzards was strolling the edge of the water, not acting hungry nor vicious but just on a tour, I reckon. The sun was setting, but the water didn't cast no shine at all. It had a dim and scummy look, so flat and still that you'd be tempted to try to walk across it, if any human could bear seeing what lay on the other side. "Don't seek it, my children, don't seek it." I han't sought it, but now the devil had sent me there, and all I knew to do was hold my guitar close to me and watch those buzzards a-picking and a-pecking and wait for it to get dark. And Lord, what would this place be like in the dark?

But the guitar did feel good up against me thataway, like it had stored up all the songs I ever wrote or sung to comfort me in a hard time. I thought about those field hands a-pointing my way, and about Ezekiel sweating along behind his mule, and the way he grabbed aholt of my shoulder and swung me around. And I remembered the new song I had been fooling with all day in my head while I was following that li'l peckerwood in the Terraplane.

"Well, boys," I told the buzzards, "if the devil's got some powers I reckon I got some, too. I didn't expect to be playing no blues after I was dead. But I guess that's all there is to play now. 'Sides, I've played worse places."

I started humming and strumming, and then just to warm up I played "Rambling on My Mind" cause it was, and "Sweet Home Chicago" cause I figured I wouldn't see that town no more, and "Terraplane Blues" on account of that damn car. Then I sang the song I had just made up that day.

*I'm down in Beluthahatchie, baby,*
*Way out where the trains don't run*
*Yes, I'm down in Beluthahatchie, baby,*
*Way out where the trains don't run*
*Who's gonna take you strolling now*
*Since your man he is dead and gone*

*My body's all laid out mama*
*But my soul can't get no rest*
*My body's all laid out mama*
*But my soul can't get no rest*
*Cause you'll be sportin with another man*
*Lookin for some old Mr. Second Best*

*Plain folks got to walk the line*
*But the Devil he can up and ride*
*Folks like us we walk the line*
*But the Devil he can up and ride*
*And I won't never have blues enough*
*Ooh, to keep that Devil satisfied.*

When I was done it was black dark and the crickets was zinging and everything was changed.

"You can sure get around this country," I said, "just a-sitting on your ass."

I was in a cane-back chair on the porch of a little wooden house, with bugs smacking into an oil lamp over my head. Just an old cropper place, sitting in the middle of a cotton field, but it had been spruced up some. Somebody had swept the yard clean, from what I could see of it, and on a post above the dipper was a couple of yellow flowers in a nailed-up Chase & Sanborn can.

When I looked back down at the yard, though, it wan't clean

anymore. There was words written in the dirt, big and scrawly like from someone dragging his foot.

## DON'T GET A BIG HEAD JOHN
## I'LL BE BACK

Sitting on my name was those two fat old hound dogs. "Get on with your damn stinking talking selves," I yelled, and I shied a rock at them. It didn't go near as far as I expected, just sorta plopped down into the dirt, but the hounds yawned and got up, snuffling each other, and waddled off into the dark.

I stood up and stretched and mumbled. But something was still shifting in the yard, just past where the light was. Didn't sound like no dogs, though.

"Who that? Who that who got business with a wore out dead man?"

Then they come up toward the porch a little closer where I could see. It was a whole mess of colored folks, men in overalls and women in aprons, granny women in bonnets pecking the ground with walking sticks, younguns with their bellies pookin out and no pants on, an old man with Coke-bottle glasses and his eyes swimming in your face nearly, and every last one of them grinning like they was touched. Why, Preacher Dodds woulda passed the plate and called it a revival. They massed up against the edge of the porch, crowding closer in and bumping up against each other, and reaching their arms out and taking hold of me, my lapels, my shoulders, my hands, my guitar, my face, the little ones aholt of my pants legs—not hauling on me or messing with me, just touching me feather light here and there like Meemaw used to touch her favorite quilt after she'd already folded it to put away. They was talking, too, mumbling and whispering and saying, "Here he is. We heard he was coming and here he is. God bless you friend, God bless you brother, God bless you son." Some of the womenfolks was crying, and there was Ezekiel, blowing his nose on a rag.

"Y'all got the wrong man," I said, directly, but they was already heading back across the yard, which was all churned up now, no words to read and no pattern neither. They was looking back at me and smiling and touching, holding hands and leaning into each other, till they was all gone and it was just me and the crickets and the cotton.

Wan't nowhere else to go, so I opened the screen door and went on in the house. There was a bed all turned down with a feather pillow, and in the middle of the checkered oilcloth on the table was a crock of molasses, a jar of buttermilk, and a plate covered with a rag. The buttermilk was cool like it had been chilling in the well, with water beaded up on the sides of the jar. Under the rag was three hoecakes and a slab of bacon.

When I was done with my supper, I latched the front door, lay down on the bed and was just about dead to the world when I heard something else out in the yard—swish, swish, swish. Out the window I saw, in the edge of the porch light, one old granny woman with a shuck broom, smoothing out the yard where the folks had been. She was sweeping it as clean as for company on a Sunday. She looked up from under her bonnet and showed me what teeth she had and waved from the wrist like a youngun, and then she backed on out of the light, swish swish swish, rubbing out her tracks as she went.

South Carolina native **Andy Duncan** was a twenty-nine-year-old newspaperman turned N.C. State University graduate student when he attended Clarion West 1994. In the first week, indignant that a classmate said no one ever needed to write another deal-with-the-Devil story, Duncan retreated to his Seattle University dorm room, sat at Eileen Gunn's typewriter, and wrote "Beluthahatchie." It became his first fiction sale (to Gardner Dozois at *Asimov's Science Fiction Magazine*), his first Hugo nominee, and the title story of his first collection, which won his first World Fantasy Award. Duncan since has taught Clarion West and Clarion; his second collection *The Pottawatomie Giant* was published in 2012. An assistant professor of English at Frostburg State University in Maryland, he also teaches in the University of Alabama Honors College.

# Elizabeth Hand
# on Andy Duncan

One always remembers a first encounter with a great writer's work. In the case of Andy Duncan, it's impossible for me to separate the work from the writer, or the words on the page from the voice—Andy's voice—in my head. It's one of the great voices in contemporary fiction, and by that I don't just mean the beauty of Andy's language, or the originality of his vision and characterizations, all of which are exceptional and, in the case of his characters, among the most memorable I've ever encountered.

What I'm talking about here is the sound of Andy's voice reading his own work, an experience on par with listening to Flannery O'Connor read "A Good Man is Hard to Find." Which comparison is neither far-fetched nor coincidental—listen to Andy reading from his recent story "Close Encounters," then listen to O'Connor. Then read Andy's homage to the ten-year-old O'Connor, "Unique Chicken Goes in Reverse." Then read everything else he's ever written.

I met Andy in 1994, when he was a student at Clarion West and I was an instructor. I knew right from the get-go that I couldn't teach him anything, and told him as much when we had our first formal one-on-one meeting. I'd already been blown away by his story in progress, but what I remember just as vividly was hearing Andy's voice for the first time. In our initial group meeting, I asked the students what their favorite books were. Andy's response was a honeyed drawl: "Flannery O'Connor and *Alice's Adventures in Wonderland*."

At that moment, I knew he was the real deal. I felt as though I'd stumbled into the Cavern Club circa 1962 as the Beatles walked onstage.

Since then, Andy's become one of the best-known and best-loved writers of fantastic literature on the planet, receiving multiple World Fantasy Awards and the Theodore Sturgeon Award. And I wouldn't be surprised if his reputation extends beyond (or below) our planet, to some of the far-flung places he writes about. I read and reread everything of Andy's that I can get my hands on, including (of course) "Beluthahatchie." The truth is, I'd walk over hot coals to read Andy's stories (and I'd run over hot coals to hear him read them aloud himself). Fortunately, I don't have to, and if you're holding this book right now, neither do you.

**Elizabeth Hand** is the author of many novels, including *Winterlong*, *Waking the Moon*, *Glimmering*, and *Mortal Love*, as well as three collections of stories, including the recent *Saffron and Brimstone*. Her fiction has received the Nebula, World Fantasy, Mythopoeic, Tiptree, and International Horror Guild Awards, and her novels have been selected as New York Times and Washington Post Notable Books.

# Another Word for Map Is Faith

## Christopher Rowe

### 1996

The little drivers threw baggage down from the top of the bus and out from its rusty undercarriage vaults. This was the last stop. The road broke just beyond here, a hundred yards short of the creek.

With her fingertip, Sandy traced the inked ridge northeast along the map, then rolled the soft leather into a cylinder and tucked it inside her vest. She looked around for her pack and saw it tumbled together with the other cartographers' luggage at the base of a catalpa tree. Lucas and the others were sorting already, trying to lend their gear some organization, but the stop was a tumult of noise and disorder.

The high country wind shrilled against the rush of the stony creek; disembarkees pawed for their belongings and tried to make sense of the delicate, coughing talk of the unchurched little drivers. On the other side of the valley, across the creek, the real ridge line—the *geology*, her father would have said disdainfully—stabbed upstream. By her rough estimation it had rolled perhaps two degrees off the angle of its writ mapping. Lucas would determine the exact discrepancy later, when he extracted his instruments from their feather and wax paper wrappings.

"Third world *bullshit*," Lucas said, walking up to her. "The transit services people from the university paid these little schemers before we ever climbed onto that deathtrap, and now they're asking for the fare." Lucas had been raised near the border, right outside the last town the bus had stopped at, in fact, though he'd dismissed the notion of visiting any family. His patience with the locals ran inverse to his familiarity with them.

"Does this count as the third world?" she asked him. "Doesn't there have to be a general for that? Rain forests and steel ruins?"

Lucas gave his half-grin—not quite a smirk—acknowledging her reduction. Cartographers were famous for their willful ignorance of social expressions like politics and history.

"Carmen paid them, anyway," he told her as they walked towards their group. "Probably out of her own pocket, thanks be for wealthy dilettantes."

"Not fair," said Sandy. "She's as sharp as any student in the seminar, and a better hand with the plotter than most post-docs, much less grad students."

Lucas stopped. "I hate that," he said quietly. "I hate when you separate yourself; go out of your way to remind me that you're a teacher and I'm a student."

Sandy said the same thing she always did. "I hate when you forget it."

Against all odds, they were still meeting the timetable they'd drawn up back at the university, all those months ago. The bus pulled away in a cloud of noxious diesel fumes an hour before dark, leaving its passengers in a muddy camp dotted with fire rings but otherwise marked only by a hand lettered sign pointing the way to a primitive latrine.

The handful of passengers not connected with Sandy's group had melted into the forest as soon as they'd found their packages. ("Salt and sugar," Lucas had said. "They're backwoods people—hedge shamans and survivalists. There's every kind of lunatic out here.") This left Sandy to stand by and pretend authority while the Forestry graduate student whose services she'd borrowed showed them all how to set up their camps.

Carmen, naturally, had convinced the young man to demonstrate tent pitching to the others using her own expensive rig as an example. The olive-skinned girl sat in a camp chair folding an onionskin scroll back on itself and writing in a wood-bound notebook while the others struggled with canvas and willow poles.

"Keeping track of our progress?" Sandy asked, easing herself onto the ground next to Carmen.

"I have determined," Carmen replied, not looking up, "that we have traveled as far from a hot water heater as is possible and still be within Christendom."

Sandy smiled, but shook her head, thinking of the most remote places she'd ever been. "Davis?" she asked, watching her student's reaction to mention of that unholy town.

Carmen, a Californian, shuddered but kept her focus. "There's a naval base in San Francisco, sí? They've got all the amenities, surely."

Sandy considered again, thinking of cold camps in old mountains, and of muddy jungle towns ten days' walk from the closest bus station.

"Cape Canaveral," she said.

With quick, precise movements, Carmen folded a tiny desktop over her chair's arm and spread her scroll out flat. She drew a pair of calipers out from her breast pocket and took measurements, pausing once to roll the scroll a few turns. Finally, she gave a satisfied smile and said, "Only 55 miles from Orlando. We're almost twice that from Louisville."

She'd made the mistake Sandy had expected of her. "But Orlando, Señorita Reyes, is Catholic. And we were speaking of Christendom."

A stricken look passed over her student's face, but Sandy calmed her with exaggerated conspiratorial looks left and right. "Some of your fellows aren't so liberal as I am, Carmen. So remember where you are. Remember *who* you are. Or who you're trying to become."

Another reminder issued, Sandy went to see to her own tent.

The Forestry student gathered their wood, brought them water to reconstitute their freeze-dried camp meals, then withdrew to his own tent far back in the trees. Sandy told him he was welcome to spend the evening around their fire—"You built it after all," she'd said—but he'd made a convincing excuse.

The young man pointed to the traveling shrine her students had erected in the center of their camp, pulling a wooden medallion from beneath his shirt. "That Christ you have over there, ma'am," he said. "He's not this one, is he?"

Sandy looked at the amulet he held, gilded and green. "What do you have there, Jesus in the Trees?" she asked, summoning all her professional courtesy to keep the amusement out of her voice. "No, that's not the Christ we keep. We'll see you in the morning."

They didn't, though, because later that night, Lucas discovered that the forest they were camped in wasn't supposed to be there at all.

He'd found an old agricultural map somewhere and packed it in with their little traveling library. Later, he admitted that he'd only pulled it out for study because he was still sulking from Sandy's clear signal he wouldn't be sharing her tent that night.

Sandy had been leading the rest of the students in some prayers and thought exercises when Lucas came up with his mouldering old quarto. "Tillage," he said, not even bothering to explain himself before he'd foisted the book off on his nearest fellow. "All the acreage this side of the ridge line is supposed to be under tillage."

Sandy narrowed her eyes, more than enough to quiet any of her charges, much less Lucas. "What's he got there, Ford?" she asked the thin undergraduate who now held the book.

"Hmmmm?" said the boy; he was one of those who fell instantly and almost irretrievably into any text and didn't look up. Then, at an elbow from Carmen, he said, "Oh! This is ... " He turned the book over in his hands, angled the spine toward one of the oil lamps and read, "This is *An Agricultural Atlas of Clark County, Kentucky*."

"'County?'" said Carmen. "*Old* book, Lucas."

"But it's *writ*," said Lucas. "There's nothing superseding the details of it and it doesn't contradict anything else we brought about the error. Hell, it even confirms the error we came to correct." Involuntarily, all of them looked up and over at the apostate ridge.

"But what's this about tillage," Sandy said, giving him the opportunity to show off his find even if was already clear to her what it must be.

"See, these plot surveys in the appendices didn't get accounted for in the literature survey we're working from. The book's listed as a source, but only as a supplemental confirmation. It's not just the ridge that's wrong, it's the stuff growing down this side, too. We're supposed to be in grain fields of some kind down here in the flats, then it's pasturage on up to the summit line."

A minor find, sure, but Sandy would see that Lucas shared authorship on the corollary she'd file with the university. More importantly, it was an opportunity before the hard work of the days ahead.

"We can't do anything about the hillsides tonight, or any of the acreage beyond the creek," she told them. "But as for these glades here ..."

It was a simple exercise. The fires were easily set.

In the morning, Sandy drafted a letter to the Dean of Agriculture while most of her students packed up the camp. She had detailed a few of them to sketch the corrected valley floor around them, and she'd include those visual notes with her instructions to the Dean, along with a copy of the writ map from Lucas's book.

"Read that back to me, Carmen," she said, watching as Lucas and Ford argued over yet another volume, this one slim and bound between paper boards. It was the same back country cartographer's guide she'd carried on her own first wilderness forays as a grad student. They'd need its detailed instructions on living out of doors without the Tree Jesus boy to help them.

"'By my hand,'" read Carmen, "'I have caused these letters to be writ. Blessings on the Department of Agriculture and on you, Dean. Blessings on Jesus Sower, the Christ you serve.'"

"Skip to the end, dear." Sandy had little patience for the formalities of academic correspondence, and less for the pretense at holiness the Agriculturalists made with their little fruiting Christ.

"'So, then, it is seen in these texts that Cartography has corrected the error so far as in our power, and now the burden is passed to you and your brethren to complete this holy task, and return the land to that of Jesus's vision.'" Carmen paused. "Then you promise to remember the Dean in your prayers and all the rest of the politesse."

"Good. Everything observed. Make two copies and bring the original to me for sealing when you're done."

Carmen turned to her work and Sandy to hers. The ashen landscape extending up the valley was still except for some ribbons twisting in a light breeze. The ribbons were wax sealed to the parchment banner her students had set at first light, the new map of the valley floor drawn in red and black against a cream background. Someone had found the the blackened disc of the Forestry student's medallion and leaned it against the base of the banner's staff and Sandy wondered if it had been Carmen, prone to sentiment, or perhaps Lucas, prone to vague gestures.

By midmorning, the students had readied their gear for the march up the ridge line and Carmen had dropped Sandy's package for the university in the mailbox by the bus stop. Before they hoisted their backpacks, though, Sandy gathered them all for fellowship and prayer.

"The gymnasiums at the university have made us fit enough for this task," and here she made a playful flex with her left arm, earning rolled eyes from Lucas and a chuckle from the rest. "The libraries have given us the woodscraft we need, and the chapels have given us the sustenance of our souls."

Sandy swept her arm north to south, indicating the ridge. "When I was your age, oh so long ago—" and a pause here for another ripple of laughter, acknowledgment of her dual status as youngest tenured faculty member at the university and youngest ordained minister in the curia. "When I was your age, I was blessed with the opportunity to go to the Northeast, traveling the lands beyond the Susquehanna, searching out error."

Sandy smiled at the memory of those times—*could they be ten years gone already?* "I traveled with men and women strong in the Lord, soldiers and scholars of God. There are many errors in the Northeast."

*Maps so brittle with age that they would flake away in the cold winds of the Adirondack passes, so faded that only the mightiest of prayers would reveal Jesus's true intentions for His world.*

"But none here in the heartlands of the Church, right? Isn't that what our parish priests told us growing up?" The students recognized that she was beginning to teach and nodded, murmured assent.

"Christians, there *is* error here. There is error right before our eyes!" Her own students weren't a difficult congregation to hook, but she was gratified nonetheless by the gleam she caught in most of their eyes, the calls, louder now, of "Yes!" and "I see it! I see the lie!"

"I laid down my protractor, friends, I know exactly how far off north Jesus mapped this ridge line to lay," she said, sweeping her arm in a great arc, taking in the whole horizon, "and that ridge line sins by two degrees!"

"May as well be two *hundred*!" said Carmen, righteous.

Sandy raised her hand, stopped them at the cusp of celebration instead of loosing them. "Not yet," she said. "It's tonight. It's tonight we'll sing down the glory, tonight we'll make this world the way it was mapped."

The march up the ridge line did not go as smoothly as Sandy might have wished, but the delays and false starts weren't totally unexpected. She'd known Lucas—a country boy after all—would take the lead, and she'd guessed that he would dead-end them into a crumbling gully or two before he picked the right route through the brambles. If he'd been some kind of natural-born hunter he would never have found his way to the Lord, or to education.

Ford and his friends—all of them destined for lecture halls and libraries, not fieldwork—made the classic, the *predicted* mistake she'd specifically warned against in the rubric she'd distributed for the expedition. "If we're distributing 600 pounds of necessities across twenty-two packs," she asked Ford, walking easily beside him as he struggled along a game trail, "how much weight does that make each of us responsible for?"

"A little over twenty-seven pounds, ma'am," he said, wheezing out the reply.

"And did you calculate that in your head like a mathematician or did you remember it from the syllabus?" Sandy asked. She didn't press too hard, the harshness of the lesson was better imparted by the straps cutting into his shoulders than by her words.

"I remembered it," Ford said. And because he really did have the makings of a great scholar and great scholars are nothing if not owners of their own errors, he added, "It was in the same paragraph that said not to bring too many books."

"Exactly," she said, untying the leather cords at the top of his pack and pulling out a particularly heavy looking volume. She couldn't resist looking at the title page before dropping it into her own pack.

"*Unchurched Tribes of the Chiapas Highlands: A Bestiary.* Think we'll make it to Mexico on this trip, Ford?" she asked him, teasing a little.

Ford's faced reddened even more from her attention than it had from the exertions of the climb. He mumbled something about migratory patterns then leaned into the hike.

If most of the students were meeting their expectations of themselves and one another, then Carmen's sprightly, sure-footed bounding up the trail was a surprise to most. Sandy, though, had seen the girl in the gym far more frequently than the other students, most of whom barely met the minimum number of visits per week required by their advising committees. Carmen was as much an athlete as herself, and the lack of concern the girl showed about dirt and insects was refreshing.

So it was Carmen who summitted first, and it was her that was looking northeast with a stunned expression on her face when Sandy and Lucas reached the top side by side. Following Carmen's gaze,

Lucas cursed and called for help in taking off his heavily laden pack before he began unrolling the oilcloth cases of his instruments.

Sandy simply pursed her lips and began a mental review of her assets: the relative strengths and weaknesses of her students, the number of days worth of supplies they carried, the nature of the curia-designed instruments that Lucas exhibited a natural affinity for controlling. She began to nod. She'd marshaled more than enough strength for the simple tectonic adjustment they'd planned, she could set her own unquestionable faith against this new challenge if it revealed any deficiencies among her students. She would make a show of asking their opinions, but she already knew that this was a challenge she could meet.

Ford finally reached the top of the ridge line, not so much climbing as stumbling to the rocky area where the others were gathering. Once he looked up and around, he said, "The survey team that found the error in the ridge's orientation, they didn't come up here."

"They were specifically scouting for projects that the university could handle," said Sandy. "If they'd been up here, they would have called in the Mission Service, not us."

Spread out below them, ringed in tilled fields and dusted with a scattering of wooden fishing boats, was an unmapped lake.

Sandy set Ford and the other bookish scholars to cataloguing all of the texts they'd smuggled along so they could be integrated into her working bibliography. She hoped that one of them was currently distracted by waterways the way that Ford was distracted by fauna.

Lucas set their observation instruments on tripods in an acceptably devout semicircle and Sandy permitted two or three of the others to begin preliminary sight-line measurements of the lake's extent.

"It turns my stomach," said Lucas, peering through the brass tube of a field glass. "I grew up seeing the worst kind of blasphemy, but I could never imagine that anyone could do something like this."

"You need to work on that," said Sandy. Lucas was talking about the landscape feature crosshaired in the glass, a clearly artificial earth-works dam, complete with a retractable spillway. "Missionaries see worse every day."

Lucas didn't react. He'd never abandoned his ambition, even after she'd laughed him down. *Our sisters and brothers in the Mission Service*, she'd said with the authority that only someone who'd left that order could muster, *make up in the pretense of zeal what they lack in scholarship and access to the divine. Anyone can move a mountain with whips and shovels.*

The sketchers showed her their work, which they annotated with Lucas's count and codification of architectural structures, fence lines, and crops. "Those are corn cribs," he said. "That's a meeting house. That's a mill."

This was the kind of thing she'd told him he should concentrate on. The best thing any of them had to offer was the overlay of their own personal ranges of unexpected expertise onto the vast body of accepted Cartography. Lucas's barbaric background, Ford's holographic memory, Carmen's cultured scribing. Her own judgment.

"They're *marmotas*!" said Ford. They all looked up at where he'd been awkwardly turning the focus wheel on one of the glasses. "Like in my book!" He wasn't one to flash a triumphant grin, which Sandy appreciated. She assented to the line of inquiry with a nod and he hurried over to the makeshift shelf that some of his friends had been using to stack books while they wrote their list.

The unchurched all looked alike to Sandy, differing only in the details of their dress, modes of transportation, and to what extent the curia allowed interaction with them. In the case of the little drivers, for example, tacit permission was given for commercial exchange because of their ancient control of the bus lines. But she'd never heard of *marmotas*, and said so.

"They're called 'rooters' around here," said Lucas. "I don't know what Ford's on about. I've never heard of them having a lake, but they've always come into the villages with their vegetables, so far as I know."

"Not always," said Carmen. "There's nothing about any unchurched lineages in the glosses of the maps we're working from. They're as new as that lake."

Sandy recognized that they were in an educable moment. "Everybody come here, let's meet. Let's have a class."

The students maneuvered themselves into the flatter ground within the horseshoe of instruments, spreading blankets and pulling out notebooks and pens. Ford lay his bestiary out, a place marked about a third of the way through with the bright yellow fan of a fallen gingko leaf.

"Carmen's brought up a good point," said Sandy, after they'd opened with a prayer. "There's no cartographical record of these diggers, or whatever they're called, along the ridge line."

"I don't think it matters, necessarily, though," said Carmen. "There's no record of the road up to the bus stop, either, or of Lucas's village. 'Towns and roads are thin scrims, and outside our purview.'"

Sandy recognized the quote as being from the autobiography of a radical cleric intermittently popular on campus. It was far from writ, but not heretical by any stretch of the imagination and, besides, she'd had her own enthusiasms for colorful doctrinal interpretations when she was younger. She was disappointed that Carmen would let her tendency toward error show so plainly to the others but let it pass, confident that one of the more conservative students would address it.

"Road building doesn't affect landscape?" asked Lucas, on cue. "The Mapmaker *used* road builders to cut canyons all over the continent. Ford, maybe Carmen needs to see the cutlines on your contour maps of the bus routes."

Before Ford, who was looking somewhat embarrassed by the exchange, could reply, Carmen said, "I'm not talking about the Mapmaker, Lucas, I'm talking about your *family*, back in the village we passed yesterday."

"Easy, Carmen," said Sandy. "We're getting off task here. The question at hand isn't *whether* there's error. The error is clear. We can feel the moisture of it on the breeze blowing up the hill right now." Time to shift directions on them, to turn them on the right path before they could think about it.

"The question," she continued, "is how much of it we plan to correct." Not *whether* they'd correct, don't leave that option for them. The debate she'd let them have was over the degree of action they'd take, not whether they'd take any at all.

The more sophisticated among them—Ford and Carmen sure, but even Lucas, to his credit—instantly saw her tack and looked at her with eyebrows raised. Then Lucas reverted to type and actually dared to say something.

"We haven't prepared for anything like this. That lake is more than a mile across at its broadest!"

"A mile across, yes," said Sandy, dismissively. "Carmen? What scale did you draw your sketch of the valley in?"

Carmen handed her a sheaf of papers. "24K to one. Is that all right?"

"Good, good," said Sandy. She smiled at Ford. "That's a conversion even I can do in my head. So ... if I compare the size of the *dam*—" and she knitted her eyebrows, calculating. "If I compare the dam to the ridge, I see that the ridge we came to move is about three hundred times the larger."

Everyone began talking at once and at cross purposes. A gratifying number of the students were simply impressed with her cleverness and seemed relaxed, sure that it would be a simple matter now that they'd been shown the problem in the proper perspective. But Carmen was scratching some numbers in the dirt with the knuckle of her right index finger and Ford was flipping through the appendix of one of his books and Lucas ...

Lucas stood and looked down over the valley. He wasn't looking at the lake and the dam, though, or even at the village of the unchurched creatures who had built it. He was looking to his right, down the eastern flank of the ridge they stood on, down the fluvial valley towards where, it suddenly occurred to Sandy, he'd grown up, towards the creek side town they'd stopped in the day before.

Ford raised his voice above an argument he'd been having with two or three others. "Isn't there a question about what that much water will do to the topography downstream? I mean, I know hydrology's a pretty knotty problem, theologically speaking, but we'd have a clear hand in the erosion, wouldn't we? What if the floodwaters subside off ground that's come unwrit because of something that we did?"

"That *is* a knotty problem, Ford," said Sandy, looking Lucas straight in the eye. "What's the best way to solve a difficult knot?"

And it was Lucas who answered her, nodding. "Cut through it."

Later, while most of the students were meditating in advance of the ceremony, Sandy saw Carmen moving from glass to glass, making minute focusing adjustments and triangulating different views of the lake and the village. Every so often, she made a quick visual note in her sketchbook.

"It's not productive to spend too much time on the side effects of an error, you know," Sandy said.

Carmen moved from one instrument to the next. "I don't think it's all that easy to determine what's a side effect and what's ... okay," she said.

Sandy had lost good students to the distraction she could see now in Carmen. She reached out and pivoted the cylinder down, so that its receiving lens pointed straight at the ground. "There's nothing to see down there, Carmen."

Carmen wouldn't meet her eye. "I thought I'd record—"

"Nothing to see, nothing to record. If you could go down and talk to them you wouldn't understand a word they say. If you looked in their little huts you wouldn't find anything redemptive; there's no cross hanging in the wall of the meeting house, no Jesus of the Digging Marmots. When the water is drained, we won't see anything along the lake bed but mud and whatever garbage they've thrown in off their docks. The lake doesn't have any secrets to give up. You know that."

"Ford's books—"

"Ford's books are by anthropologists, who are halfway to being witch doctors as far as most respectable scholars are concerned, and who keep their accreditation by dint of the fact that their field notes are good intelligence sources for the Mission Service. Ford reads them because he's got an overactive imagination and he likes stories too much—lots of students in the archive concentration have those failings. Most of them grow out of it with a little coaxing. Like Ford will, he's too smart not to. Just like *you're* too smart to backslide into your parents' religion and start looking for souls to save where there are no souls to be found."

Carmen took a deep breath and held it, closed her eyes. When she opened them, her expression had folded into acquiescence. "It is not the least of my sins that I force you to spend so much time counseling me, Reverend," she said formally.

Sandy smiled and gave the girl a friendly squeeze of the shoulder. "Curiosity and empathy are healthy, and valuable, señorita," she said. "But you need to remember that there are proper channels to focus these things into. Prayer and study are best, but drinking and carousing will do in a pinch."

Carmen gave a nervous laugh, eyes widening. Sandy could tell that the girl didn't feel entirely comfortable with the unexpected direction of the conversation, which was, of course, part of the strategy for handling backsliders. Young people in particular were easy to refocus on banal and harmless "sins" and away from thoughts that could actually be dangerous.

"Fetch the others up here, now," Sandy said. "We should set to it."

Carmen soon had all twenty of her fellow students gathered around Sandy. Lucas had been down the eastern slope far enough to gather some deadwood and now he struck it ablaze with a flint and steel from his travel kit. Sandy crumbled a handful of incense into the flames.

Ford had been named the seminar's lector by consensus, and he opened his text. "Blessed are the Mapmakers ... " he said.

"For they hunger and thirst after righteousness," they all finished.

Then they all fell to prayer and singing. Sandy turned her back to them—congregants more than students now—and opened her heart to the land below her. She felt the effrontery of the unmapped lake like a caul over her face, a restriction on the land that prevented breath and life.

Sandy showed them how to test the prevailing winds and how to bank the censers in chevrons so that the cleansing fires would fall onto the appropriate points along the dam.

Finally, she thumbed an ashen symbol onto every wrist and forehead, including her own, and lit the oils of the censer *primorus* with a prayer. When the hungry flames began to beam outward from her censer, she softly repeated the prayer for emphasis, then nodded her assent that the rest begin.

The dam did not burst in a spectacular explosion of mud and boulders and waters. Instead, it atrophied throughout the long afternoon, wearing away under their prayers even as their voices grew hoarse. Eventually, the dammed river itself joined its voice to theirs and speeded the correction.

The unchurched in the valley tried for a few hours to pull their boats up onto the shore, but the muddy expanse between the water and their lurching docks grew too quickly. They turned their attention to bundling up the goods from their mean little houses then, and soon a line of them was snaking deeper into the mountains to the east, like a line of ants fleeing a hill beneath a looking glass.

With the ridge to its west, the valley fell into evening shadow long before the cartographers' camp. They could still see below though, they could see that, as Sandy had promised Carmen, there were no secrets revealed by the dying water.

**Christopher Rowe** has been a finalist for the Hugo, Nebula, World Fantasy and Theodore Sturgeon Awards. His stories have been frequently reprinted, translated into a half-dozen languages around the world, and praised by the *New York Times Book Review*.

His early fiction was collected in a chapbook, *Bittersweet Creek and Other Stories*, by Small Beer Press. His first novel, *Sandstorm*, was published by Wizards of the Coast in 2011. He is a student at the Bluegrass Writers Studio, the MFA program of Eastern Kentucky University, and lives in a hundred-year-old house in Lexington, Kentucky, with his wife, novelist Gwenda Bond.

# Terry Bisson
# on Christopher Rowe

I remember this guy.

Every Clarion class arrives festooned with favorites. Instructors whisper. Watch this one, or that one. One special talent or two at most; the ones to watch out for, already slinging sparks. The ones with flash or promise, the ones who sparkle or strut, who wear their guns outside their pants for all the honest world to feel.

Rowe wasn't one of these. But we shared an accent and an origin: he was a fellow Kentuckian, a country boy really, with a modesty that marked a certain self assurance. A bit of a rube, a bit of a gentleman; a familiar and comfortable mix in the Upper Mid South. So I noticed him. Maybe even worried about him a little. Because I knew what he was after. Not simply fame or fortune or the agreeable ability to astonish or please readers, but a life in literature. A fool's errand perhaps but a familiar one, to me at least.

What instructors like best are students with shopworn ideas and clunky needy prose, colorfulish characters, plywood dialogue: grist for the workshop to mill. Clarion is stingy with these, but a precious few are always provided.

Rowe wasn't one of these either. He already knew how to tell a story, and had the words to tell it with. He was in the top rank from jump, and quite comfortable being there. Already quite publishable, thank you. I could see not only talent but ability, not only ambition but the boldness to run with it. Generous with his peers, all he needed to develop was ruthlessness with his own work. And his knives were already pretty sharp.

He didn't waste any time. Today, greedily anthologized, he's in the top rank of SF's short-form stars. His strong suit is one that I feel Clarion helped encourage. Rowe understands that what you leave out is what makes what you leave in work. As this lean but expansive little story shows.

So I was right. (I sometimes am.) But enough about me.

Let us pray.

**Terry Bisson** is primarily known for his Hugo and Nebula Award winning science fiction short stories. He also writes novels, screenplays, comics, and non-fiction. Other projects include co-authoring "Car Talk" with NPR's Click and Clack. He lives in Oakland, California, where he hosts a monthly author reading series in San Francisco.

# The Adventures of Captain Black Heart Wentworth

## A Nautical Tail

Rachel Swirsky

2005

### I. Burial at Sea

With a splash, the body of Cracked Mack the Lack went overboard. Captain Black Heart Wentworth, Rat Pirate of the Gully by the Oak, stared after Mack into the turgid brown waters. Wentworth's first mate, Whiskers Sullivan of the beady eyes and greedy paws, slunk deckside, muttering madly about the pitter patter of fleas rushing along his spine so loud he couldn't sleep or shit or make water—and when a rat can't shit or make water, tis a dark day indeed.

Cracked Mack the Lack had been the last of their dastardly crew. Sully'd found him that morning, gone tail over snout in the stern. Arsenic done him in. Mack had a taste for it, reminded him of that crack in the wall called home when papa took the boys out of a morning to learn their way in the world: how to tweak a cat's whiskers and pry cheese from between spring-loaded jaws. Now Mack was gone, wrapped in a spider web shroud to decay in his watery grave.

"We two rat jacks is all that's left," Wentworth said to Sully. "A ship with but two pirates is hardly a pirate ship at all."

Sully swiveled one ear toward his captain's voice. He scratched his head with his back foot.

"Tis time for a new mission," said Wentworth. "This old girl's been plundering these shores since you and I were press-ganged pups. We coarsened our hair on this route. Its bounty allowed our balls to grow low and pendulous.

"But now, I say, enough! Enough of hustling gulls, robbing their garbage as if twas treasure. Enough of gobbling eggs and spooking minnows. Like our venerable ancestors who carried the plague across Europe on their backs, we must spread our scourge throughout the seven seas! You hark?"

Sully scrabbled in circles, claws scratching on leaf-planks. His naked tail whipped; his beady eyes sparkled; his snout raised to sniff the invigorating maritime breeze. Whether he danced for joy or to exorcise the demon fleas what haunted him was anyone's guess.

## II. Launch

Wentworth oversaw the repairs which would see them off to parts unknown. Finest acorns restocked the cannon. Deadfall to replank the deck was collected from the base of the Great Oak on the riverbank, the tree with bark too slick for any cat to climb, where ancestral rats had taken refuge through dark winters. Fresh twigs, roots, and tubers replaced the rotting hull, bound together with whiskers plucked from captured hounds. The old anchor was replaced with a ripe plum, plucked from a pie still cooling on the windowsill belonging to the tabby Sharp Tooth. Under Wentworth's supervision, Sully secured the fruit to a catgut line and dropped it to the riverbottom.

As for the ragged pelts hanging from the fishspine mast, Wentworth ordered them taken down.

"Tis the banner of death what sees us off," said Wentworth. "Our flag should be the same."

Wentworth ordered that a black squirrel should be caught and skinned, one with fur fine as the down on a mother rat's breast and dark as Wentworth's withered heart. Muttering and grumbling, Sully hunted squirrels through the windswept grass. He cornered his quarry near the briar patch, ignoring the squirrel's prayers and promises. He dispatched the creature merciful quick: with but an exhalation of Sully's fetid breath, the squirrel perished.

They hung the pelt—skull and femurs attached—and prepared to launch.

In the stern, Sully stood watch, grumbling to his fleas. Standing at the snail-shell wheel, Wentworth opened the rusty trunk that had belonged to the captain before him, and the captain before him. He pulled out an ancient map. Looking to the overhanging stars, he guided the ship toward a place marked in the shaking script of a rat close to death: The Open Seas.

The ship plunged through dark waters, ghastly sail billowing in the wind, black-furred tail trailing behind them like the hem of death's own garment. Above hung the moon, green as finest rotting cheese.

### III. Battle

Dawn rose over the water, shards of reflected orange and rose mingling with foam. The ship bobbed through the estuary leading into the sea. Frogs and toads leapt, squelching, through the mud. Sully drew his scimitar to teach the tadpoles a thing or two about pirates, but Wentworth stayed his hand. "Wait til they have legs. Tis fair play," he advised.

Midmorning waters deepened to cobalt. Sully filled his tin cup and used the water to salt his dried meat ration. The treeline thinned to a distant green fringe.

"At last, the sea," said Wentworth. "I feel its goodness deep in my piratical bones."

Sully appeared to agree, or at least the mad twinkle brightened in his eye.

In the afternoon, they caught sight of a duck followed by a line of puffy yellow ducklings.

"Stand down!" shouted Wentworth, brandishing his sword. "We demand treasure! Give us your eggs and nest lining! Lay algae and water bugs at our feet."

The duck turned a matte eye on him and gave an uncomprehending honk.

"A rebel, eh?" Wentworth turned to Sully. "To the cannons, rat!"

The first shot fired across mama's feathered bow. She flapped her wings, but surrendered no treasure.

"Down the fleet!" ordered Wentworth.

The cannon boomed. One, two, three fluffy chicks disappeared into a puff of yellow feathers. Mama honked her outrage. She flew at the ship, pecking the prow. The ship careened beneath ardent avian assault. The whittled ears of the rat maiden figurehead snapped free. Wentworth ducked as they crashed around his head. Sully slammed against the hull and slumped.

"Retreat!" shouted Wentworth. He scrambled over Sullivan's unconscious form and wrenched the wheel to the left. The ship veered. The duck flapped after them, feet dragging in the waves, then skidded back to her remaining youngsters.

### IV. Uncharted Waters

Sully plucked splinters from his fur. "No lasting damage, eh?" said Wentworth.

They sailed til the water turned the steely grey of their swords. Overhead, web-winged creatures wheeled through the sky. "Wok, wok," they called, "Jabberwock."

Sully tested the depths by dropping anchor. The catgut line unspooled til it broke.

Wentworth went to fill his flask and found the supply of good brisk drink had pitched overboard. Ah, and the water barrels were gone, too.

He found Sully perched on the side of the boat, fishing with the broken catgut line. "We're to die out here," said Wentworth. "There's no booze left and no water neither."

Something tugged at Sully's line. He staggered back to ho-heave-ho.

Up on deck came a-sprawling a strange creature with a fish's bright green tail and the furry, cherubic face of a rat maid not long weaned.

"My whiskers," said Wentworth, "a merrat!"

She was slender for a ratly creature, but huge for a fish. Where her fur merged into scales, it flushed deep emerald like a branch giving way to leaves. Six pink shells covered the delights of her nipples.

Fancies of seduction raced through Wentworth's brain. Sully had other ideas. Drawing his saber, he slashed her tender throat. Her dying squeak rose high above her thumping death throes.

That evening they dined on roast fish while Sully wove himself a coat from the merrat's fur. Twas too close to cannibalism for Wentworth's gut, but a mad rat like Sullivan would slay his mother for her pelt.

"You're a cruel rat, Sully," said Wentworth.

Sully looked up, whiskers twitching. Wentworth could almost see the fleas rushing through his fur.

"Maybe your fleas'll move from your pelt to hers," suggested Wentworth.

Laughter danced in the inky wells of Sully's eyes. Baring the yellowed squares of his teeth, he ripped off a chunk of the merrat's pelt and threaded the needle he'd carved of her bone.

On the horizon, Wentworth glimpsed a white tentacle glowing in the pale dusk. "A monster! Rat your station! It's like to be guarding a hoard."

### V. Here There Be Krakens

Wentworth ordered Sullivan to quiet their running. They cut silently through darkening waters, hushed as a coward's footsteps.

They sailed round the tentacle like a peninsula, for twas almost as massive. Suckers big as pampered housecats pulsed, tasting the briny air.

"We'll sail to its center," Wentworth told Sullivan. "I'd lay ingots the beast's treasure lies near its heart."

The monster's head rose from the ocean like the great white dome of a cathedral. It was garbed in seaweed and encrusted with barnacles. A vast obsidian eye stared with diffuse gaze at the horizon.

Wentworth fetched his best harpoon, point honed to the soul of sharpness, and aimed at the creature. He threw strong, but false. His harpoon sank into the waves.

The wind of its passing woke the monster. Its great, murky eye flashed alert. The massive head reared, barnacles snapping off and falling into the sea. A tentacle crashed across the ship, knocking the wheel askew. A second wrapped Wentworth in its sinuous grip.

Undaunted, Wentworth drew his dagger and hacked away. Green blood burned Wentworth's fur and sprayed across the ocean surface like oil. The tentacle pulsed with pain, squeezing tighter. At last, Wentworth hacked the tentacle through and thumped onto the deck.

Behind him, Sully led another tentacle in circles. It wrapped around the fishspine mast like a maypole.

Wentworth dashed to Sully's side. "Faster! Faster!" he called.

They whirled in a merry, desperate dance. The tentacle spiraled tighter and tighter 'til white flesh strained.

"Keep running her round," shouted Wentworth. He ran to the merrat's corpse where Sully's half-sewn coat lay, wet and bedraggled. He heaved the coat toward the mast.

Feeling coarse, soaked rat fur, the monster grasped and pulled. The mast came loose in its formidable grip. It dragged both pelt and mast toward gaping maw, stabbing its throat with splintered fish spine. Green blood spurted. It began to sink.

Doused in burning blood, Wentworth and Sullivan danced a celebratory jig. Over the noise of massive tentacles sliding into the water, the pirates heard a female's distressed wail.

"Help! Help!"

## VI. Rescue

A pea-green skipper floated beside the nearest tentacle, in danger of being submerged in its wake. Wentworth directed Sullivan to the wheel. "Swiftly, rat," he ordered, buttoning his waistcoat.

They veered toward the small vessel, its deck obscured by churning waters. Wentworth knotted the catgut line and threw it down.

What vision of loveliness awaited them? Wentworth wondered. A sleek sable tail-swinger with cherry-red eyes? A midnight-furred scrambler with whiskers fine as dandelion fluff?

He felt a hitch in the catgut line as the fair maiden trusted her weight to him. "Thank you, kind sir," said she, coming into view: a green-eyed, ginger-coated, ravishing damsel of a ... cat.

## VII. Dinner at the Captain's Table

They gathered round a knotted pine table stolen from a child's dollhouse. Oil lamps fueled by finest seal fat cast orange light across their repast of roast fish and "recycled" water.

"Avoid the drink," Wentworth advised their guest. "'Tis less than potable."

The cat pulled a flask from her lacy garter. "I come supplied for all occasions." Feline she might be, but she still seemed a lady, bonnet and petticoat pristine. "Gin. Would you like a snifter?"

Wentworth grunted. Was it his imagination or had Sullivan polished the bones on his necklace? Did his flea-ridden fur seem fluffier from, perhaps, a mid-ocean bath?

"I'm Pussy La Chat," said the ginger jezebel. "My story is terrible sad. A fortnight ago, I set off with my bridegroom hoping to be married by the turkey on the hill. Alas, now, my love is gone, and I'm alone." She smiled demurely. Lamplight could not help but glisten on her fangs. "How lucky I am to have found two strong sailors."

She set her paw on the table. Wentworth noted the fetching white sock on her foreleg.

Now Wentworth came to think of it, her tail had a rather shapely curve, and her green eyes—well, was not green the color of leaves and grass and cool spring meadows?

"Lucky and lovely," he agreed.

Sullivan glared jealously at his Captain.

"I wonder," said Pussy, voice honeyed with purr, "if I might join your crew. Weak though I am, perhaps I could be of some small assistance."

"That could be arranged."

"Purrfect."

Wentworth loosened his ascot. "Would you care to join me for a moonlight stroll?"

"Would that I could, Captain, but I find myself accounted for this evening." Pussy perked her ears. "Your first mate has offered to show me the constellations. Perhaps another time?"

Sullivan offered his arm to the feline intruder. She *mrrowwed*, fur ruffling prettily along her back. Oh, Wentworth had seen the signs of love before. How fast women fell. How illogical and intractable their affections.

He drained his goblet. Blast. He shouldn't have let Sully slay the merrat.

## VIII. A Better Battle

Pussy spotted the galleon. "A nautical masterpiece," said Wentworth, admiring the five masts and graceful lateen sail. Plump, well-dressed hamsters bustled along deck.

"To the cannons!" called Wentworth.

Sully paused, shoulders hunched.

"To the cannons!" Wentworth repeated. "Are you a rat or a mouse?"

Hesitantly, Pussy licked her paw. "Your first mate has regaled me with your adventures," she began. "Your aggressive strategy, while admirable, may not be wise."

"Is that what Sully said?"

Under his Captain's betrayed gaze, Sullivan slunk away.

"Innovation is a sailor's way!" Pussy continued. "Else we'd all sail battered skiffs, like me and my poor bridegroom." She sniffed, dabbing her eye.

Wentworth tugged down his waistcoat. "What's your suggestion?"

"Deception!" Pussy licked her chops. "Good nautical men are always eager to assist their fellow voyagers."

"As we assisted you?"

"Our mast is gone. Our figurehead broken. I must say, we're quite a sight."

Grudgingly, Wentworth assented. He and Sullivan secreted themselves beneath the fallen sail, awaiting Pussy's signal.

"We must not allow Pussy to come between us," whispered Wentworth. "We're pirates. We kill without remorse. We do not romance. You hark?"

Sully pricked his ears.

"Good."

Dimly, they heard the galleon nearing. Pussy called, "Oh, sirs! Alack and alas, my ship has been caught in a storm, and all hands lost save me! Help, help!"

In low squeaks, the hamsters considered their options. "What's she worth in salvage?" "We'll get but a pittance for the leaves." "But a gross for the wheel!" Planks creaked as they boarded.

"Now!" shouted Pussy.

Wentworth and Sullivan dashed out, sabers flashing. The merchant's captain drew a fancy fencing foil. "I'll save you, milady!" he shouted. Pussy devoured him in a gulp.

A pretentious poof of a hamster flung a knife at Pussy's tail. Fast as a hopping mad flea, Sully chopped off the fellow's whiskers, tail, and head.

Wentworth made short work of the other quivering wretches. Those who surrendered were marched off the plank with a satisfying splash.

Wentworth surveyed the tatters of his once-sturdy vessel. He turned to the galleon. "The time's come to jump ship."

## IX. Treasure at Last

"Pearls!" said Pussy. "Rubies!"

"Sapphires, gold, tea and tin." Wentworth rushed between over-flowing trunks. "We're rich, rich, rich!"

He tossed a handful of gems, dancing in their glittering fall. "Ow."

Pussy turned. "What's wrong?"

Sully returned from exploring the ship's bowels, brandishing a master-crafted, jewel-encrusted sword—yet twas the object in Sully's other paw that caught Wentworth's eye.

Wentworth relieved Sullivan of the vintage wine. "Nothing," he said. "Nothing at all."

They drank into the night. Sully and Pussy curled up on a silk rug. Abandoned, the wine bottle emptied its dregs onto fine silk. Amid so much bounty, no one paid heed.

"This is so nice," said Pussy. A pearl necklace looped thrice around her neck. Her claws shone with diamonds.

Wentworth wore the hamster captain's tri-corner hat and tiny velvet waistcoat, unbuttoned. "We should sell our bounty and find a tropical island. We'll have servants and order everyone about. If anyone defies us, our blades will drink their blood!"

"That sounds lovely." Pussy rolled across the rug, paws in the air. "Captain Wentworth, will you marry Sullivan and me?"

The evening's joy bled away like the wine. Wentworth paced to the hull, gazing down at the roiling black sea. "What happened to your last bridegroom?"

Pussy burped. A white feather flew from her mouth. "Nevermind that." She joined Wentworth at the hull. "Here, I want you to have this."

She drew from her petticoats a metal object. It glinted in starlight.

"Tis my runcible spoon. My bridegroom and I ate our last meal from it. It's very precious to me."

Wentworth admired the runcible spoon. "No one's ever given me a gift before. Not without a threat."

Pussy purred. "Will you marry us?"

Wentworth glanced at Sully. He stood, paws folded at his waist, whiskers clean and tidy. For the first time in years, he wasn't twitching.

"Very well."

Wentworth married them there, beneath the green crescent moon. Seeing the two of them, rapturous and silhouetted by starlight, a tear came to Wentworth's crusty pirate's eye.

## X. A Brewing Storm

Wentworth woke with a headache. He grabbed the wine and took a swig.

Above, the rosy tint of dawn illuminated the dark underbellies of storm clouds. Distant lightning flashed across the horizon. Thunder followed.

"Storm!" cried Wentworth. He rushed to the captain's cabin where Pussy and Sullivan had made their honeymoon suite. He burst through the door. "No time to lose! A dickens of a squall is on the way!"

He fell silent. Pussy stood over the bed, mouth stretched to reveal shining, dagger-sharp teeth. Sully lay helpless on the sheets, still snoring.

"Stop, you wretch!" Drawing his dagger, Wentworth ran at the cat. She mewled and leapt away.

"You've the wrong idea," began Pussy.

"Cat!" shouted Wentworth. "Feline! Kitten! Domesticated animal!"

Sullivan woke. He jumped to his feet, drawing his sword. He looked between his wife and his friend, unsure which to attack.

Wentworth jabbed at Pussy. "This felis domesticus was about to make you a snack!"

"Do nothing hasty, my beloved," said Pussy. "We can work this out."

Mad eyes bright, Sully charged his friend. Wentworth was too stunned to move. The blade's tip drew close to his fur.

With a burst of lightning like a thousand firecrackers, the ship tilted. Sully's blade clattered to the floor. Wentworth was thrown to the ground after it. Pussy clamored over him, escaping to the deck.

"After her," said Wentworth.

## XI. Lightning Strikes

He found the false feline standing by the mast, long white gown wetted to her body.

"I didn't mean to hurt him!" she called into the wind. "Tis just— that flashing tail, that delectable fur, that delicious, rapid heartbeat! Oh, the trials of a cat in love."

"Is that what happened to your former bridegroom?"

"Tis true, I've succumbed to temptation in the past, but not this time! I would have remembered my vows!"

Sully crawled after Wentworth. His eyes were black as the tumbling waves. He twitched beneath a seething mass of fleas.

"My fate is in your paws," Pussy called to him.

Another lightning bolt crashed into the ship. It lit the mast from tip to deck where Pussy stood. Her dress turned ashen. The odor of burned fur filled the air.

Sully rushed to her side. "Don't comfort the harlot," called Wentworth. "There's no time."

Thunder rumbled. The mast creaked. As it fell, Wentworth pushed Sullivan aside. It crashed across the deck. The ship heaved and tilted. Gems and silks slid into the water. The bow tipped into the waves, prow pointing straight up toward the hidden sun.

Wentworth scrabbled for purchase. He pulled the runcible spoon from his sleeve and stuck it into a groove between planks. He gripped it, hind paws dangling over the water.

Pussy fell past him. Her claws slipped, stuck. Sully shivered on her back, twitches so bad they'd become convulsions. Fleas flashed around his body.

Pussy began to slip. "Hold tight," she yelled.

Her claws pulled free. She scrambled, regained her grip. She couldn't support them both.

Sully's eyes blazed past the black of waves and nighttime. They were black as madness now, black as the rotten cheese at the back of the moon.

He let go.

"No!" shouted Pussy and Wentworth, simultaneously.

Sully slid into the water, naked tail cresting the waves before disappearing.

## XII. Rat Overboard

The storm cleared to bright, azure sky. Pussy knelt, weeping. Wentworth inventoried the ship to see what treasure remained.

"The jewels are gone. And the rugs and gold and tea and tin and wine. But it looks like some silver survived. Enough to buy a new boat, maybe. A small one."

"Tis my fault," sobbed Pussy. "If I hadn't been tempted, if you hadn't found me, the three of us might have sheltered together."

Long ago as a press-ganged pup, Wentworth had made a vow of solidarity with those who found themselves prematurely estranged from their loved ones. He would not kill orphans or widows. But oh, he was tempted.

"No, we wouldn't," he said. "You'd have eaten him."

Pussy's bitter tears mingled with the drying ocean water on deck. "O, my dark one, my fleet one, my mad dancing one, with eyes black as a moonless night, and fur soft as the master's blanket."

"Should we drink the wine or save it to sell?" asked Wentworth.

"O, that you should die like this, at the hour of my ignominy, sacrificing your noble life for mine!"

"Drink it, I think," said Wentworth.

"Oh, my love! I can't go on without you!"

With a clatter of her claws on the leaf-planks, Pussy mounted the side of the ship. She stood like a figurehead, gown rustling in the wind, tail billowing behind her. Then the leap, and with a splash of spray, she was gone.

Wentworth gazed after her. This journey had been one of death. Cracked Mack had died. Sullivan had died. Even Pussy, poor pirate though she'd been, had taken a watery grave. Wentworth pulled the runcible spoon from his pocket and heaved it overboard. Without the damn thing, he'd be dead too, and maybe it would have been for the best.

## XIII. Adrift

Weakened by the storm, exhausted timbers broke apart. The captain's quarters capsized, taking the silver with them. The deck cracked into sections. Wentworth clung to the planks beneath him as they split off like a raft.

Long hours passed. A circling gull woke Wentworth's hope he might be approaching land til the bird pitched dead into the sea. Wentworth fished out its corpse and dined upon it.

Wet and miserable, Wentworth lay down and waited to die. He considered his many sins. As a ratling, he'd oft squabbled with his siblings, nipping their whiskers to make off with their breadcrumbs. He'd swindled apples from pups and woven lies odiferous as rotten cheese. He'd nipped the teats that fed him.

For all that, he didn't think he'd been a bad rat. A bit nasty. A bit merciless. A bit bloodthirsty. No rodent is without flaws.

When he heard the rush of water pushed aside by a well-made prow, he thought perhaps he was gone to heaven. Sharp steel jabbing his ribs set him straight.

"Slavers, eh?" he asked.

"Silence, rat," replied the sword-wielding ferret, cruel nose twitching. He turned tail and two fat guineas marched Wentworth aboard their rickety vessel.

Palm trees swayed on the horizon, black against the sunset. Wentworth stared slack-jawed, aghast that he'd come so close to freedom.

A guinea caught him looking. "That thar's Sweet Summer Isle. They grow sugar thar. You'll spend the rest of yer life workin' the plantations."

He gave a dry and brutal laugh, cuffed Wentworth round the ear for good measure, and led him below decks whence he chained the poor rat to a dank cell wall for the remainder of the journey.

## XIV. Deserted Island

But what kind of pirate would Captain Black Heart Wentworth, Oppressor of Puppies and Terror of Things That Go Squeak, be if he couldn't slip free of rusty handcuffs? He knocked out the guinea guard with his own sword and with thundering footsteps marched deckside to conquer his craven captors.

At port, Wentworth sold the slavers for good gold coin and bought a plantation. When no other rat would purchase the cowards, Wentworth reacquired them at a price much reduced and forced them to labor sunup to sundown.

One afternoon, as summer sun shimmered on the sand, Wentworth was surprised to see two familiar figures staggering from the sea. Pussy, fur patched and ears a-tatter, clung to a skinnier flealess Sullivan. Over a feast of tropical fruit, Pussy explained how they'd come to these sunny shores.

Pussy had leapt into the water contrite and ready to die, until accosted by hungry cannibals who dragged her to their camp. Nearby, Sully, having been found inedible, was imprisoned in a cage. When the cannibals dunked Pussy in their wicked cauldron, Sully drew on nameless reserves of strength to wrench apart the cage bars. Quickly, he slew the cannibals and fled with his bride to their captor's ship which they converted to their own piratical ends. Ah, but theft and murder felt wrong without Wentworth to oversee it. The wedded couple spent their gold-strewn hours listless and mournful til they heard rumors of a wealthy white rat with a scurvy temper who ran a tropical sugar plantation. With haste, Pussy and Sully set off, til not two days from the island, their ship was lost to a freak whirlpool. Pussy and Sully swam for shore. Sharks circled and tropical undertows threatened to drag them under, but lo, they arrived at last on this very beach.

Past slights forgiven, Wentworth embraced his long-lost friends. In the sugar cane fields, even the ferret and his crew of guineas, now tanned and sore from their months of punishing labor, wept sentimental tears til Wentworth ordered them back to work.

## XV. Piratical Epilogue

So it came to be that the world was not menaced by rat pirates. Port cities flourished unafraid, reaping rich cargos of coffee and tea, sugar and salt, wood and silk and spices and precious stones. Unaccosted gold flowed through marine arteries, sustaining the vast fatherly arms of empires. By turbulent sea, churning river, or trickling tributary, trade reached even the most insignificant peoples stranded in the remotest, uncivilized reaches of the globe.

Sully held Pussy as they sat together on the white sand, admiring the sunset over the water. Wentworth threatened a cowardly guinea with his sword if he did not immediately dash to fetch a goblet of rum and mango juice. The creature scurried off. A smile stirred beneath Wentworth's whitening whiskers. Ah, sun and sand and sea air. Ah, the goodness of reclining on a beach with friends.

**Rachel Swirsky** is a graduate of the Iowa Writers Workshop where she learned how to A) write and B) endure the cold. She currently lives in Bakersfield where she is A) continuing to write and B) enduring the heat. She aspires to someday live in a temperate zone. Her fiction has appeared in numerous magazines and anthologies, including Tor.com and *Clarkesworld,* and been nominated for the Hugo, the World Fantasy, the Sturgeon and the Locus Awards. In 2010, "The Lady Who Plucked Red Flowers Beneath the Queen's Window" won the Nebula Award for best novella. Her collection *How the World Became Quiet: Myths of the Past, Present, and Future* is forthcoming from Subterrnean Press in late September, 2013.

# Andy Duncan
# on Rachel Swirsky

Somewhere in the second week of Clarion West 2005, I decided I better not tell Rachel Swirsky how good she was. Sure, I praised her writing. There was no other response to "Heartstrung," which I read in typescript that week, two years ahead of the readers of *Interzone*. I also did my best to treat her not as a student but as a new colleague I'd just met. But I kept to myself The Speech, the one about how well-known she was going to be five years hence. I mean, she was how old, 22? I didn't want to intimidate her, shut her down—though Rachel didn't strike me, then or now, as easily intimidated. And five years later, when she was a Hugo, Nebula, and Sturgeon Award finalist, I wished I had written down and postmarked my earlier predictions, so I could prove that just once, I was a seer.

In short, I'm not surprised that she's my first student to win a Nebula Award, nor that she's my first student to hold elected office in the Science Fiction and Fantasy Writers of America. As a group, Clarion West 2005 was unusually talented and vocal, but Rachel nevertheless stood out as an agenda-setter, a classroom advocate for feminism and genre inclusiveness, a one-on-one adviser and counselor to many of us. Whenever I'm lucky enough to see her on the circuit, or to read one of her luminous stories, I am reminded: This is why I teach, to see the future.

**Andy Duncan** is a science fiction and fantasy writer whose work frequently deals with Southern themes. Duncan attended Clarion West in 1994, and returned to teach there in 2005. His fiction has won the Theodore Sturgeon Award, two World Fantasy Awards, and has been nominated for both the Hugo and the Nebula Award.

# A Boy in Cathyland

David Marusek

1992

For as long as he could remember, the boy had watched such fiery pieces of space junk streak across the southern sky. This one, low on the horizon, would be a fragment of the Rialoto Platform. The Rialoto Platform, or so he'd learned in school, had been like a giant raft floating on the sea of air that surrounded the Earth. It had been many times larger than the village and had supported as many people as lived in Provideniya, the regional capital. But this raft and dozens more like it had been shattered to bits, and every so often a jagged piece or frozen human body would hurtle to Earth like a shooting star. Each time he saw one, Mikol would squeeze his eyes shut—as he did now—and make a desperate wish with all his young heart that once, just one time, a piece would fall somewhere nearby, and he could go examine it with his own two eyes and thus appease the clawing demands of his curiosity.

When he opened his eyes, the tragic debris was gone. No matter, he'd see more before too long. According to his schoolteacher, Mikol would be an old man with a long, grey beard before the last shard fell.

Mikol removed the plastic pail brimming with cool spring water and set the empty one under the pipe. Out of the corner of his eye he noticed movement on the valley floor far below him. There was a cloud of dust on the river road, horsemen riding in loose formation. "Raz, dva, tri," he counted them, "chetyre, p'at', shest'." It was, no doubt, the Patrol. Villagers had been expecting it for weeks, and here it was.

Carefully, so as not to spill the water, Mikol toted two full pails up the narrow bluff path. At the top he called, "Babushka Katia, Patrul' idet!" But she was bent over a hoe and paid him no mind. He looked down the valley again and saw that the riders, small as gnats, had turned onto the track that mounted the ridge. This cabin would be their first stop. They would arrive in a couple of hours.

"Babushka Katia," he called again as he threaded his way through the garden maze of cabbages and kohlrabi, potatoes and beets. "Patrul'," he said, placing the pails at her feet.

Cathy straightened her back and consulted the sun's position in the sky. Patrol or no Patrol, the garden was thirsty. "Esche vody," she said, handing the boy two empty pails and two pebbles. He was a good boy and a tireless helper, and she paid him in carrots. Four pebbles to the carrot, redeemable whenever he decided to quit for the day and go home. He dropped the pebbles into his pocket and hurried off with the empty pails.

Over the last ten years, subsistence had become Cathy's full-time occupation. The garden, once a hobby, had become the cornerstone of her survival. As luck would have it, she had received a shipment of Denali seeds just before the world went all to hell. They were hybrid seeds, especially gengineered for the cold soil of the subarctic. During the short summer, when the sun hung on the horizon continuously day and night, these seeds exploded with growth. And the vegetables they produced kept well throughout the long winter in her root cellar beneath the cabin floor.

The villagers—to whom she was and would always be a foreigner—were greatly impressed by the bounty and hardiness of her harvests. In exchange for seed stock, they eagerly helped her extend her garden to the forest edge and beyond. They felled trees and pulled stumps, hauled wagonloads of manure, wood ash, and river soil up the ridge to tame her raw earth.

Now she had a half-hectare under cultivation. She bartered her surplus for losos'—sliced into narrow strips and smoked over alder until the meat was as hard and pellucid as wax—and for snowshoe hare and rock grouse. She bartered for thread and fur, tea, sugar, home-distilled vodka, and all the little necessities that brought joy to a solitary life.

Still, she was old—almost two hundred—and without periodic treatment, her strong body was beginning to fail. Soon, while she was still able, she would have to cross the mountains to the crazy world beyond in order to partake in the blessings of geriatric medicine.

When the dumification patrol arrived, Cathy ordered Mikol home, but instead the boy hid in the thick willow brush at the forest edge. The soldiers sat on their horses while their officer dismounted and stood under the sunflowers that lined the garden path. He was a handsome young man with the blunt features and reddish skin of the local population. He wore shiny, black riding boots and a brown republican uniform. "Zdravstvuite," he called politely to Cathy as she hauled a bundle of weeds to the fire pit. When she turned to him, he smiled and nodded his head. "Razreshite nam pozhaluista, delat' osmotr vashei vysokoi tekhniki."

"No problem," Cathy said and left the garden. The young officer's polite request was a pleasant formality, she knew, and in no way necessary. They would inspect her property whether she granted them permission or not. She skirted the men and their horses—there was a dog, too, a German shepherd—and led the officer to the khizhina where she kept her fusion generator. It was the camping model she had brought with her fifteen years ago when she'd bought this place. It put out five kilowatts, more than enough to power her modest lifestyle: an electric stove, lights, a radio. The officer gave it hardly a glance.

"Mozhet byt' vy menia ne ponimaete," he said, searching her face for signs of cleverness. "Nas interesuet vysokai tekhnika—*hi-tech*."

Oh, she knew exactly what kind of tech they were after. The smart kind. The willful kind. The kind she had dazzled the villagers with when she'd first arrived. The kind that had briefly conquered the world. The officer went to the door of her cabin and waited for her. "Mozhno?" he said.

"Of course," she said and opened it for him. As she did so, her hand trembled, which surprised her. She knew what she was risking here, but she'd made up her mind a long time ago. And she'd rehearsed for this inspection, even practicing her answers in front of the mirror. This was no time to grow feeble-hearted.

The officer waved for his men to dismount. Two joined them in the cabin, while the others searched the grounds and outbuildings. Their manner was respectful but thorough. They opened all her cupboards and drawers, moved furniture, tapped floor and walls for hollow places, discovered and searched the root cellar. One soldier poked the wand of a sniffer into narrow spaces and sampled the air by squeezing a rubber bulb. "Ogo!" Cathy said, pointing to the sniffer. "Armii razreshena *hi-tech*."

"Eto ne *hi-tech*," said the soldier patiently, as he undoubtedly had hundreds of times before. He opened the back of the device's handle to expose its electronics. Old-fashioned tin solder flashed in the light. Silicon chips sat like spiders on a printed circuit board. The plastic case was embossed with Chinese characters. "Smotrite," he said, "nizkai tekhnika—*lo-tech*."

"I see," said Cathy, following her careful script. "Vas interesuet elektro-khimicheskaia pasta. Why didn't you say so? Idite za mnoi." She led them outside to the scarecrow guarding the north side of the garden. All of the soldiers followed. "Vot moia *hi-tech*," she said.

The men laughed, for indeed the scarecrow was hi-tech. It had holo emitters for eyes and a satellite dish for a hat, wore an all-weather jacket, sensi-tread shoes, and a belt valet. She had decked it out with all her smart appliances after smashing their processors and breaking open their paste capsules.

"Eto dolzhno byt' samoe umnoe chuchelo, kotoroe ia videl," said the officer, but Cathy could tell he wasn't entirely satisfied. In the village, they would have told him about her houseputer and its thousands of simulacra—a whole virtual community of Artificial People who had once occupied her property and shared her life. Her Cathyland. The villagers would remember Cathyland.

So she consulted her mental script and said, "Vam nraviatsia moi aniutiny glazki?" She pointed toward the flowers on the picnic table.

"Krasivo," the officer said and went for a closer look, not at the flowers, but at the flower pots. They were made from houseputer containers, each originally designed to hold a liter of electro-neural paste. Now they contained garden dirt and hybrid pansies. There were three of them. The villagers would have reported three. "Krasivo," the officer repeated. He ordered his men to mount up. He thanked her for her cooperation.

"Ne za chto," she replied graciously.

When they were ready to leave, the handler called his dog, but it was nowhere to be seen. He whistled, and the dog whined from around the cabin. The soldiers dismounted, and Cathy followed them to where the dog was pawing through her compost pile.

"Bad dog! Make him stop!" she said. "Kakoe bezobrazie!" The dog ignored her and eagerly dug into the rotting compost.

The dog's handler leashed him and tried to pull him away, but the animal snuffled stubbornly at the pile. "Izvinite," the officer said to Cathy. "Moi soldaty uberut eto." But instead of ordering his men to clean up the dog's mess, he nodded to the soldier with the sniffer.

The soldier plunged the wand deep into the compost pile and squeezed the bulb. In a moment the results appeared on the display. "Nichego net," he announced, and Cathy tried to mask her relief.

"You should try to feed your dog better," she grumbled and bent to gather up the scattered compost.

The officer watched her for a long while. Finally, he ordered a man to go to the horses for a spade. The soldier returned with a camp spade that he unfolded and used to scrape away the compost pile. It was slow going, and the soldier began to sweat. With the compost removed, the soldier glanced at the officer. The officer nodded, and the soldier began to dig. When he had dug a hole a half-meter deep, he looked again at the officer. The camp spade was ill-suited for major excavation, and his hands were beginning to blister.

Too late Cathy realized that she had watched every spadeful of dirt being removed, while the officer had been watching her. She had shown too much interest. She should have offered to go into the cabin to prepare them something cool to drink.

"Glubzhe," said the officer, and the soldier continued to dig.

Even now it was not too late. Even now Cathy could surrender the contraband and save her own life. They would punish her, but they would have to let her live. That was their law. The soldier in the shallow pit paused to ease his back. And though Cathy stood directly in front of him, his eyes avoided her. He bent to his labor again, and the dirt continued to fly.

They found the containers at one-and-a-half meters, brought them up, and pried open the lids. The paste glittered in the sunlight, revealing the nebular craze of trillions of neural synapses. The soldiers gaped at the sight, and Cathy thought, "Now here's the test." Would these underpaid recruits of a distant government hold fast to duty? Or would they be swayed by greed? She did not doubt that they had destroyed plenty of microcapsules of paste during their rambling patrol of the province, but here was *three liters* of the stuff. Even reprocessed, this haul could make them all as rich as czars. Surely there was a black market for *hi-tech*. Surely there were rich madmen still eager to posses Artificial People again no matter the international ban. Already the soldiers were passing secret glances behind their officer's back.

Not that the fate of Cathy's simulacra made much difference now: her own fate had been sealed the moment they'd unearthed the containers. She turned and searched the willow brush behind her yard for Mikol. The boy shouldn't have to witness this. She prayed that he had left for home.

A soldier unsheathed his knife. Followed by a second soldier, and a third. But it wasn't mutiny. They plunged their blades into the containers and stirred the paste. They could not be as rich as czars, for where could soldiers spend such wealth? They poured the paste out on the ground and scraped it from the sides of the containers. "I'm sorry," Cathy thought as a soldier doused the puddle with gasoline. "I tried. I'm sorry. Good-bye." The burning paste sizzled and gave off thick, black smoke.

The officer assembled his men in a line facing Cathy. He read something from a card in a faltering voice. Clearly he did not relish this part of his duty, and for that Cathy pitied him. She looked one last time at her little cabin. She heard a breeze moving through the tops of the tall spruce trees.

Mikol, hidden in dense foliage, did not flinch. On the contrary, he watched steadfastly, for he knew he would be asked many times in his life to relate this very scene in all its detail. The innostranka did not cry for mercy but waited bravely. The lieutenant pointed the gun into her ear. It made a little popping sound, not the big boom Mikol had expected. She fell immediately but scrabbled on the ground a bit. The soldiers left her for the villagers to bury. They mounted their horses and headed up the ridge road to the next homestead.

And thus a heavy responsibility befell the boy. He must run home and tell his people of the tragedy before news of it spread. A treasure lay unclaimed in neatly cultivated rows, and he had worked too hard for it to end up in some other family's soup pot. When Mikol was sure the soldiers were gone, he left his hiding place, but he did not start for home at once. First he went into the now vacant cabin and pulled from a shelf the tin can in which he knew the innostranka kept a handful of coins. He took these and replaced them with the dozen pebbles he had earned that morning. He left the cabin, but still he did not start for home. First he went around to look at her where she had fallen, to see up close with his own two eyes where the bullet went in and where it came out. And maybe to touch it with a stick. Just once.

*Russian translation by Trina Mamoon*

**David Marusek** writes science fiction in a cabin in Fairbanks, Alaska. His work has appeared in *Playboy, Nature, MIT Technology Review, Asimov's,* and other periodicals and anthologies and has been translated into ten languages. His two novels and clutch of short stories have earned him numerous award nominations and have won the Theodore Sturgeon and Endeavour awards. His current novel project, *Camp Tribulation,* is a tale of love, faith, and alien invasion set in the Alaskan bush.

# Pat Cadigan
# on David Marusek

David Marusek was in the first Clarion West class I ever faced, back in 1992. He had come down to Seattle from somewhere outside of Fairbanks, Alaska, where he had been living, quietly and austerely, writing stories in his spare time.

That year's class was a motley, and very talented bunch. David was the quietest. He contributed to every discussion but otherwise did nothing to call attention to himself. Eventually, the time came for our one-on-one meeting. By then, I had one of his stories, a very short piece called "The Earth Is On The Mend," and my first question to him was, "What are you doing here?"

Like David, the story was deceptively quiet. The language, spare but loaded, delivered a revelatory moment disguised as a brief description of a day in the life of a survivor of a global disaster, the details of which can only be inferred by the reader.

"A Boy In Cathyland" is another day in a life after some unnamed worldwide catastrophe. The life is strange: the setting and the people are foreign, strangers to each other as well as to us—in fact, most of the characters don't speak English and there is no explicit translation. But none is necessary; we understand all of them, human to human. Strange people are, in the end, just people.

I'm willing to bet you'll read this story more than once, to get at every fleeting aroma and flavour, every morsel of nuance, to hope for the boy, to mourn Cathy, to try to imagine what Cathyland must have been like. This is exactly what a short story should be.

I kept in touch with most of the 1992 class, including David. He went back to his home in the Alaskan countryside where he continued to write wonderful stories that attracted a lot of favourable attention from readers and critics alike. In the late 90s, despite his preference for simple country living, my husband and I managed to lure him to London. During the six months he spent in our spare room, he began work on his first novel, *Counting Heads*.

If that sounds like I'm bragging, I am.

However, I'm not claiming I had anything to do with what he wrote. David has always had an extraordinary instinct for story—not just for what it is but for what it means, for why we tell stories in the first place.

That's a rare gift and I'm happy to say David is making the most of it.

**Pat Cadigan** is a American born science fiction author who has lived in England since 1996. She has won a number of awards, including the Arthur C. Clarke Award in 1992 and in 1995 for her novels *Synners* and *Fools*.

# The Water Museum

## Nisi Shawl

### 1992

When I saw the hitchhiker standing by the sign for the Water Museum, I knew he had been sent to assassinate me. First off, that's what the dogs were saying as I slowed to pick him up. Girlfriend, with her sharp, little, agitated bark, was quite explicit. Buddy was silently trying to dig a hole under the back seat, seeking refuge in the trunk. I stopped anyway.

Second off, the man as much as told me so his own self. He opened up the passenger door of my midnight-blue '62 Mercury and piled in with his duffel bag and his jeans and white tee and his curly brown hair tucked under a baseball cap. "Where you going?" I asked, as soon as he was all settled and the door shut.

"Water Museum," he said. "Got an interview for a job there." That was confirmation, 'cause I wasn't hiring just then. Way too early in the year for that; things don't pick up here till much later in the spring. Even then, my girls and me handle most of whatever work comes up. Even after Albinia, my oldest, took herself off ten years ago, I never hired no more than a couple locals to tide us over the weekends. And this guy wasn't no local. So he was headed where he had no business to be going, and I could think of only the one reason why.

But I played right along. "What part?" I asked him, pulling back out on the smooth one-lane blacktop.

It took him a second to hear my question. "What do you mean, what part? They got different entrances or something?"

"I mean the Water Museum is three, four miles long," I told him.

Three point two miles, if you want to be exact, but I didn't. "You tell me where you want to go there, and I'll get you as close as I can."

I twisted around to get a good look at the dogs. Buddy had given up his tunnel to the trunk. He was lying on the floor, panting like a giant, asthmatic weight-lifter. His harness jingled softly with every whuffling breath. Girlfriend was nowhere in sight.

The hitchhiker twisted in his seat, too. "Nice animal," he said uneasily, taking in Buddy's shiny, tusky-looking teeth. "Sheepdog?"

"Nope. Otterhound. Lotta people make that mistake, though. They do look alike, but otterhound's got a finer bone structure, little different coloring."

"Oh."

We started the long curve down to the shore. I put her in neutral and let us glide, enjoying the early morning light. It dappled my face through the baby beech leaves like butter and honey on a warm biscuit.

On this kind of bright, sunshiny spring morning, I found it hard to credit that a bunch of men I didn't even know were bent on my destruction. Despite the evidence to the contrary sitting right there next to me on the plaid, woven vinyl seat cushion, it just did not make sense. What were they so het up about? Their lawns? Browned-off golf courses, which shouldn'ta oughta been there in the first place? Ranches dried to dust and blowing away ... yeah, I could see how it would disturb folks to find the land they thought they owned up and left without em. I just did not agree with their particular manner of settling the matter.

I drove quietly with these thoughts of mine awhile, and my killer sat there just as quiet with his. Then we came to that sweet little dip, and the turn under the old viaduct, and we were almost there. "You figured out yet where you're headed?" I asked.

"Uhh, no, ma'am. Just drop me off by the offices, I guess ... "

"Offices ain't gonna be open this early," I told him. "Not till noon, between Labor Day and Memorial Weekend. C'mon, I got nothing better to do, I'll give you a tour."

"Well, uhh, that's nice, ma'am, but I, uh, but don't go out of your way or anything ... "

I looked at him, cocked my chin, and grinned my best country-girl grin, the one that makes my cheeks dimple up and my eyelashes flutter. "Why, it'd be a pleasure to show you around the place!" By this time we were to the parking lot. I pulled in and cut the ignition, and before he could speak another word I had opened my door. "Let's go."

The hitchhiker hesitated. Buddy whined and lumbered to his feet, and that must have decided him. With what I would call alacrity he sprang out on his side of the car onto the gravel. Ahh, youth.

I let Buddy out the back. Instead of his usual sniff and pee routine, he stuck close to me. Girlfriend was still nowhere in sight. The hitchhiker was looking confusedly around the clearing. At first glance the steps are hard to pick out, and the trail up into the dunes is faint and overgrown.

I grabbed my wool ruana and flung it on over my shoulders, rearranging my neckerchiefs and headscarves. "You got a jacket, young man?" I asked him. "Shirtsleeves're all right here, but we're gonna catch us a nice breeze down by the Lake."

"Um, yeah, in my—" He bent over the front seat and tugged at something on the floor. "In my duffel, but I guess it's stuck under here or something."

Came a low, unmistakable growl, and he jumped back. I went around to his side. "Don't worry, I'll get it out for you," I said. "Girlfriend!" I bent over and grabbed one green canvas corner of my assassin's duffel bag and pulled. This is Girlfriend's favorite game. We tussled away for a few minutes. "She's small, but she's fierce," I commented as I took a quick break. "You got any food in there, a sandwich or something?"

"No. Why?"

"I just noticed she had the zipper open some."

The hitchhiker got a little pale and wispy-looking when he heard that. He stayed that way till I retrieved his duffel and gave it to him to rummage through. He took his time finding his jean jacket, and by the time he'd dug it out and put it on he looked more solid and reassured.

So now I knew where his gun was. Should I let him keep it? He'd be a lot easier to handle without a pistol in his fist. Then again, the thing might not even be loaded, depending on how soon he'd been planning on meeting up with me; simpler for him to explain an empty gun to any cops stopped him hitching rides. And I'd be able to get him relaxed faster if he was armed.

He threw the bag over his shoulder, and I locked the car. Girlfriend had already started up the trail. Of course he wanted me to walk ahead of him, but Buddy just looked at him with his dark, suspicious eyes and Mr. Man decided it would be okay if this time he was the one to go first.

I love the dance I chose when I made this path, the wending and winding of the way. As we climbed, we left the beech trees behind and ascended into the realm of grass and cherries, of white-backed poplar leaves, soft as angel fuzz. Poison ivy shone waxily, warningly, colored like rich, red wine.

We walked right past my offices. They look like part of the dune crest, coming at em from this side. I cast em that way, wound em round with roots, bound em with stems and sprinkled pebbles lightly over the top. The windows are disguised as burrows, with overhangs and grass growing down like shaggy eyebrows.

My assassin's Nikes made soft little drumming sounds on the boardwalk, following the click of Girlfriend's nails round to the blow-out and the observation deck. The promised breeze sprang up, ruffling our fur and hair. I watched my killer's reaction to his first sight of the Museum.

His shoulders straightened and relaxed, though I hadn't noticed they were crooked before that. He walked up and leaned against the wooden rail. "All that water ... " he said.

I came up and joined him. "Yes," I said. "All that water." From the deck you can see it, as much as can be seen from down here on the Earth. Shadows still hung beneath us, but further out the Great Lake sparkled splendidly. Waves were dancing playfully, like little girls practicing ballet. They whirled and leapt and tumbled to rest just beyond the short terminal dunes five hundred feet below where we stood. "All that water. And all of it is sweet."

I took my killer gently by the arm and led him to the river side. That's where the work I've done is easiest to take in: the floating bridges over Smallbird Marsh, the tanks and dioramas and such. "Where you from, kid?" We started down the steps.

"Colorado."

"Pretty?"

"It used to be. When I was little, back before the drought got bad."

I stopped at a landing and waited for Buddy to catch up. He's all right on a hillside, but this set of stairs is steep and made out of slats. They give under his weight a bit, and that makes him take them slow and cautious, ears flapping solemnly with every step.

I smiled at my assassin and he smiled shyly back. It occurred to me then that he might not know who I am. I mean, I do present a pretty imposing figure, being a six-six strawberry blonde and not exactly overweight, but on the fluffy side. I'd say I'm fairly easy to spot from a description. But maybe they hadn't bothered to give him one.

I dropped his arm and motioned him on ahead. "By the bye," I called out, once he was well on his way. "I don't believe I caught your name. Mine's Granita. Granita Bone."

He sorta stopped there for a sec and put his hand out, grabbing for a railing I'd never had installed. Well, I thought, at least they told the poor boy that much.

"Jasper Smith," he said, then turned around to see how I took it.

I nodded down at him approvingly. Jasper rang a nice change on Granita, and the Smith part kinda balanced out its oddness. "Pleased to meet you, Jasper." Girlfriend barked up at us from the foot of the stairs. "All right," I shouted down at her, "I'm a-coming, I'm a-coming."

"Sheltie," I explained to my killer. "Herding animal. Makes her nervous to see us spread out like this." By that time Buddy had caught up and passed me. He knew this walk. I followed him down.

At the bottom, I chose the inland path, past pools of iridescent black blooming with bright marsh marigold. Stabilizing cedars gave way to somber hemlock, still adrip with the morning's dew.

"Water Music," I told Jasper, just before our first stop.

"I don't—"

"Hush up, then, and you will." Even the dogs knew to keep quiet here. It fell constantly, a bit more hesitant than rain. Notes in a spatter, a gentle jingle, a high and solitary ping! ping! ping! Liquid runs and hollow drums grew louder and louder until we reached the clearing and stood still, surrounded.

It was the tank and windmill that drew him first, though there's nothing so special about them. I went over with him and undid the lock so the blades could catch the morning's breeze. The tank's got a capacity of about four hundred gallons; small, but it usually lasts me a day or two.

With the pump going, the pipe up from the river started in to sing. It's baffled and pierced; totally inefficient, but gorgeous to my ears. From the other pipes and the web of hose overhead, drops of water continued to gather and fall—on glass and shells, in bowls and bottles, overflowing or always empty, on tin and through bamboo, falling, always falling.

Adding to the symphony, Girlfriend lapped up a drink from a tray of lotuses.

"Wow, Granita, this is really, uh, elaborate," said Jasper when he'd pretty much done looking around.

"Do you like it?" I asked.

"Yeah, but isn't it kinda, umm, kinda wasteful?"

I shrugged. "Maybe. But like my mama always said, 'You don't never know the usefulness of a useless thing.'" Right then I just about washed my hands of good ole Jasper. But he hadn't even seen any of the other exhibits, so I decided I'd better postpone judgment. My assassins did tend to have a wide stripe of utilitarianism to em. At least at first. Couldn't seem to help it.

Buddy stood where the trail began again, panting and whining and wagging his whole hind end. He was looking forward to the next stop, hoping to catch him a crawdad. The fish factory's never been one of my favorite features of the place, but Buddy loved it, and it turned out to be a big hit with Jasper, too. He took a long, long look at the half-glazed ponds that terraced down the dune. Me and some of the girls had fixed up burnt wood signs by the path, explaining the contents of each one, but Jasper had to climb up all the ladders and see for himself. He disappointed me by flashing right past all my pretty koi. Can you believe it was the catfish that caught his fresh little fancy? He must have spent twenty minutes to check out those mean, ugly suckers. Though, to give him his credit, he dallied a fair while with Yertle and that clan, too.

Meanwhile, me and the dogs kept waiting on my killer to make his move.

We looped under the deserted highway and came back by Summer Spring Falls and the Seven Cauldrons, then started across the marsh over the floating bridges, which Buddy doesn't like anymore than the stairs. Maybe it's the way the wicker that I wove em from sorta sags, or the dark breezes stirring up between the chinks, or the gaps you have to hop over going from one section to the next.

The breeze picked up again as we headed towards the beach. Small clouds, light on their feet, flickered past the sun.

I let him get behind me. Wicker creaks. I could hear his footsteps hesitate, sinking lower as he stood trying to decide was this the time and place. We were alone, he had a good clean line of sight, nothing but the wind between his aim and my broad back. But when he stilled and I turned, his hand wasn't doing nothing but resting on the zipper of his duffel bag, and that wasn't even open yet. His eyes were focused over my head, far off in space or time. He was listening.

Red-winged blackbirds. Sweet and pure, their songs piped up, trilling away into silence, rising again from that pool of quiet, sure and silver, pouring over and over into my ears. "When I was a boy ... " said Jasper. I waited. In a moment he started again. "When I was a boy, there was a creek and a swamp, where the river used to be. I didn't know, I thought it was just a fun place to play. Some birds there, they sang just like this."

Well, making allowance for a few inaccuracies (swamp for marsh, and the bird songs had to vary a *little*), this sounded pretty much like his truth. And it made actual sense to me, not like them pipeline dreams of those cowboys sent him here. Now we were getting somewhere. Closer. He'd be making his attack real soon.

I turned back around and trudged a little more slowly along the baskety surface of the bridge. The back of my neck crawled and itched, like itty bitty Jaspers and Granitas were walking all over it. I kept myself in hand, though, breathing deep and regular, balanced on the bubbling well of power beneath my feet, telling myself soon—soon—

He didn't stop, he just slowed down a hair. I didn't hear any zipper, either, but when I turned again he had finally pulled his goddamn gun out and it was pointed straight at me. Was it loaded, then? He seemed to think so.

My chest cramped up and my temperature dropped like I'd been dumped head first into Superior. I could wind up contributing my vital nitrogen and phosphorus content to the cycle like right *now*. I let my fright sag me down and grabbed the rails as his eyes hardened and his gun hand tensed. He was a lefty.

With a sudden lurch I threw myself against the side of the bridge and tipped us all into the cool, ripe waters of Smallbird Marsh. The gun cracked off one shot, just before we all made a nice big splash. I shrugged out of my ruana and kicked off my clogs and I knew I'd be okay. Fluff floats. Buddy woofed and Girlfriend yapped, all happy and accounted for.

Girlfriend and I pulled ourselves right up onto the next basket, but the menfolks stayed in a while longer. Buddy loves to swim, and he's good at it, too. Jasper was floundering, though, wrapped up in weeds and trying to breathe mud. By the time I got him hauled out he wasn't more than half conscious. Still had a grip on that gun, though. I pried it loose and tossed it back.

Now how to get him back up to the offices? I thought about it while I whipped a few of my scarves around his wrists and elbows and ankles and knees. My sash in a slip knot 'round his throat for good measure. I shoved him till he sat mostly upright. "Ain't this a fucking mess?" I asked him, tilting his head so he could see the tipped over basket, then back around to me. "I *just* had my hair done, got the dogs back from the groomer's *yesterday*, now you pull this stunt! What in the name of every holy thing were you trying to do?"

"Kill you." His voice was rough, sort of a wheeze now from coughing up marsh water.

"Well, duh. Yeah. Question is what you thought that was supposed to accomplish?" He just stuck out his bottom lip. Put me in mind of Albinia, age eight.

"Ain't I done told your bosses, time and again, getting rid of me is gonna do em not one whit of good? Ain't I told em how it's the oracle decides whether or not the Water Museum's ever gonna open up a pipeline and exercise its rights to sell? And if I hadn't told em, ain't it right there in our charter, a matter of public record for every passing pissant to read it if he remembers his A-B-Cs? Well, ain't it?"

My killer kinda shrunk his shoulders in. Breeze picked up some, rustling the reeds. I'm pretty well insulated, but Jasper couldn't help a little shiver. That was all I got out of him that while, though.

I left him and walked a couple of baskets to the boathouse for a life jacket. Had to untie his arms to get it on, and he wanted to wrestle then, having dried out enough to get his dander up. I got a hold on his nice new necktie and pulled. Finished bundling him up while he was trying to recall if he still knew how to breathe. I gave us both a chance to calm down, then dumped him back in the marsh.

Good thing I had Buddy's harness on him. I whistled him over, hooked up Jasper's life jacket and we were on our way once more.

"You're in luck," I told my assassin. "Usually we skip this part of the tour, but I noticed you gronking all the technical dingle-dangles. So I figure you'll get a large charge out of our sewage treatment facilities."

The jacket worked fine. Buddy paddled joyfully along next to the bridges. He likes to make himself useful.

It wasn't far to the settling ponds. I gave Jasper plenty of chances to tell me about Colorado wildlife and the dying riparian ecosystem, but he didn't seem to be in the mood. He was mostly silent, excepting the odd snort when Buddy kicked up too big a wake.

Really, the ponds weren't that bad. Joy, my youngest daughter, got the Museum a contract with a local trailer park, but they're pretty much dormant till early May. Right then, the park was mostly empty, just a few old retirees, so the effluent came mainly from my offices and the tanks of a couple friends.

I glossed over that, though, in my lecture. I concentrated instead on wind-driven aeration paddles, ultra-sound and tank resonance, and oh, yes, our patented, prize-winning, bacteriophagic eels. As the ponds got murkier and murkier, Jasper's gills got greener and greener, so to speak. He held up well. I had dragged him over two locks, and had him belly down on the third when he broke.

"Nonononono!" he gibbered at me. "What is it, what is it, don't let it touch me, please!" I bent over and looked where he was looking. Something was floating in the water. I fished it out. One end of a cucumber had my killer sobbing out his heart and wriggling like a worm with eyes to see the hook.

People are funny.

Girlfriend came up and sniffed the piece of cucumber. It was kind of rotten, and after all, she is a dog. I threw it back to the eels, unhitched Buddy's harness and rolled Jasper over on his back. "You ready to come clean?" I asked him. He nodded desperately.

I wasted quite a few minutes trying to untie the wet silk knotted around his ankles. Then I got disgusted and sawed it through with my car keys. Still left him hobbled at the knees as I marched him off to the laundry room.

We came in through the "Secret Tunnel," what the girls like to call it. Really, it's just a old storm sewer from under the highway. But when I excavated the place and found how close it passed, I annexed the pipe onto my basement there. Handy, sometimes. Grate keeps out most of the possum and nutrias. The big ones, anyways. I locked that into place and set Jasper down on a bench next to the washer, under the skylight.

I nabbed a towel off the steam rack and wrecked it rubbing Buddy down. Took off his poor harness while carefully considering my killer.

He looked a sorrowful mess. His tee shirt was gonna need some enzyme action before you could come anywhere's close to calling it white again, and his jeans and jacket weren't never gonna smell clothesline fresh no more, no matter what. His hat was gone, his hair matted down with algae and such. His eyes were red from crying, his upper lip glistened unbecomingly, and the rest of him steamed in the cool laundry room air.

I prayed for a washday miracle.

"Jasper," I told him, "you are in a terrible spot right now." He nodded a couple times, agreeable as any schoolchild. "Sometimes, the only way outta danger is in. You gotta go through it to get to the other side. You gotta sink to swim.

"I'm telling you honest and true that in spite of what went on out there I bear you absolutely no grudges. You believe me?" Again the nod. "Good. Try to bear it in mind over the next few days."

I reached my shears down from the shelf above his head and cut away the rest of where I'd tied him up: hands first, elbows next, then knees. Those were some nice scarves, too. One my favorite. I was sure hoping he'd be worth it.

"Strip," I told him. He only hung back a second, then he put off his modesty or pride or whatever, and the rest of his wet, useless things right after. Girlfriend tried to run off with a sock but I made her bring it back. "Dump that shit in the washer." I had him set it to low, hot wash, cold rinse, add my powder, and switch on. He didn't seem to know his way around the control panel, and I wondered who'd been taking care of him back home.

Pale goose pimples ain't exactly my cup of vodka, but Jasper was a nice enough looking young man. Given the circumstances. I admired his bumptious little backside as I scooted him on ahead of me over to the Sunshower. Light shafted down through the glass, glittering off the walls of black sand that lined its path for all of two hundred and fifty feet. It was midday by then, and the water pretty warm. He stayed under there a good, long while. I could tell he was finished when he started to look for a way to turn it off. Weren't none, of course. It ain't my job to tell the water when to stop, only to help it through the flow. And naturally, any little deviations I do participate in ain't nothing like what them so called "Water Interest" cowboys got in mind.

"Leave it, Jasper," I told him, motioning him on with my shears. Girlfriend gruffed a little bit to underline the suggestion. We took him along the hall past the Glowing Pool and the steps down to the Well. Later, on his way out, I planned on stopping to offer him a sweet, cold dipperful. Like drinking a cup of stars.

Gradually, the way we walked kept getting darker, the skylights scarcer and more spaced out. Joy and Gerrietta's mosaics running up and down the walls barely glittered by the time we hit the Slipstream, and I heard Jasper gasp as he stepped into swiftly moving water. "Keep going," I told him, and he sloshed obediently on ahead. The dogs were between us, now.

Somewhere close by came the sound of icebergs calving, the underwater songs of whales. I barely heard them as I fumed to myself, wondering if I loaded up a fleet of helicopters to drop off leaflets and trained a flock of condors to fly across the whole United States with a banner in their beaks, if I could make them idiots realize they were not gonna get their Great Lakes pipeline open by killing me off.

Maybe the first few assassins were just to put a touch of fear on me. Maybe they thought the oracle wasn't nothing but a sham, and I could be bullied into letting them use the Museum's exclusive access.

For a while there, looked like they really did want to kill me. With my oldest girl, Albinia, off in the wild blue yonder, there'd be a bit of a legal tussle over the Directorship. Guess they might of planned to take advantage of the confusion ensuing upon my untimely demise.

Lately, most of their moves they seemed to make just purely to annoy me. Sending out an amateur like this here Jasper—

Up ahead, the sloshing stopped. My killer stood waiting for us on the ledge, in the dark.

"Here's where you'll be staying." I opened the door to the Dressing Room. He didn't seem much taken with the place. Sure, the ceiling's kind of low, 'cept for that two hundred foot skylight. And you got to sleep on the floor or in the sandpit. But that sand is soft, and nice and warm on account of the solar heat-exchanger underneath. "I'll give you a little while in here by yourself to figure out what you're gonna be when you come out. Say, a week maybe. Then I'll come back and you can tell me what you'll be needing."

"But—food, water!"

"They're here." He looked around at the bare driftwood walls. "You doubting my word? You're a bright boy, Jasper, I'm sure you'll find where they're at in plenty time."

"I don't understand. You're not trying to torture me are you? I mean, if you want a confession I've already—"

"You don't understand? Then let me explain. I don't need a confession. I got that the first time them cowboys sent someone up here to murder me, fourteen years agone. That's right, Jasper, you are by no means the first hired killer I met up with, though you have got to be the most naive by a crane's holler. *Hitchhiking* to the *hit*? Talk about your sore thumbs!"

Jasper turned red from the collarbone up. "My van broke down in Bliss."

"Yeah, well, guess you couldn't afford a rental, and probably just as conspicuous to get one of them, anyways. But you coulda just given up. Couldn't you?"

That's when my killer started in again about the blackbirds, and added a sheep farm and I don't know what all else. It wasn't the sense of his words I paid attention to: none of them ever had much worth listening to to say at this point. The Earth owed them a living, and a silver teat to suck. And it better be a mighty long dug, 'cause it wasn't supposed to dry up, no matter how hard them cowboys chewed.

They all seemed to need to give their little speeches, though, so I had got used to sitting politely and listening to the kinds of sounds they made. Rattles and grates and angry, poisonous buzzings was what they usually come up with.

Jasper surprised me with an awful good imitation of a red-winged blackbird. Lower register, of course. But his voice trilled up and spilled over the same way, throbbing sweet and pure, straight from his poor little heart. A pretty song, but he was singing it to the wrong audience.

Once, I was one of the richest women on this continent. Powerball winnings. I took and built the Water Museum, then finessed an old congressman of a lover of mine into pushing through our charter. He secured us the sole, exclusive rights to be selling off the Great Lakes' water to irrigate them thirsty Western states.

Or not.

Didn't them cowboys kick up a dust storm! Kept us real busy for a while there, in the courts and on the talkiest of the talk shows.

I'm not rich no more. What I didn't use building the Museum or fighting to protect our charter, I wound up giving us as a donation. Not so famous no more, neither. And important? Not in the least.

During the season, I sell tickets and polish windows, hand out sea-weed candy to unsuspecting kids. Nothing but that would stop because I died, much less if I changed my feeble mind.

I sighed. Jasper had finished his aria, and I prepared to shut the door. Then, shears still held tight, and Buddy close and attentive at hand, I did the funniest thing. I kissed him, right on his damp, still-kinda-smelly forehead. He looked up at me, and he done something funny, too. He smiled. I smiled again, but neither of us said a thing. I backed out, still careful, and locked him in. I have a sneaky suspicion this one *might* turn out to be interesting. When he's good and ready.

1992 alumna **Nisi Shawl's** collection *Filter House* won the 2009 James Tiptree, Jr. Award. Her work has been published at *Strange Horizons*, in *Asimov's SF Magazine*, and in anthologies including *Dark Matter, River, Dark Faith,* and *The Other Half of the Sky*.

She edited *Bloodchildren: Stories by the Octavia E. Butler Scholars*, and co-edited *Strange Matings: Octavia E. Butler, Science Fiction, Feminism, and African American Voices*. With classmate Cynthia Ward she co-authored *Writing the Other: A Practical Approach*.

Shawl is a cofounder of the Carl Brandon Society and serves on the Board of Directors of the Clarion West Writers Workshop. Her website is www.nisishawl.com.

# Nancy Kress
# on Nisi Shawl

It's funny, the things you remember about a person decades later. I've known Nisi Shawl ever since she was a student in the very first Clarion West class I taught, in 1992. Since then we've been together at many parties, dinners, Clarion West functions. Yet two things remain clear in my mind from that first meeting long ago.

First, she made me a pair of earrings. White translucent beads, and I wore them often and for a long time until, in the way of earrings, I lost one. The second thing, more significant, is that she was one of the strongest writers there.

She still is. "The Water Museum" is a lovely story, rich with what we have not yet lost but might, and distressingly soon. I grew up near the Great Lakes (Buffalo, New York). I remember them so polluted and scummy that a canal off of Lake Erie actually caught fire—the water itself burning. I remember the long slow decades of clean-up. And I remember, not that long ago, the first rumblings of political dissatisfaction that the United States's treaty with Canada, who owns half the water rights, forbids diversion of water from the Lakes to those American states already in need of it. The only exception is supposed to be for the city of Chicago, grandfathered in at the time of the treaty. This treaty is going to be a source of considerable future conflict.

"The Water Museum" is just as notable for what it celebrates as for what it mourns. We have all experienced the transcendent beauty and peace of waterfalls, marshes, small hidden pools in the forest. If that hasn't happened to you recently, then let this story remind you of, as Nisi so poignantly phrases it, the "dance" of living water.

**Nancy Kress** is the author of 26 books: sixteen science fiction novels, three fantasy novels, four short story collections, and three books on writing. Her fiction has won five Nebula Awards, two Hugos, a Sturgeon, and a John W. Campbell Memorial Award.

# The Evolution of Trickster Stories Among the Dogs of North Park After the Change

Kij Johnson

1987

North Park is a backwater tucked into a loop of the Kaw River: pale dirt and baked grass, aging playground equipment, silver-leafed cottonwoods, underbrush—mosquitoes and gnats blackening the air at dusk. To the south is a busy street. Engine noise and the hissing of tires on pavement mean it's no retreat. By late afternoon the air smells of hot tar and summertime river-bottoms. There are two entrances to North Park: the formal one, of silvered railroad ties framing an arch of sorts; and an accidental little gap in the fence, back where Second Street dead-ends into the park's west side, just by the river.

A few stray dogs have always lived here, too clever or shy or easily hidden to be caught and taken to the shelter. On nice days (and this is a nice day, a smell like boiling sweet corn easing in on the south wind to blunt the sharper scents), Linna sits at one of the faded picnic tables with a reading assignment from her summer class and a paper bag full of fast food, the remains of her lunch. She waits to see who visits her.

The squirrels come first, and she ignores them. At last she sees the little dust-colored dog, the one she calls Gold.

"What'd you bring?" he says. His voice, like all dogs' voices, is hoarse and rasping. He has trouble making certain sounds. Linna understands him the way one understands a bad lisp or someone speaking with a harelip.

(It's a universal fantasy, isn't it?—that the animals learn to speak, and at last we learn what they're thinking, our cats and dogs and horses: a new era in cross-species understanding. But nothing ever works out quite as we imagine. When the Change happened, it affected all the mammals we have shaped to meet our own needs. They all could talk a little, and they all could frame their thoughts well enough to talk. Cattle, horses, goats, llamas; rats, too. Pigs. Minks. And dogs and cats. And we found that, really, we prefer our slaves mute.

(The cats mostly leave, even ones who love their owners. Their pragmatic sociopathy makes us uncomfortable, and we bore them; and they leave. They slip out between our legs and lope into summer dusks. We hear them at night, fighting as they sort out ranges, mates, boundaries. The savage sounds frighten us, a fear that does not ease when our cat Klio returns home for a single night, asking to be fed and to sleep on the bed. A lot of cats die in fights or under car wheels, but they seem to prefer that to living under our roofs; and as I said, we fear them.

(Some dogs run away. Others are thrown out by the owners who loved them. Some were always free.)

"Chicken and French fries," Linna tells the dog, Gold. Linna has a summer cold that ruins her appetite, and in any case it's too hot to eat. She brought her lunch leftovers, hours old but still lukewarm: half of a Chik-fil-A and some French fries. He never takes anything from her hand, so she tosses the food onto the ground just beyond kicking range. Gold likes French fries, so he eats them first.

Linna tips her head toward the two dogs she sees peeking from the bushes. (She knows better than to lift her hand suddenly, even to point or wave.) "Who are these two?"

"Hope and Maggie."

"Hi, Hope," Linna says. "Hi, Maggie." The dogs dip their heads nervously as if bowing. They don't meet her eyes. She recognizes their expressions, the hurt wariness: she's seen it a few times, on the recent strays of North Park, the ones whose owners threw them out after the Change. There are five North Park dogs she's seen so far: these two are new.

"Story," says the collie, Hope.

## 2. One Dog Loses Her Collar.

This is the same dog. She lives in a little room with her master. She has a collar that itches, so she claws at it. When her master comes home, he ties a rope to the collar and takes her outside to the sidewalk. There's a busy street outside. The dog wants to play on the street with the cars, which smell strong and move very fast. When her master tries to take her back inside, she sits down and won't move. He pulls on the rope and her collar slips over her ears and falls to the ground. When she sees this, she runs into the street. She gets hit by a car and dies.

This is not the first story Linna has heard the dogs tell. The first one was about a dog who's been inside all day and rushes outside with his master to urinate against a tree. When he's done, his master hits him, because his master was standing too close and his shoe is covered with urine. *One Dog Pisses on a Person.* The dog in the story has no name, but the dogs all call him (or her: she changes sex with each telling) One Dog. Each story starts: "This is the same dog."

The little dust-colored dog, Gold, is the storyteller. As the sky dims and the mosquitoes swarm, the strays of North Park ease from the underbrush and sit or lie belly-down in the dirt to listen to Gold. Linna listens, as well.

(Perhaps the dogs always told these stories and we could not understand them. Now they tell their stories here in North Park, as does the pack in Cruz Park a little to the south, and so across the world. The tales are not all the same, though there are similarities. There is no possibility of gathering them all. The dogs do not welcome eager anthropologists with their tape recorders and their agendas.

(The cats after the Change tell stories as well, but no one will ever know what they are.)

When the story is done, and the last of the French fries eaten, Linna asks Hope, "Why are you here?" The collie turns her face away, and it is Maggie, the little Jack Russell, who answers: "Our mother made us leave. She has a baby." Maggie's tone is matter-of-fact: it is Hope who mourns for the woman and child she loved, who compulsively licks her paw as though she were dirty and cannot be cleaned.

Linna knows this story. She's heard it from the other new strays of North Park: all but Gold, who has been feral all his life.

(Sometimes we think we want to know what our dogs think. We don't, not really. Someone who watches us with unclouded eyes and sees who we really are is more frightening than a man with a gun. We can fight or flee or avoid the man, but the truth sticks like pine sap. After the Change, some dog owners feel a cold place in the pit of their stomachs when they meet their pets' eyes. Sooner or later, they ask their dogs to find new homes, or they forget to latch the gate, or they force the dogs out with curses and the ends of brooms. Or the dogs leave, unable to bear the look in their masters' eyes.

(The dogs gather in parks and gardens, anywhere close to food and water where they can stay out of people's way. Cruz Park ten blocks away is big, fifteen acres in the middle of town, and sixty or more dogs already have gathered there. They raid trash or beg from their former owners or strangers. They sleep under the bushes and bandstand and the inexpensive civic sculptures. No one goes to Cruz Park on their lunch breaks any more.

(In contrast North Park is a little dead-end. No one ever did go there, and so no one really worries much about the dogs there. Not yet.)

### 3. One Dog Tries to Mate.

This is the same dog. There is a female he very much wants to mate with. All the other dogs want to mate with her, too, but her master keeps her in a yard surrounded by a chain-link fence. She whines and rubs against the fence. All the dogs try to dig under the fence, but its base is buried too deep to find. They try to jump over, but it is too tall for even the biggest or most agile dogs.

One Dog has an idea. He finds a cigarette butt on the street and tucks it in his mouth. He finds a shirt in a dumpster and pulls it on. He walks right up to the master's front door and presses the bell-button. When the master answers the door, One Dog says, "I'm from the men with white trucks. I have to check your electrical statico-pressure. Can you let me into your yard?"

The man nods and lets him go in back. One Dog takes off his shirt and drops the cigarette and mates with the female. It feels very nice, but when he is done and they are still linked together, he starts to whine.

The man hears and comes out. He's very angry. He shoots One Dog and kills him. The female tells One Dog, "You would have been better off if you had found another female."

The next day after classes (hot again, and heavy with the smell of cut grass), Linna finds a dog. She hears crying and crouches to peek under a hydrangea, its blue-gray flowers as fragile as paper. It's a Maltese with filthy fur matted with twigs and burrs. There are stains under her eyes and she is moaning, the terrible sound of an injured animal.

The Maltese comes nervous to Linna's outstretched fingers and the murmur of her voice. "I won't hurt you," Linna says. "It's okay."

Linna picks the dog up carefully, feeling the dog flinch under her hand as she checks for injuries. Linna knows already that the pain is not physical; she knows the dog's story before she hears it.

The house nearby is massive, a graceful collection of Edwardian gingerbread work and oriel windows and dark green roof tiles. The garden is large, with a low fence just tall enough to keep a Maltese in. Or out. A woman answers the doorbell: Linna can feel the Maltese vibrate in her arms at the sight of the woman: excitement, not fear.

"Is this your dog?" Linna asks with a smile. "I found her outside, scared."

The woman's eyes flicker to the dog and away, back to Linna's face.

"We don't have a dog," she says.

(We like our slaves mute. We like to imagine they love us, and they do. But they are also with us because freedom and security war in each of us, and sometimes security wins out. They do love us. But.)

In those words Linna has already seen how this conversation will go, the denials and the tangled fear and anguish and self-loathing of the woman. Linna turns away in the middle of the woman's words and walks down the stairs, the brick walkway, through the gate and north, toward North Park. The dog's name is Sophie. The other dogs are kind to her.

(When George Washington died, his will promised freedom for his slaves, but only after his wife had also passed on. A terrified Martha freed them within hours of his death. Though the dogs love us, thoughtful owners can't help but wonder what they think when they sit on the floor beside our beds as we sleep, teeth slightly bared as they pant in the heat. Do the dogs realize that their freedom hangs by the thread of our lives? The curse of speech—the things they could say and yet choose not to say—makes that thread seem very thin.

(Some people keep their dogs, even after the Change. Some people have the strength to love, no matter what. But many of us only learn the limits of our love when they have been breached. Some people keep their dogs; many do not.

(The dogs who stay seem to tell no stories.)

### 4. One Dog Catches Possums.

This is the same dog. She is very hungry because her master forgot to feed her, and there's no good trash because the possums have eaten it all. "If I catch the possums," she says, "I can eat them now and then the trash later, because then they won't be getting it all."

She knows that possums are very hard to catch, so she lies down next to a trash bin and starts moaning. Sure enough, when the possums come to eat trash, they hear her and waddle over.

"Oh, oh oh," moans the dog. "I told the rats a great secret and now they won't let me rest."

The possums look around but they don't see any rats. "Where are they?" the oldest possum asks.

One Dog says, "Everything I eat ends up in a place inside me like a giant garbage heap. I told the rats and they snuck in, and they've been there ever since." And she let out a great howl. "Their cold feet are horrible!"

The possums think for a time and then the oldest says, "This garbage heap, is it large?"

"Huge," One Dog says.

"Are the rats fierce?" says the youngest.

"Not at all," One Dog tells the possums. "If they weren't inside me, they wouldn't be any trouble, even for a possum. Ow! I can feel one dragging bits of bacon around."

After whispering among themselves for a time, the possums say, "We can go in and chase out the rats, but you must promise not to hunt us ever again."

"If you catch any rats, I'll never eat another possum," she promises.

One by one the possums crawl into her mouth. She eats all but the oldest, because she's too full to eat any more.

"This is much better than dog food or trash," she says.

(Dogs love us. We have bred them to do this for ten thousand, a hundred thousand, a million years. It's hard to make a dog hate people, though we have at times tried, with our junkyard guards and our attack dogs.

(It's hard to make dogs hate people, but it is possible.)

Another day, just at dusk, the sky an indescribable violet. Linna has a hard time telling how many dogs there are now: ten or twelve, perhaps. The dogs around her snuffle, yip, bark. One moans, the sound of a sled dog trying to howl. Words float up: *dry, bite, food, piss.*

The sled dog continues its moaning howl, and one by one the others join in with drawn-out barks and moans. They are trying to howl as a pack, but none of them know how to do this, nor what it is supposed to sound like. It's a wolf-secret, and they do not know any of those.

Sitting on a picnic table, Linna closes her eyes to listen. The dogs outyell the trees' restless whispers, the river's wet sliding, even the hissing roaring street. Ten dogs, or fifteen. Or more: Linna can't tell, because they are all around her now, in the brush, down by the Kaw's muddy bank, behind the cottonwoods, beside the tall fence that separates the park from the street.

The misformed howl, the hint of killing animals gathered to work efficiently together—it awakens a monkey-place somewhere in her amygdala or even deeper, stained into her genes. Adrenaline hits hot as panic. Her heart beats so hard that it feels as though she's torn it. Her monkey-self opens her eyes to watch the dogs through pupils constricted enough to dim the twilight; it clasps her arms tight over her soft belly to protect the intestines and liver that are the first parts eaten; it tucks her head between her shoulders to protect her neck and throat. She pants through bared teeth, fighting a keening noise.

Several of the dogs don't even try to howl. Gold is one of them. (The howling would have defined them before the poisoned gift of speech; but the dogs have words now. They will never be free of stories, though their stories may free them. Gold may understand this.

(They were wolves once, ten thousand, twenty thousand, a hundred thousand years ago. Or more. And before we were men and women, we were monkeys and fair game for them. After a time we grew taller and stronger and smarter: human, eventually. We learned about fire and weapons. If you can tame it, a wolf is an effective weapon, a useful tool. If you can keep it. We learned how to keep wolves close.

(But we were monkeys first, and they were wolves. Blood doesn't forget.)

After a thousand heartbeats fast as birds', long after the howl has decayed into snuffling and play-barks and speech, Linna eases back into her forebrain. Alive and safe. But not untouched. Gold tells a tale.

## 5. One Dog Tries to Become Like Men.

This is the same dog. There is a party, and people are eating and drinking and using their clever fingers to do things. The dog wants to do everything they do, so he says, "Look, I'm human," and he starts barking and dancing about.

The people say, "You're not human. You're just a dog pretending. If you wanted to be human, you have to be bare, with just a little hair here and there."

One Dog goes off and bites his hairs out and rubs the places he can't reach against the sidewalk until there are bloody patches where he scraped off his skin, as well.

He returns to the people and says, "Now I am human," and he shows his bare skin.

"That's not human," the people say. "We stand on our hind legs and sleep on our backs. First you must do these things." One Dog goes off and practices standing on his hind legs until he no longer cries out loud when he does it. He leans against a wall to sleep on his back, but it hurts and he does not sleep much. He returns and says, "Now I am human," and he walks on his hind legs from place to place.

"That's not human," the people say. "Look at these, we have fingers. First you must have fingers."

One Dog goes off and he bites at his front paws until his toes are separated. They bleed and hurt and do not work well, but he returns and says, "Now I am human," and he tries to take food from a plate.

"That's not human," say the people. "First you must dream, as we do."

"What do you dream of?" the dog asks.

"Work and failure and shame and fear," the people say.

"I will try," the dog says. He rolls onto his back and sleeps. Soon he is crying out loud and his bloody paws beat at the air. He is dreaming of all they told him.

"That dog is making too much noise," the people say and they kill him.

Linna calls the Humane Society the next day, though she feels like a traitor to the dogs for doing this. The sky is sullen with the promise of rainstorms, and even though she knows that rain is not such a big problem in the life of a dog, she worries a little, remembering her own dog when she was a little girl, who had been terrified of thunder.

So she calls. The phone rings fourteen times before someone picks it up. Linna tells the woman about the dogs of North Park. "Is there anything we can do?"

The woman barks a single unamused laugh. "I wish. People keep bringing them—been doing that since right after the Change. We're packed to the rafters—and they *keep* bringing them in, or just dumping them in the parking lot, too chickenshit to come in and tell anyone."

"So—" Linna begins, but she has no idea what to ask. She can see the scene in her mind, a hundred or more terrified angry confused grieving hungry thirsty dogs. At least the dogs of North Park have some food and water, and the shelter of the underbrush at night.

The woman has continued "—they can't take care of themselves—"

"Do you know that?" Linna asks, but the woman talks on.

"—and we don't have the resources — "

"So what do you do?" Linna interrupts. "Put them to sleep?"

"If we have to," the woman says, and her voice is so weary that Linna wants suddenly to comfort her. "They're in the runs, four and five in each one because we don't have anywhere to put them, and we can't get them outside because the paddocks are full; it smells like you wouldn't believe. And they tell these stories—"

"What's going to happen to them?" Linna means all the dogs, now that they have speech, now that they are equals.

"Oh, hon, I don't know." The woman's voice trembles. "But I know we can't save them all."

(Why do we fear them when they learn speech? They are still dogs, still subordinate. It doesn't change who they are or their loyalty.

(It is not always fear we run from. Sometimes it is shame.)

## 6. One Dog Invents Death.

This is the same dog. She lives in a nice house with people. They do not let her run outside a fence and they did things to her so that she can't have puppies, but they feed her well and are kind, and they rub places on her back that she can't reach.

At this time, there is no death for dogs, they live forever. After a while, One Dog becomes bored with her fence and her food and even the people's pats. But she can't convince the people to allow her outside the fence.

"There should be death," she decides. "Then there will be no need for boredom."

(How do the dogs know things? How do they frame an abstract like *thank you* or a collective concept like *chicken*? Since the Change, everyone has been asking that question. If awareness is dependent on linguistics, an answer is that the dogs have learned to use words, so the words themselves are the frame they use. But it is still *our* frame, *our* language. They are still not free.

(Any more than we are.)

It is a moonless night, and the hot wet air blurs the streetlights so that they illuminate nothing except their own glass globes. Linna is there, though it is very late. She no longer attends her classes and has switched to the dogs' schedule, sleeping the afternoons away in the safety of her apartment. She cannot bring herself to sleep in the dogs' presence. In the park, she is taut as a strung wire, a single monkey among wolves; but she returns each dusk, and listens, and sometimes speaks. There are maybe fifteen dogs now, though she's sure more hide in the bushes, or doze, or prowl for food.

"I remember," a voice says hesitantly. (*Remember* is a frame; they did not "remember" before the word, only lived in a series of nows longer or shorter in duration. Memory breeds resentment. Or so we fear.) "I had a home, food, a warm place, something I chewed—a, a blanket. A woman and a man and she gave me all these things, patted me." Voices in assent: pats remembered. "But she wasn't always nice. She yelled sometimes. She took the blanket away. And she'd drag at my collar until it hurt sometimes. But when she made food she'd put a piece on the floor for me to eat. Beef, it was. That was nice again."

Another voice in the darkness: "Beef. That is a hamburger." The dogs are trying out the concept of *beef* and the concept of *hamburger* and they are connecting them.

"*Nice* is not being hurt," a dog says.

"Not-nice is collars and leashes."

"And rules."

"Being inside and only coming out to shit and piss."

"People are nice and not nice," says the first voice. Linna finally sees that it belongs to a small dusty black dog sitting near the roots of an immense oak. Its enormous fringed ears look like radar dishes. "I learned to think and the woman brought me here. She was sad, but she hit me with stones until I ran away, and then she left. A person is nice and not nice."

The dogs are silent, digesting this. "Linna?" Hope says. "How can people be nice and then not nice?"

"I don't know," she says, because she knows the real question is, *How can they stop loving us?*

(The answer even Linna has trouble seeing is that *nice* and *not-nice* have nothing to do with love. And even loving someone doesn't always mean you can share your house and the fine thread of your life, or sleep safely in the same place.)

### 7. One Dog Tricks the White-Truck Man.

This is the same dog. He is very hungry and looking through the alleys for something to eat. He sees a man with a white truck coming toward him. One Dog knows that the white-truck men catch dogs sometimes, so he's afraid. He drags some old bones out of the trash and heaps them up and settles on top of them. He pretends not to see the white-truck man but says loudly, "Boy that was a delicious man I just killed, but I'm still starved. I hope I can catch another one."

Well, that white-truck man runs right away. But someone was watching all this from her kitchen window and she runs out to the man and tells him, "One Dog never killed a man! That's just a pile of bones from my barbeque last week, and he's making a mess out of my backyard. Come catch him."

The white-truck man and the person run back to where One Dog is still gnawing on one of the bones in his pile. He sees them and guesses what has happened, so he's afraid. But he pretends not to see them and says loudly, "I'm still starved! I hope that human comes back soon with that white-truck man I asked her to get for me."

The white-truck man and the woman both run away, and he does not see them again that day.

"Why is she here?"

It's one of the new dogs, a lean Lab-cross with a limp. He doesn't talk to her but to Gold, and Linna sees his anger in his liquid brown eyes, feels it like a hot scent rising from his back. He's one of the half-strays, an outdoor dog who lived on a chain. It was no effort at all for his owner to unhook the chain and let him go; no effort for the Lab-cross to leave his owner's yard and drift across town killing cats and raiding trash cans, and end up in North Park.

There are thirty dogs now and maybe more. The newcomers are warier around her than the earlier dogs. Some, the ones who have taken several days to end up here, dodging police cruisers and pedestrians' Mace, are actively hostile.

"She's no threat," Gold says.

The Lab-cross says nothing but approaches with head lowered and hackles raised. Linna sits on the picnic table's bench and tries not to screech, to bare her teeth and scratch and run. The situation is as charged as the air before a thunderstorm. Gold is no longer the pack's leader—there's a German Shepherd dog who holds his tail higher—but he still has status as the one who tells the stories. The German Shepherd doesn't care whether Linna's there or not; he won't stop another dog from attacking if it wishes. Linna spends much of her time with her hands flexed to bare claws she doesn't have.

"She listens, that's all," says Hope: frightened Hope standing up for her. "And brings food sometimes." Others speak up: *she got rid of my collar when it got burrs under it. She took the tick off me. She stroked my head.*

The Lab-cross's breath on her ankles is hot, his nose wet and surprisingly warm. Dogs were once wolves; right now this burns in her mind. She tries not to shiver. "You're sick," the dog says at last.

"I'm well enough," Linna says through clenched teeth.

Just like that the dog loses interest and turns back to the others.

(Why does Linna come here at all? Her parents had a dog when she was a little girl. Ruthie was so obviously grateful for Linna's love and the home she was offered, the old quilt on the floor, the dog food that fell from the sky twice a day like manna. Linna wondered even then whether Ruthie dreamt of a Holy Land, and what that place would have looked like. Linna's parents were kind and generous, denied Ruthie's needs only when they couldn't help it; paid for her medical bills without too much complaining; didn't put her to sleep until she became incontinent and messed on the living-room floor.

(Even we dog-lovers wrestle with our consciences. We promised to keep our pets forever until they died; but that was from a comfortable height, when we were the masters and they the slaves. Some Inuit tribes believe all animals have souls—except for dogs. This is a convenient stance. They could not use their dogs as they do—beat them, work them, starve them, eat them, feed them one to the other— if dog's were men's equals.

(Or perhaps they could. Our record with our own species is not so exemplary.)

## 8. One Dog and the Eating Man.

This is the same dog. She lives with the Eating Man, who eats only good things while One Dog has only dry kibble. The Eating Man is always hungry. He orders a pizza but he is still hungry, so he eats all the meat and vegetables he finds in the refrigerator. But he's still hungry, so he opens all the cupboards and eats the cereal and noodles and flour and sugar in there. And he's still hungry. There is nothing left, so he eats all One Dog's dry kibble, leaving nothing for One Dog.

So One Dog kills the Eating Man. "It was him or me," One Dog says. The Eating Man is the best thing One Dog has ever eaten.

Linna has been sleeping the days away so that she can be with the dogs at night, when they feel safest out on the streets looking for food. So now it's hot dusk, a day later, and she's just awakened in tangled sheets in a bedroom with flaking walls: the sky a hard haze, air warm and wet as laundry. Linna is walking past Cruz Park, on her way to North Park. She has a bag with a loaf of day-old bread, some cheap sandwich meat, and an extra order of French fries. The fatty smell of the fries sticks in her nostrils. Gold never gets them any more, unless she saves them from the other dogs and gives them to him specially.

She thinks nothing of the blue and red and strobing white lights ahead of her on Mass Street until she gets close enough to see that this is no traffic stop. There's no wrecked car, no distraught student who turned left across traffic because she was late for her job and was T-boned. Half a dozen police cars perch on the sidewalks around the park, and she can see reflected lights from others otherwise hidden by the park's shrubs. Fifteen or twenty policemen stand around in clumps, like dead leaves caught for a moment in an eddy and freed by some unseen current.

Everyone knows Cruz Park is full of dogs—sixty or seventy according to today's editorial in the local paper, each one a health and safety risk—but very few dogs are visible at the moment, and none look familiar to her, either as neighbors' ex-pets or wanderers from the North Park pack.

Linna approaches an eddy of policemen; its elements drift apart, rejoin other groups.

"Cruz Park is closed," the remaining officer says to Linna. He's a tall man with a military cut that makes him look older than he is.

It's no surprise that the flashing lights, the cars, the yellow CAUTION tape, and the policemen are about the dogs. There've been complaints from the people neighboring the park—overturned trashcans, feces on the sidewalks, even one attack when a man tried to grab a stray's collar and the stray fought to get away. Today's editorial merely crystalized what everyone already felt.

Linna thinks of Gold, Sophie, Hope. "They're just dogs."

The officer looks a little uncomfortable. "The park is closed until we can address current health and safety concerns." Linna can practically hear the quote marks from the official statement.

"What are you going to do?" she asks.

He relaxes a little. "Right now we're waiting for Animal Control. Any dogs they capture will go to Douglas County Humane Society, they'll try to track down the owners—"

"The ones who kicked the dogs out in the first place?" Linna asks. "No one's gonna want these dogs back, you know that."

"That's the procedure," he says, his back stiff again, tone harsh. "If the Humane—"

"Do you have a dog?" Linna interrupts him. "I mean, did you? Before this started?"

He turns and walks away without a word.

Linna runs the rest of the way to North Park, slowing to a lumbering trot when she gets a cramp in her side. There are no police cars up here, but yellow plastic police tape stretches across the entry: CAUTION. She walks around to the side entrance, off Second Street. The police don't seem to know about the break in the fence.

### 9. One Dog Meets Tame Dogs.

This is the same dog. He lives in a park, and eats at the restaurants across the street. On his way to the restaurants one day, he walks past a yard with two dogs. They laugh at him and say, "We get dog food every day and our master lets us sleep in the kitchen, which is cool in the summer and warm in the winter. And you have to cross Sixth Street to get food where you might get run over, and you have to sleep in the heat and the cold."

The dog walks past them to get to the restaurants, and he eats the fallen tacos and French fries and burgers around the dumpster. When he sits by the restaurant doors, many people give him bits of food; one person gives him chicken in a paper dish. He walks back to the yard and lets the two dogs smell the chicken and grease on his breath through the fence. "Ha on you," he says, and then goes back to his park and sleeps on a pile of dry rubbish under the bridge, where the breeze is cool. When night comes, he goes looking for a mate and no one stops him.

(Whatever else it is, the Change of the animals—mute to speaking, dumb to dreaming—is a test for us. We pass the test when we accept that their dreams and desires and goals may not be ours. Many people fail this test. But we don't have to, and even failing we can try again. And again. And pass at last.

(A slave is trapped, choiceless and voiceless; but so is her owner. Those we have injured may forgive us, but how can we know? Can we trust them with our homes, our lives, our hearts? Animals did not forgive before the Change; mostly they forgot. But the Change brought memory, and memory requires forgiveness, and how can we trust them to forgive us?

(And how do we forgive ourselves? Mostly we don't. Mostly we pretend to forget, and hope it becomes true.)

At noon the next day, Linna jerks awake, monkey-self already dragging her to her feet. Even before she's fully awake, she knows that what woke her wasn't a car's backfire. It was a shotgun blast, and it was only a couple of blocks away, and she already knows why.

She drags on clothes and runs to Cruz Park, no stitch in her side this time. The flashing police cars and CAUTION tape and men are all still there, but now she sees dogs everywhere, twenty or more laid flat near the sidewalk, the way dogs sleep on hot summer days. Too many of the ribcages are still; too many of the eyes open, dust and pollen already gathering.

Linna has no words, can only watch speechless; but the men say enough. First thing in the morning, the Animal Control people went to Dillon's grocery store and bought fifty one-pound packages of cheap hamburger on sale, and they poisoned them all, and then scattered them around the park. Linna can see little blue styrene squares from the packaging scattered here and there, among the dogs.

The dying dogs don't say much. Most have fallen back on the

ancient language of pain, wordless yelps and keening. Men walk among them, shooting the suffering dogs, jabbing poles into the underbrush looking for any that might have slipped away.

People come in cars and trucks and on bicycles and scooters and on their feet. The police officers around Cruz Park keep sending them away—"a health risk" says one officer: "safety," says another, but the people keep coming back, or new people.

Linna's eyes are blind with tears; she blinks and they slide down her face, oddly cool and thick.

"Killing them is the answer?" says a woman beside her. Her face is wet as well, but her voice is even, as if they are debating this in a class, she and Linna. The woman holds her baby in her arms, a white cloth thrown over its face so that it can't see. "I have three dogs at home, and they've never hurt anything. Words don't change that."

"What if they change?" Linna asks. "What if they ask for real food and a bed soft as yours, the chance to dream their own dreams?"

"I'll try to give it to them," the woman says, but her attention is focused on the park, the dogs. "They can't do this!"

"Try and stop them." Linna turns away tasting her tears. She should feel comforted by the woman's words, the fact that not everyone has forgotten how to love animals when they are no longer slaves, but she feels nothing. And she walks north, carved hollow.

## 10. One Dog Goes to the Place of Pieces.

This is the same dog. She is hit by a car and part of her flies off and runs into a dark culvert. She does not know what the piece is, so she chases it. The culvert is long and it gets so cold that her breath puffs out in front of her. When she gets to the end, there's no light and the world smells like cold metal. She walks along a road. Cold cars rush past but they don't slow down. None of them hit her.

One Dog comes to a parking lot which has nothing in it but the legs of dogs. The legs walk from place to place, but they cannot see or smell or eat. None of them is her leg, so she walks on. After this she finds a parking lot filled with the ears of dogs, and then one filled with the assholes of dogs, and the eyes of dogs and the bodies of dogs; but none of the ears and assholes and eyes and bodies are hers, so she walks on.

The last parking lot she comes to has nothing at all in it except for little smells, like puppies. She can tell one of the little smells is hers, so she calls to it and it comes to her. She doesn't know where the little smell belongs on her body, so she carries it in her mouth and walks back past the parking lots and through the culvert.

One Dog cannot leave the culvert because a man stands in the way. She puts the little smell down carefully and says, "I want to go back."

The man says, "You can't unless all your parts are where they belong."

One Dog can't think of where the little smell belongs. She picks up the little smell and tries to sneak past the man, but the man catches her and hits her. One Dog tries to hide it under a hamburger wrapper and pretend it's not there, but the man catches that, too.

One Dog thinks some more and finally says, "Where does the little smell belong?"

The man says, "Inside you."

So One Dog swallows the little smell. She realizes that the man has been trying to keep her from returning home but that the man cannot lie about the little smell. One Dog growls and runs past him, and returns to our world.

There are two police cars pulled onto the sidewalk before North Park's main entrance. Linna takes in the sight of them in three stages: first, she has seen police everywhere today, so they are no shock; second, they are *here*, at *her* park, threatening *her* dogs, and this is like being kicked in the stomach; and third, she thinks: *I have to get past them.*

North Park has two entrances, but one isn't used much. Linna walks around to the little narrow dirt path from Second Street.

The park is never quiet. There's busy Sixth Street just south, and the river and its noises to the north and east and west; trees and bushes hissing with the hot wind; the hum of insects.

But the dogs are quiet. She's never seen them all in the daylight, but they're gathered now, silent and loll-tongued in the bright daylight.

There are forty or more. Everyone is dirty, now. Any long fur is matted; anything white is dust-colored. Most of them are thinner than they were when they arrived. The dogs face one of the tables, as orderly as the audience at a string quartet; but the tension in the air is so obvious that Linna stops short.

Gold stands on the table. There are a couple of dogs she doesn't recognize in the dust nearby: flopped flat with their sides heaving, tongues long and flecked with white foam. One is hunched over; he drools onto the ground and retches helplessly. The other dog has a scratch along her flank. The blood is the brightest thing Linna can see in the sunlight, a red so strong it hurts her eyes.

The Cruz Park cordon was permeable, of course. These two managed to slip past the police cars. The vomiting one is dying.

She realizes suddenly that every dog's muzzle is swiveled toward her. The air snaps with something that makes her back-brain bare its teeth and scream, her hackles rise. The monkey-self looks for escape, but the trees are not close enough to climb (and she is no climber), the road and river too far away. She is a spy in a gulag; the prisoners have little to lose by killing her.

"You shouldn't have come back," Gold says.

"I came to tell you—warn you." Even through her monkey-self's defiance, Linna weeps helplessly.

"We already know." The pack's leader, the German Shepherd dog, says. "They're killing us all. We're leaving the park."

She shakes her head, fighting for breath. "They'll kill you. There are police cars on Sixth—they'll shoot you however you get out. They're *waiting*."

"Will it be better here?" Gold asks. "They'll kill us anyway, with their poisoned meat. We *know*. You're afraid, all of you—"

"I'm not—" Linna starts, but he breaks in.

"We smell it on everyone, even the people who take care of us or feed us. We have to get out of here."

"They'll *kill* you," Linna says again.

"Some of us might make it."

"Wait! Maybe there's a way," Linna says, and then: "I have stories."

In the stifling air, Linna can hear the dogs pant, even over the street noises. "People have their own stories," Gold says at last. "Why should we listen to yours?"

"We made you into what we wanted; we *owned* you. Now you are becoming what *you* want. You belong to yourselves. But we have stories, too, and we learned from them. Will you listen?"

The air shifts, but whether it is the first movement of the still air or the shifting of the dogs, she can't tell.

"Tell your story," says the German Shepherd.

Linna struggles to remember half-read textbooks from a sophomore course on folklore, framing her thoughts as she speaks them. "We used to tell a lot of stories about Coyote. The animals were here before humans were, and Coyote was one of them. He did a lot of stuff, got in a lot of trouble. Fooled everyone."

"I know about coyotes," a dog says. "There were some by where I used to live. They eat puppies sometimes."

"I bet they do," Linna says. "Coyotes eat everything. But this wasn't *a* coyote, it's *Coyote*. The one and only."

The dogs murmur. She hears them work it out: *Coyote* is the same as *this is the same dog.*

"So. Coyote disguised himself as a female so that he could hang out with a bunch of females, just so he could mate with them. He pretended to be dead, and then when the crows came down to eat him, he snatched them up and ate every one! When a greedy man was keeping all the animals for himself, Coyote pretended to be a very rich person and then freed them all, so that everyone could eat. He—" She pauses to think, looks down at the dogs all around her. The monkey-fear is gone: she is the storyteller, the maker of thoughts. They will not kill her, she knows. "Coyote did all these things, and a lot more things. I bet you'll think of some, too.

"I have an idea of how to save you," she says. "Some of you might die, but some chance is better than no chance."

"Why would we trust you?" says the Lab-cross who has never liked her, but the other dogs are with her. She feels it, and answers.

"Because this trick, maybe it's even good enough for Coyote. Will you let me show you?"

We people are so proud of our intelligence, but that makes it easier to trick us. We see the white-truck men and we believe they're whatever we're expecting to see. Linna goes to U-Haul and rents a pickup truck for the afternoon. She digs out a white shirt she used to wear when she ushered at the concert hall. She knows *clipboard with printout* means *official responsibilities*, so she throws one on the dashboard of the truck.

She backs the pickup to the little entrance on Second Street. The dogs slip through the gap in the fence and scramble into the pickup's bed. She lifts the ones that are too small to jump so high. And then they arrange themselves carefully, flat on their sides. There's a certain amount of snapping and snarling as later dogs step on the ears and ribcages of the earlier dogs, but eventually everyone is settled, every-one able to breathe a little, every eye tight shut.

She pulls onto Sixth Street with a truck heaped with dogs. When the police stop her, she tells them a little story. Animal Control has too many calls these days: cattle loose on the highways, horses leaping fences that are too high and breaking their legs; and the dogs, the scores and scores of dogs at Cruz Park. Animal Control is renting trucks now, whatever they can find. The dogs of North Park were slated for poisoning this morning.

"I didn't hear about this in briefing," one of the policemen says. He pokes at the heap of dogs with a black club; they shift like dead meat. They reek; an inexperienced observer might not recognize the stench as mingled dog-breath and shit.

Linna smiles, baring her teeth. "I'm on my way back to the shelter," she says. "They have an incinerator." She waves an open cell phone at him, and hopes he does not ask to talk to whoever's on the line, because there is no one.

But people believe stories, and then they make them real: the officer pokes at the dogs one more time and then wrinkles his nose and waves her on.

Clinton Lake is a vast place, trees and bushes and impenetrable brambles ringing a big lake, open country in every direction. When Linna unlatches the pickup's bed, the dogs drop stiffly to the ground, and stretch. Three died of overheating, stifled beneath the weight of so many others. Gold is one of them, but Linna does not cry. She knew she couldn't save them all, but she has saved some of them. That has to be enough. And the stories will continue: stories do not easily die.

The dogs can go wherever they wish from here, and they will. They and all the other dogs who have tricked or slipped or stumbled to safety will spread across the Midwest, the world. Some will find homes with men and women who treat them not as slaves but as friends freeing themselves, as well. Linna herself returns home with little shivering Sophie and sad Hope.

Some will die, killed by men and cougars and cars and even other dogs. Others will raise litters. The fathers of some of those litters will be coyotes. Eventually the Changed dogs will find their place in the changed world.

(When we first fashioned animals to suit our needs, we treated them as if they were stories and we the authors, and we clung desperately to an imagined copyright that would permit us to change them, sell them, even delete them. But some stories cannot be controlled. A wise author or dog owner listens, and learns, and says at last, "I never knew that.")

## 11. One Dog Creates the World.

This is the same dog. There wasn't any world when this happens, just a man and a dog. They lived in a house that didn't have any windows to look out of. Nothing had any smells. The dog shit and pissed on a paper in the bathroom, but not even this had a smell. Her food had no taste, either. The man suppressed all these things. This was because the man didn't want One Dog to create the universe and he knew it would be done by smell.

One night One Dog was sleeping and she felt the strangest thing that any dog has ever felt. It was the smells of the world pouring from her nose. When the smell of grass came out, there was grass outside. When the smell of shit came out, there was shit outside. She made the whole world that way. And when the smell of other dogs came out, there were dogs everywhere, big ones and little ones all over the world.

"I think I'm done," she said, and she left.

**Kij Johnson** is the author of several novels, including *The Fox Woman* and *Fudoki*, and a short story collection, *At the Mouth of the River of Bees*. She has won the Hugo, World Fantasy, Sturgeon, and Crawford Awards, and is a three-time winner of the Nebula Award. She splits her time between Seattle and Lawrence, where she is a professor of creative writing at the University of Kansas.

# Ursula K. LeGuin
# on Kij Johnson

She was in my last Clarion class, and at one of the workshops at the Flight of the Mind, where she was working on the marvelous tale of love and transformation that took form as both a short story and a novel. To me she is and will always be Fox Woman.

I don't recall that there was anything I could teach her at those workshops; it was pretty much a matter of saying, "Wow. Go on!"

Even so, when she published *At the Mouth of the River of Bees*, I was amazed not only at the power and beauty of the stories, but at their exuberant variety. Kijland is immense. It includes Elfland, Japan, and other more or less fantastic parts of the Earth, as well as quite realistic places that are not on Earth, and also, most wonderfully, the realest and least known world of all—the one where the other animals live.

This story takes you there, but it takes you the hard way, through something I believe only two kinds of animal, humans and ants, have made a practice of: slavery. It's a story about language, and about stories, and about bondage and freedom. We are no longer the masters of dogs who have learned to speak as we speak, but "the words themselves are the frame they use. But it is still our frame, our language. They are still not free. (Any more than we are.)"

Sometimes I think the best stories are the ones that have no answers, but ask a question in a way that lets us begin to see a glimpse of what the question really is ...

**Ursula K. Le Guin** has written novels, children's books, and short stories, mainly in the genres of fantasy and science fiction. She has been awarded over 11 Hugo and Nebula Awards, the Science Fiction and Fantasy Writers of America Grand Master Award, and a World Fantasy Lifetime Achievement. Her novel *The Farthest Shore* won the 1973 National Book Award.

# The Lineaments of Gratified Desire

Ysabeau S. Wilce

2002

*Abstinence sows sand all over*
*The ruddy limbs & flowing hair*
*But Desire Gratified*
*Plants fruit of life & beauty there.*

William Blake

## I. Stage Fright

Here is Hardhands up on the stage, and he's cheery cherry, sparking fire, he's as fast as a fox-trotter, stepping high. Sweaty blood dribbles his brow, bloody sweat stipples his torso, and behind him the Vortex buzzsaw whines, its whirling outer edge black enough to cut glass. The razor in his hand flashes like a heliograph as he motions the final Gesture of the invocation. The Eye of the Vortex flutters, but its perimeter remains firmly within the structure of Hardhands' Will and does not expand. He ululates a Command, and the Eye begins to open, like a pupil dilating in sunlight, and from its vivid yellowness comes a glimpse of scales and horns, struggling not to be born.

Someone tugs at Hardhands' foot. His concentration wavers. Someone yanks on the hem of his kilt. His concentration wiggles, and the Vortex wobbles slightly like a run-down top. Someone tugs on his kilt-hem, and his concentration collapses completely, and so does the Vortex, sucking into itself like water down a drain. There goes the Working for which Hardhands has been preparing for the last two weeks, and there goes the Tygers of Wrath's new drummer, and there goes their boot-kicking show.

Hardhands throws off the grasp with a hard shake, and looking down, prepares to smite. His lover is shouting upward at him, words that Hardhands can hardly hear, words he hopes he can hardly hear, words he surely did not hear a-right. The interior of the club is toweringly loud, noisy enough to make the ears bleed, but suddenly the thump of his heart, already driven hard by the strength of his magickal invocation, is louder.

Relais, pale as paper, repeats the shout. This time there is no mistaking what he says, much as Hardhands would like to mistake it, much as he would like to hear something else, something sweet and charming, something like: you are the prettiest thing ever born, or the Goddess grants wishes in your name, or they are killing themselves in the streets because the show is sold right out. Alas, Relais is shouting nothing quite so sweet.

"What do you mean you can not find Tiny Doom?" Hardhands shouts back. He looks wildly around the congested club, but it's dark and there are so many of them, and most of them have huge big hair and huger bigger boots. A tiny purple girl-child and her stuffy pink pig have no hope in this throng; they'd be trampled under foot in a second. That is exactly what Hardhands had told the Pontifexa earlier that day; no babysitter, he, other business, other pleasures, no time to take care of small children, not on this night of all nights: The Tygers of Wrath's biggest show of the year. Find someone else.

Well, talkers are no good doers, they say, and talking had done no good, all the yapping growling barking howling in the world had not changed the Pontifexa's mind: it's Paimon's night off, darling, and she'll be safe with you, Banastre, I can trust my heir with no one else, my sweet boy, do your teeny grandmamma this small favor and how happy I shall be, and here, kiss-kiss, I must run, I'm late, have a wonderful evening, good luck with the show, be careful with your invocation, cheerie-bye my darling.

And now see:

Hardhands roars: "I told you to keep an eye on her, Relais!"

He had too, he couldn't exactly watch over Tiny Doom (so called because she is the first in stature and the second in fate), while he was invoking the drummer, and with no drummer, there's no show (no show damn it!) and anyway if he's learned anything as the grandson of the Pontifexa of Califa, it's how to delegate.

Relais shouts back garbled defense. His eyes are whirling pie-plates. He doesn't mention that he stopped at the bar on his way to break the news and that there he downed four Choronzon Delights (hold the delight, double the Choronzon) before screwing up the courage to face his lover's ire. He doesn't mention that he can't exactly remember the last time he saw Little Tiny Doom except that he thinks it might have been about the time when she said that she had to visit El Casa de Peepee (oh cute) and he'd taken her as far as the door to the loo, which she had insisted haughtily she could do alone, and then he'd been standing outside, and gotten distracted by Arsinoë Fyrdraaca, who'd sauntered by, wrapped around the most gorgeous angel with rippling red wings, and then they'd gone to get a drink, and then another drink, and then when Relais remembered that Tiny Doom and Pig were still in the potty and pushed his way back through the crush, Tiny Doom and Pig were not still in the potty anymore.

And now, here:

Up until this very second, Hardhands has been feeling dandy as candy about this night: his invocation has been powerful and sublime, the blood in his veins replaced by pure unadulterated Magickal Current, hot and heavy. Up until this very second, if he clapped his hands together, sparks would fly. If he sang a note, the roof would fall. If he tossed his hair, fans would implode. Just from the breeze of the Vortex through his skin, he had known this was going to be a charm of a show, the very pinnacle of bombast and bluster. The crowded club still hums with cold fire charge, the air still sparks, cracking with glints of magick: yoowza. But now all that rich bubbly magick is curdling in his veins, his drummer has slid back to the Abyss, and he could beat someone with a stick. Thanks to an idiot boyfriend and a bothersome five-year-old his evening has just tanked.

Hardhands' perch is lofty. Despite the roiling smoke (cigarillo, incense, and oil), he can look out over the big big hair, and see the club is as packed as a cigar box with hipsters eager to see the show. From the stage Hardhands can see a lot, his vision sharpened by the magick he's been mainlining, and he sees: hipsters, b-boys, gothicks, crimson-clad officers, a magistra with a jaculus on a leash, etc. He does not see a small child or a pink pig or even the tattered remnants of a small child and a pink pig or even, well, he doesn't see them period.

Hardhands sucks in a deep breath and uses what is left of the Invocation still working through his veins to shout: "--!"

The syllable is vigorous and combustible, flowering in the darkness like a bruise. The audience erupts into a hollering hooting howl. They think the show is about to start. They are ready and geared. Behind Hardhands, the band also mistakes his intention, and despite the lack of drummer, kicks in with the triumphant blare of a horn, the delirious bounce of the hurdy-gurdy.

"--!" This time the shout sparks bright red, a flash of coldfire that brings tears to the eyes of the onlookers. Hardhands raises an authoritative hand towards the band, crashing them into silence. The crowd follows suit and the ensuing quiet is almost as ear-shattering.

"--." This time his words provide no sparkage, and he knows that his Will is fading under his panic. The club is dark. It is full of large people. Outside it is darker still and the streets of South of the Slot are wet and full of dangers. No place for a Tiny Doom and her Pig, oh so edible, to be wandering around, alone. Outside it the worst night of the year to be wandering alone anywhere in the City, particularly if you are short, stout, and toothsome.

"--!" This time Hardhands' voice, the voice which has launched a thousand stars, which has impregnated young girls with monsters and kept young men at their wanking until their wrists ache and their members bleed, is scorched and rather squeaky:

"Has anyone seen my wife?"

## II. Historical Notes

Here's a bit of background. No ordinary night, tonight, not at all. It's Pirate's Parade and the City of Califa is afire—in some places actually blazing. No fear, tho', bucket brigades are out in force, for the Pontifexa does not wish to lose her capital to revelry. Wetness is stationed around the things that the Pontifexa most particularly requires not to burn: her shrines, Bilskinir House, Arden's Cake-O-Rama, the Califa National Bank. Still, even with these bucket brigades acting as damper, there's fun enough for everyone. The City celebrates many holidays, but surely Pirates' Parade ranks as Biggest and Best.

But why pirates and how a parade? Historians (oh fabulous professional liars) say that it happened thusly: Back in the day, no chain sealed the Bay of Califa off from sea-faring foes and the Califa Gate sprang wide as an opera singer's mouth, a state of affairs good for trade and bad for security. Chain was not all the small city lacked: no guard, no organized militia, no blood thirsty Scorchers regiment to stand against havoc, and no navy. The City was fledgling and disorganized, hardly more than a village, and plump for the picking.

One fine day, Pirates took advantage of Califa's tenderness, and sailed right through her Gate, and docked at the Embarcadero, as scurvy as you please. From door to door they went, demanding tribute or promising wrath, and when they were loaded down with booty they went well satisfied back to their ships to sail away.

But they didn't get far. While the pirates were shaking down the householders, a posse of quiet citizens crept down to the docks and sabotaged the poorly guarded ships. The pirates arrived back at the docks to discover their escape boats sinking, and when suddenly the docks themselves were on fire, and their way off the docks was blocked, and then they were on fire too, and that was it.

Perhaps Califa had no army, no navy, no militia, but she did have citizens with grit and cleverness, and grit and cleverness trump greed and guns every time. Such a clever victory over a pernicious greedy foe is worth remembering, and maybe even repeating, in a fun sort of way, and thus was born a roistering day of remembrance when revelers dressed as pirates gallivant door to door demanding candy booty, and thus Little Tiny Doom has muscled in on Hardhands' evening. With Grandmamma promised to attend a whist party, and Butler Paimon's night off, who else would take Tiny Doom, (and the resplendently costumed Pig) on candy shakedown? Who but our hero, as soon as his show is over and his head back down to earth, lucky boy?

Well.

The Blue Duck and its hot dank club-y-ness may be the place to be when you are tall and trendy and your hearing is already shot, but for a short kidlet, big hair and loud noises bore, and the cigarillo smoke scratches. Tiny Doom has waited for Pirates' Parade for weeks, dreaming of pink popcorn and sugar squidies, chocolate manikins and jacksnaps, praline pumpkin seeds and ginger bombs: a sackful of sugar guaranteed to keep her sick and speedy for at least a week. She can wait no longer.

Shortness has its advantage; trendy people look up their noses, not down. The potty is filthy and the floor yucky wet; Tiny Doom and Pig slither out the door, right by Relais, so engaged in his conversation with a woman with a boat in her hair that he doesn't even notice the scram. Around elbows, by tall boots, dodging lit cigarettes and drippy drinks held low and cool-like, Tiny Doom and Pig achieve open air without incident and then, sack in hand, set out for the Big Shakedown.

"*Rancy Dancy is no good,*" she sings as she goes, swinging Pig, who is of course, too lazy to walk, "*Chop him up for firewood ... When he's dead, boil his head and bake it into gingerbread ... *"

She jumps over a man lying on the pavement, and then into the reddish pool beyond. The water makes a satisfying SPLASH and tho' her hem gets wet, she is sure to hold Pig up high so that he remains dry. He's just getting over a bad cold and has to care for his health, silly Pig he is delicate, and up past his bedtime, besides. Well, it is only once a year.

Down the slick street, Tiny Doom galumphs, Pig swinging along with her. There are shadows ahead of her and shadows behind, but after the shadows of Bilskinir House (which can sometimes be *grabby*) these shadows: so what? There's another puddle ahead, this one dark and still. She pauses before it, and some interior alarum indicates that it would be best to jump over, rather than in. The puddle is wide, spreading across the street like a strange black stain. As she gears up for the leap, a faint rippling begins to mar the mirror-like surface.

"Wah! Wah!" Tiny Doom is short, but she has lift. Holding her skirt in one hand, and with a firm grip upon Pig, she hurtles herself upward and over, like a tiny tea cosy levering aloft. As she springs, something wavery and white snaps out of the stillness, snapping towards her like the crack of a whip. She lands on the other side, and keeps scooting, beyond the arm's reach. Six straggly fingers, like pallid parsnips, waggle angrily at her, but she's well beyond their grip.

"*Tell her, smell her! Kick her down the cellar,*" Tiny Doom taunts, flapping Pig's ears derisively. The scraggly arm falls back, and then another emerges from the water, hoisting up on its elbows, pulling a slow rising bulk behind it: a knobby head, with knobby nose and knobby forehead and a slowly opening mouth that shows razor sharp gums and a pointy black tongue, unrolling like a hose. The tongue has length where the arms did not, and it looks gooey and sticky, just like the salt licorice Grandmamma loves so much. Tiny Doom cares not for salt licorice one bit and neither does Pig, so it seems prudent to punt, and they do, as fast as her chubby legs can carry them, further down the slickery dark street.

### III. Irritating Children

Here is Hardhands in the alley behind the club, taking a deep breath of brackish air, which chills but does not calm. Inside, he has left an angry mob, who've had their hopes dashed rather than their ears blown. The Infernal Engines of Desire (opening act) has come back on stage and is trying valiantly to suck up the slack, but the audience is not particularly pacified. The Blue Duck will be lucky if it doesn't burn. However, that's not our hero's problem; he's got larger fish frying.

He sniffs the air, smelling: the distant salt spray of the ocean; drifting smoke from some bonfire; cheap perfume; his own sweat; horse manure. He closes his eyes and drifts deeper, beyond smell, beyond scent, down down down into a wavery darkness that is threaded with filaments of light which are not really light, but which he knows no other way to describe. The darkness down here is not really darkness either, it's the Magickal Current as his mind can envision it, giving form to the formless, putting the indefinable into definite terms. The Current bears upon its flow a tendril of something familiar, what he qualifies, for lack of a better word, as a taste of obdurate obstinacy and pink plush, fading quickly but unmistakable.

The Current is high tonight, very high. In consequence, the Aeyther is humming, the Aeyther is abuzz; the line between In and Out has narrowed to a width no larger than a hair, and it's an easy step across—but the jump can go either way. Oh this would have been the very big whoo for the gig tonight; musickal magick of the highest order, but it sucks for lost childer out on the streets. South of the Slot is bad enough when the Current is low: a sewer of footpads, dollymops, blisters, mashers, cornhoes, and others is not to be found elsewhere so deep in the City even on an ebb-tide day. Tonight, combine typical holiday mayhem with the rising magickal flood and Goddess knows what will be out, hungry and yummy for some sweet tender kidlet chow. And not even regular run of the mill niblet, but prime grade A best grade royalty. The Pontifexa's heir, it doesn't get more yummy than that—a vampyre could dare sunlight with that bubbly blood zipping through his veins, a ghoul could pass for living after gnawing on that sweet flesh. It makes Hardhands' manly parts shrivel to think upon the explanation to Grandmamma of Tiny Doom's loss and the blame sure to follow.

Hardhands opens his eyes, it's hardly worth wasting the effort of going deep when everything is so close the surface tonight. Behind him, the iron door flips open and Relais flings outward, borne aloft on a giant wave of disapproving noise. The door snaps shut, cutting the sound in a brief echo which quickly dies in the coffin narrow alley-way.

"Did you find her?" Relais asks, holding his fashionable cuffs so they don't trail on the mucky cobblestones. Inside his brain is bouncing with visions of the Pontifexa's reaction if they return home minus Cyrenacia. Actually, what she is going to say is the least of his worries; it is what she might do that really has Relais gagging. He likes his lungs exactly where they are: inside his body, not flapping around outside.

Hardhands turns a white hot look upon his lover and says: "If she gets eaten, Relais, I will eat you."

Relais' father always advised saving for a rainy day and though the sky above is mostly clear, Relais is feeling damp. He will check his bankbook when they get home, and reconsider Sweetie Fyrdraaca's proposition. He's been Hardhands' leman for over a year now: blood sacrifices, coldfire-singed clothing, throat tearing invocations, corn-meal gritty sheets, murder. He's had enough. He makes no reply to the threat.

Hardhands demands, not very politely: "Give me my frockcoat."

Said coat, white as snow, richly embroidered in white peonies and with cuffs the size of tablecloths, well, Relais had been given that to guard too, and he now has a vague memory of hanging it over the stall door in the pisser, where hopefully it still dangles, but probably not.

"I'll get it—" Relais fades backward, into the club, and Hardhands lets him go.

For now.

For now, Hardhands takes off his enormous hat, which had remained perched upon his gorgeous head during his invocation via a jeweled spike of a hairpin, and speaks a word into its upturned bowl. A green light pools up, spilling over the hat's capacious brim, staining his hand and the sleeve below with drippy magick. Another commanding word, and the light surges upward and ejects a splashy elemental, fish-tail flapping.

"Eh, boss—I thought you said I had the night off," Alfonso complains. There's lip rouge smeared on his fins and a clutch of cards in his hand. "It's Pirates' Parade."

"I changed my mind. That wretched child has given me the slip and I want you to track her."

Alfonso grimaces. Ever since Little Tiny Doom trapped him in a bowl of water and fed him fishy flakes for two days, he's avoided her like fluke-rot.

"Why worry your good luck, boss—"

Hardhands does not have to twist. He only has to look like he is going to twist. Alfonso zips forward, flippers flapping and Hardhands, after draining his chapeau of Current and slamming it back upon his grape, follows.

### IV. Who's There?

Here is The Roaring Gimlet, sitting pretty in her cozy little kitchen, toes toasting on the grate, toast toasting on the tongs, drinking hot ginger beer, feeling happily serene. She's had a fun-dandy evening. Citizens who normally sleep behind chains and steel bolts, dogs a-prowl and guns under their beds, who maybe wouldn't open their doors after dark if their own mothers were lying bleeding on the threshold, these people fling their doors widely and with gay abandon to the threatening cry of "Give us Candy or We'll Give you the Rush."

Any other night, at this time, she'd still be out in the streets, looking for drunken mashers to roll. But tonight, all gates were a-jar and the streets a high tide of drunken louts. Out by nine and back by eleven, with a sack almost too heavy to haul, a goodly load of sugar, and a yummy fun-toy, too. Now she's enjoying her happy afterglow from a night well-done. The noises from the cellar have finally stopped, she's finished the crossword in *The Alta Califa*, and as soon as the kettle blows, she'll fill her hot water bottle and aloft to her snuggly bed, there to dwell the rest of the night away in kip.

Ah, Pirates' Parade, best night of the year.

While she's waiting for the water to bubble, she's cleaning the tool whence comes her name: the bore is clotted with icky stuff and the Gimlet likes her signature clean and sharply shiny. Clean hands, clean house, clean heart, the Gimlet's pappy always said. Above the fireplace, Pappy's flat representation stares down at his progeny, the self-same gimlet clinched in his hand. The Roaring Gimlet is the heir to a fine family tradition and she does love her job.

What's that a-jingling? She glances at the clock swinging over the stove. It's almost midnight. Too late for visitors, and anyway, everyone knows the Roaring Gimlet's home is her castle. Family stays in, people stay out, so Daddy Gimlet always said. Would someone? No, they wouldn't. Not even tonight, they would not.

Jingle jingle.

The cat looks up from her perch on the fender, perturbed.

Heels down, the Gimlet stands aloft, and tucks her shirt back into her skirts, ties her dressing gown tight, bounds up the ladder-like kitchen stairs to the front door. The peephole shows a dimly lit circle of empty cobblestones. Damn it all to leave the fire for nothing. As the Gimlet turns away, the bell dances again, jangling her into a surprised jerk.

The Roaring Gimlet opens the door, slipping the chain, and is greeted with a squirt of flour right in the kisser, and a shrieky command:

"Give us the Candy or We'll give you the Rush!"

The Gimlet coughs away the flour, choler rising, and beholds before her, knee-high, a huge black feathered hat. Under the hat is a pouty pink face, and under the pouty pink face, a fluffy farthingale that resembles in both color and points an artichoke, and under that, purple dance shoes, with criss-crossy ribbands. Riding on the hip of this apparition is a large pink plushy pig, also wearing purple criss-crossy dance shoes, golden laurel leaves perched over floppy piggy ears.

It's the Pig that the Gimlet recognizes first, not the kid. The kid, whose public appearances have been kept to a minimum (the Pontifexa is wary of too much flattery, and as noted, chary of her heir's worth) could be any kid, but there is only one Pig, all Califa knows that, and the kid must follow the Pig, as day follows night, as sun follows rain, as fortune follows the fool.

"Give us the CANDY or we'll GIVE YOU THE RUSH!" A voice to pierce glass, to cut right through the Gimlet's recoil, all the way down to her achy toes. The straw-shooter moves from *present* to *fire*; while Gimlet was gawking, reloading had occurred, and another volley is imminent. She's about to slam shut the door, she cares not to receive flour or to give out yum, but then, door-jamb held halfway in hand, she stops. An idea, formed from an over-abundance of yellow nasty novellas and an under-abundance of good sense, has leapt full-blown from Nowhere to the Somewhere that is the Roaring Gimlet's calculating brain. So much for sugar, so much for swag: here then is a price above rubies, above diamonds, above chocolate, above, well, Above All. What a pretty price a pretty piece could fetch. On such proceeds the Gimlet could while away her elder days in endless sun and fun-toys.

Before the kid can blow again, the Gimlet grins, in her best granny way, flour feathering about her, and says, "Well, now, chickiedee, well now indeed. I've no desire to be rushed, but you are late and the candy is—"

She recoils, but not in time, from another spurt of flour. When she wipes away the flour, she is careful not to wipe away her welcoming grin. "But I have more here in the kitchen, come in, tiny pirate, out of the cold and we shall fill your sack full."

"Huh," says the child, already her husband's Doom and about to become the Roaring Gimlet's, as well. "GIVE ME THE CANDY—"

Patience is a virtue that the Roaring Gimlet is well off without. She peers beyond the kid, down the street. There are people about but they are: drunken people, or burning people, or screaming people, or carousing people, or running people. None of them appear to be observant people, and that's perfecto. The Gimlet reaches and grabs.

"Hey!" says the Kid. The Pig does not protest.

Tiny Doom is stout, and she can dig her heels in, but the Gimlet is stouter and the Gimlet has two hands free, where Tiny Doom has one, and the Pig is too flabby to help. Before Tiny Doom can shoot off her next round of flour, she's yanked and the door is slammed shut behind her, bang!

## V. Bad Housekeeping

Here is Hardhands striding down the darkened streets like a colossus, dodging fire, flood, and fighting. He is not upset, oh no indeedy. He's cool and cold and so angry that if he touched tinder it would burst into flames, if he tipped tobacco it would explode cherry red. And there's more than enough ire to go around, which is happy because the list of Hardhands' blame is quite long.

Firstly: the Pontifexa for making him take Cyrenacia with him. What good is it to be her darling grandson when he's constantly on doodie-detail? Being the only male Haðraaða should be good for: power, mystery, free booze, noli me tangare, first and foremost, the biggest slice of cake. Now being the only male Haðraaða is good for: marrying small torments, kissing the Pontifexa's ass, and being bossed into wife-sitting. He almost got Grandmamma once; perhaps the decision should be revisited.

Secondly: Tiny Doom for not standing still. When he gets her, he's going to paddle her, see if he doesn't. She's got it coming, a long time coming and perhaps a hot hinder will make her think twice about, well, think twice about everything. Didn't he do enough for her already? He married her, to keep her in the family, to keep her out of the hands of her nasty daddy, who otherwise would have the prior claim. Ungrateful kidlet. Perhaps she deserves whatever she gets.

Thirdly: Relais for being such an utter jackass that he can't keep track of a four year old. Hardhands has recently come across a receipt for an ointment that allows the wearer to walk through walls. For which, this sigil requires three pounds of human tallow. He's got a few walls he wouldn't mind flitting right through and at last, Relais will be useful.

Fourthly: Paimon. What need has a domicilic denizen for a night off anyway? He's chained to the physical confines of the House Bilskinir by a sigil stronger than life. He should be taking care of the Heir to the House Bilskinir, not doing whatever the hell he is doing on his night off which he shouldn't be doing anyway because he shouldn't be having a night off and when Hardhands is in charge, he won't, no sieur.

Fifthly: Pig. Ayah, so, well, Pig is a stuffy pink plush toy, and can hardly be blamed for anything, but what the hell, why not? Climb on up, Pig, there's always room for one more!

And ire over all: his ruined invocation, for which he had been purging starving dancing and flogging for the last two weeks, all in preparation for what would surely be the most stupendous summoning in the history of summoning. It's been a stellar group of daemons that Hardhands has been able to force from the Aeyther before, but this time he had been going for the highest of the high, the loudest of the loud, and the show would have been sure to go down in the annals of musickology and his name, already famous, would become gigantic in its height. Even the Pontifexa was sure to be impressed. And now ...

The streets are full of distraction but neither Hardhands nor Alfonso are distracted. Tiny Doom's footprints pitty-patter before them, glowing in the gloam like little blue flowers, and they follow, avoiding burning brands, dead horses, drunken warblers, slithering servitors, gushing water pipes, and an impromptu cravat party and, because of their glowering concentration, they are avoided by all the aforementioned, in turn. The pretty blue footprints dance, and leap, from here to there, and there to here, over cobblestone and curb, around corpse and copse, by Cobweb's Palace and Pete's Clown Diner, by Ginger's Gin Goint and Guerrero's Helado, and other blind tigers so blind they are nameless also, dives so low that just walking by will get your knickers wet. The pretty prints don't waver, don't dilly-dally, and then suddenly, they turn towards a door, broad and barred, and they stop.

At the door, Hardhands doesn't bother knocking, and neither does Alfonso, but their methods of entry differ. Alfonso zips through the wooden obstruction as though it is neither wooden nor obstructive. Hardhands places palm down on wood, and via a particularly loud Gramatica exhortation, blows the door right off its hinges. His entry is briefly hesitated by the necessity to chase after his chapeau, having blown off also in the breeze of Gramatica, but once it is firmly stabbed back on his handsome head, onward he goes, young Hardhands, hoping very much that something else will get in his path, because, he can't deny it: exploding things is Fun.

The interior of the house is dark and dull, not that Hardhands is there to critique the décor. Alfonso has zipped ahead of him, coldfire frothing in his wake. Hardhands follows the bubbly pink vapor, down a narrow hallway, past peeling paneling, and dusty doorways. He careens down creaky stairs, bending head to avoid braining on low ceiling, and into a horrible little kitchen.

He wrinkles his nose. Our young hero is used to a praeterhuman amount of cleanliness, and here there is neither. At Bilskinir House even the light looks as though it's been washed, dried and pressed before hung in the air. In contrast, this pokey little hole looks like the back end of a back end bar after a particularly festive game of Chew the Ear. Smashed crockery and blue willow china crunches under boot, and the furniture is bonfire ready. A faint glow limns the wreckage, the after-reflection of some mighty big magick. The heavy sour smell of blackberries wrinkles in his nose. Coldfire dribbles from the ceiling, whose plaster cherubs and grapes look charred and withered.

Hardhands pokes at a soggy wad of clothes lying in a heap on the disgusting floor. For one testicle-shriveling moment he thought that he saw black velvet amongst the sog; he does, but it's a torn shirt, not a puffy hat.

All magickal acts leave a resonance behind, unless the magician takes great pains to hide: Hardhands knows every archon, hierophant, sorceress, bibliomatic, and avatar in the City, but he don't recognize the author of this Working. He catches a drip of coldfire on one long finger and holds it up his lips: salt-sweet-smoky-oddly familiar but not enough to identify.

"Pigface pogo!" says our hero. He has put his foot down in slide and almost gone face down in a smear of glass and black goo—mashy blackberry jam, the source of the sweet stench. Flailing un-heroically he regains his balance, but in doing so grabs at the edge of an over-turned settle. The settle has settled backwards, cock-eyed on its back feet, but Hardhands' leverage rocks it forward again, and, hello, here's the Gimlet—well, parts of her anyway. She is stuck to the bench by a flood of dried blood, and the expression on her face is doleful, and a little bit surprised.

"Pogo pigface on a pigpogopiss! Who the hell is that?"

Alfonso yanks the answer from the Aethyr. "The Roaring Gimlet, petty roller and barn stamper. You see her picture sometimes in the post office."

"She don't look too roaring to me. What the hell happened to her?"

Alfonso zips closer, while Hardhands holds his sleeve to his sensitive nose. The stench of metallic blood is warring with the sickening sweet smell of the crushed blackberries, and together a pleasuring perfume they do not make.

"Me, I think she was chewed," Alfonzo announces after close inspection. "By something hungry and mad."

"What kind of something?"

Alfonso shrugs. "Nobody I know, sorry, boss."

As long as Doom is not chewed, Hardhands cares naught for the chewy-ness of others. He uneasily illuminates the fetid shadows with a vivid Gramatica phrase, but thankfully no rag-like wife does he see, tossed aside like a discarded tea-towel, nor red wet stuffy Pig-toy, only bloody jam and magick-bespattered walls. He'd never admit it, particularly not to a yappy servitor, but there's a warm feeling of relief in his toes that Cyrenacia and Pig were not snacked upon. But if they were not snacked upon, where the hell are they, oh irritation.

There, in the light of his sigil-sign: two dainty feet stepped in jammy blood, hopped in disgust, and then headed up the back stairs, the shimmer of Bilskinir blue shining faintly through the rusty red. Whatever got the Gimlet did not get his wife and pig, that for sure, that's all he cares about, all he needs to know, and the footprints are fading, too: onward.

At the foot of the stairs, Hardhands poises. A low distant noise drifts out of the floor below, like a bad smell, a rumbly agonized sound that makes his tummy wiggle.

"What is that?"

A wink of Alfonso's tails and top-hat and here's his answer: "There's some guy locked in the cellar, and he's—he's in a bad way, and I think he needs our help—"

Hardhands is not interested in guys locked in cellars, nor in their bad ways. The footprints are fading, and the Current is still rising, he can feel it jiggling in his veins. Badness is on the loose—is not the Gimlet proof of that?—and Goddess Califa knows what else, and Tiny Doom is alone.

## VI. Sugar Sweet

Here is Hardhands, hot on the heels of the pretty blue footsteps skipping along through the riotous streets. Hippy-hop, pitty-pat. The trail takes a turning, into a narrow alley and Hardhands turns with it, leaving the sputtering street lamps behind. Before the night was merely dark: now it's darkdarkdark. He flicks a bit of coldfire from his fingertips, blossoming a ball of luminescence that weirdly lights up the crooked little street, broken cobbles and black narrow walls. The coldfire ball bounces onward, and Hardhands follows. The footprints are almost gone: in a few more moments they will be gone, for a lesser magician they would be gone already.

And then, a drift of song:

*"Hot corn, hot corn! Buy my hot corn!*
*Lovely and sweet, Lovely and Warm!"*

Out of the shadow comes a buttery smell, hot and wafting, the jingling of bells, friendly and beckoning: a Hot Corn Dolly, out on the prowl. The perfume is delightful and luscious and it reminds

Hardhands that dinner was long since off. But Hardhands does not eat corn (while not fasting, he's on an all meat diet, for to clean his system clear of sugar and other poisons), and when the Hot Corn Dolly wiggles her tray at him, her green ribbon braids dancing, he refuses.

The Corn Dolly is not alone, her sisters stand behind her, and their wide trays, and the echoing wide width of their farthingale skirts, flounced with patchwork, jingling with little bells, form a barricade that Hardhands, the young gentleman, can not push through. The Corn Dolly skirts are wall-to-wall and their ranks are solid and only rudeness will make a breach.

"I cry your pardon, ladies," he says, in feu de joie, ever courteous, for is not the true mark of a gentleman his kindness towards others, particularly his inferiors? "I care not for corn, and I would pass."

*"Buy my hot corn, deliciously sweet,*
*Gives joy to the sorrowful and strength to the weak."*

The Dolly's voice is luscious, ripe with sweetness. In one small hand she holds an ear of corn, dripping with butter, fragrant with the sharp smell of chile and lime, bursting up from its peeling of husk like a flower, and this she proffers towards him. Hardhands feels a southerly rumble, and suddenly his mouth is full of anticipatory liquid. Dinner was a long long time ago, and he has always loved hot corn, and how can one little ear of corn hurt him? And anyway, don't he deserve some solace? He fumbles in his pocket, but no divas does he slap; he's the Pontifexa's grandson, and not in the habit of paying for his treats.

The Dolly sees his gesture and smiles. Her lips are glistening golden, as yellow as her silky hair, and her teeth, against the glittering, are like little nuggets of white corn.

*"A kiss for the corn, and corn for a kiss,*
*One sweet with flavor, the other with bliss"* she sings, and the other dollies join in her harmony, the bells on their square skirts jingling. The hot corn glistens like gold, steamy and savory, dripping with yum. A kiss is a small price to pay to sink his teeth into savory. He's paid more for less and he leans forward, puckering.

The dollies press in, wiggling their oily fingers and humming their oily song, enfolding him in the husk of their skirts, their hands, their licking tongues. His southerly rumble is now a wee bit more southerly, and it's not a rumble, it's an avalanche. The corn rubs against his lips, slickery and sweet, spicy and sour. The chili burns his lips, the butter soothes them, he kisses, and then he licks, and then he bites into a bliss of crunch, the squirt of sweetness cutting the heat and the sour. Never has he tasted anything better, and he bites again, eagerly, butter oozing down his chin, dripping onto his shirt. Eager fingers stroke his skin, he's engorged with the sugar-sweetness, so long denied, and now he can't get enough, each niblet exploding bright heat in his mouth, his tongue, his head, he's drowning in the sweetness of it all.

And like a thunder from the Past, he hears ringing in his head the Pontifexa's admonition, oft repeated to a whiny child begging for hot corn, spun sugar, spicy taco or fruit cup, sold on the street, in marvelous array but always denied because: *you never know where it's been.* An Admonition drummed into his head with painful frequency, all the other kidlets snacked from the street vendors with reckless abandon, but not the Pontifexa's grandson, whose tum was deemed too delicate for common food and the common bugs it might contain.

Drummed well and hard it would seem, to suddenly recall now, with memorable force, better late than never. Hardhands snaps open eyes and sputters kernels. Suddenly he sees true what the Corn Dollies' powerful glamour has disguised under a patina of butter and spice: musky kernels and musky skin. A fuzz of little black flies encircles them. The silky hair, the silky husks are slick with mold. The little white corn teeth grin mottled blue and green, and corn worms spill in a white wiggly waterfall from gaping mouths.

"Arrgg," says our hero, managing to keep the urp down, heroically. He yanks and flutters, pulls and yanks, but the knobby fingers have him firm, stalk to stalk. He heaves, twisting his shoulders, spinning and ducking: now they have his shirt, but he is free.

"---------!" he bellows, at the top of his magickal lungs. The word explodes from his head with an agonizing aural thud. The Corn Dollies sizzle and shriek, but he doesn't wait around to revel in their popping. Now he's a fleet footed fancy boy, skedaddling as fast as skirts will allow; to hell with heroics, there's no audience about, just get the hell out. He leaves the shrieking behind him, fast on booted heels, and it's a long heaving pause later, when the smell of burned corn no longer lingers on the air, that he stops to catch breath and bearings. His heart, booming with Gramatica exertion, is starting to slow, but his head, still thundering with a sugary rush, feels as though it might implode right there on his shoulders, dwindle down a pinprick of pressure, diamond hard. The sugar pounds in his head, beating his brain into a ploughshare of pain, sharp enough to cut a furrow in his skull.

He leans on a scaly wall and sticks a practiced finger down his gullet. Up heaves corn, and bile, and blackened gunk, and more gunk. The yummy sour-lime-butter taste doesn't have quite the same delicious savor coming up as it did going down, nor is his shuddering now quite so delightful. He spits and heaves, and heaves and spits, and when his inside is empty of everything, including probably most of his internal organs, he feels a wee bit better. Not much, but some. His ears are cold. He puts a quivery hand to his head; his hat is gone.

The chapeau is not the only thing to disappear, Tiny Doom's tiny footprints, too, have faded. Oh for a drink to drive the rest of the stale taste of rotting corn from his tonsils. Oh for a super duper purge to scour the rest of the stale speed of sugar from his system. Oh for a bath, and bed, and deep sweet sleep. He's had a thin escape, and he knows it: the Corn Sirens could have drained him completely, sucked him as a dry as a desert sunset, and Punto Finale for the Pontifexa's grandson. Now it's going to take him weeks of purifications, salt-baths and soda enemas to get back into whack. Irritating. He's also irked at the loss of his shirt; it was brand-new, he'd only worn it once, and the lace on its sleeves had cost him fifty-eight divas in gold. And his hat, bristling with angel feathers, its brim bigger than an apple pancake. He's annoyed at himself, sloppy-sloppy-sloppy.

The coldfire track has sputtered and no amount of Gramatica kindling can spark it alight; it's too late, too gone, too long. Alfonso, too, is absent of summoning and when Hardhands closes his eyes and clenches his fists to his chest, sucks in deep lungs of air, until the Current bubbles in his veins like the most sparkling of red wines, he knows why: the Current has flowed so high now that even the lowliest servitors can ride it without assistance, are strong enough to avoid constraint and ignore demand. He'd better find the kid soon, with the Current this high, only snackers will now be out, anyone without skill or protection—the snackees—will have long since gone home, or been eaten. Funtime for humans is over, and funtime for Others just begun.

Well, that's fine, Alfonso is just a garnish, not necessary at all. Is not Tiny Doom his own blood? Does not a shared spark run through their veins? He closes eyes again, and stretches arms outward, palms upward and he concentrates every split second of his Will into a huge vaporous awareness which he flings out over Califa like a net. Far far at the back of his throat, almost a tickle, not quite a taste, he finds the smell he is looking for. It's dwindling, and it's distant, but it's there and it's enough. A tiny thread connecting him to her, blood to blood, heat to heat, heart beat to heart beat, a tiny threat of things to come when Tiny Doom is not so Tiny. He jerks the thread with infinitesimal delicacy. It's thin, but it holds. It's thin, but it can never completely break.

He follows the thread, gently, gently, down darkened alleys, past shuttered facades, and empty stoops. The streets are slick with smashed fruit, but otherwise empty. He hears the sound of distant noises, hooting, hollering, braying mule, a fire bell, but he is alone. The buildings grow sparser, interspaced with empty lots. They look almost like rows of tombstones, and their broken windows show utterly black. The acrid tang of burning sugar tickles his nose, and the sour-salt smell of marshy sea-water; he must be getting closer to the bay's soggy edge. Cobblestones give way to splintery corduroy which gives way to moist dirt, and now the sweep of the starry sky above is unimpeded by building facades; he's almost out of the City, he may be out of the City now, he's never been this far on this road and if he hadn't absolute faith in the Haðraaða family bond, he'd be skeptical that Tiny Doom's chubby little legs had made it this far either.

But they have. He knows it.

Hardhands pauses, cocking his head: a tinge suffuses his skin, a gentle breeze that isn't a breeze at all, but the galvanic buzz of the Current. The sky above is now obscured by wafts of spreading fog, and, borne distantly upon that breeze, a vague tune. Musick.

Onward, on prickly feet, with the metallic taste of magick growing thicker in the back of his throat. The music is building crescendo, it sounds so friendly and fun, promising popcorn, and candied apples, fried pies. His feet prickle with these promises, and he picks up the pace, buoyed on by the rollicking musick, allowing the musick to carry him onward, towards the twinkly lights now beckoning through the heavy mist.

Then the musick is gone, and he blinks, for the road has come to an end as well, a familiar end, although unexpected. Before him looms a giant polychrome monkey head, leering brightly. This head is two stories high, it has flapping ears and wheel-size eyes, and its gaping mouth, opened in a silent howl, is large enough for a gaggle of school children to rush through, screaming their excitement.

Now he knows where he is, where Tiny Doom has led him too, predictable, actually, the most magical of all childhood places: *Woodward's Garden, Fun for All Occasions, Not Occasionally but Always.*

How oft has Hardhands been to Woodward's (in cheerful daylight), and ah the fun he has had there, (in cheerful daylight): The Circular Boat and the Mystery Manor, the Zoo of Pets, and the Whirla-Gig. Pink popcorn and strawberry cake, and Madam Twanky's Fizzy Lick-A-Rice Soda. Ah, Woodward's Garden and the happy smell of sun, sugar, sweat, and sizzling meat. But at Woodward's, the fun ends at sundown, as evening's chill begins to rise, the rides begin to shut, the musick fades away and everyone must go, exiting out the Monkey's Other End. Woodward's is not open at night.

But here, tonight, the Monkey's Eyes are open, although his smile is a grimace, less Welcome and more Beware. The Monkey's Eyes roll like red balls in their sockets, and at each turn they display a letter:

"F" "U" "N" they spell in flashes of sparky red. Something skitters at our boy's ankles and he jumps: scraps of paper flickering like shredded ghosts. The Monkey's Grin is fixed, glaring, in the dark it does not seem at all like the Gateway to Excitement and Adventure, only Digestion and Despair. Surely even Doom, despite her ravenous adoration of the Circular Boat, would not be tempted to enter the hollow throat just beyond the poised glittering teeth. Despite the promise of the Monkey's Rolling Eyes there is no Fun here.

Or is there? Look again. Daylight, a tiara of letters crowns the Monkey's Head, spelling Woodward's Garden in cheery lights. But not tonight, tonight the tiara is a crown of spikes, whose glittering red letters proclaim a different title: *Madam Rose's Flower Garden.*

Hardhands closes his eyes against the flashes, feeling all the blood in his head blushing downward into his pinchy toes. Madam Rose's Flower Garden! It cannot be. Madam Rose's is a myth, a rumor, an innuendo, a whisper. A prayer. The only locale in Califa where entities, it is said, can walk in the Waking World without constraint, can move and do as their Will commands, and not be constrained by the Will of a magician or adept. Such mixing is proscribed, it's an abomination, against all laws of nature, and until this very second, Hardhands thought, mere fiction.

And yet apparently not fiction at all. The idea of Tiny Doom in such environs sends Hardhands' scalp a-shivering. This is worse than having her out on the streets. Primo child-flesh, delicious and sweet, and plump full of such energy as would turn the most mild-mannered elemental into a rival of Choronzon, the Daemon of Dispersion. Surrounded by dislocated elementals and egregores, under no obligation and bound by no sigil, indulging in every depraved whim. Surely the tiresome child did not go forward to her own certain doom.

But his burbling tum, his swimming head, knows she did.

If he were not Banastre Haðraaða, the Grand Duque of Califa, this is the point where he'd turn about and go home. First he might sit upon the ground, right here in the dirt, and wallow for a while in discouragement, then he'd rise, dust, and retreat. If he were not himself,

344 **Ysabeau S. Wilce**

but someone else, someone lowly, he might be feeling pretty low.

For a moment, he is not himself, he is cold and tired and hungry and ready for the evening to end. It was fun to be furious, his anger gave him forward motion and will and fire, but now he wants to be home in his downy-soft bed with a yellow nasty newsrag and a jorum of hot wine. If Wish could be made Will in a heartbeat, he'd be lying back on damask pillows, drowning away to happy dreamland.

Before he can indulge in such twaddle, a voice catches his attention.

"Well, now, your grace. Slumming?"

Then does Hardhands notice a stool, and upon the stool a boy sitting, legs dangling, swinging copper-toed button boots back and forth. A pocketknife flashes in his hand; shavings flutter downward. He's tow-headed, and blue-eyed, freckled and tan, and he's wearing a polka-dotted kilt, a redingcote, and a smashed bowler. A smoldering stogie hangs down from his lips.

"I beg your pardon?"

"Never mind, never mind. Are you here for the auction?"

Hardhands replies regally: "I am looking for a child and a pink pig."

The boy says, brightly, "Oh yes, of course. They passed this way some time ago, in quite a hurry."

Hardhands makes move to go inside, but is halted by the red velvet rope which is action as barrier to the Monkey's mouth.

"Do you have a ticket? It's fifteen divas, all you can eat and three trips to the bar."

Remembering his empty pockets, Hardhands says loftily: "I'm on the List."

The List: Another powerful weapon. If you are on it, all to the good. If not, back to the Icy Arrogance. But when has Hardhands not been on the list? Never! Unthinkable!

"Let me see," says the Boy. He turns out pockets, and thumps his vest, fishes papers, and strings, candy and fish-hooks, bones and lights, a white rat, and a red rubber ball. "I know I had something—Ahah!" This ahah is addressed to his hat, what interior he is excavating and out of which he draws a piece of red foolscap. "Let me see ... um ... *Virex the Sucker of Souls, Zigurex Avatar of Agony, Valefor Teller of Tales*, no, I'm sorry your grace, but you are not on the list. That will be fifteen divas."

"Get out of my way."

Hardhands takes a pushy step forward, only to find that his feet can not come off the ground. The Boy, the Gatekeeper, smells like human but he has powerful praeterhuman push.

"Let me by."

"What's the magick word?"

"--------." This word should blossom like fire in the sultry air, it should spout lava and sparks and smell like burning tar. It should shrink the Boy down to stepping-upon size.

It sparks briefly, like a wet sparkler, and gutters away.

He tries again, this time further up the Gramatica alphabet, heavier on the results.

"--------." This word should suck all the light out of the world, leaving a blackness so utter the Boy will be gasping for enough breath to scream.

It casts a tiny shadow, like a gothick's smile, and then brightens.

"Great accent," says the Boy. He is grinning sympathetically, which enrages Hardhands even more, because he is the Pontifexa's grandson and there's nothing to be sorry about for THAT. "But not magickal enough."

Hardhands is flummoxed, this is a first, never before has his magick been stifled, tamped, failed to light. Gramatica is tricky, it is true. In the right mouth the right Gramatica word will explode the Boy into tiny bits of bouncing ectoplasm, or shatter the air as though it were made of ice, or turn the moon into a tulip. The right word in the wrong mouth, a mouth that stops when it should glottal or clicks when it should clack, could turn his tummy into a hat, roll back time, or turn his blood to fire. But, said right or said wrong, Gramatica never does nothing. His tummy is, again, tingling.

The Boy is now picking his teeth with the tip of his knife. "I give you a hint. The most magickal word of them all."

What more magick than ----------? Is there a more magickal word that Hardhands has never heard of? He's an adept of the sixth order, he's peeked into the Abyss, surely there is no Super Special Magickal Word hidden from him yet—he furrows his pure white brow into unflattering wrinkles, and then, a tiny whiny little voice in his head says: *what's the magick word, Bwannie, what's the magick word?*

"Please," Hardhands says. "Let me pass, please."

"With pleasure," the Boy says. "But I must warn you. There are ordeals."

"No ordeal can be worse than listening to you."

"One might think so," the boy says. "You have borne my rudeness so kindly, your grace, that I hate to ask you for one last favor, but I fear I must."

Hardhands glares at the boy, who smiles sheepishly.

"Your boots, your grace. Madama doesn't care for footwear on her clean carpets. I shall give you a ticket, and give your boots a polish and they'll be nice and shiny for you, when you leave."

Hardhands does not want to relinquish his heels, which may only add an actual half an inch in height, but are marvelous when it comes to mental stature, who can not help but swagger in red-topped jack-boots, champagne shiny and supple as night?

He sighs, bending. The grass below is cool against our hero's hot feet, once liberated happily from the pinchy pointy boots (ah vanity, thy name is only sixteen years old) but he'd trade the comfort, in a second, for height.

He hops and kicks, sending one boot flying at the kid (who catches it easily) and the other off into the darkness.

"Mucho gusto. Have a swell time, your grace."

Hardhands stiffens his spine with arrogance and steps into the Monkey's Mouth.

### VII. Time's Trick

Motion moves in the darkness around him, a glint of silver, to one side, then the other, then in front of him: he jumps. Then he realizes that the form ahead of him is familiar: his own reflection. He steps forward, and the Hardhands before him resolves into a Hardhands behind him, while those to other side move with him, keeping pace. For a second he hesitates, thinking to run into mirror, but an outstretched arm feels only empty air, and he steps once, again, then again, more confidently. His reflection has disappeared; ahead is only darkness.

So he continues on, contained with a hollow square of his own reflections, which makes him feel a bit more cheerful, for what can be more reassuring but an entire phalanx of your own beautiful self? Sure, he looks a bit tattered: bare chest, sticky hair, blurred eyeliner, but it's a sexy tattered, bruised and battered, and slightly forlorn. He could start a new style with this look: *After the Deluge*, it could be called, or, *A Rough Night*.

Of course Woodward's has a hall of mirrors too, a horrifying place where the glasses stretch your silver-self until you look like an emaciated crane, or squash you down, round as a beetle. These mirrors continue, as he continues, to show only his perfect self, disheveled, but still perfect. He laughs, a sound which, pinned in on all sides as it is, quickly dies. If this is the Boy's idea of an Ordeal, he's picked the wrong man. Hardhands has always loved mirrors, so much so that he has them all over his apartments: on his walls, on his ceilings, even, in his Conjuring Closet, on the floor. He's never met a reflection of himself he didn't love, didn't cherish, cheered up by the sight of his own beauty—what a lovely young man, how blissful to be me!

He halts and fumbles in his kilt-pocket for his favorite lip rouge (*Death in Bloom*, a sort of blackish pink) and reapplies. Checks his teeth for color, and blots on the back of his hand. Smoothes one eyebrow with his fingertip, and arranges a strand of hair so it is more fetchingly askew—then leans in, closer. A deep line furrows behind his eyes, a line where he's had no line before, and there, at his temple, is that a strand of gray amidst the silver? His groping fingers feel only smoothness on his brow, he smiles and the line vanishes, he grips the offending hair and yanks: in his grasp it is as pearly as ever. A trick of the poor light then, and on he goes, but sneaking glances to his left and right, not from admiration, but from concern.

As he goes, he keeps peeking sideways and at each glance, he quickly looks away again, alarmed. Has he always slumped so badly? He squares his shoulders, and peeks again. His hinder, it's huge, like he's got a caboose under his kilt, and his chin, it's as weak as custard. No, it must just be a trick of the light, his hinder is high and firm, and his chin as hard and curved as granite, he's overstressed and overwrought and he still has all that sugar in his system. His gaze doggedly forward, he continues down the silver funnel, picks up his feet, eager, perhaps for the first time ever, to get away from a mirror.

The urge to glance is getting bigger and bigger, and Hardhands has, before, always vanquished temptation by yielding to it, he looks again, this time to his right. There, he is as lovely as ever, silly silly. He grins confidently at himself, that's much better. He looks behind him and sees, in another mirror, his own back looking further beyond, but he can't see what he's looking at or why.

Back to the slog, and the left is still bugging him, he's seeing flashes out of the corner of his eye, and he just can't help it, he must look: his eyes, they are sunken like marbles into his face, hollow as a sugar skull, his skin tightly pulled, painted with garish red cheekbones. Blackened lips pull back from grayish teeth—his pearly white teeth!—He chatters those pearly whites together, his bite is firm and hard. He looks to the right and sees himself, as he should be.

Now he knows, don't look to the left, keep to the right and keep focused, the left is a mirage, the right is reality. The left side is a horrible joke and the right side is true, but even as he, increasing his steps to almost a run (will this damn hallway never end?), the Voice of Vanity in his head is questioning that assertion. Perhaps the right side is the horrible joke, and the left side the truth, perhaps he has been blind to his own flaws, perhaps—

This time: he is transfixed at the image which stares back, as astonished as he is: he's an absolute wreck. His hair is still and brittle, hanging about his knobby shoulders like salted sea grass. His ice blue eyes look cloudy, and the thick black lines drawn about them serve only to sink them deeper into his skull. Scars streak lividly across his cheeks. Sunken chest and tattoos faded into blue and green smudges, illegible on slack skin. He's too horrified to seek reassurance in the mirror now behind him, he's transposed on the horror before him: the horror of his own inevitable wreckage and decay. The longer he stares the more hideous he becomes. The image blurs for a moment, and then blood blooms in his hair, and dribbles from his gaping lips, his shoulders are scratched and smudged with black, his eyes starting from his skull. He is surrounded by swirling snow, flecks of which sputter on his eyelashes, steam as they touch his skin. The shaft of an arrow protrudes from his throat.

"Oh how bliss to me," the Death's Head croaks, each word a bubble of blood.

With a shout, Hardhands raises his right fist and punches. His fist meets the glass with a nauseous jolt of pain that rings all the way down to his toes. The glass bows under his blow but doesn't crack. He hits again, and his corpse reels back, clutching itself with claw-like hands. The mirror refracts into a thousand diamond shards, and Hardhands throws up his other arm to ward off glass and blood. When he drops his shield, the mirrors and their Awful Reflection are gone.

He stands on the top of stairs, looking out over a tumultuous vista: there's a stage with feathered denizens dancing the hootchie-coo. Behind the hootchie-coochers, a band plays a ferocious double-time waltz. Couples slide and twist and turn to the musick, their feet flickering so quickly they spark. The scene is much like the scene he left behind at the Blue Duck, only instead of great big hair, there are great big horns, instead of sweeping skirts there are sweeping wings, instead of smoke there is coldfire. The musick is loud enough to liquefy his skull, he can barely think over its howling sweep.

The throng below whirls about in confusion—denizens, demons, egregores, servitors—was that a Bilskinir-Blue Bulk he saw over there at the bar, tusks a-gleaming, Butler Paimon on his damn night-off? No matter even if it is Paimon, no holler for help from Hardhands, oh no. Paimon would have to help him out, of course, but Paimon would tell the Pontifexa for sure, for Paimon, in addition to being the Butler of Bilskinir, is a suck-up. No thanks, our hero is doing just fine on his own.

A grip pulls at Hardhands' soft hand, he looks down into the wizened grinning face of a monkey. Hardhands tries to yank from the grasp, the monkey has pretty good pull, which he puts into gear with a yank, that our hero has little choice but to follow. A bright red cap shaped like a flowerpot is affixed to Sieur Simian's head by a golden cord, and he's surprisingly good at the upright; his free hand waves a path through the crowd, pulling Hardhands behind like a toy.

The dancers slide away from the monkey's push, letting Hardhands and his guide through their gliding. By the band, by the fiddler, who is sawing away at his fiddle as though each note was a gasp of air and he a suffocating man, his hair flying with sweat, his face burning with concentration. Towards a flow of red velvet obscuring a doorway, and through the doorway into sudden hush, the cessation of the slithering music leaving sudden silence in Hardhands' head.

Now he stands on a small landing, overlooking a crowded room. The Great Big Horns and Very Long Claws etc. are alert to something sitting upon a dais at the far end of the room. Hardhands follows their attention and goes cold all the way to his bones.

Upon the dais is a table. Upon the table is a cage. Within the cage: Tiny Doom.

## VIII. Cash & Carry

The bidding has already started. A hideous figure our hero recognizes as Zigurex the Avatar of Agony is flipping it out with a dæmon whose melty visage and dribbly hair Hardhands does not know. Their paddles are popping up and down, in furious volley to the furious patter of the auctioneer:

" ... unspoiled untouched pure one hundred percent kid-flesh plump and juicy tender and sweet highest grade possible never been spanked whacked or locked in a closet for fifty days with no juice no crackers no light fed on honey dew and chocolate sauce ... "

(Utter lie, Tiny Doom is in a cheesy noodle phase and if it's not noodles and it's not orange then she ain't gonna eat it, no matter the dire threat.) Tiny Doom is barking, frolicking about the cage happily, she's the center of attention, she's up past her bedtime and she's a *puppy*. It's fun!

The auctioneer is small, delicate, and apparently human, although Hardhands is willing to bet that she's probably none of these at all, and she has the patter down: "Oh she's darling oh she's bright she'll fit on your mantel, she'll sleep on your dog-bed, she's compact and cute now, and ah the blood you can breed from her when she's older. What an investment, sell her now, sell her later, you're sure to repay your payment a thousand times over and a free Pig as garnish can you beat the deal—and see how bright she does bleed."

The minion hovering above the cage displays a long length of silver tipped finger and then flicks downward. Tiny Doom yelps, and the rest of the patter is lost in Hardhands' roar as he leaps forward, pushing spectators aside: "THAT IS MY WIFE!"

His leap is blocked by bouncers, who thrust him backwards, but not far. Ensues: rumpus, with much switching and swearing and magickal sparkage. Hardhands may have Words of Power, and a fairly Heavy Fist for one so fastidious but the bouncers have Sigils of Impenetrableness or at least Hides of Steel, and one of them has three arms, and suction cups besides.

"THAT IS MY WIFE!" Hardhands protests again, now pinned. "I demand that you release her to me."

"It's careless to let such a tempting small morsel wander the streets alone, your grace." Madam Rose cocks her head, her stiff wire head-dress jingling, and the bouncers release Hardhands.

He pats his hair; despite the melee, still massively piled, thanks to Paimon's terrifically sticky hair pomade. The suction cups have left little burning circles on his chest and his bare toes feel a bit tingly from connecting square with someone's tombstone-hard teeth, but at least he solaces in the fact that one of the bouncers is dripping whitish ooze from puffy lips and the other won't be breeding children anytime soon;

just as hard a kick, but much more squishy. The room's a wreck, too, smashed chairs, crumpled paper, spilled popcorn, oh dear, too bad.

"She's my wife to be, as good as is my wife, and I want her back." He makes movement towards the cage, which is now terribly quiet, but the bouncers still bar the way.

Zigurex upsteps himself, then, looming over Hardhands, who now wishes he had been more insistent about the boots: "Come along with the bidding; it's not all night, you see, the tide is rising and the magick will soon sail."

The other dæmon, who is both squishy and scaly, bubbles his opinion, as well. At least Hardhands assumes it is his opinion, impossible to understand his blubbering, some obscure dialect of Gramatica, or maybe just a very bad accent, anyway who cares what he has to say anyway, not Hardhands, not at all.

"There is no bidding, she's not for sale, she belongs to me, and Pig, too, and we are leaving," he says.

"Do you bid?" Madam Rose asks.

"No I do not bid. I do not have to bid. She is my wife."

"One hundred fifty!" Zigurex says, last-ditch.

The Fishy Thing counters the offer with a saliva spray glug.

"He offers two hundred," says Madam Rose, "what do you offer?"

"Two hundred!" says Hardhands, outraged. "I've paid two hundred for a pot of lip rouge. She's worth a thousand if she's worth a diva—"

Which is exactly of course the entirely wrong thing to say but his outrage has gotten the better of his judgment, which was already impaired by the outrage of being manhandled like a commoner to begin with, and which also might not have been the best even before then.

Madam Rose smiles. Her lips are sparkly pink and her teeth are sparkly black. "One thousand divas, then, for her return! Cash only. Good night good night and come again!"

She claps her hands, and the bouncers start to press the disappointed bidders into removing.

"Now look here—" says Hardhands. "You can't expect me to buy my own wife, and even if you could expect me to buy my own wife, I won't. I insist that you hand her over right this very second and impede me no longer."

"Is that so?" Madam Rose purrs. The other bidders retreat easily, perhaps they have a sense of where this is all going and decide it's wise to get out of the way whilst there is still a way to get out of. Even Sieur Squishy and Zigurex go, although not without several smoldering backways looks on the part of the Avatar of Agony, obviously a sore loser. Madam Rose sits herself down upon a velvet-covered chair, and waves Hardhands to do the same, but he does not. A majordomo has uprighted the brazier and repaired the smoldering damage, decanted tea into a brass teapot and set it upon a round brass tray. Madam Rose drops sugar cubes into two small glasses and pours over: spicy cinnamon, tangy orange.

Hardhands ignores the tea; peers into the cage to access damage.

"Pig has a tummy ache, and wants to go home, Bwannie." The fat little lip is trembling and despite himself, Hardhands is overwhelmed by the tide of adorableness, that he should, being a first rate magician and poet, be inoculated against. She is so like her mother, oh his darling sister, sometimes it makes him want to cry.

He retreats into gruff. "Ayah, so well, Pig should not have had so much candy. And nor should Pig have wandered off alone."

"He is bad," agrees Doom. "Very bad."

"Sit tight and do not cry. We will go home soon. Ayah?"

"Ayah." She sniffs, but holds the snuffle, little soldier.

Madam Rose offers Hardhands a seat, which he does not sit upon, and a glass, which he waves away, remembering anew the Pontifexa's advice, and also not trusting Madam's sparkle grin. He's heard of the dives where they slide sleep into your drink; you gulp down happily and wake up six hours later minus all you hold dear and a splitting headache, as well. Or worse still, gin-joints that sucker you into one little sip, and then you have such a craving that you must have more and more, but no matter how much you have, it shall never be enough. He'll stay dry and alert, thank you.

"I have no time for niceties, or social grace," he says. "I will take my wife and pig, and leave."

"One thousand divas is not so great a sum to the Pontifexa's grandson," Madam Rose observes. "And it's only right that I should recoup some of my losses—look here, I shall have to redecorate, and fashionable taste, as your grace knows, is not cheap."

"I doubt there is enough money in the world to buy you good taste, madama, and why should I pay for something that is mine?"

"Now who owns who, really? *She* is the Heir to the House Haðraaða, and one day she'll be Pontifexa. *You* are just the boy who does. By rights all of us, including you, belong to her, in loyalty and in love. I do wish you would sit, your grace." Madam Rose pats the pillow beside her, which again he ignores.

This statement sets off a twinge of rankle because it is true. He answers loftily, "We are all the Pontifexa's obedient servants, and are happy to bend ourselves to her Will, and her Will in the matter of her Heir is clear. I doubt that she would be pleased to know of the situation of this night."

Madam Rose sets her red cup down. An ursine-headed minion offers her a chocolate, gently balanced between two pointy bear-claws. She opens red lips, black teeth, long red throat, and swallows the chocolate without a chew.

"I doubt," she says, "that the Pontifexa shall be pleased at tonight's situation at all. I do wish you would sit, your grace. I feel so small, and you so tall, so high above. And do sample, your grace. I assure you that my candy has no extra spice to it, just wholesome goodness you will find delicious. You have my word upon it."

Hardhands sits, and takes the chocolate he is offered. He's already on the train bound for Purgelandia, he might as well make the journey worth the destination. The Minion twinkles azure bear eyes at him. Bears don't exactly have the right facial arrangement to smirk, but this bear is making a fine attempt, and Hardhands thinks what a fine rug Sieur Oso would make, stretched out before a peaceful fire. In the warmth of his mouth, the chocolate explodes into glorious peppery chocolate yum. For a second he closes his eyes against the delicious darkness, all his senses receding into sensation of pure bliss dancing on his tongue.

"It is good chocolate, is it not?" Madam Rose asks. "Some say such chocolate should be reserved for royalty and the Goddess. But we do enjoy it, no?"

"What do you want?" Hardhands asks, and they both know that he doesn't just mean for Tiny Doom.

"Putting aside, for the moment, the thousand divas, I want nothing more than to be of aid to you, your grace, to be your humble servant. It is not what I may want from you but what you can want from me."

"That I have told you."

"Just that?"

In the cage, Tiny Doom is silent and staring, she may be a screamer, but she does, thankfully, know when to keep her trap shut.

"I can offer you no other assistance? Think on it, your grace. You are an adept, and you traffic with denizens of the deep, through the force of your Will. I am not an adept, I also have traffic with those same denizens."

The second chocolate tangs his tongue with the sour-sweet brightness of lime. "Contrary to all laws of Goddess and nature," he says thickly, when the brilliant flavor has receded enough to allow speech. "Your traffic is obscene. It is not the same."

"I didn't say it was the same, I said we might complement each other, rather than compete. Do you not get tired of your position, your grace? You are so close, and yet so far. The Pontifexa's brightest boy, but does she respect you? Does she trust you? This little girl, is she not the hitch in your git-along, the sand in your shoe? Leave her with me, and she'll never muss your hair again, or wrinkle your cravat."

"I don't recall inviting you to comment upon my personal matters," says Hardhands, à la prince. "And I don't recall offering you my friendship either."

"I cry your pardon, your grace. I only offer my thoughts in the hope—"

He's tired of the game now, if he had the thousand divas he'd fork them over, just to be quit of the entire situation, it was fun, it was cool, it's not fun it's not cool, he's bored, the sugar is drilling a spike through his forehead and he's done.

"I'll write you a draft, and you'll take it, and we shall leave, and that's the end of the situation," Hardhands says loftily.

Madam Rose sighs, and sips her tea. Another sigh, another sip.

"I'm sorry, your grace, but if you can not pay, then I must declare your bid null, and reopen the auction. Please understand my position. It is, and has always been, the policy of this House to operate on a cash basis; I'm sure you understand why—taxes, a necessary evil, but perhaps more evil than necessary." Madam Rose smiles at him, and sips again before going on. "My reputation rests upon my policies, and that I apply them equally to all. Duque of Califa or the lowliest servitor, all are equal within my walls. So you see, if I allow you license I have refused others, how shall it appear then?"

"Smart," answers our hero. "Prudent. Wise."

Madam Rose laughs. "Would that others might consider my actions in that light, but I doubt their charity. No, I'm sorry, your grace. I have worked hard for my name. I can not give it up, not for you or for anyone."

She puts her tea glass down and clicks her tongue, a sharp snap that brings Sieur Bear to her side. "The Duque has decided to withdraw his bid; please inform Zigurex that his bid is accepted and he may come and claim his prize."

Hardhands looks at Doom in her cage, her wet little face peers through the bars. She smiles at him, she's scared but she has confidence that Bwannie will save her, Bwannie loves her. Bwannie has a sense of déjà vu; hasn't he been here before, why is it his fate to always give in to her, little monster? Tiny Doom, indeed.

"What do you want?" he repeats.

"Well," Madam Rose says brightly. "Now that you mention it. The Pontifexina is prime, oh that's true, but I know one more so. More mature, more valuable, more ready."

Now it's Hardhands' turn to sigh, which he does, and sip, wetting parched throat, now not caring if the drink be drugged, or not. "You'll let her go? Return her safe and sound?"

"Of course, your grace. You have my word on it."

"Not a hair on her head or a drop from her veins or a tear from her eye? Not a scab, or nail, or any part that might be later used against her? Completely whole? Untouched, unsmudged, no tricks?"

"As you say."

Hardhands puts his glass down, pretending resignation. "All right then. You have a deal."

Of course he don't really give in, but he's assessed that perhaps it's better to get Doom out of the way. He can play rough enough if it's only his own skin involved, but why take the chance of her collateral damage? When she's out of the way, he calculates, and Madam Rose's guard is down, then we'll see, oh yes, we'll see.

Madam Rose's shell-white hand goes up to her lips, shading them briefly behind two slender fingers. Then the fingers flip down and flick a shard of spinning coldfire towards him. Hardhands recoils, but too late. The airy kiss zings through the air like an arrow of outrageous fortune and smacks him right in the middle of Death in Bloom. The kiss feels like a kick to the head, and our hero and his chair flip backwards, the floor rising to meet his fall, but not softly. The impact sends his bones jarring inside his flesh, and the jarring is his only movement for the sigil has left him shocked and paralyzed.

He can't cry out, he can't flinch, he can only let the pain flood down his palate and into his brain, in which internal shouting and swearing is making up for external silence. He can't close his eyes either, but he closes his outside vision and brings into inside focus the bright sharp words of a sigil that should suck all the energy from Madam Rose's sigil, blow it into a powderpuff of oblivion.

The sigil burns bright in Hardhands' eyes, but it is also trapped and cannot get free. It sparks and wheels, and he desperately tries to tamp it out, dumping colder, blacker sigils on top of its flare, trying to fling it outward and away, but it's stuck firmly inside his solar plexus, he can fling it nowhere. It's caught in his craw like a fish bone, and he's choking but he can't choke because he cannot move. The sigil's force billows through him: it is twisting his entrails into knots, his bones into bows, it's flooding him with a fire so bright that it's black, with a fire so cold that it burns and burns and burns, his brain boils and then: nothing.

## IX. Thy Baited Hook

Here is Hardhands, returning to the Waking World. His blood is mud within his veins, he can barely suck air through stifled lungs and there's a droning in his ears, no not droning, humming, Tiny Doom:

*"Kick her bite her that's the way I'll spite her! Kick her bite her that's the way I'll spite her! Kick her bite her that's the way I'll spite her!"*

The view aloft is raven-headed angels, with ebony black wings swooping loops of brocade across a golden ceiling. Then the view aloft is blocked by Tiny Doom's face; she still has the sugar mustache, and her kohl has blurred, cocooning her blue eyes in smoky blackness. Her hat is gone.

"Don't worry, Bwannie," she pats his stiff face with a sticky hand, "Pig will save us."

His brain heaves but the rest of him remains still. The frame of his body has never before been so confining. Diligent practice has made stepping his mind from his flesh an easy accomplishment, are there not times when a magician's Will needs independence from his blood and bones? But never before has he been stuck, nor run up against sigils harder and more impenetrable than his own. Lying in the cage of his own flesh he is feeling helpless, and tiny, and it's a sucky feeling, not at all suited to his stature of Pontifexa's grandson, first rate magician and—

"I will bite you," says Doom.

"I doubt that," is the gritty answer, a deep rumble: "My skin is thick as steel and your teeth will break."

"Ha! I am a shark and I will bite you."

"Not if I bite you first, little lovely, nip your sweet tiny fingers, crunch crunch each one, oh so delicious, what a snack. Come here, little morsel."

The weight of Tiny Doom suddenly eases off his chest, but not without kicking and gripping, holding on to him in a vise-like grip, oww, her fingers dig like nails into his leg but to no avail. Tiny Doom is wrenched off of him, and in the process he's wrenched sideways, now he's got a nice view of the grassy floor, a broken teapot, and, just on the edge, someone's feet. The feet are shod in garish two-tone boots: magenta upper and orange toe-cap. Tiny Doom screams like a rabbit, high and horrible.

"You'll bruise her," says a voice from above the feet. "And then the Pontifexa will be chuffed."

"I shall not hurt her one jot if she's a good girl, but she should shut her trap, a headache I am getting."

Good for her, Tiny Doom does not shut her trap, she opens her trap wider and shoots the moon, with a piercing squeal that stabs into Hardhands' unprotected ears like an awl, slicing all the way down to the center of his brain. With a smack, the shriek abruptly stops.

Two pretty little bare feet drift into Hardhands' view. "Stop it, you two. She must be returned in perfect condition, an' I get my deposit back. It's only the boy that the Pontifexa wants rid of; the girl is still her heir. Leave her alone, or I shall feed you both into my shredder. Chop chop. The guests are waiting and he must be prepared."

"She squirms," complains the Minion.

Madam Rose, sternly: "You, little madam, stop squirming. You had fun being a puppy, and cupcakes besides, and soon you shall be going home to your sweet little bed. How sad Grandmamma and Paimon shall be if I must give them a bad report of your behavior."

Sniffle, sniff. "But I want Bwannie."

"Never you mind Bwannie for now, here have a Choco-Sniff, and here's one for Pig, too."

Sniff, sniffle. "Pig don't like Choco-Sniffs."

Hardhands kicks, but it's like kicking air, he can feel the movement in his mind, but his limbs stay stiff and locked. And then his mind recoils: What did Madam Rose say about the Pontifexa? Did he hear a-right? Deposit? Report?

"Here then is a jacksnap for Pig. Be a good girl, eat your candy and then you shall kiss Bwannie good-bye."

Whine: "I want to go with Bwannie!"

"Now, now," Madam Rose's cheery tone tingles with irritation, but she's making a good show of not annoying Tiny Doom into another session of shrieking. "Now, Bwannie must stay here, and you must go home—do not start up with the whining again, it's hardly fitting for the Pontifexa's heir to cry like a baby, now is it? Here, have another Choco-Sniff."

Then more harshly, "You two, get the child ready to be returned and the boy prepared. I shall be right back."

The pretty feet float from Hardhands' view and a grasp attaches to Hardhands' ankle. Though his internal struggle is mighty, externally he puts up no fuss at all. Flipped over by rough hands, he sees above him the sharp face of a Sylph, pointy eyes, pointy nose, pointy chin. Hands are fumbling at his kilt buckles; obscurely he notices that the Sylph has really marvelous hair, it's the color of fresh caramel and it smells, Hardhands notices as the Sylph bends over to nip at his neck, like new-mown grass. A tiny jolt of pretty pain, and warm wetness dribbles down his neck.

"Ahhh ... " the Sylph sighs, "you should taste this, first rate knock-back."

"Madama said be nice."

"I am being nice, as nice as pie, as nice as he is. Nice and sweet," The Sylph licks at Hardhands' neck again; its tongue is scrape-y, like a cat's, and it hurts in a strangely satisfying way. "Sweet sweet darling boy. He is going to bring our garden joy. What a deal she has made. Give the girl, but keep the boy, he's useful to us, even if she don't want him anymore. A good trick he'll turn for Madama. Bright boy."

Hardhands is hoisted aloft, demon claws at his ankles and his wrists, slinging him like a side of beef on the way to the barbeque pit. His eyes are slitted open, his head dangling downward, he can see only a narrow slice of floor bobbing by. A carpet patterned with entwined snakes, battered black and red tiles, white marble veined with gold. He's watching all this, with part of attention, but mainly he's running over and over again what Madam Rose had said about the Pontifexa. Was it possible to be true? Did Grandmamma set him up? Sell him out? Was this all a smokescreen to get him out of her hair, away from her treasure? He will not believe it, he will not believe it, it cannot be true!

Rough movement drops Hardhands onto the cold floor, and metal clenches his ankles. The bracelets bite into his flesh as he is hoisted aloft, and all the blood rushes to his head in a explosion of pressure. For a second, even his slit of sight goes black, but then, just as suddenly, he finds he can open his eyes all the way. He rolls eyeballs upward, and sees retreating minion backs. He rolls eyes downward and sees polished marble floor and the tangled drape of his own hair, Paimon's pomade having finally given up. The gryves are burning bright pain into his ankles, and he's swaying slightly from some invisible airflow, but the movement is kind of soothing and his back feels nice and stretched out. If it weren't for being the immobilization, and obvious bait, hanging upside-down could be kind of fun.

Our hero tries to wiggle, but can't, tries to jiggle but is still stuck. He doesn't dare try another sigil and risk blowing his brains out, and without the use of his muscles he cannot gymnastic himself free. He closes his internal eyes, slips his consciousness into darkness, and concentrates. His Will pushes and pushes against the pressure that keeps him contained, focuses into a single point that must burn through. After a second, a minute, an eternity, all bodily sensation—the burn of the gyres, the stretch of his back, the pressure of his bladder, the breeze on his face—slips away, and his Will floats alone on the Current.

Away from the strictures of his body, Hardhands' consciousness can take any form that he cares to mold it to, or no form at all, a spark of himself drifting on the Currents of Elsewhere. But such is his fondness for his own form, even Elsewhere, that when he steps lightly from the flesh hanging like a side of beef, he coalesces into a representation of himself, in every way identical to his corporeal form, although with lip rouge that will not smudge, and spectacularly elevated hair.

On Elsewhere feet, Hardhands' fetch turns to face its meaty shell, and is rather pleased with the view; even dangling upside down, he looks pretty darn good. Elsewhere, the sigil that has caged Hardhands' motion is clearly visible as a pulsating net of green and gold, interwoven at the interstices with splotches of pink. A Coarctation Sigil, under normal circumstances no stronger than pie, but given magnitude by the height of the Current, and Hardhands' starchy condition. The fetch, however, is not limited by starch, and the Current just feeds its strength. Dismantling the constraint is the work of a matter of seconds, and after the fetch slides back into its shell, it's a mere bagatelle to contort himself down and free.

Casting free of the gyres with a splashy Gramatica command, Hardhands rubs his ankles, and then stands on tingly feet. Now that he has the leisure to inspect the furnishings, he sees there are no furnishings to inspect because the room, while sumptuously paneled in gorgeous tiger-eye maple, is empty other than a curvy red velvet chaise. The only ornamentations are the jingly chains dangling from the ceiling. The floor is bare stone, cold beneath his bare feet. And now, he notices that the flooring directly under the dangle is dark and stained, with something that he suspects is a combination of blood, sweat, and tears.

Places to go and praterhuman entities to fry, no time to linger to discover the truth of his suspicions. Hardhands turns to make his exit through the sole door, only to find that the door is gone, and in its place, a roiling black Vortex, as black and sharp as the Vortex that he himself had cut out of the Aeyther, only hours before. He is pushed back by the force of the Vortex, which is spiraling outward, not inward, thus indicating that Something is coming, rather than trying to make him go.

The edges of the Vortex glow hot-black, the wind that the Vortex is creating burns his skin; he shields his eyes with his hand, and tries to stand upright, but his tingly feet can not hold against the force, and he falls. The Vortex widens, like a surprised eye, and a slit of light appears pupil-like in its darkness. The pupil widens, becomes a pupa, a cocoon, a shell, an acorn, an egg, growing larger and larger and larger until it fills the room with unbelievable brightness, with a scorching heat that is hotter than the sun, bright enough to burn through Hardhands' shielding hand. Hardhands feels his skin pucker, his eyes shrivel, his hair start to smolder, and then just as he is sure he is about to burst into flames, the light shatters like an eggshell, and Something has arrived.

Recently, Hardhands' Invocations have grown quite bold, and, after some bitter tooth and nails, he's pulled a few large fish into his circle. But those are as like to This as a fragment of beer bottle is to a faceted diamond. He knows, from the top of his pulsating head to the tips of his quivering toes that this is no servitor, no denizen, no elemental. Nothing this spectacular can be called, corralled, or compelled. This apparition can be nothing but the highest of the high, the blessed of the blessed: the Goddess Califa herself.

How to describe what Hardhands sees? Words are too simple, they cannot do justice to Her infinite complexity, she's Everything and Nothing, both fractured and whole. His impressions are blurred and confused, but here's a try. Her hair is ruffled black feathers, it is slickery green snakes, it is as fluffy and lofty as frosting. Her eyes— one, two, three, four, maybe five—are as round and polished as green apples, are long tapered crimson slits, they are as flat white as sugar. She's as narrow as nightfall, She's as round as winter, She's as tall as moonrise, She's shorter than love. Her feet do not crush the little flowers, She is divine, She is fantastic.

She simply is.

Hardhands has found his footing only to lose it again, falling to his knees before her, her fresh red smile as strong as a kick to the head, to the heart. Hardhands is smitten, no not smitten, he's smote, from the tingly tingly top of his reeling head to the very tippy tip of his tingling toes. He's freezing and burning, he's alive, he's dying, he's dead. He's hypmooootized. He gapes at the Goddess, slack-jawed and tight-handed, wanting nothing more than to reach out and grasp at her perfection, bury himself in the ruffle of her feathers. Surely a touch of Her hand would spark such fire in him that he would catch alight and perish in a blaze of exquisite agony but it would be worth it, oh it would be worth every cinder.

The Goddess's mouth opens, with a flicker of a velvet tongue and the glitter of a double row of white teeth. The Gramatica that flows from Her mouth in a sparkly ribband is as crisp and sweet as a summer wine, it slithers over Hardhands' flushed skin, sliding into his mouth, his eyes, his ears, and filling him with a dark sweet rumble.

"Georgiana's toy," the Goddess purrs. He didn't see Her move but now She is poured over the chaise like silk, and the bear-head minion is offering bowls of snacks, ice cream sundaes, and magazines. "Chewable and sweet, ah lovely darling yum."

Hardhands has forgotten Georgiana, he's forgotten Tiny Doom, he's forgotten Madam Rose, he's forgotten himself, he's forgotten his exquisite manners—no not entirely, even the Goddess's splendor can not expunge good breeding. He toddles up onto sweaty feet, and sweeps the floor with his curtsy.

"I am your obedient servant, your grace," he croaks.

The Goddess undulates a languid finger and he finds himself following Her beckon, not that he needs to be beckoned, he can barely hold himself aloof, wants nothing more than to throw himself forward and be swallowed alive. The Goddess spreads Her wings, Her arms, Her legs, and he falls into Her embrace, the prickle of the feathers closing over his bare skin, electric and hot.

## X. Doom Acts

Here is Tiny Doom howling like a banshee, a high-pitched shriek that usually results in immediate attention to whatever need she is screaming for: more pudding, longer story, hotter bath, bubbles. The Minion whose arm she is slung under must be pitch deaf because her shrieks have not the slightest impact upon him. He continues galumphing along, whistling slightly, or perhaps that is just the breeze of his going, which is a rapid clip.

She tries teeth, her fall-back weapon and always effective, even on Paimon whose blue skin is surprisingly delicate. The Minion's hide is as chewy as rubber and it tastes like salt licorice. Spitting and coughing, Tiny Doom gives up on the bite. Kicking has no effect other than to bruise her toes and her arms are too pinned for hitting, and, down the stairs they go, bump bump, Bwannie getting further and further away. Pig is jolting behind them, she's got a grip on one dangly ear, but that's all, and his bottom is hitting each downward stump, but he's too soft to thump.

An outside observer might think that Doom is wailing for more candy, or perhaps is just over-tired and up past her bedtime. Madam Rose certainly thought that her commotion was based in over-tiredness, plus a surfeit of sugar, and the Bouncer thinks it's based in spoiled-ness, plus a surfeit of sugar, but they are both wrong. Sugar is Doom's drug of choice, she's not allowed it officially, but unofficially she has her ways (she knows exactly in what drawer the Pontifexa's secretary keeps his stash of Crumbly Crem-O's and Jiffy-Ju's, and if that drawer is empty, Relais can be relied upon to have a box of bon-bons hidden from Hardhands in the bottom of his wardrobe), and so her system can tolerate massive quantities of the stuff before hyper-activity and urpyness sets in.

No. She is wailing because every night, at tuck-in time, after the Pontifexa has kissed her, and kissed Pig and together they have said their prayers, then Paimon sits on the edge of Tiny Doom's big white frilly bed and tells her a story. It's a different story every night, Paimon's supply of fabulosity being apparently endless, but always with the same basic theme:

Kid is told what To Do.

Kid does Not Do what Kid is told To Do.

Kid gets into Bad Trouble with various Monsters.

Kid gets Eaten.

The End, yes you may have one more drink of water, and then no more excuses and it's lights out, and to sleep. Now.

Tiny Doom loves these stories, whose Directives and Troubles are always endlessly inventively different, but which always turn out the same way: with a Giant Monstrous Burp. She knows that Paimon's little yarns are for fun only, that Kids do not really get eaten when they do not do what they are told, for she does not do what she is told all the time, and she's never been eaten. Of course, no one would dare eat her anyway, she's the Heir to the Pontifexa, and has Paimon and Pig besides. Paimon's stories are just stories, made to deliciously shiver her skin, so that afterwards she lies in the haze of the nightlight, cuddled tight to Pig's squishiness, and knows that she is safe.

But now, tonight, she's seen the gleam in Madam Rose's eye and seen the look she gave her minions and Tiny Doom knew instantly that Bwannie is in Big Trouble. This is not bedtime, there is no Paimon, and no nightlight, and no drink of water. This is all true Big Trouble and Tiny Doom knows exactly where Big Trouble ends. Now she is scared, for Bwannie and for herself, and even for Pig, who would make a perfect squishy demon dessert.

Thus, shrieking.

"Bwaaaaaaaaaaaaaaaaaaaaanie!" Doom cries, "Bwaaaaaaaaaaanie!"

They jump the last step, Tiny Doom jolting bony hip, oww, and then round a corner. Doom sucks in the last useless shriek. Her top half is hanging half over the servitor's shoulder and her dangling-down head is starting to feel tight, plus the shrieking has left her breathless, so for a few seconds she gulps in air. Gulping, her nose running yucky yuck. She wiggles, whispers, and lets go of Pig.

He plops down onto the dirty floor, hinder up and snout down, and then they round another corner and he's gone.

She lifts her head, twisting her neck, and there's the hairy interior of a pointy ear.

She shouts: "Hey, minion!"

"I ain't listening," says the Minion. "You can shout all you want, but I ain't listening. Madam told me not to listen and I ain't."

"I gotta pee!"

"You gotta wait," the Minion says. "You be home soon and then you can pee in your own pot. And you ain't gotta shout in my ear. You make my brain hurt, you loudness little bit, you."

"I gotta pee right now!" Doom, still shouting, anyway, just in case there are noises behind them. "I'M GONNA PEE NOW!"

The Minion stops and shifts Tiny Doom around like a sack full of flour, and breathes into her face. "You don't pee on me, loudness."

Like Paimon, the Minion has tusks and pointy teeth but Paimon's tucks are polished white and his teeth sparkle like sunlight, and his breath smells always of cloves. The Minion's tusks are rubbed and worn, his teeth yucky yellow and he's got bits of someone caught between them.

Doom wrinkles her nose and holds her breath and says in a whine: "I can't help it, I have to go, my hot chocolate is all done." Her feet are dangling and she tries to turn the wiggle into a kick, but she can't quite reach the Minion's soft bits, and her purple slippers wiggle at empty air.

"You pee on me and I snack you up, nasty baby." The Minion crunches spiny fangs together, clashing sparks. "Delish!"

"You don't dare!" says Tiny Doom stoutly. "I am the Pontifexina and my grandmamma would have your knobby hide if you munch me!!"

"An' I care, little princess, if you piss me wet, I munch you dry—"

"---------" whispers Tiny Doom and spits. She's got a good wad going, and it hits the Minion right on the snout.

The Minion howls and drops her. She lands on stingy sleepy feet, falls over, and then scrambles up, stamping. The Minion is also stamping, and holding his hairy hands to his face; under his clawing fingers smoke is steaming. He careens this way and that, Doom dodging around his staggers, and then she scoots by him, and back the way they had just come.

Tiny Doom runs as fast as her fat little legs will run, her heart pounding because she is now in Big Trouble, and she knows if the Minion quits dancing and starts chasing, she's going to be Eaten too. The hot word she spit burned her tongue and that hurts too, and where's Pig? She goes around another corner, thinking she'll see the stairs that they came down, but she doesn't, she sees another long hallway. She turns around to go back, and then the Minion blunders towards her, his face a melt-y mess, and she reverses, speedily.

*"I dance around in a ring and suppose and the secret sits in the middle and knows."* She sings very quietly to herself as she runs.

Carpet silent under her feet; a brief glimpse of another running Doom reflected off a glass curio cabinet; by a closed door, the knob turns but the door will not open. She can feel the wind of closing in beating against her back, but she keeps going. The demon is shouting mean things at her, but she keeps going.

*"You dance around in a ring and suppose and the secret sits in the middle and knows."*

A door opens and a wer-flamingo trips out, stretching its longneck out; Doom dodges around its spindly legs, ignoring yelps. Ahead, more stairs, and there she aims, having no other options, can't go back and there's no where to go sideways.

At the top of the stairs, Doom pauses and finally looks behind. The Minion has wiped most of his melt off, livid red flares burn in his eye sockets and he looks pretty mad. The were-flamingo has halted him, and they are wrangling, flapping wings against flapping ears. The Minion is bigger but the were-flamingo has a sharp beak—rapid fire pecking at the Minion's head. The Minion punches one humongous fist and down the flamingo goes, in a flutter of pink feathers.

"I snack you, spitty baby!" the Minion howls and other things too mean for Doom to hear.

*"We dance around in a ring and suppose and the secret sits in the middle and knows."*

Doom hoists herself up on the banister, squeezing her tummy against the rail. The banister on the Stairs of Infinite Demonstration, Bilskinir's main staircase, is fully sixty feet long. Many is the time that Doom has swooped down its super-polished length, flying miles through the air, at the end to be received by Paimon's perfect catch. This rail is much shorter, and there's no Paimon waiting, but here we go!

She flings her legs over, and slides off. Down she goes, lickety-split, bumping over splinters, but still getting up a pretty good whoosh. Here comes the demon, waving angry arms, he's too big to slide, so he galumphs down the stairs, clumpty clump, getting closer. Doom hits the end of the banister and soars onward another five feet or so, then ooph, hits the ground, owww. She bounces back upward, and darts through the foyer and into the mudroom beyond, pulling open her pockets as she goes.

Choco-sniffs and jack-snaps skitter across the parquet floor, rattling and rolling. Sugarbunnies and beady-eyes, jimjoos and honeybuttons scatter like shot. Good-bye crappy candy, good-bye yummy candy, good-bye.

*"I DANCE AROUND A RING AND SUPPOSE AND THE SECRET SITS IN THE MIDDLE AND KNOWS."*

Ahead, a big red door, well barred and bolted, but surely leading Out. The bottom bolt snaps back under her tiny fingers, but the chains are too high and tippy-toe, hopping, jumping will not reach them. The demon is down the stairs, he's still shouting and steaming, and the smell of charred flesh is stinky indeed.

A wall rack hangs by the door, and from it coats and cloaks dangle like discarded skins; Doom dives into the folds of cloth and becomes very small and silent. She's a good hider, Tiny Doom, she's learned against the best (Paimon).

Her heart pounds thunder in her ears, and she swallows her panting. When Paimon makes discovery (*if* he makes discovery), it means only bath-time, or mushy peas, or toenail clipping. If the demon finds her, Pontifexina or not, it's snicky snack time for sure. She really did have to potty too, pretty bad. She crosses her ankles and jiggles her feet, holding.

In the other room, out of sight, comes yelling, shouting, roaring and then a heavy thud that seems to shake the very walls. The thud reverberates and then fades away.

Silence.

Stillness.

Tiny Doom peeks between the folds. Through the archway she sees rolling candy and part of a sprawled bulk. Then the bulk heaves, hooves kicking. The demon's lungs have re-inflated and he lets out a mighty horrible roar—the nastiest swear word that Tiny Doom has ever heard. Doom, who had poked her head all the way out for a better view, yanks back, just in time. The Word, roiling like mercury, howls by her, trailing sparks and smelling of shit.

A second roar is gulped off in mid-growl, and turns into a shriek, which is then muffled in thumping and slurping, ripping, and chomping. Doom peeks again: the demon's legs are writhing, wiggling, and kicking. A thick stain spreads through the archway, gooey and green. Tiny Doom wiggles her way out of the velvet and runs happily towards the slurping sound.

## XI. Desire Gratified

Inside the Goddess's embrace, Hardhands is dying, he's crying, he's screaming with pleasure, with joy, crying his broken heart out. He's womb-enclosed, hot and smothering, and reduced to his pure essence. He has collapsed to a single piercing pulsing point of pleasure. He has lost himself, but he has found everything else.

And then his ecstasy is interrupted by another piercing sensation: pain. Not the exquisite pain of a well placed needle, or perfectly laid lash, but an ugly pain that gnaws into his pleasurable non-existence in an urgent painful way. He wiggles, tossing, but the pain will not go away, it only gnaws deeper, and with each razor nibble it slices away at his ecstasy. And as he is torn away from the Goddess's pleasure, he is forced back into himself, and the wiggly body-bound part of himself realizes that the Goddess is sucking him out of life. The love-torn spirit part of him does not care. He struggles, trying to dive down deeper into the bottomless divine love, but that gnawing pain is tethering him to the Waking World, and he can't kick it free.

Then the Goddess's attention lifts from him, like a blanket torn away. He lies on the ground, the stones slick and cold against his bare skin. The echo of his loss pounds in his head, farrier-like, stunning him. A shrill noise pierces his agony, cuts through the thunder, a familiar high-pitched whine:

"Ya! Ya! Ya!"

His eyes are filled with sand; it takes a moment of effort before his nerveless hands can find his face, and knuckle his vision clear. Immediately he sees: Tiny Doom, dancing with the bear-headed Minion. Sieur Oso is doing the Mazorca, a dance which requires a great deal of jumping and stamping, and he's got the perfect boots to make the noise, each one as big as horse's head. Tiny Doom is doing the Ronde-loo, weaving round and round Sieur Oso her circular motion too sick-making for Hardhands to follow.

Then he realizes: no, they are not dancing, Sieur Oso is trying to squash Tiny Doom like a bug, and she, rather than run like a sensible child, is actually taunting him on. Oh Haðraaða!

Dimly Tiny Doom's husband sparks the thought that perhaps he should help her, and he's trying to figure out where his feet are, so as to arise to this duty, when his attention is caught by a whirl, not a whirl, a Vortex the likes of which he has never before seen, a Vortex as black as ink, but streaked hot pink, and furious furious. Though he can see nothing but the cutting blur of the spin, he can feel the force of the fight within; the Goddess is battling it out with something, something strong enough to give her a run for her divas, something tenacious and tough.

"Bwannie! Bwannie!" cries Doom. She is still spinning, and the Minion is starting to look tuckered, his stomps not so stompy anymore, and his jeers turned to huffy puffs. Foam is dribbling from his muzzle, like whipped cream.

Hardhands ignores Tiny Doom.

"------" Hardhands grates, trying to throw a Word of encouragement into the mix, to come to his darling's aid. The Word is a strong one, even his weakened state, but it bounces off the Vortex, harmless, spurned, just as he has been spurned. The Goddess cares nothing for Hardhands' love, for his desire, he chokes back tears, and staggers to his feet, determined to help somehow, even if he must cast himself into the fire to do so.

Before he can do anything so drastic, there is the enormous sound of suction sucking in. For a split second, Hardhands feels himself go as flat as paper, his lungs suck against his chest, his bones slap into ribands, his flesh becomes as thin as jerky. The Current pops like a cork, the world re-inflates and Hardhands is round and substantial again, although now truly bereft. The Goddess is gone.

The Vortex has blushed pink now, and its spin is slowing, slower, slower, until it is no longer a Vortex, but a little pink blur, balanced on pointy toes, ears flopping—what the hell? Pig?

He has gone insane, or blind, or both? In one dainty pirouette Pig has soared across the room and latched himself to the Minion's scraggly throat. Suddenly invigorated, Sieur Oso does a pirouette of his own, upward, gurgling.

"What is going on—!" Madam Rose's voice raises high above the mayhem-noises, then it chokes. She has stalled in the doorway, more minions peering from behind her safety. Tiny Doom has now attached to Sieur Oso's hairy ankle and her grip—hands and teeth—are not dislodged by his antic kicking, though whether the Minion is now dancing because Tiny Doom is gnawing on his ankle or because his throat is a massive chewy-mess, it's hard to say. Pig disengages from Sieur Oso and leaps to Madam Rose, who clutches him to her bosom in a maternal way, but jerkily, as though she wants less of his love, not more. Her other slaveys have scarpered, and now that the Goddess is gone, Hardhands sees no particular reason to linger either.

He flings one very hard Gramatica word edgewise at the antic bear. Sieur Oso jerks upward, and his surprised head sails backwards, tears through the tent wall, and is gone. Coldfire founts up from the stump of his neck, sizzling and sparky. Hardhands grabs Tiny Doom away from the Minion's forward fall, and she grasps onto him monkey-wise, clinging to his shoulders.

"Pig!" she screams, "Pig!"

Madam Rose manages to disentangle Pig, and flings him towards Hardhands and Tiny Doom. Pig sails through the air, his ears like wings, and hits Hardhands' chest with a soggy thud and then tumbles downward. Madam Rose staggers, she is clutching her throat, her hair has fallen down, drippy red. Above her, the tent ceiling is flickering with tendrils of coldfire, it pours down around her like fireworks falling from the sky, sheathing her bones in glittering flickering flesh. The coldfire has spread to the ceiling now, scorching the raven angels, and the whole place is going to go: coldfire doesn't burn like non-magickal fire, but it is hungry and does consume, and Hardhands has had enough consumption for tonight. Hefting Tiny Doom up higher on his shoulder, he turns about to retreat (run away).

"Pig! Pig!" Tiny Doom beats at his head as he ducks under the now flickering threshold, "PIG!"

The coldfire has raced across the roof beyond him and the antechamber before him is a heaving weaving maelstrom of magick, the Current bubbling and sucking, oh it's a shame to let such yummy power go to waste, but now is perhaps not the time to further test his control. Madam Rose staggers out of the flames, the very air around her is bubbling and cracking, spitting Abyss through cracks in the Current, black tendrils that coil and smoke.

Tiny Doom, still screaming: "Pig!"

Hardhands jumps and weaves through the tentacles of flame, flinging banishings as he goes, and the tendrils snap away. He's not going to stop for Pig, Pig is on his own, Hardhands can feel the Current boiling, in a moment there will be too much magick for the space to contain, there is going to be a giant implosion and he's had enough implosions for one night, too. Through the dining room they run, scattering cheese platters, waiters, cocktails and conservationists, crunching crackers underfoot, knocking down a minion—there—open veranda doors, and beyond those doors, the sparkle of hurdy-gurdy lights. Doom clinging to his head like a pinchy hat, he leaps over the bar, through breaking bottles and scattered ice, and through the doors, into blessed cool air. There ahead—the back of the Monkey's Head—keeping running, through gasps and a pain in his side.

Through the dark throat—for a second Hardhands thinks that for sure the Grin will snap shut, and they will be swallowed forever, but no, he leaps the tombstone teeth and they are clear. The sky above turns sheet white, and the ground shifts beneath his feet in a sudden bass roll. He sits down hard in the springy grass, lungs gasping. Tiny Doom collapses from his grasp and rolls like a little barrel across the springy turf. The stars wink back in, as though a veil has been drawn back, and suddenly Hardhands is limp with exhaustion. The Current is gone. The Monkey's Grin still grins, but his glittering letter halo is gone, and his eyes are dim. Madam Rose's is gone, as well.

Well, good riddance, good-bye, adios, farewell. From the Monkey's

Grin, Pig tippy-dances, pirouetting towards Doom, who receives him with happy cries of joy.

Hardhands lies on the grass and stares upward at the starry sky, and he moves his head back and forth, drums his feet upon the ground, wiggles his fingers just because he can. He feels drained and empty, and sore as hell. The grass is crispy cool beneath his bare sweaty back, and he could just lie there forever. Behind the relief of freedom, however, there's a sour sour taste.

He was set up. The whole evening was nothing but a gag. His grandmother, his darling sweet grandmother whom he did not kill out of love, respect, and honor, whom he pulled back from the brink of assassination because he held her so dear, his grandmamma sold him to Madam Rose.

Him, Hardhands, sold!

The Pontifexa has played them masterfully: Relais' incompetence, Tiny Doom's greed, Madam Rose's cunning, and his own sense of duty and loyalty. He'd gone blindly in to save Tiny Doom and she was the bait and he the stupid stupid prey, all along.

He, Hardhands, expendable! Can he believe it?

Tiny Doom is ignored but she is also insistent: "Bwannie—get up! Pig wants to go home!"

For a second our hero is wracked with sorrow, he takes a deep breath that judders his bones, and closes his eyes. The darkness is sparked with stars, flares of light caused by the pressure of holding the tears back. But under the surface of his sorrow, he feels an immense longing, longing not for the Pontifexa, or hot water, or for Relais' comforting embrace, or even for waffles. Compared to this longing, the rest of his feelings—anger, sorrow, guilt, love—are nothing. He should be already plotting his revenge, his payback, his turn-about-is-fair-play, but instead he is alive with thoughts of sweeping black wings, and spiraling hair, and the unutterable blissful agony of Desire.

"Pig wants a waffle, Bwannie! And I must potty, I gotta potty now!"

Hardhands opens his eyes to a dangly pink snout. Pig's eyes are small black beads, and his cotton stitched mouth is a bit red around the edges, as though he's smeared his lipstick. He smells of salty-iron blood and the peachy whiff of stale coldfire. He looks satisfied.

"Would you please get Pig out of my face?" Hardhands says wearily. The mystery of how Pig fought and defeated a goddess is beyond him right now; he'll consider that later.

Tiny Doom pokes him. She is jiggling and bobbing, with her free hand tightly pressed. She has desires ungratified of her own; her bladder may be full, but her candy sack is empty. "Pig wants you to get up. He says Get Up Now, Banastre!"

Hardhands, thinking of desire gratified, gets up.

**Ysabeau S. Wilce** is the author of the Flora Fyrdraaca young adult series, the middle volume of which, *Flora's Dare*, won the Andre Norton award. Her short fiction has appeared in *The Magazine of Fantasy & Science Fiction*, *Asimov's Science Fiction*, and various anthologies. She lives in Northern California and is currently working on a novel about Hardhands and Tiny Doom.

# Paul Park
# on Ysabeau Wilce

I taught the first week of Clarion West in 2002, a class of accomplished, interesting men and women: a sailor, a painter, an engineer, a banker, a teacher, etc., and one writer.

I am not trying to be rude. Several have since gone on to fine careers, producing novels, novellas, novelettes, novelinis, short stories, short-shorts, tweets, limericks, puns. And of course the reason they came to Clarion was because they wanted to become writers, not because they were writers already.

But one of them—I arrived on a Sunday, the first day of the workshop, and gave them overnight assignments which I read aloud in class the next day. When I was halfway through Ysa's, I was already thinking, "My work here is done. I will collect my fee and disappear into the West. Or East (that's where I'm from)—it doesn't matter."

Ysabeau seemed to rise fully formed out of the ocean-spume, like Venus, only with more clothes. She was so sure in her technique— Clarion students often worry about their "voice," the collection of instinctive or learned rhetorical devices that makes their work unique. I tell them not to fuss, or else to fuss instead about structure and content. I pretend voice is an effete notion, but I'm sort of lying. What I mean is, like many elements of good writing, it amasses as a by-product. The more you dig it out, the less it's yours.

I experience the world of this story on two levels, and one of them is made of voice: gaudy vocabularies, rhyme and rhythm, artful repetition. The characters, beguiling in themselves, the author nevertheless decorates with layers of cosmetics. The imagery, vivid in itself, she displays through super-saturated filters. This double experience provokes a double response as I move back and forth between the objects and the way I see them. Like Hardhands in the story, I stagger through off-balance, hyper-aware, drunk. But I am drunk on voice.

**Paul Park** is the author of 10 science fiction and fantasy novels and numerous short stories. His work has been nominated for the World Fantasy Award, Nebula, and other awards. He teaches writing and literature at Williams College and has also taught multiple times at the Clarion West Writers Workshop.

# Giving Back: Celebrating Thirty Years of Clarion West Graduates

## Leslie Howle

Clarion West is built on a history of a community of writers paying forward.

Vonda McIntyre attended the last of the original Clarion workshops in Clarion, Pennsylvania, in 1970. Inspired by her experience, she asked Clarion founder Robin Scott Wilson for permission to launch a Clarion West in Seattle. For three years Vonda ran exciting, successful workshops, and then the workshop fell dormant for a decade.

In 1984, local poet JT Stewart, a graduate of one of those first Clarion West workshops, approached fellow writer Marilyn Holt with the idea of re-launching Clarion West at Seattle Central Community College where she worked as an instructor. With Vonda's advice and support, they set the workshop in motion and successfully ran it at the community college in 1984 and 1985.

After two years, JT and Marilyn weren't able to continue, and the workshop might have once again fallen dormant, but with their help, a dozen or so Clarion West graduates took on the challenge of building a new, self-sustaining foundation for the workshop. They incorporated Clarion West as a not-for-profit arts education organization with a Board of Directors and paid administrator. Supported by the Clarion West Board, alumni students and instructors, and writers and friends from the local SF&F community, '84 graduate Linda Jordan-Eichner served as administrator for the workshop in its first year as a 501(c) 3 non-profit in 1986. In subsequent years, Donna Davis '84, myself, (Leslie Howle '85), and later '87 graduate David E. Myers, ran the workshop together in successive teams until Donna moved to New York. Dave and I worked as the administrative team for a dozen years, and when Dave retired in 2001, '96 graduate Neile Graham took his position and we have been together ever since. Soon new people will move into roles as administrators and Board members, and the cycle will continue.

This is what Clarion West is: a writer's workshop initiated by, and almost entirely supported by, a strong, committed community of alumni students, instructors, friends, donors, and volunteers. Every graduating class gives back in some way, whether by volunteering, serving on the Board or a committee, working as staff, participating in the Write-A-Thon, or making scholarship donations.

All of the writers who have benefited from their Clarion West experience owe a debt to the many individuals, from volunteers and donors to Board members and staff, who have kindly given of their time, energy, and heart to make the workshop what it is today. It truly has been about paying it forward. It's a beautiful thing, this community for the writers, by the writers. It's given a leg up to fantastic stories and one-of-a-kind talented writers over the past 30 years and will continue to do so on into the future, thanks to the dedication and generosity of this amazing community. Here's to the next 30 years of fantastic Clarion West stories!

Leslie Howle
Clarion West Writers Workshop Director 2013